FARMINGTON COMMUNITY LIBRARY
FARMINGTON BRANCH LIBRARY
23500 LIBERTY STREET
FARMINGTON, MI 48335-3570
(248) 553-0321

FARMINGTON COMMUNITY LIBRARY

3 0036 01375 4807

W9-BCG-551

DEC 0 2 2021

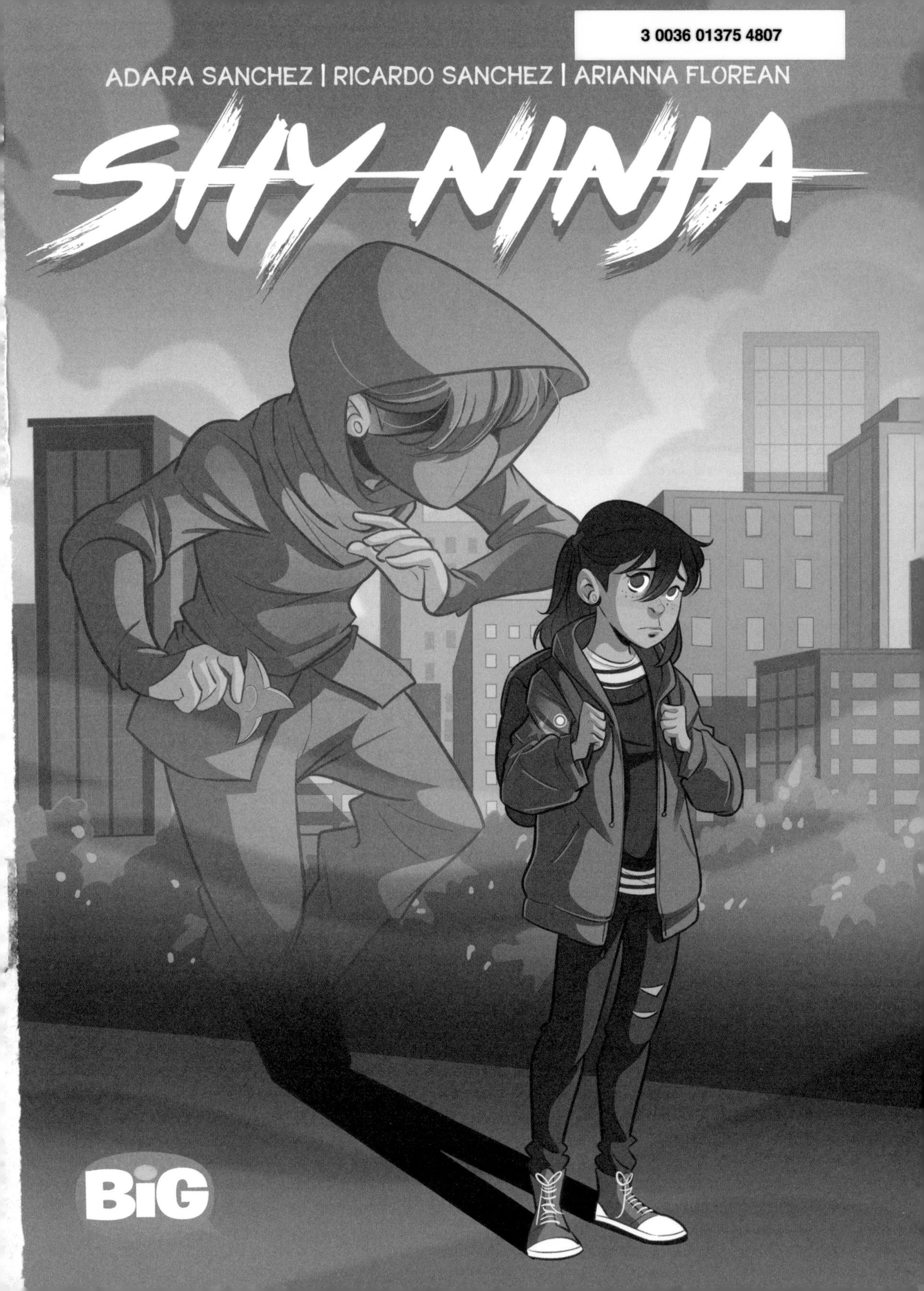
ADARA SANCHEZ | RICARDO SANCHEZ | ARIANNA FLOREAN
SHY NINJA
BiG

**ADARA SANCHEZ**
Creator

**RICARDO SANCHEZ**
Writer

**ARIANNA FLOREAN**
Art & Colors

**TOM NAPOLITANO**
Letterer

**ARIANNA FLOREAN**
Cover Artist

**Rob Levin**
**& Fabrice Sapolsky**
Editors

**Ryan Lewis**
Junior Designer

**Jerry Frissen**
Senior Art Director

**Mark Waid**
Publisher

Ricardo and Adara would like to thank Fabrice Sapolsky
for his encouragement and help bringing *Shy Ninja* to life.

Rights and Licensing - licensing@humanoids.com
Press and Social Media - pr@humanoids.com

**SHY NINJA**. Second Printing. This book is a publication of Humanoids, Inc. 8033 Sunset Blvd. #628, Los Angeles, CA 90046.
Copyright Humanoids, Inc., Los Angeles (USA). All rights reserved. Humanoids® and the Humanoids logo are registered
trademarks of Humanoids, Inc. in the U.S. and other countries.
Library of Congress Control Number: 2020952027

BiG is an imprint of Humanoids, Inc.

The story and characters presented in this publication are fictional. Any similarities to events or persons living
or dead are purely coincidental. No portion of this book may be reproduced by any means without the express written
consent of the copyright holder except for artwork used for review purposes. Printed in Latvia.

## FOREWORD

I was driving my daughter from San Francisco to San Diego for her first Comic-Con International in July 2018 when *Shy Ninja* was born. Or at least, that's when I came into the story.

We'd just passed Los Angeles and were only a few hours away from San Diego, so I was telling her what to expect: Crowds, costumes, and lots and lots of walking! I'd taken Adara to other comic conventions, but there's just nothing like the one in San Diego. I was also explaining that I'd be leaving her alone to enjoy the convention now and then so I could meet with editors to pitch them stories.

To kill the last few hours of that very long drive, and to practice my pitch, I shared with Adara the stories I'd developed and hoped to sell at Comic-Con. There were time-traveling dinosaurs, a mystery story set on an orbiting space station, and a haunted car racing around the world. Adara sort of listened to me, but her attention was focused on the sketch she was drawing on her iPad.

"What are you drawing?" I asked. She held up the iPad and showed me a hybrid robot elephant that was still in progress. It was part of a "Robot Circus" theme she was working on. She'd been developing her art skills for a few years by then, and the project she was doing was really pretty good for any artist, let alone someone her age. She went back to work, and a few miles later she mentioned that when she finished up the Robot Circus, she wanted to work on a new character, a socially awkward girl who decides to take online ninja classes. "I call her Shy Ninja," she said, and told me more about the girl's sidekicks, her adventures, and her nemesis. I was floored. It was the kind of idea that once you hear it, as a writer, you wish you'd come up with yourself.

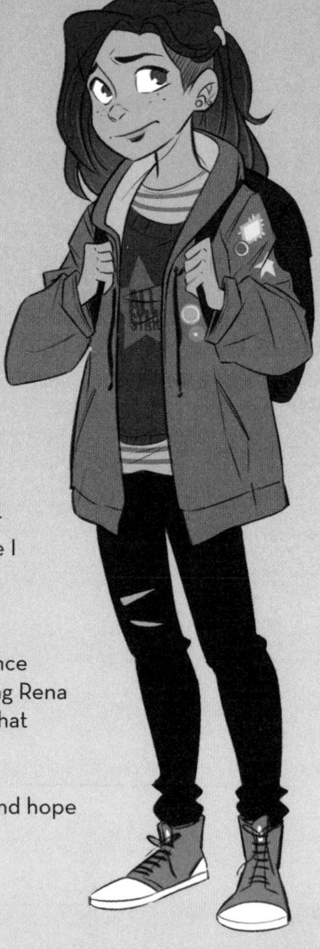

A few days later, I was sitting with Fabrice Sapolsky, my editor from BiG, the publisher of this comic book, and pitching my ideas. Dinosaurs! "Nope." Sci-fi mystery! "Boring." Haunted race car! "Been done." Then he told me that what BiG was really looking for was a story for kids that was more reality-based, less "comic booky." So I took a leap and pitched *Shy Ninja*, the story of a girl who overcomes her social anxiety disorder by becoming a ninja. His jaw dropped. He had the same reaction I did. "Sold!" he said. "Let's make it!" Then I had to admit it was my daughter's idea, so we'd have to get her permission first. "Even better!" he said. "You can work on it together!"

It took nearly a year for me to convince my daughter to have her idea made into a comic book, but convince her I did, and we started working on an outline. Being huge Harry Potter and Percy Jackson fans, we wanted to incorporate aspects of those books into the story, like a kid not knowing their true potential, but keeping it somewhat realistic: no magic, aliens, or monsters were allowed. As we developed Rena's character, Adara also suggested ideas for the villain, Rena's best friends, and how Rena might develop her ninja skills, while I wrote it up.

At Adara's second San Diego Comic-Con, she came along with me to meet with Fabrice. Together, we sold him on the story that ultimately became this book. Since then, Arianna Florean has taken over as artist and done an incredible job bringing Rena to life, while Adara and I developed the story, Rena's world, and the challenges that would face her in *Shy Ninja*.

We'd both like to thank you for joining Rena on the journey she's about to take and hope you enjoy reading it as much as we enjoyed creating it.

—Rick and Adara Sanchez

EMERGENT TECHNOLOGIES.

I'M IN.

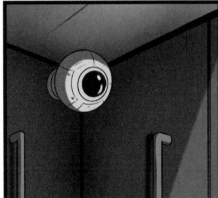

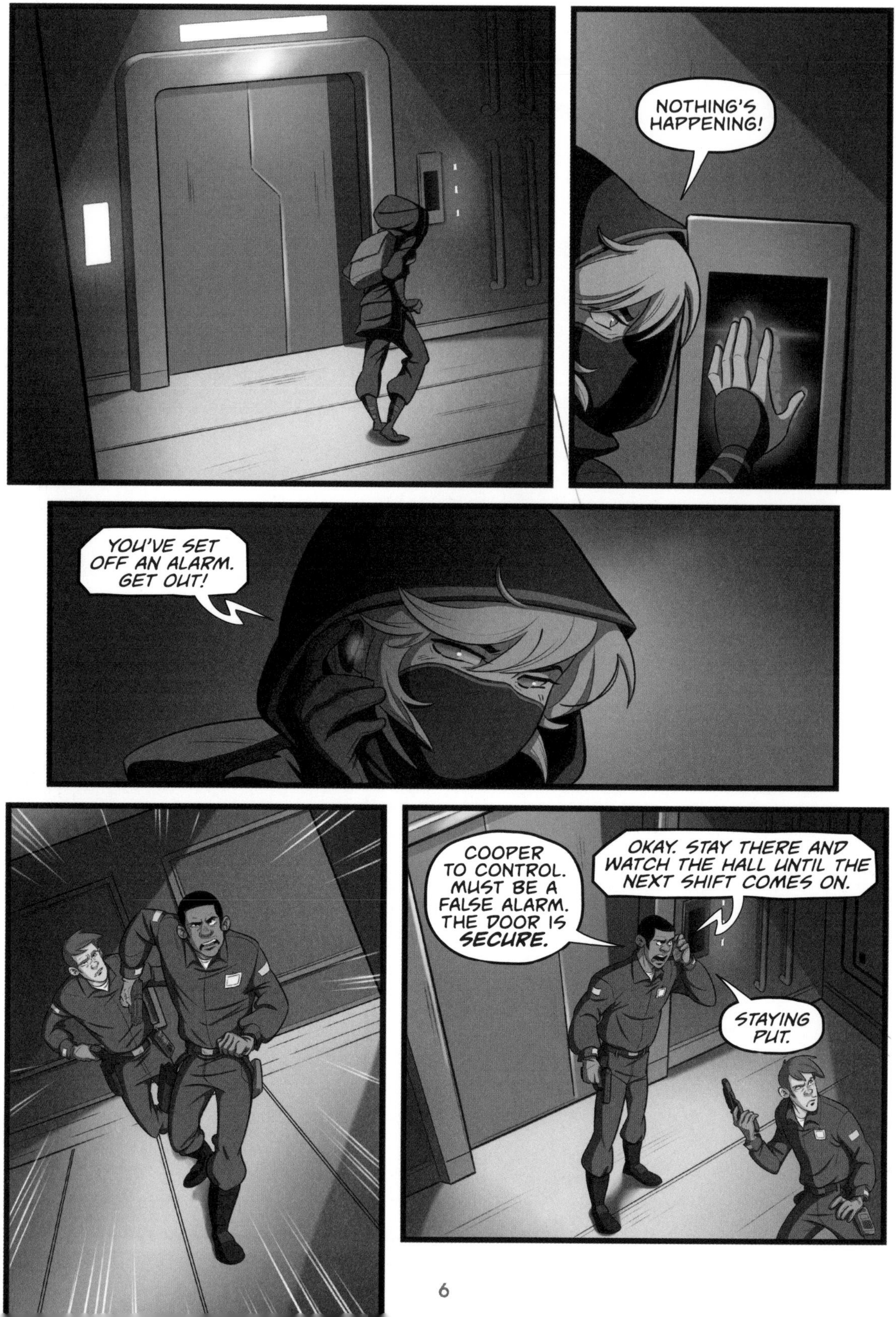
NOTHING'S HAPPENING!
YOU'VE SET OFF AN ALARM. GET OUT!
COOPER TO CONTROL. MUST BE A FALSE ALARM. THE DOOR IS SECURE.
OKAY. STAY THERE AND WATCH THE HALL UNTIL THE NEXT SHIFT COMES ON.
STAYING PUT.

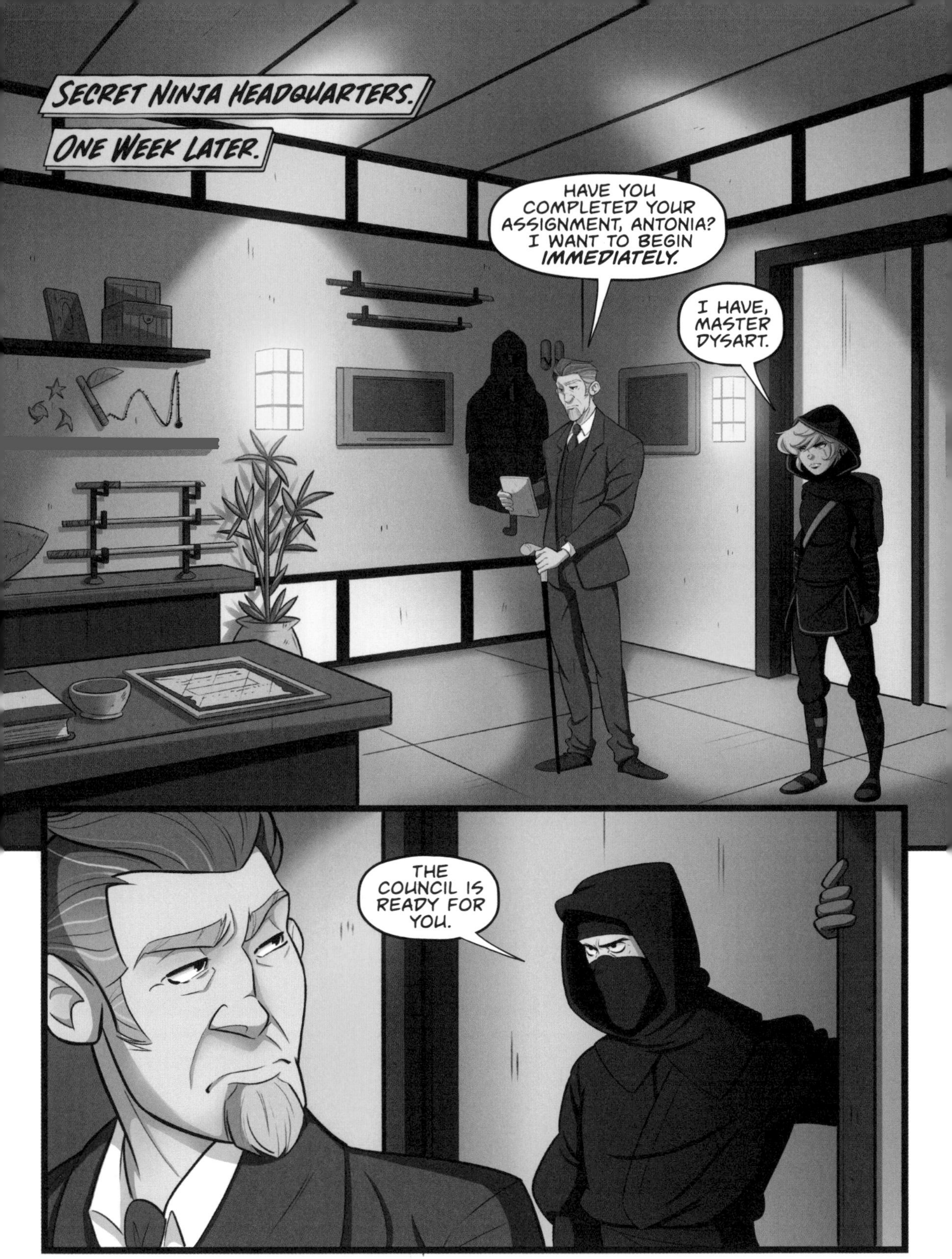
SECRET NINJA HEADQUARTERS.
ONE WEEK LATER.
HAVE YOU COMPLETED YOUR ASSIGNMENT, ANTONIA? I WANT TO BEGIN *IMMEDIATELY.*
I HAVE, MASTER DYSART.
THE COUNCIL IS READY FOR YOU.

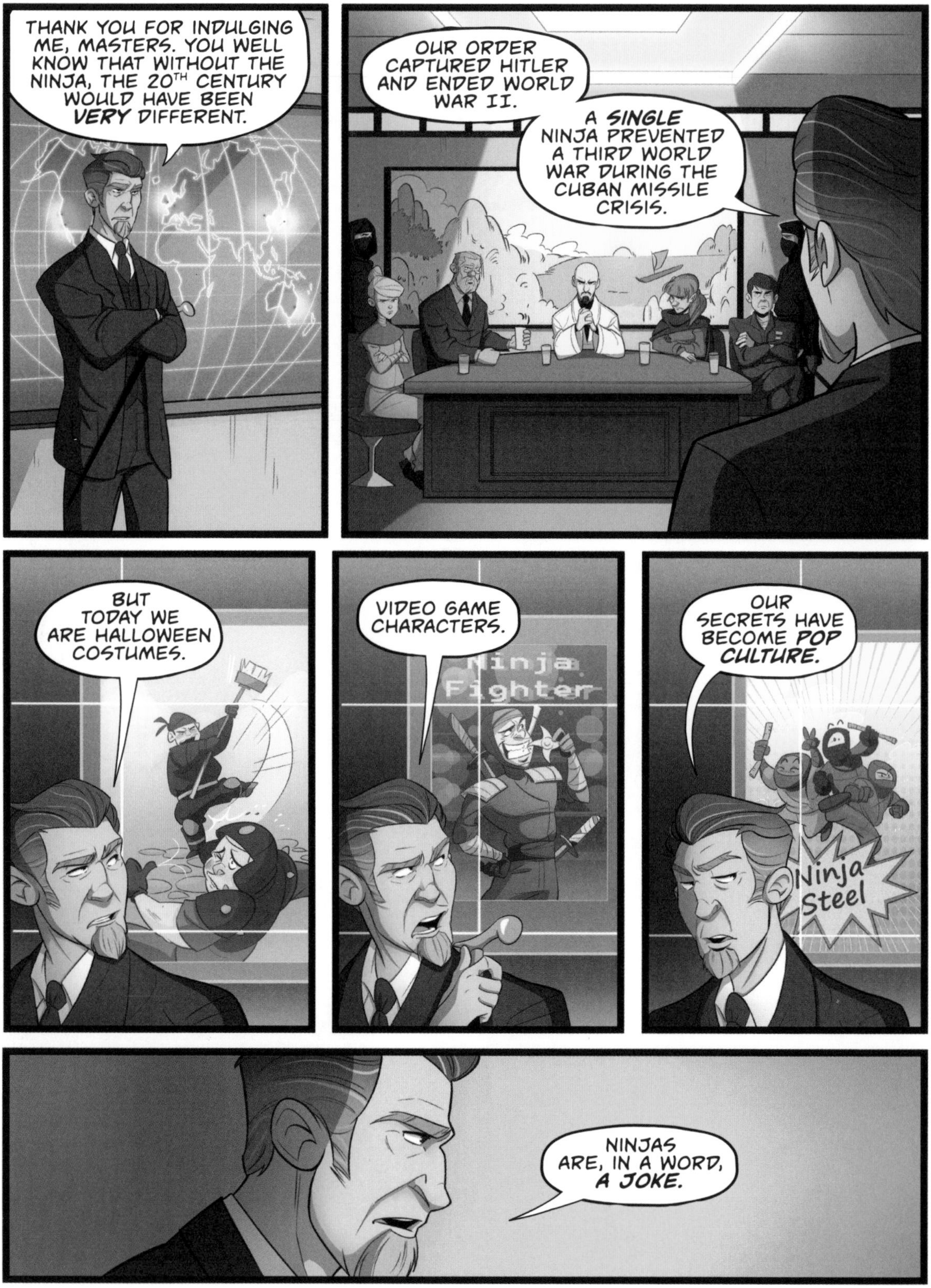
THANK YOU FOR INDULGING ME, MASTERS. YOU WELL KNOW THAT WITHOUT THE NINJA, THE 20TH CENTURY WOULD HAVE BEEN VERY DIFFERENT.
OUR ORDER CAPTURED HITLER AND ENDED WORLD WAR II.
A SINGLE NINJA PREVENTED A THIRD WORLD WAR DURING THE CUBAN MISSILE CRISIS.
BUT TODAY WE ARE HALLOWEEN COSTUMES.
VIDEO GAME CHARACTERS.
Ninja Fighter
OUR SECRETS HAVE BECOME POP CULTURE.
Ninja Steel
NINJAS ARE, IN A WORD, A JOKE.

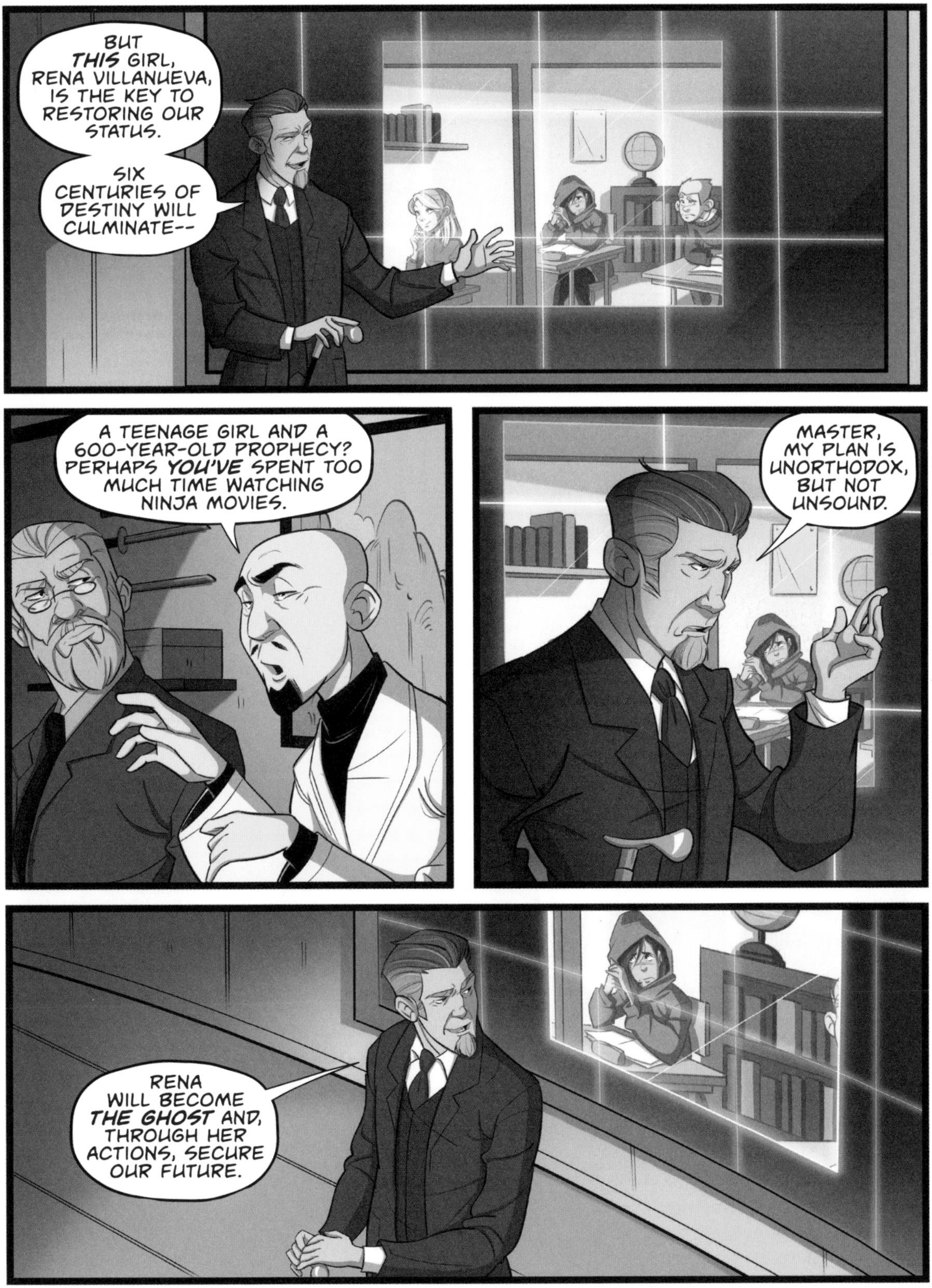
BUT THIS GIRL, RENA VILLANUEVA, IS THE KEY TO RESTORING OUR STATUS.
SIX CENTURIES OF DESTINY WILL CULMINATE--
A TEENAGE GIRL AND A 600-YEAR-OLD PROPHECY? PERHAPS YOU'VE SPENT TOO MUCH TIME WATCHING NINJA MOVIES.
MASTER, MY PLAN IS UNORTHODOX, BUT NOT UNSOUND.
RENA WILL BECOME THE GHOST AND, THROUGH HER ACTIONS, SECURE OUR FUTURE.

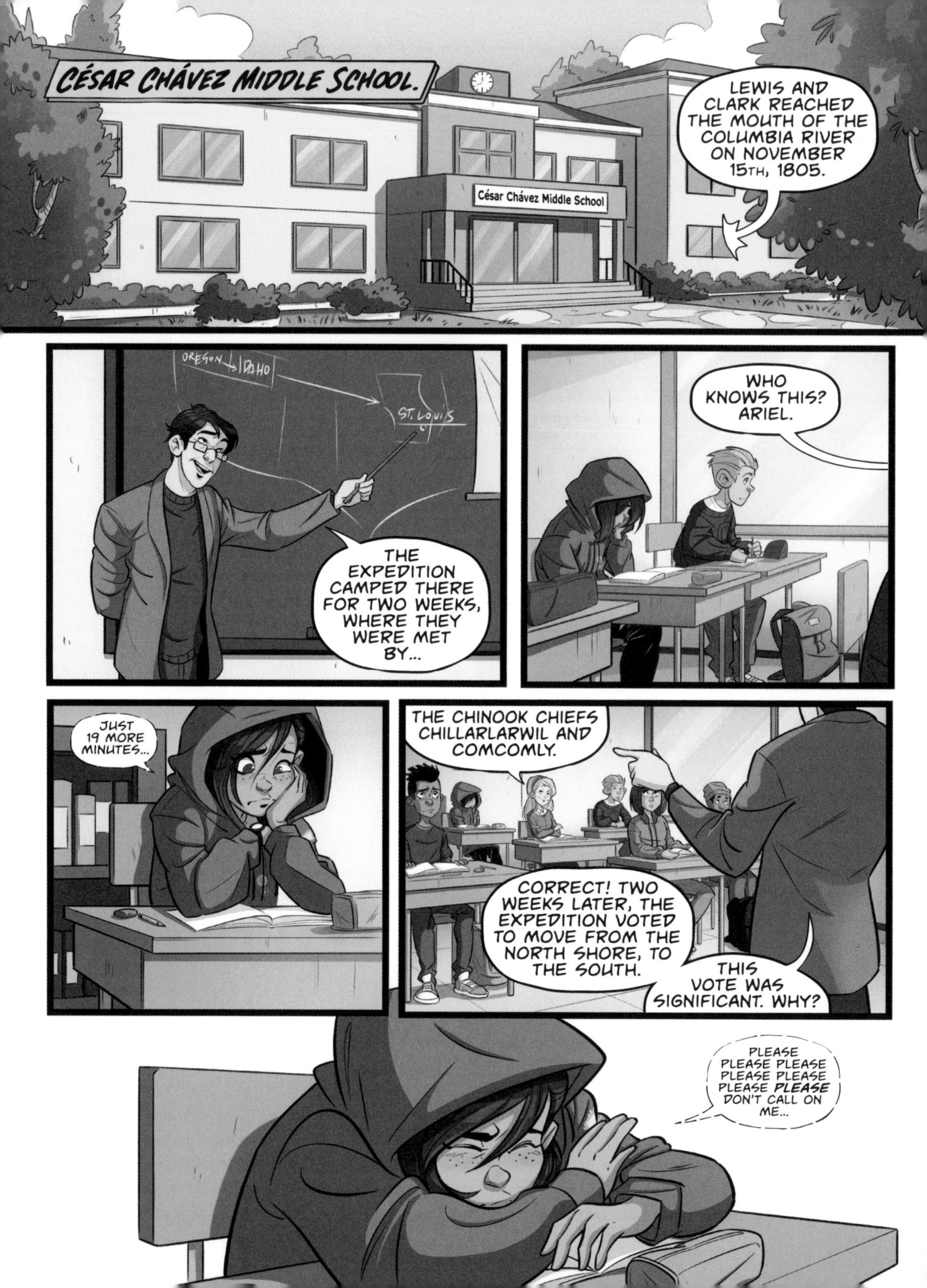
CÉSAR CHÁVEZ MIDDLE SCHOOL.
César Chávez Middle School
LEWIS AND CLARK REACHED THE MOUTH OF THE COLUMBIA RIVER ON NOVEMBER 15TH, 1805.
OREGON
IDAHO
ST. LOUIS
THE EXPEDITION CAMPED THERE FOR TWO WEEKS, WHERE THEY WERE MET BY...
WHO KNOWS THIS? ARIEL.
JUST 19 MORE MINUTES...
THE CHINOOK CHIEFS CHILLARLARWIL AND COMCOMLY.
CORRECT! TWO WEEKS LATER, THE EXPEDITION VOTED TO MOVE FROM THE NORTH SHORE, TO THE SOUTH.
THIS VOTE WAS SIGNIFICANT. WHY?
PLEASE PLEASE PLEASE PLEASE PLEASE PLEASE *PLEASE* DON'T CALL ON ME...

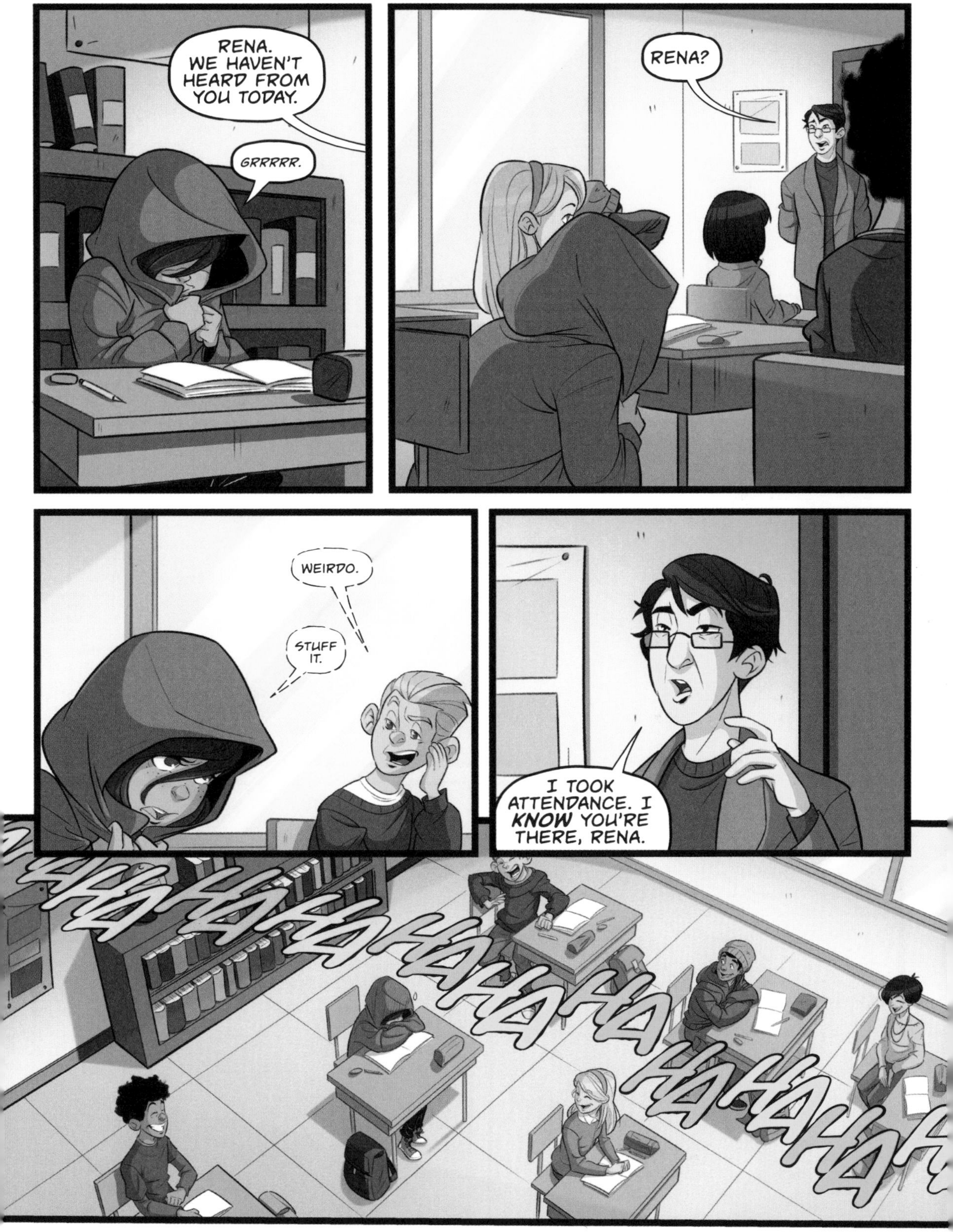
RENA. WE HAVEN'T HEARD FROM YOU TODAY.
GRRRRR.
RENA?
WEIRDO.
STUFF IT.
I TOOK ATTENDANCE. I **KNOW** YOU'RE THERE, RENA.
HAHAHAHAHAHAHAHAHAHAHAHAHA

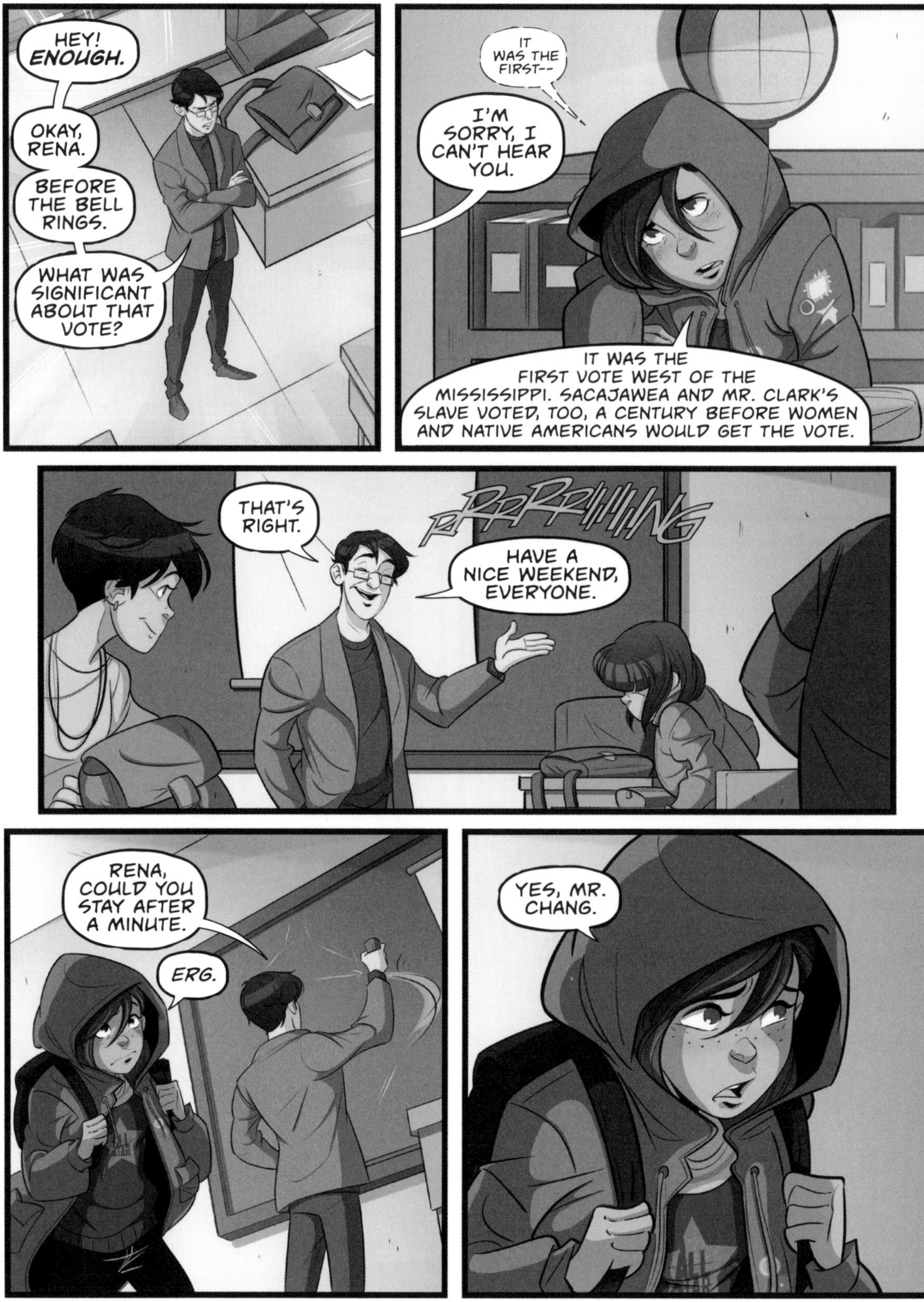
HEY! ENOUGH.
OKAY, RENA.
BEFORE THE BELL RINGS.
WHAT WAS SIGNIFICANT ABOUT THAT VOTE?
IT WAS THE FIRST--
I'M SORRY, I CAN'T HEAR YOU.
IT WAS THE FIRST VOTE WEST OF THE MISSISSIPPI. SACAJAWEA AND MR. CLARK'S SLAVE VOTED, TOO, A CENTURY BEFORE WOMEN AND NATIVE AMERICANS WOULD GET THE VOTE.
THAT'S RIGHT.
BRRRRIIIIING
HAVE A NICE WEEKEND, EVERYONE.
RENA, COULD YOU STAY AFTER A MINUTE.
ERG.
YES, MR. CHANG.

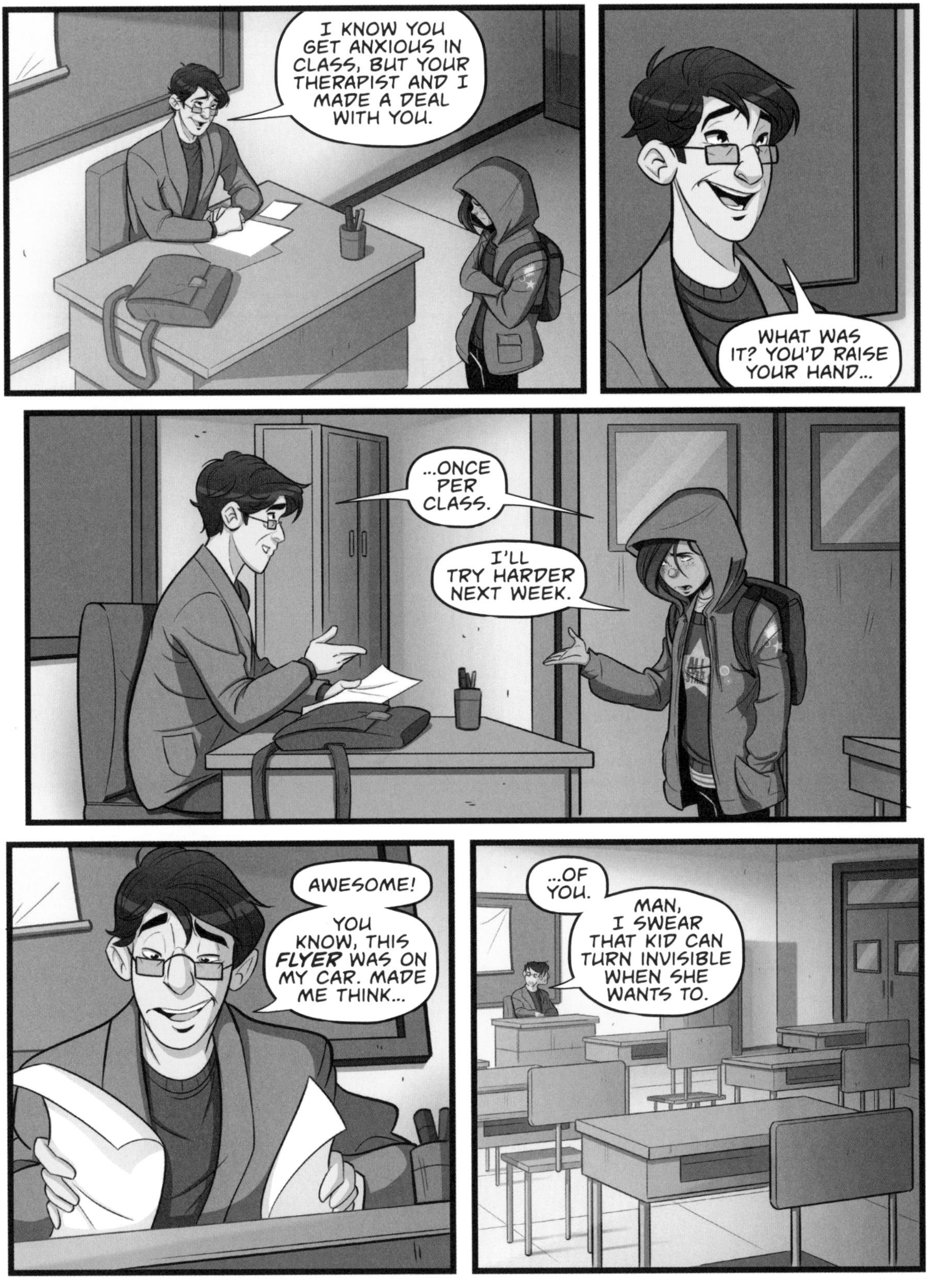
I KNOW YOU GET ANXIOUS IN CLASS, BUT YOUR THERAPIST AND I MADE A DEAL WITH YOU.
WHAT WAS IT? YOU'D RAISE YOUR HAND...
...ONCE PER CLASS.
I'LL TRY HARDER NEXT WEEK.
AWESOME!
YOU KNOW, THIS *FLYER* WAS ON MY CAR. MADE ME THINK...
...OF YOU.
MAN, I SWEAR THAT KID CAN TURN INVISIBLE WHEN SHE WANTS TO.

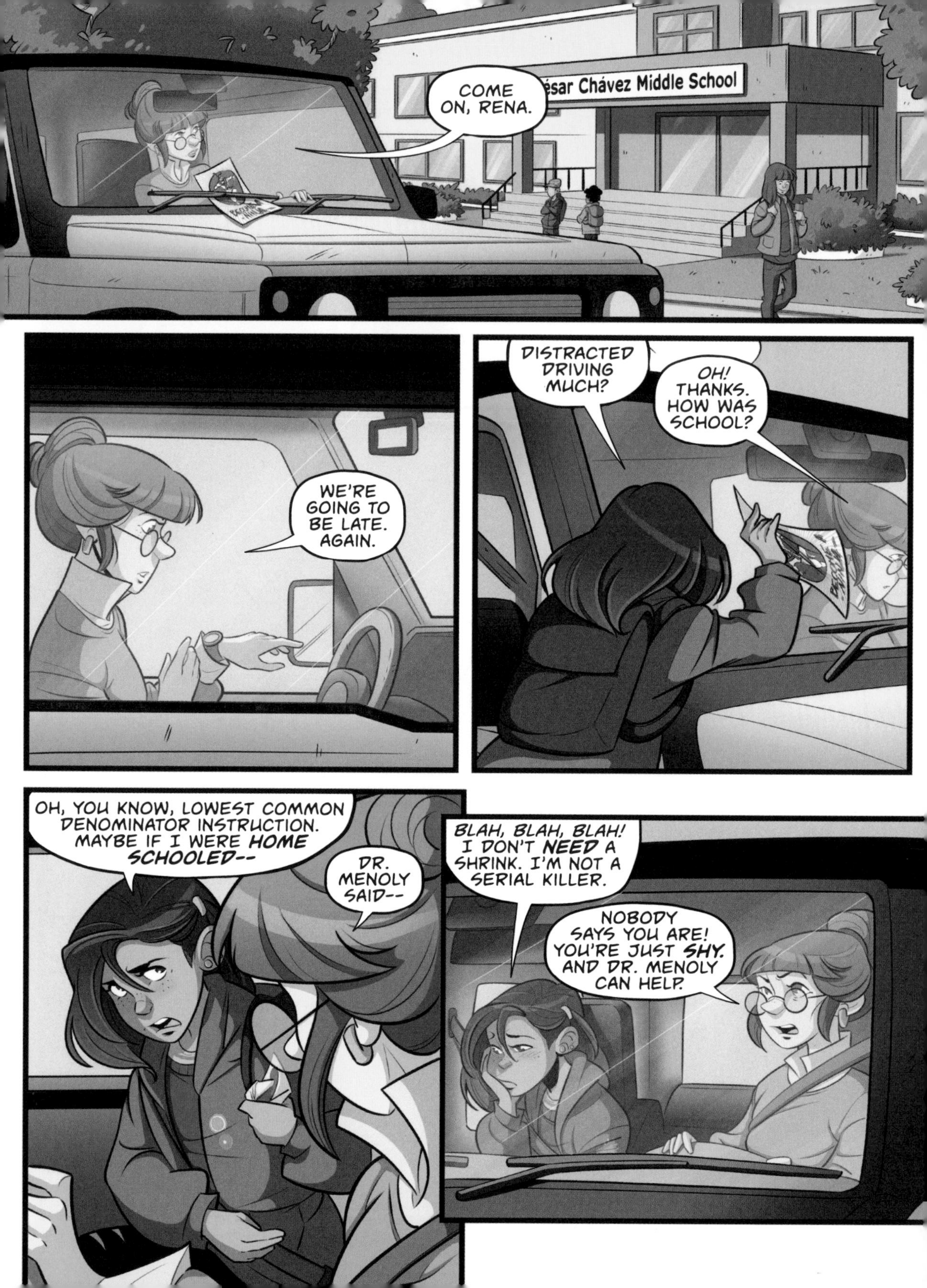
ésar Chávez Middle School
COME ON, RENA.
WE'RE GOING TO BE LATE. AGAIN.
DISTRACTED DRIVING MUCH?
OH! THANKS. HOW WAS SCHOOL?
OH, YOU KNOW, LOWEST COMMON DENOMINATOR INSTRUCTION. MAYBE IF I WERE HOME SCHOOLED--
DR. MENOLY SAID--
BLAH, BLAH, BLAH! I DON'T NEED A SHRINK. I'M NOT A SERIAL KILLER.
NOBODY SAYS YOU ARE! YOU'RE JUST SHY. AND DR. MENOLY CAN HELP.

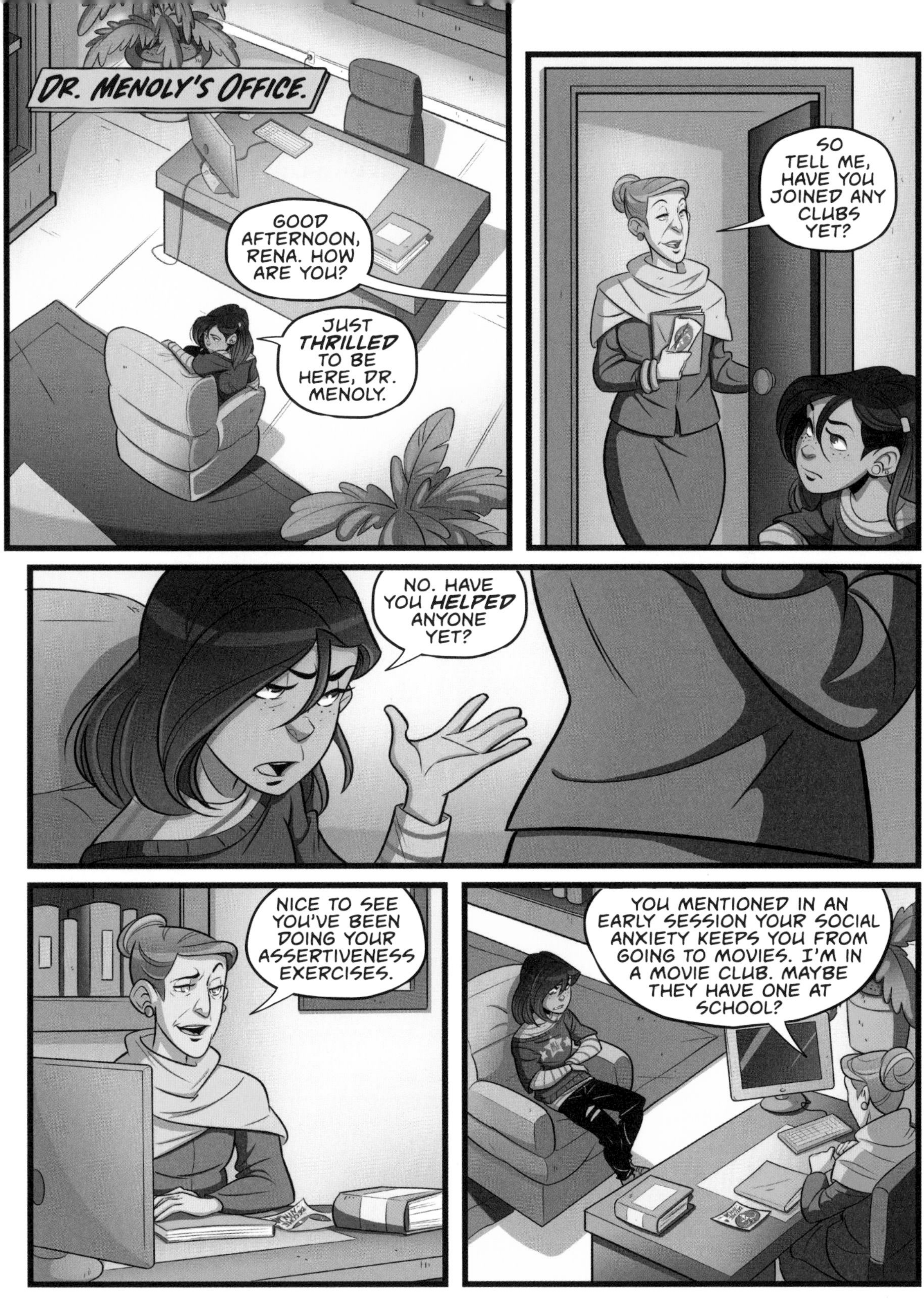

DR. MENOLY'S OFFICE.
GOOD AFTERNOON, RENA. HOW ARE YOU?
JUST THRILLED TO BE HERE, DR. MENOLY.
SO TELL ME, HAVE YOU JOINED ANY CLUBS YET?
NO. HAVE YOU HELPED ANYONE YET?
NICE TO SEE YOU'VE BEEN DOING YOUR ASSERTIVENESS EXERCISES.
YOU MENTIONED IN AN EARLY SESSION YOUR SOCIAL ANXIETY KEEPS YOU FROM GOING TO MOVIES. I'M IN A MOVIE CLUB. MAYBE THEY HAVE ONE AT SCHOOL?

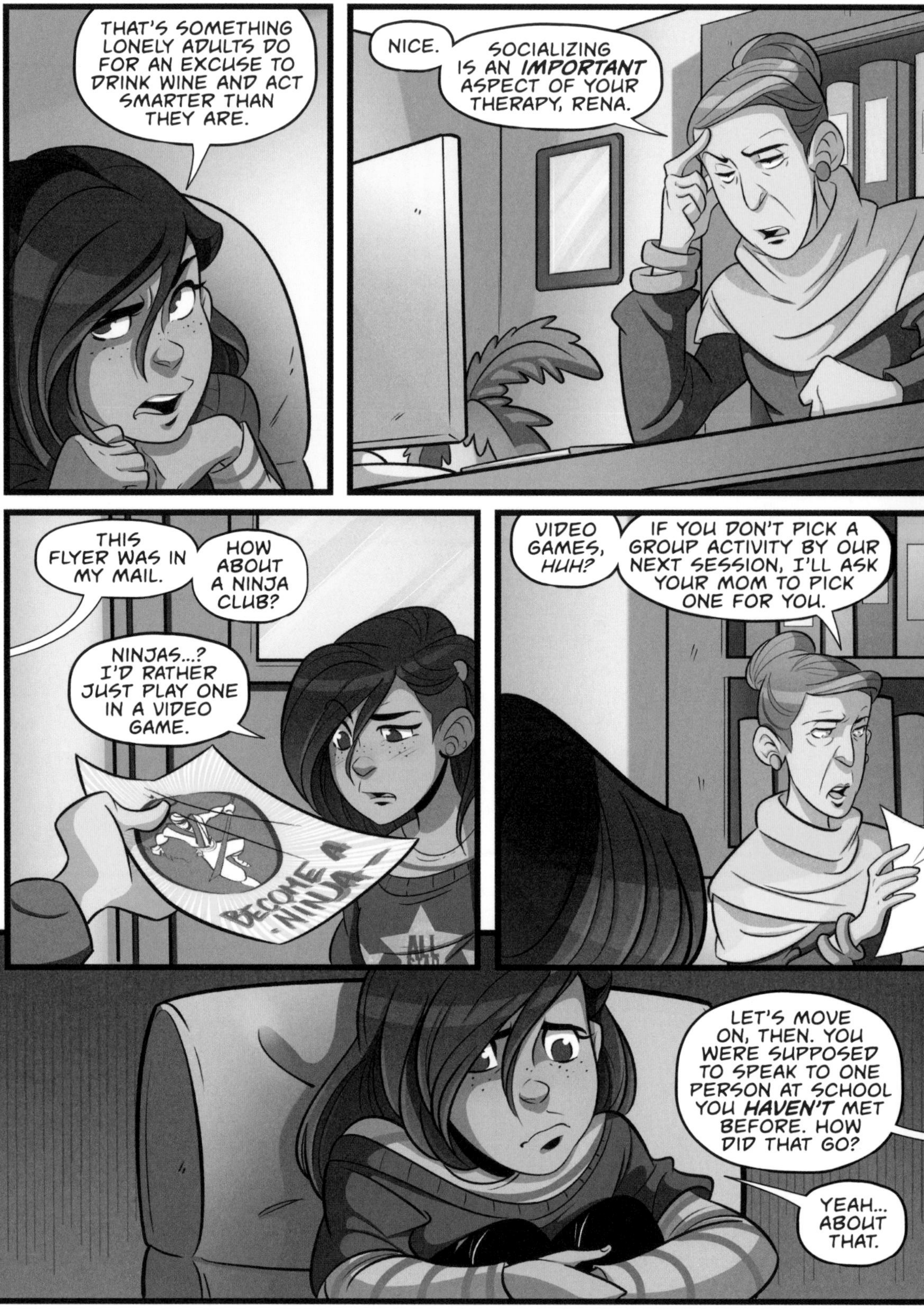
THAT'S SOMETHING LONELY ADULTS DO FOR AN EXCUSE TO DRINK WINE AND ACT SMARTER THAN THEY ARE.
NICE.
SOCIALIZING IS AN *IMPORTANT* ASPECT OF YOUR THERAPY, RENA.
THIS FLYER WAS IN MY MAIL.
HOW ABOUT A NINJA CLUB?
NINJAS...? I'D RATHER JUST PLAY ONE IN A VIDEO GAME.
BECOME A NINJA!
VIDEO GAMES, *HUH?*
IF YOU DON'T PICK A GROUP ACTIVITY BY OUR NEXT SESSION, I'LL ASK YOUR MOM TO PICK ONE FOR YOU.
LET'S MOVE ON, THEN. YOU WERE SUPPOSED TO SPEAK TO ONE PERSON AT SCHOOL YOU *HAVEN'T* MET BEFORE. HOW DID THAT GO?
YEAH... ABOUT THAT.

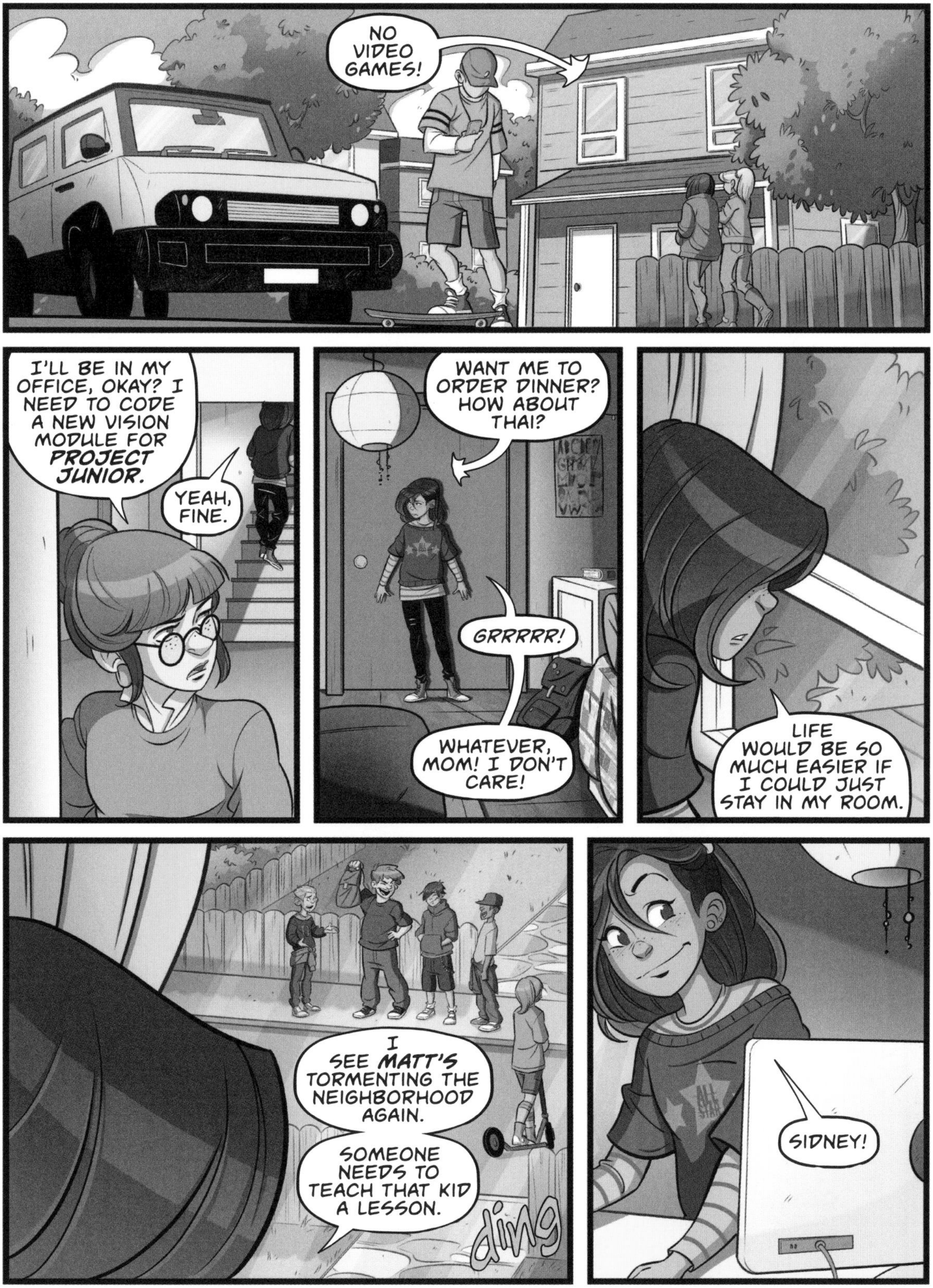
NO VIDEO GAMES!
I'LL BE IN MY OFFICE, OKAY? I NEED TO CODE A NEW VISION MODULE FOR PROJECT JUNIOR.
YEAH, FINE.
WANT ME TO ORDER DINNER? HOW ABOUT THAI?
GRRRRR!
WHATEVER, MOM! I DON'T CARE!
LIFE WOULD BE SO MUCH EASIER IF I COULD JUST STAY IN MY ROOM.
I SEE MATT'S TORMENTING THE NEIGHBORHOOD AGAIN.
SOMEONE NEEDS TO TEACH THAT KID A LESSON.
ding
SIDNEY!

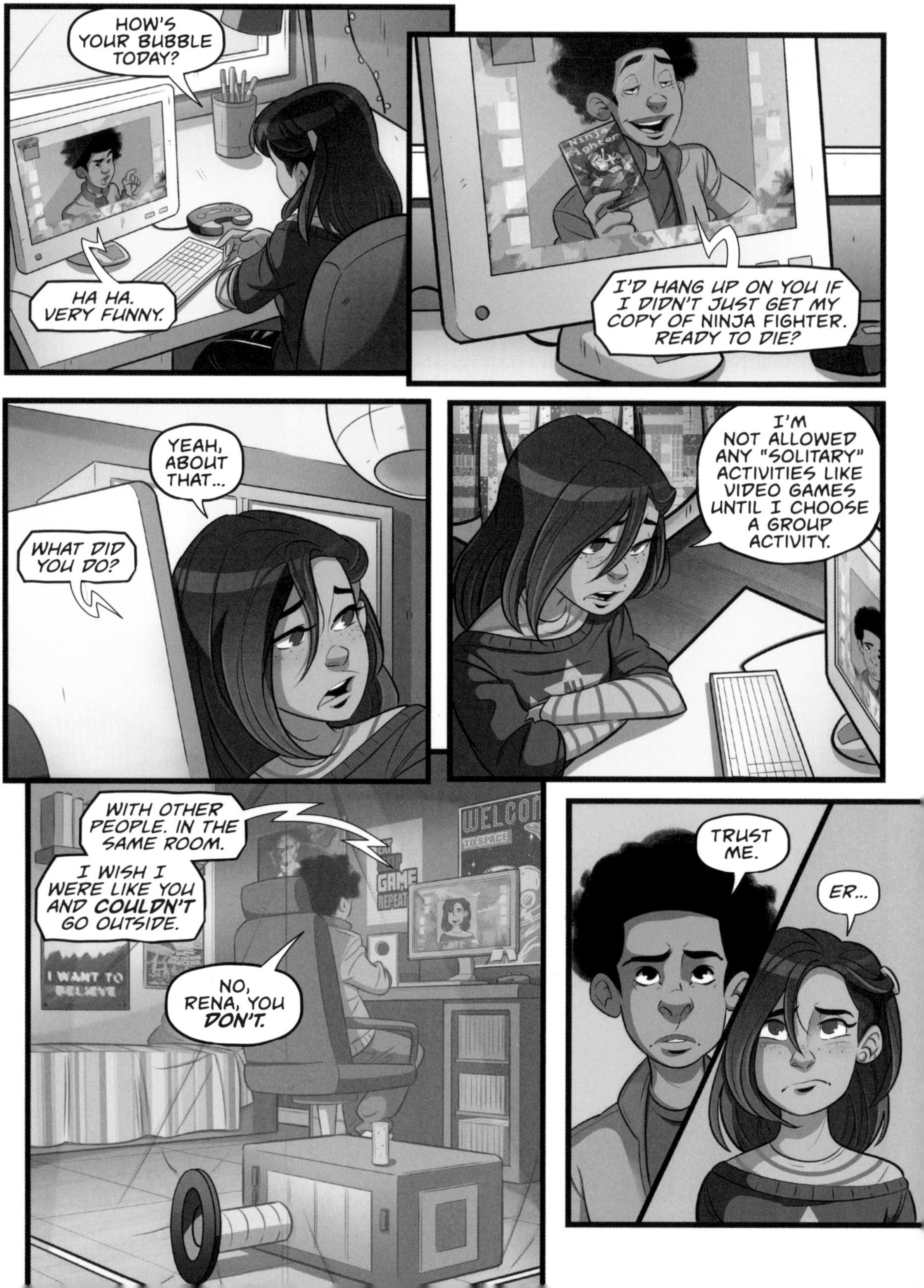
HOW'S YOUR BUBBLE TODAY?
HA HA. VERY FUNNY.
I'D HANG UP ON YOU IF I DIDN'T JUST GET MY COPY OF NINJA FIGHTER. READY TO DIE?
Ninja Fighter
YEAH, ABOUT THAT...
WHAT DID YOU DO?
I'M NOT ALLOWED ANY "SOLITARY" ACTIVITIES LIKE VIDEO GAMES UNTIL I CHOOSE A GROUP ACTIVITY.
WITH OTHER PEOPLE. IN THE SAME ROOM.
I WISH I WERE LIKE YOU AND **COULDN'T** GO OUTSIDE.
NO, RENA, YOU ***DON'T.***
WELCOME TO SPACE
GAME REPEAT
I WANT TO BELIEVE
TRUST ME.
ER...

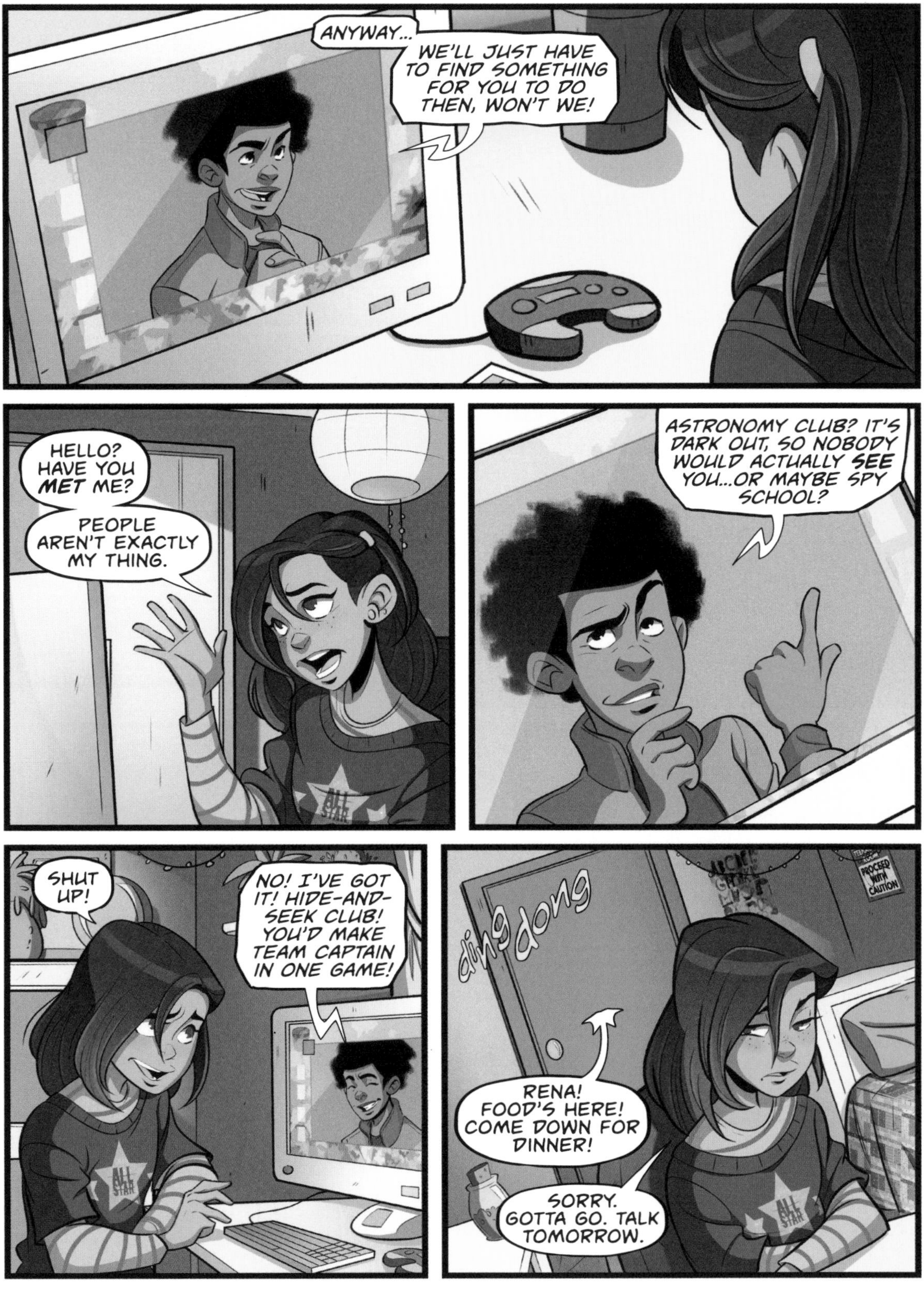
ANYWAY...
WE'LL JUST HAVE TO FIND SOMETHING FOR YOU TO DO THEN, WON'T WE!
HELLO? HAVE YOU MET ME?
PEOPLE AREN'T EXACTLY MY THING.
ASTRONOMY CLUB? IT'S DARK OUT, SO NOBODY WOULD ACTUALLY SEE YOU...OR MAYBE SPY SCHOOL?
SHUT UP!
NO! I'VE GOT IT! HIDE-AND-SEEK CLUB! YOU'D MAKE TEAM CAPTAIN IN ONE GAME!
ding dong
RENA! FOOD'S HERE! COME DOWN FOR DINNER!
SORRY. GOTTA GO. TALK TOMORROW.

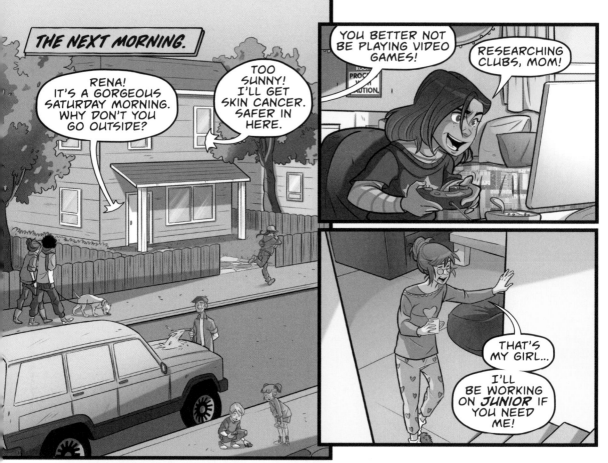

THE NEXT MORNING.

RENA! IT'S A GORGEOUS SATURDAY MORNING. WHY DON'T YOU GO OUTSIDE?

TOO SUNNY! I'LL GET SKIN CANCER. SAFER IN HERE.

YOU BETTER NOT BE PLAYING VIDEO GAMES!

RESEARCHING CLUBS, MOM!

THAT'S MY GIRL...

I'LL BE WORKING ON *JUNIOR* IF YOU NEED ME!

THAT'S MY MOM... *JUNIOR* WON'T PROGRAM ITSELF.

YOU BETTER NOT BE PLAYING *NINJA FIGHTER* WITHOUT ME.

*click*

CALLING... RENA

NOT NOW! RRRRR!

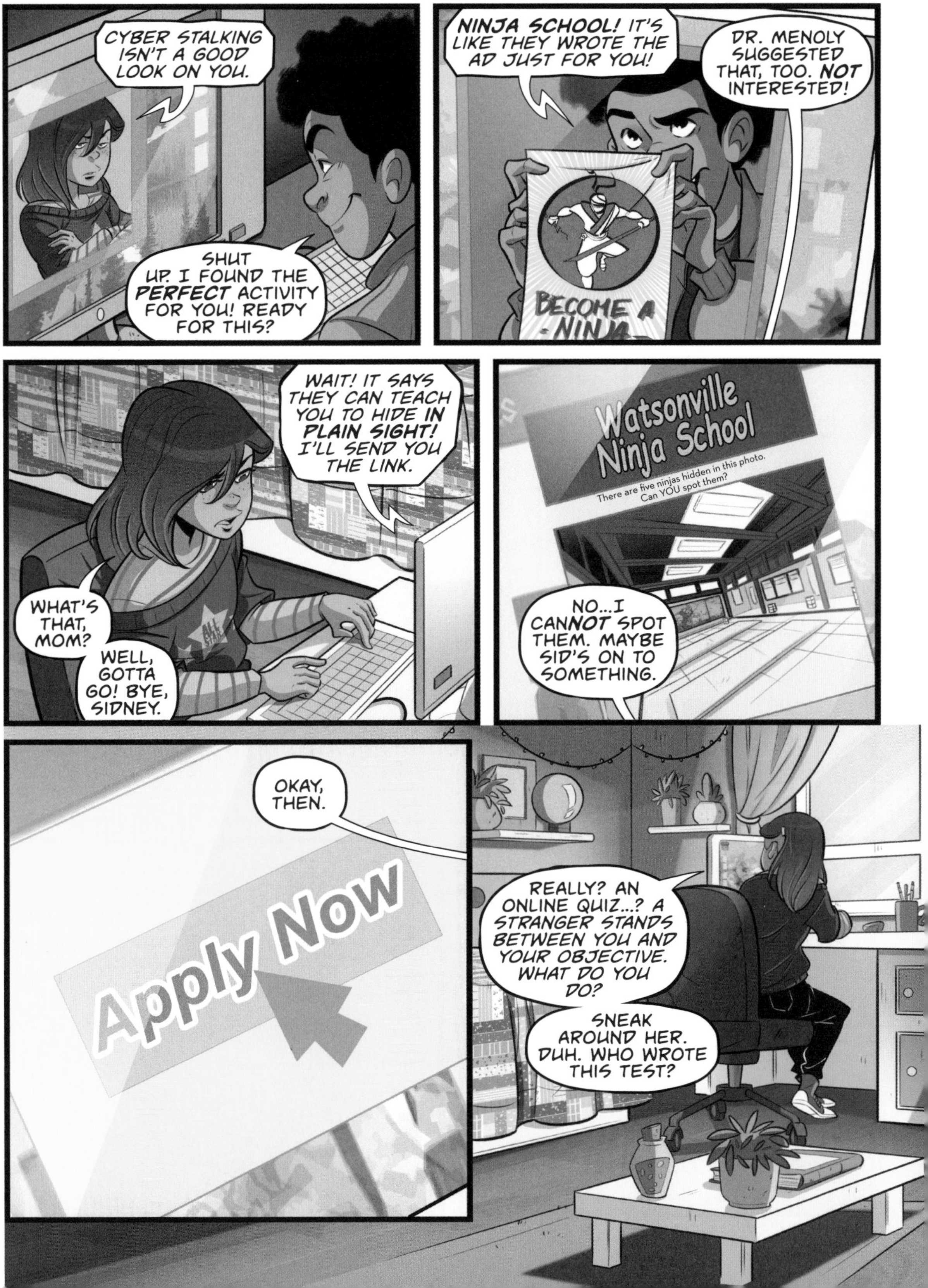
CYBER STALKING ISN'T A GOOD LOOK ON YOU.
SHUT UP. I FOUND THE PERFECT ACTIVITY FOR YOU! READY FOR THIS?
NINJA SCHOOL! IT'S LIKE THEY WROTE THE AD JUST FOR YOU!
DR. MENOLY SUGGESTED THAT, TOO. NOT INTERESTED!
BECOME A NINJA
WAIT! IT SAYS THEY CAN TEACH YOU TO HIDE IN PLAIN SIGHT! I'LL SEND YOU THE LINK.
WHAT'S THAT, MOM?
WELL, GOTTA GO! BYE, SIDNEY.
Watsonville Ninja School
There are five ninjas hidden in this photo. Can YOU spot them?
NO...I CANNOT SPOT THEM. MAYBE SID'S ON TO SOMETHING.
OKAY, THEN.
Apply Now
REALLY? AN ONLINE QUIZ...? A STRANGER STANDS BETWEEN YOU AND YOUR OBJECTIVE. WHAT DO YOU DO?
SNEAK AROUND HER. DUH. WHO WROTE THIS TEST?

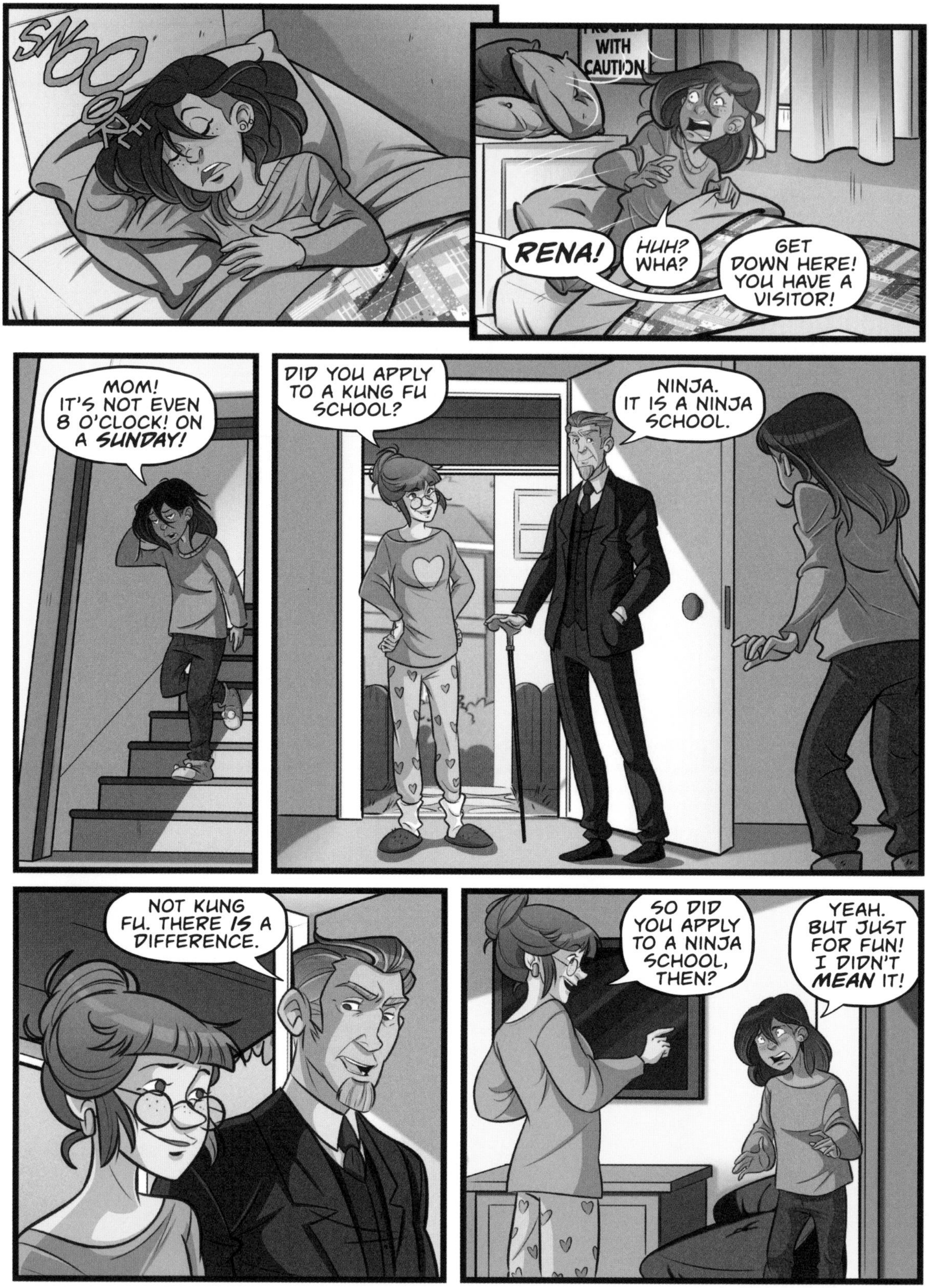
SNOORE
PROCEED WITH CAUTION
RENA!
HUH? WHA?
GET DOWN HERE! YOU HAVE A VISITOR!
MOM! IT'S NOT EVEN 8 O'CLOCK! ON A SUNDAY!
DID YOU APPLY TO A KUNG FU SCHOOL?
NINJA. IT IS A NINJA SCHOOL.
NOT KUNG FU. THERE IS A DIFFERENCE.
SO DID YOU APPLY TO A NINJA SCHOOL, THEN?
YEAH. BUT JUST FOR FUN! I DIDN'T MEAN IT!

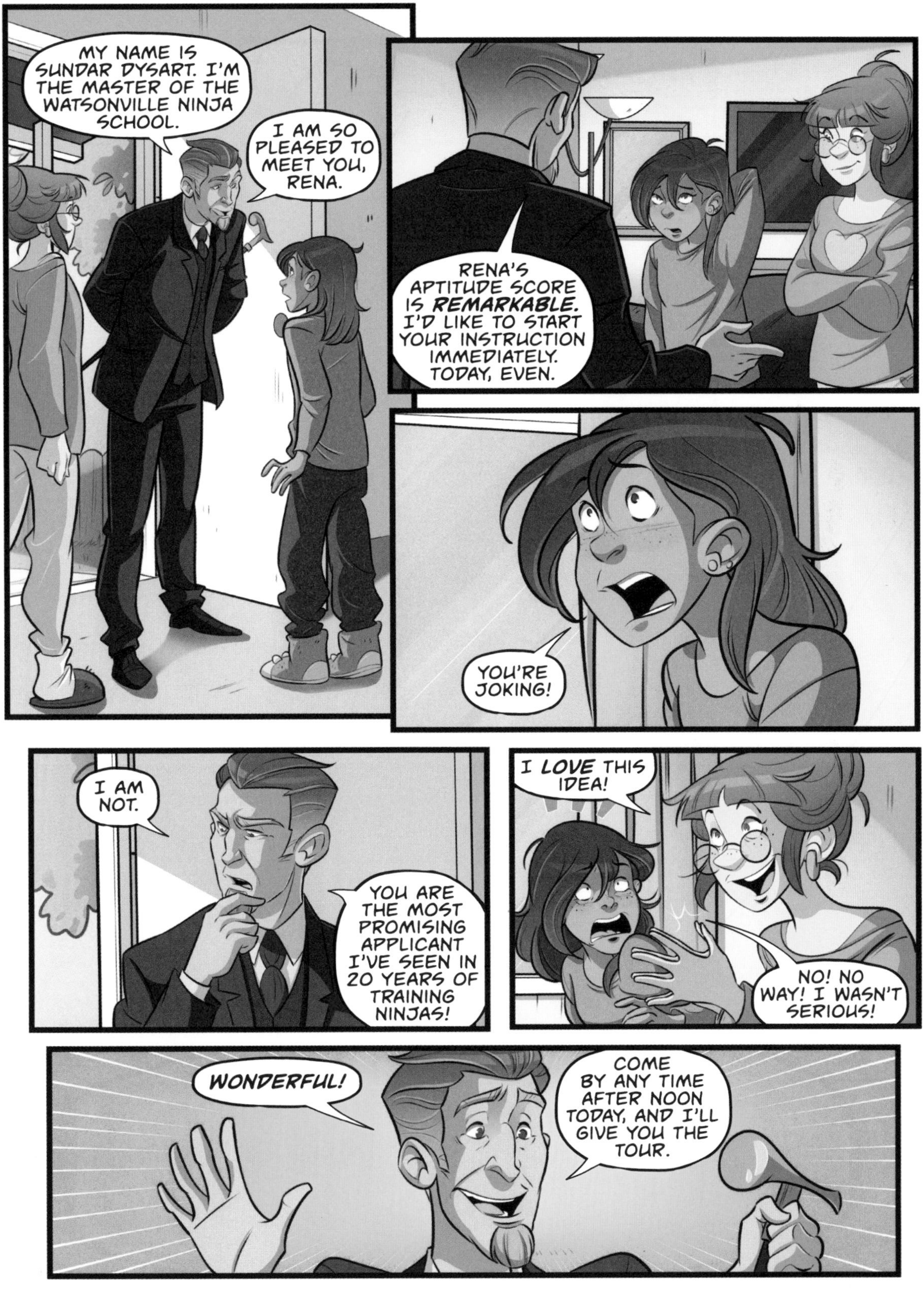
MY NAME IS SUNDAR DYSART. I'M THE MASTER OF THE WATSONVILLE NINJA SCHOOL.
I AM SO PLEASED TO MEET YOU, RENA.
RENA'S APTITUDE SCORE IS **REMARKABLE.** I'D LIKE TO START YOUR INSTRUCTION IMMEDIATELY. TODAY, EVEN.
YOU'RE JOKING!
I AM NOT.
YOU ARE THE MOST PROMISING APPLICANT I'VE SEEN IN 20 YEARS OF TRAINING NINJAS!
I **LOVE** THIS IDEA!
NO! NO WAY! I WASN'T SERIOUS!
**WONDERFUL!**
COME BY ANY TIME AFTER NOON TODAY, AND I'LL GIVE YOU THE TOUR.

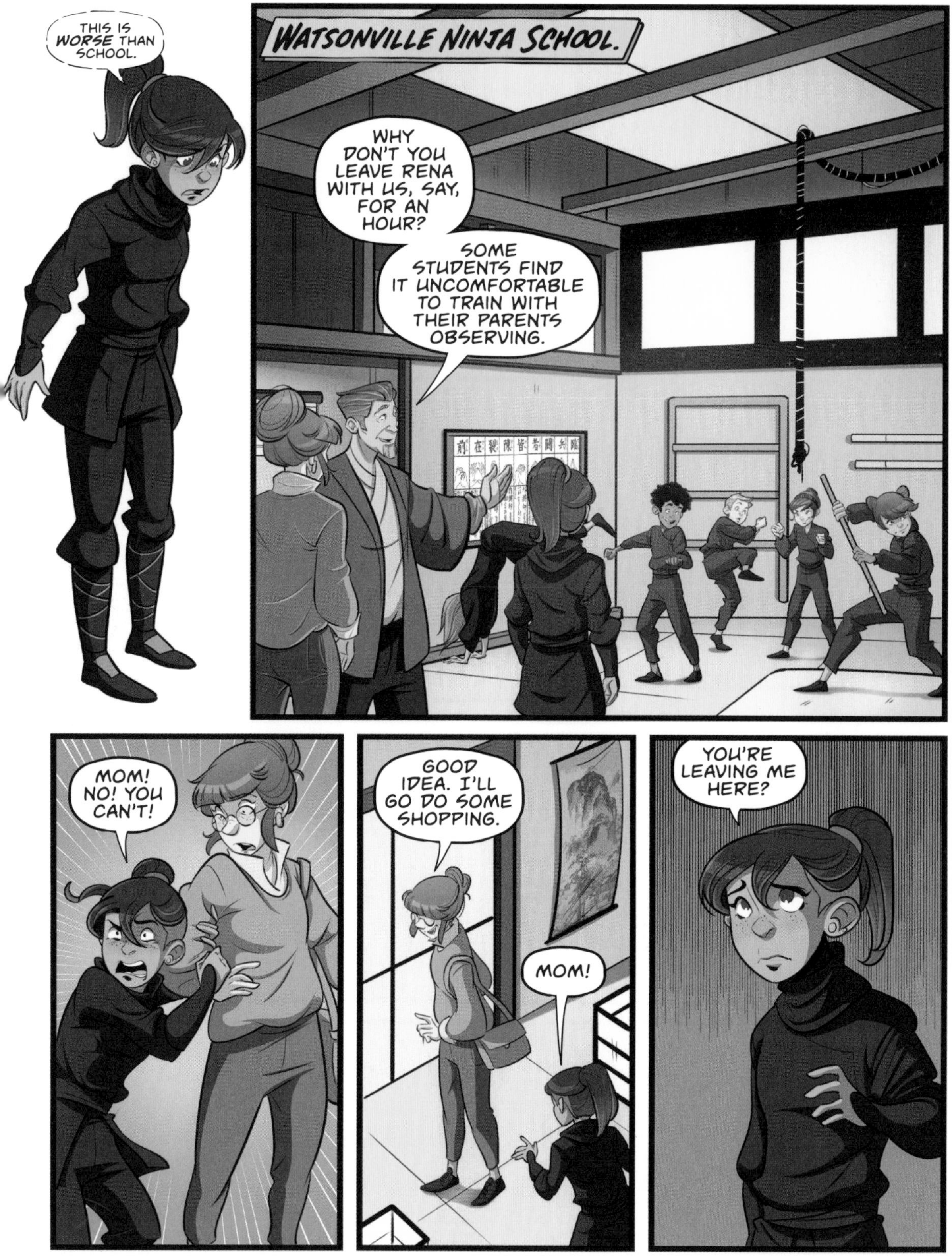
THIS IS WORSE THAN SCHOOL.
WATSONVILLE NINJA SCHOOL.
WHY DON'T YOU LEAVE RENA WITH US, SAY, FOR AN HOUR?
SOME STUDENTS FIND IT UNCOMFORTABLE TO TRAIN WITH THEIR PARENTS OBSERVING.
MOM! NO! YOU CAN'T!
GOOD IDEA. I'LL GO DO SOME SHOPPING.
MOM!
YOU'RE LEAVING ME HERE?

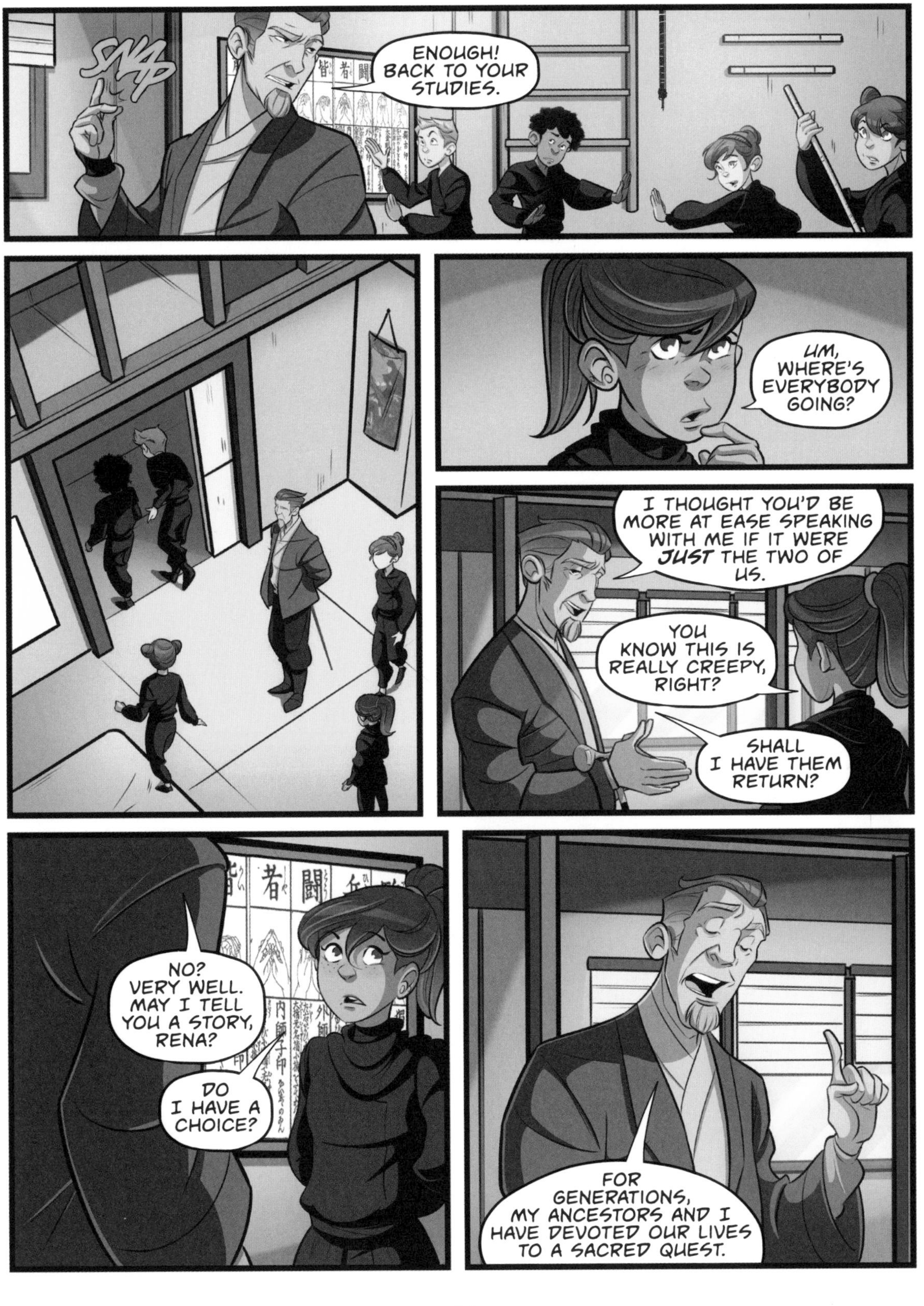
SNAP
ENOUGH! BACK TO YOUR STUDIES.
UM, WHERE'S EVERYBODY GOING?
I THOUGHT YOU'D BE MORE AT EASE SPEAKING WITH ME IF IT WERE *JUST* THE TWO OF US.
YOU KNOW THIS IS REALLY CREEPY, RIGHT?
SHALL I HAVE THEM RETURN?
NO? VERY WELL. MAY I TELL YOU A STORY, RENA?
DO I HAVE A CHOICE?
FOR GENERATIONS, MY ANCESTORS AND I HAVE DEVOTED OUR LIVES TO A SACRED QUEST.

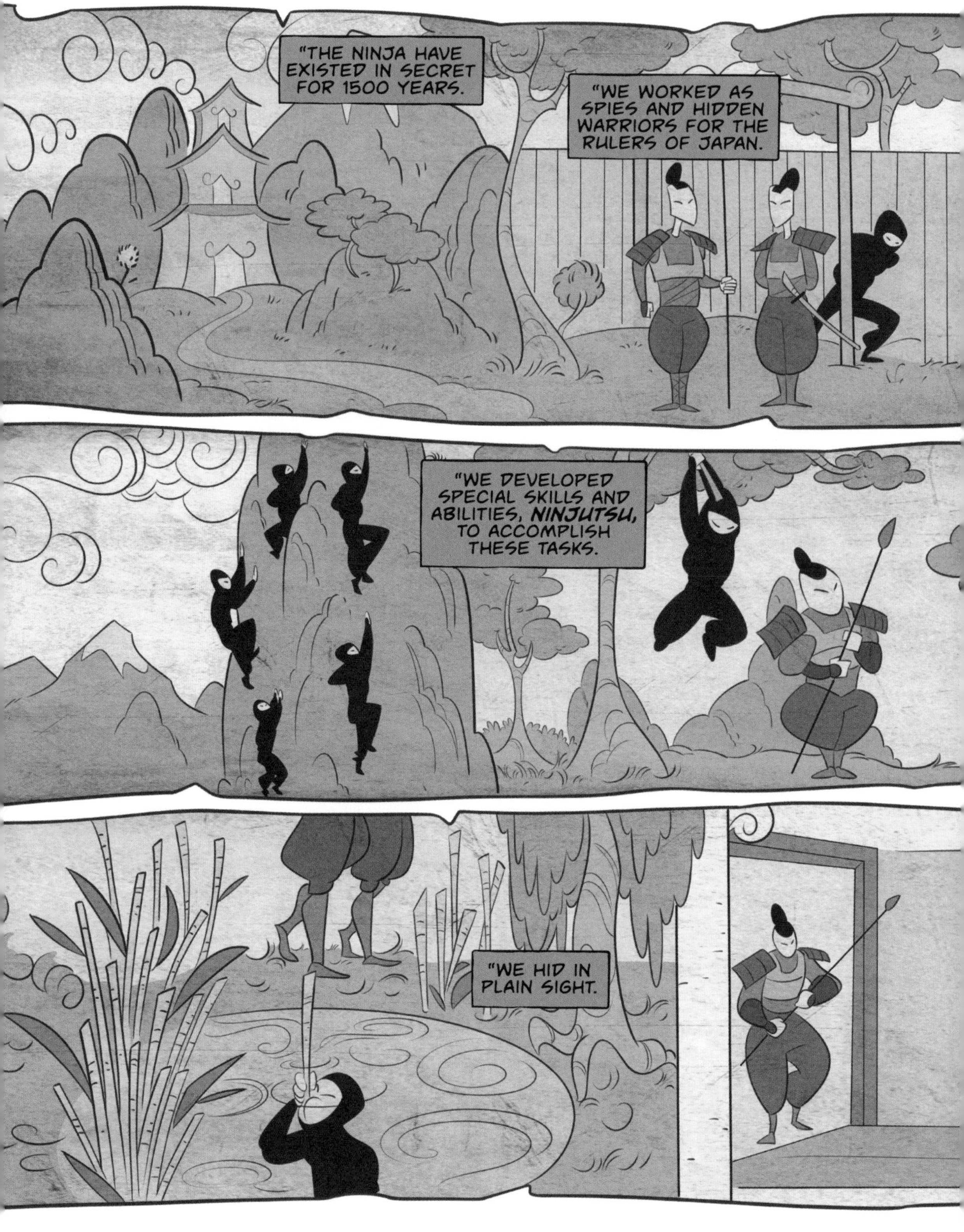
"THE NINJA HAVE EXISTED IN SECRET FOR 1500 YEARS.
"WE WORKED AS SPIES AND HIDDEN WARRIORS FOR THE RULERS OF JAPAN.
"WE DEVELOPED SPECIAL SKILLS AND ABILITIES, NINJUTSU, TO ACCOMPLISH THESE TASKS.
"WE HID IN PLAIN SIGHT.

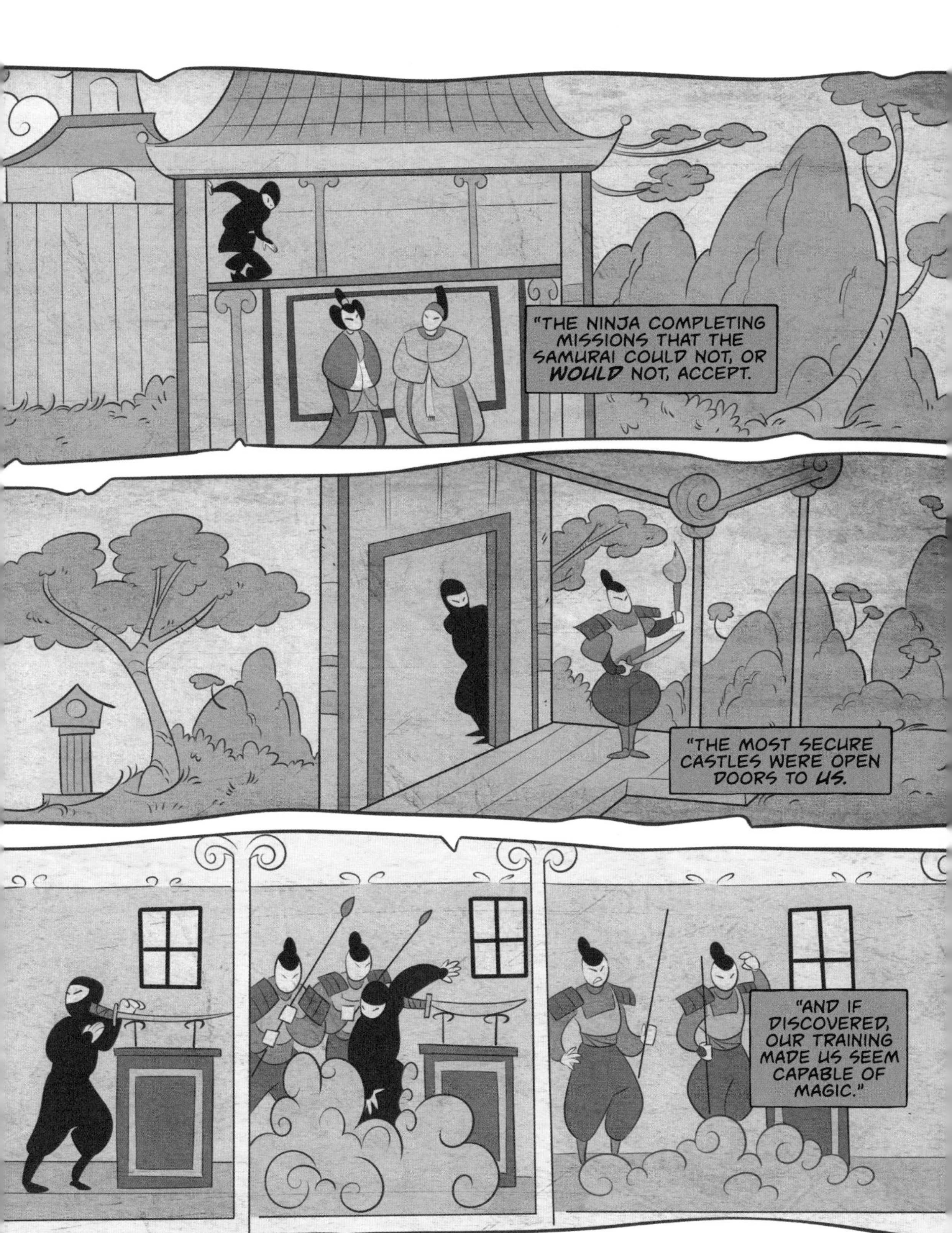
"THE NINJA COMPLETING MISSIONS THAT THE SAMURAI COULD NOT, OR WOULD NOT, ACCEPT.
"THE MOST SECURE CASTLES WERE OPEN DOORS TO US.
"AND IF DISCOVERED, OUR TRAINING MADE US SEEM CAPABLE OF MAGIC."

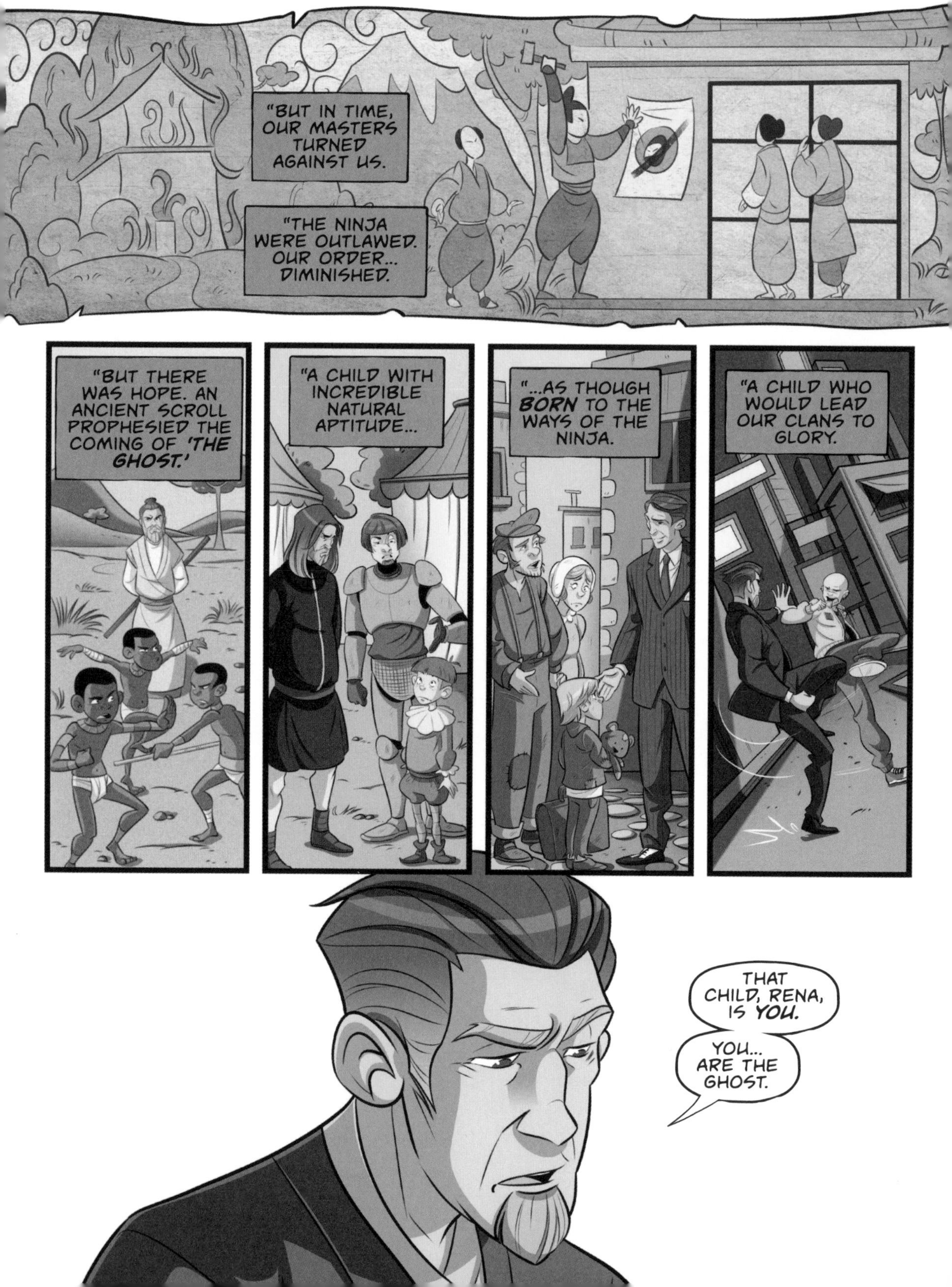
"BUT IN TIME, OUR MASTERS TURNED AGAINST US.
"THE NINJA WERE OUTLAWED. OUR ORDER... DIMINISHED.
"BUT THERE WAS HOPE. AN ANCIENT SCROLL PROPHESIED THE COMING OF *'THE GHOST.'*
"A CHILD WITH INCREDIBLE NATURAL APTITUDE...
"...AS THOUGH *BORN* TO THE WAYS OF THE NINJA.
"A CHILD WHO WOULD LEAD OUR CLANS TO GLORY.
THAT CHILD, RENA, IS *YOU.*
YOU... ARE THE GHOST.

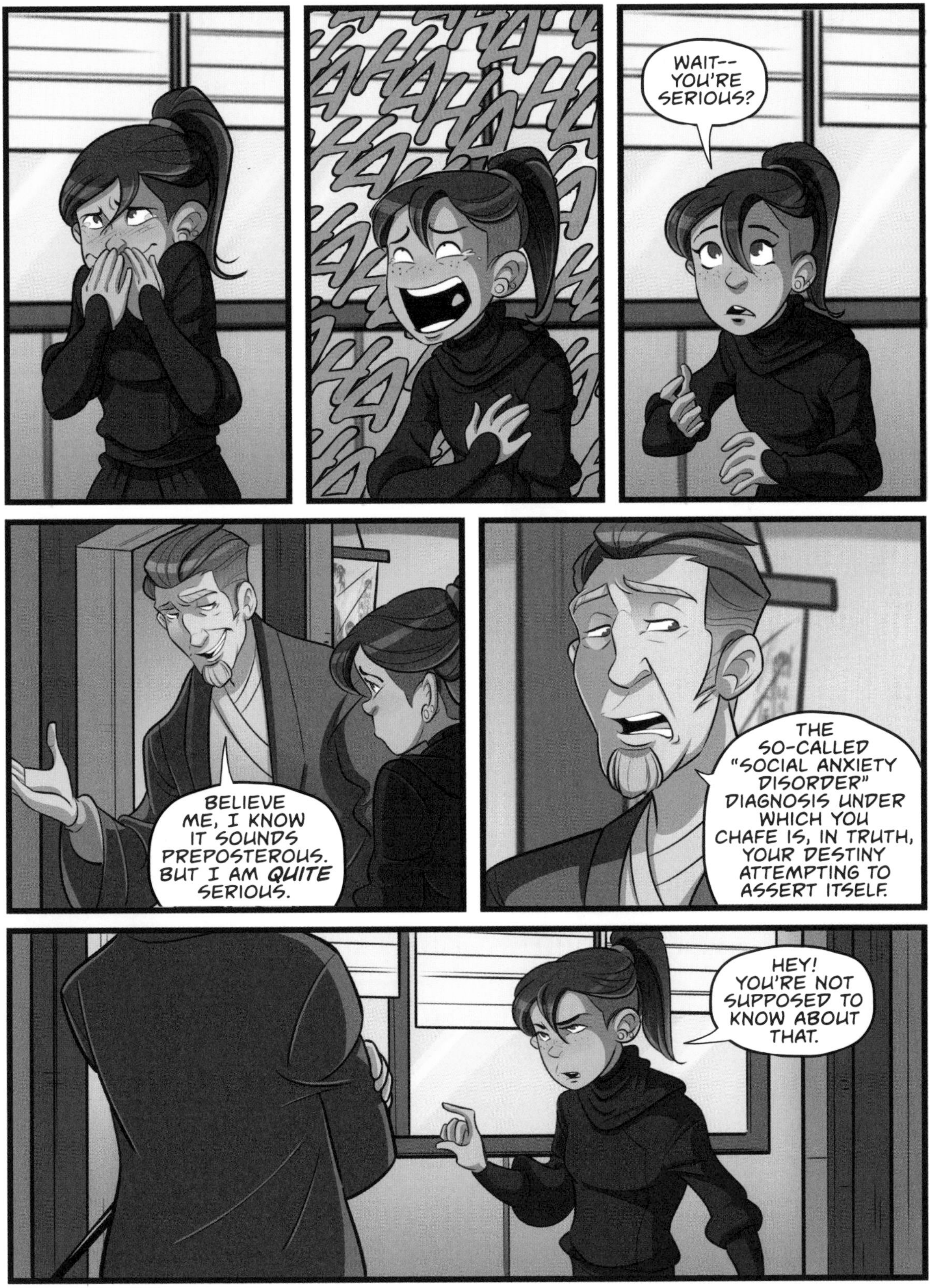
HAHAHAHA
WAIT-- YOU'RE SERIOUS?
BELIEVE ME, I KNOW IT SOUNDS PREPOSTEROUS. BUT I AM *QUITE* SERIOUS.
THE SO-CALLED "SOCIAL ANXIETY DISORDER" DIAGNOSIS UNDER WHICH YOU CHAFE IS, IN TRUTH, YOUR DESTINY ATTEMPTING TO ASSERT ITSELF.
HEY! YOU'RE NOT SUPPOSED TO KNOW ABOUT THAT.

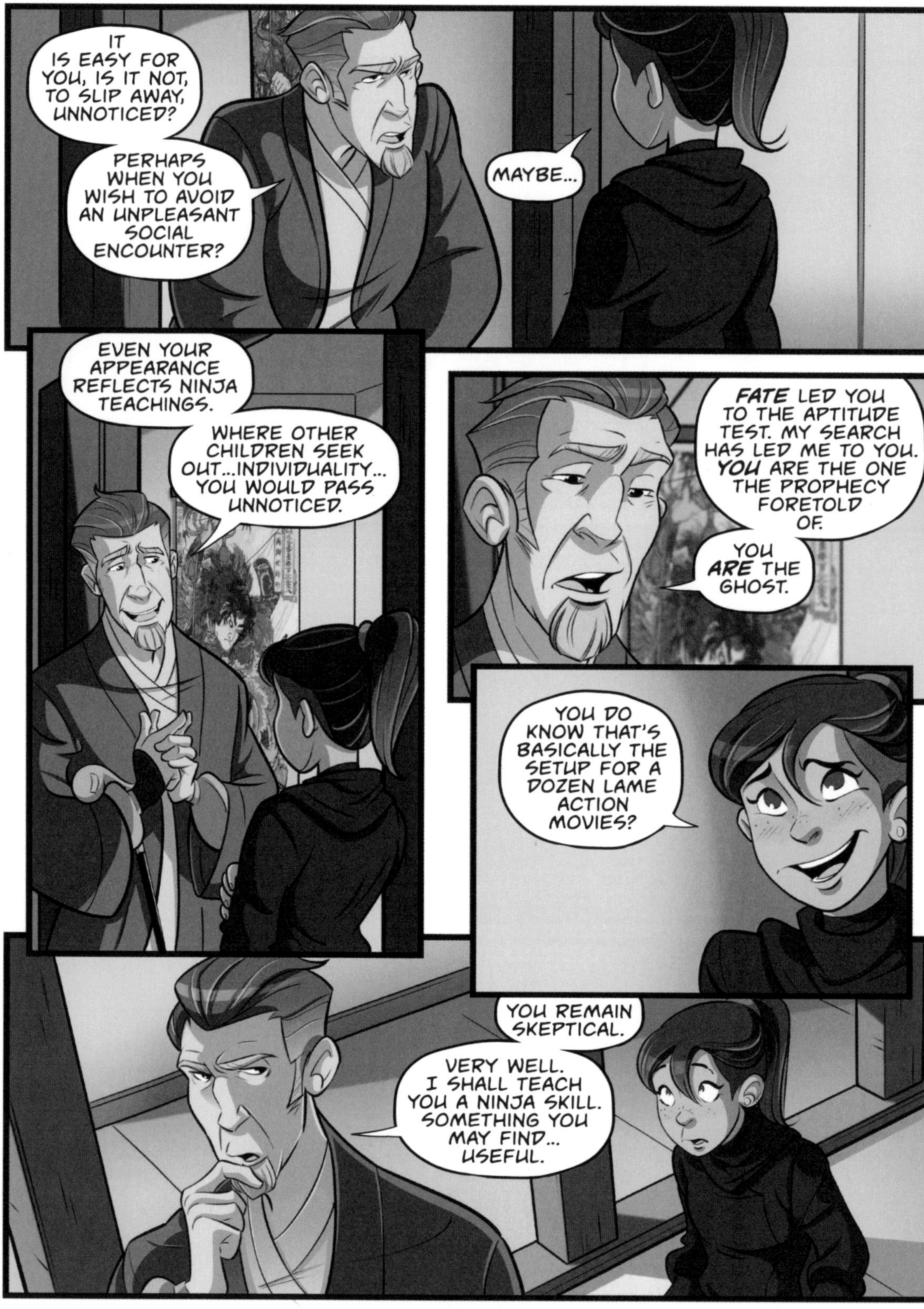

IT IS EASY FOR YOU, IS IT NOT, TO SLIP AWAY, UNNOTICED?
PERHAPS WHEN YOU WISH TO AVOID AN UNPLEASANT SOCIAL ENCOUNTER?
MAYBE...
EVEN YOUR APPEARANCE REFLECTS NINJA TEACHINGS.
WHERE OTHER CHILDREN SEEK OUT...INDIVIDUALITY... YOU WOULD PASS UNNOTICED.
FATE LED YOU TO THE APTITUDE TEST. MY SEARCH HAS LED ME TO YOU. YOU ARE THE ONE THE PROPHECY FORETOLD OF.
YOU ARE THE GHOST.
YOU DO KNOW THAT'S BASICALLY THE SETUP FOR A DOZEN LAME ACTION MOVIES?
YOU REMAIN SKEPTICAL.
VERY WELL. I SHALL TEACH YOU A NINJA SKILL. SOMETHING YOU MAY FIND... USEFUL.

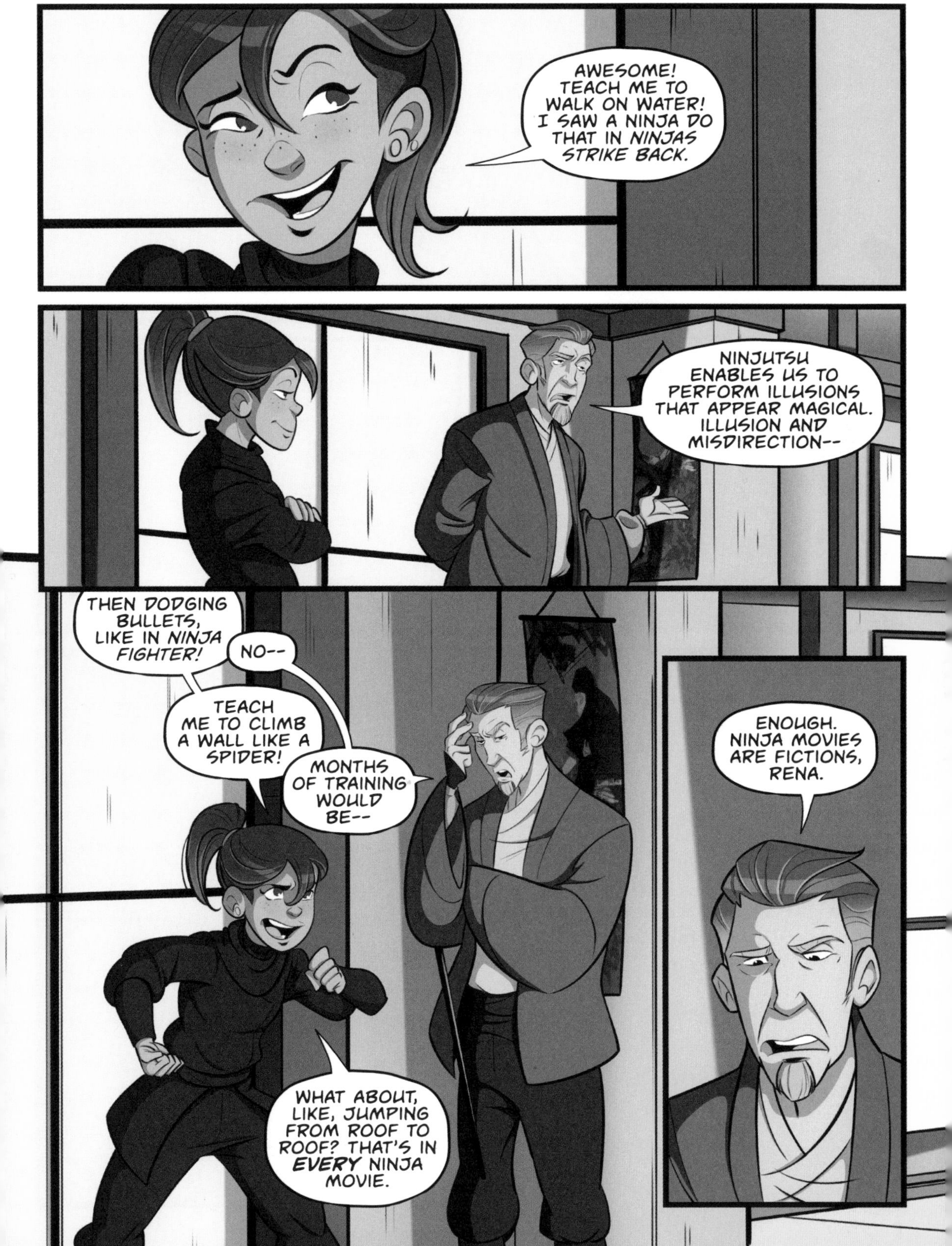
AWESOME! TEACH ME TO WALK ON WATER! I SAW A NINJA DO THAT IN *NINJAS STRIKE BACK.*
NINJUTSU ENABLES US TO PERFORM ILLUSIONS THAT APPEAR MAGICAL. ILLUSION AND MISDIRECTION--
THEN DODGING BULLETS, LIKE IN *NINJA FIGHTER!*
NO--
TEACH ME TO CLIMB A WALL LIKE A SPIDER!
MONTHS OF TRAINING WOULD BE--
WHAT ABOUT, LIKE, JUMPING FROM ROOF TO ROOF? THAT'S IN ***EVERY*** NINJA MOVIE.
ENOUGH. NINJA MOVIES ARE FICTIONS, RENA.

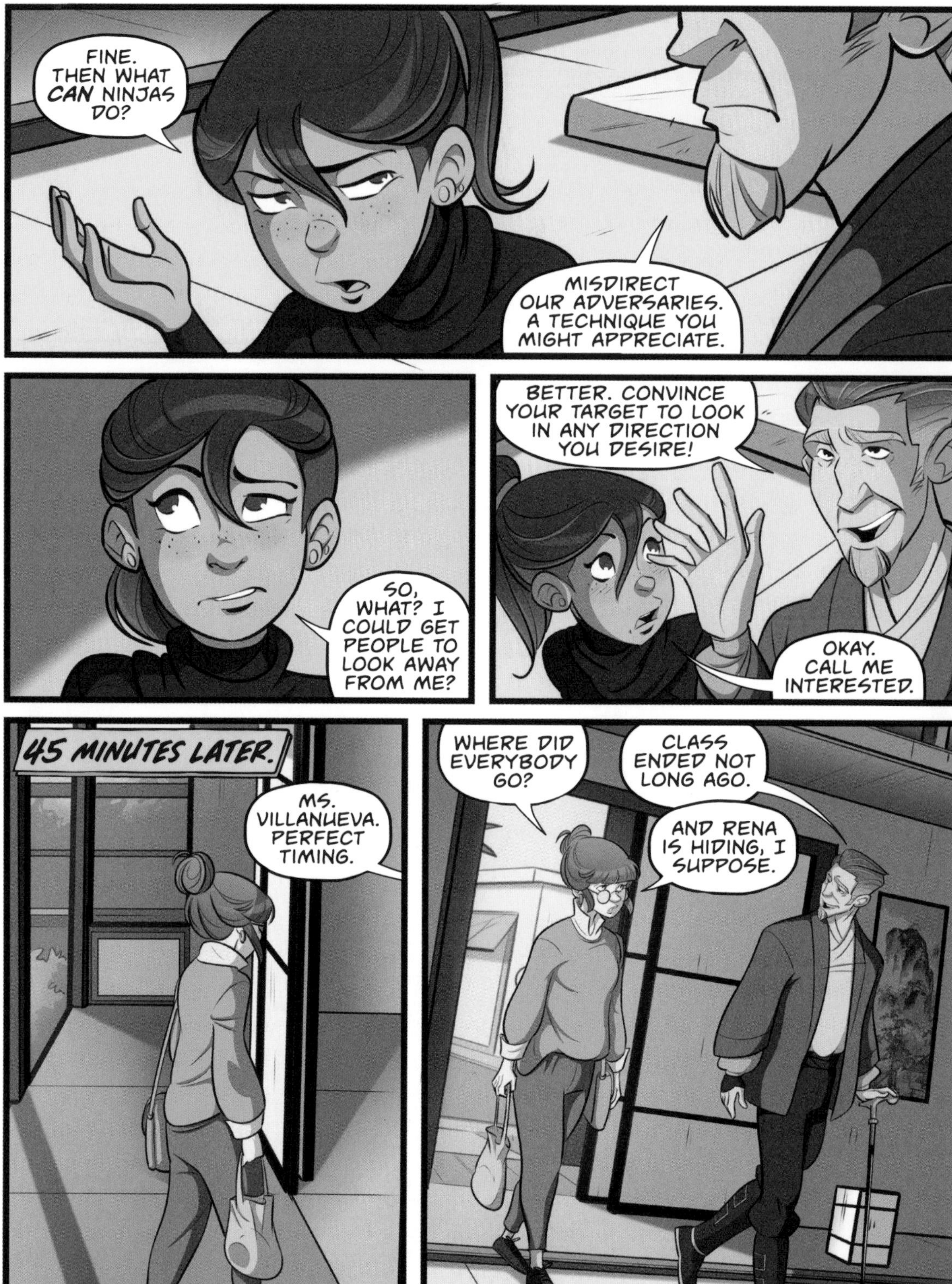
FINE. THEN WHAT CAN NINJAS DO?
MISDIRECT OUR ADVERSARIES. A TECHNIQUE YOU MIGHT APPRECIATE.
SO, WHAT? I COULD GET PEOPLE TO LOOK AWAY FROM ME?
BETTER. CONVINCE YOUR TARGET TO LOOK IN ANY DIRECTION YOU DESIRE!
OKAY. CALL ME INTERESTED.
45 MINUTES LATER.
MS. VILLANUEVA. PERFECT TIMING.
WHERE DID EVERYBODY GO?
CLASS ENDED NOT LONG AGO.
AND RENA IS HIDING, I SUPPOSE.

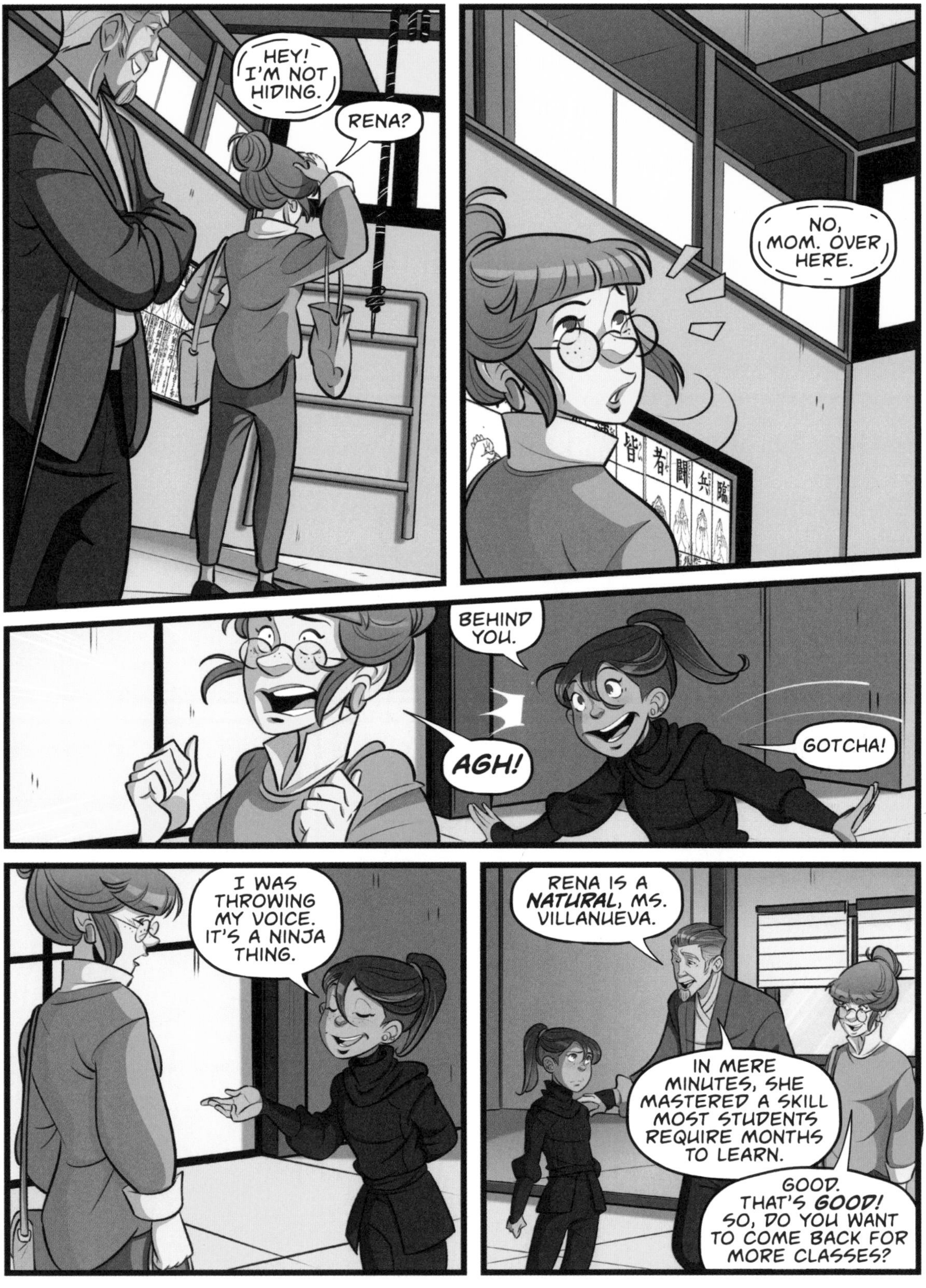
HEY! I'M NOT HIDING.
RENA?
NO, MOM. OVER HERE.
BEHIND YOU.
AGH!
GOTCHA!
I WAS THROWING MY VOICE. IT'S A NINJA THING.
RENA IS A NATURAL, MS. VILLANUEVA.
IN MERE MINUTES, SHE MASTERED A SKILL MOST STUDENTS REQUIRE MONTHS TO LEARN.
GOOD. THAT'S GOOD! SO, DO YOU WANT TO COME BACK FOR MORE CLASSES?

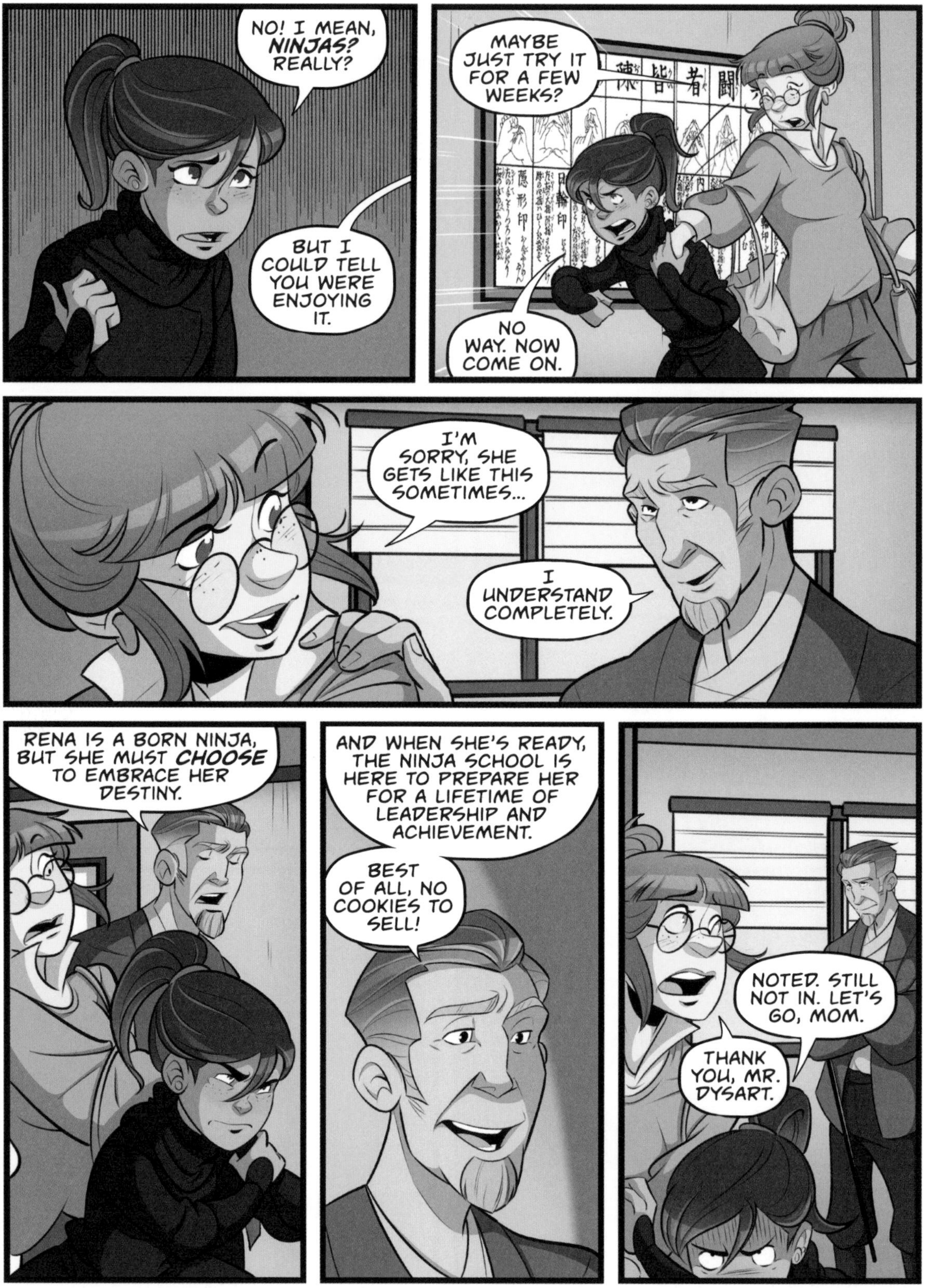
NO! I MEAN, ***NINJAS?*** REALLY?
BUT I COULD TELL YOU WERE ENJOYING IT.
MAYBE JUST TRY IT FOR A FEW WEEKS?
NO WAY. NOW COME ON.
I'M SORRY, SHE GETS LIKE THIS SOMETIMES...
I UNDERSTAND COMPLETELY.
RENA IS A BORN NINJA, BUT SHE MUST ***CHOOSE*** TO EMBRACE HER DESTINY.
AND WHEN SHE'S READY, THE NINJA SCHOOL IS HERE TO PREPARE HER FOR A LIFETIME OF LEADERSHIP AND ACHIEVEMENT.
BEST OF ALL, NO COOKIES TO SELL!
THANK YOU, MR. DYSART.
NOTED. STILL NOT IN. LET'S GO, MOM.

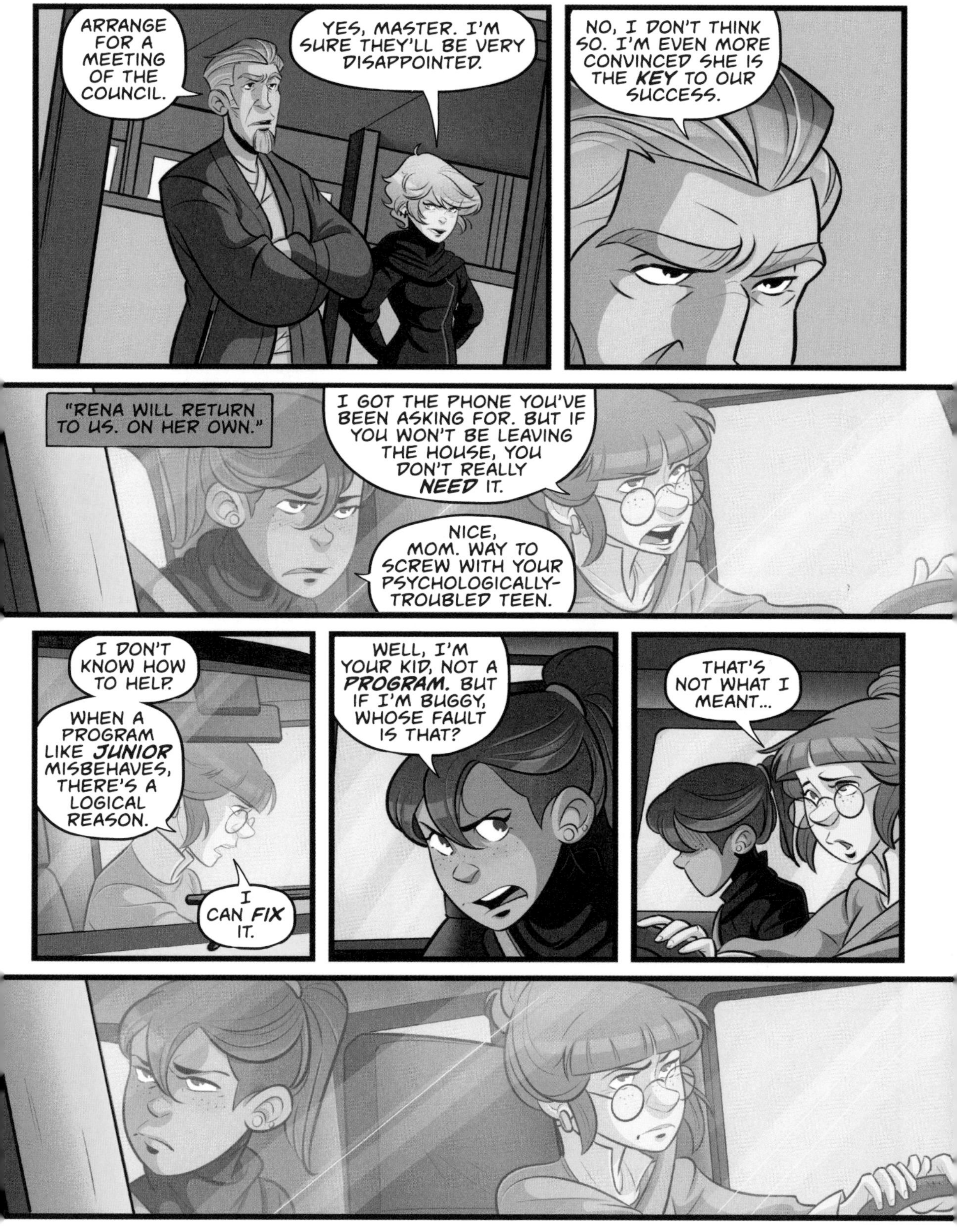
ARRANGE FOR A MEETING OF THE COUNCIL.
YES, MASTER. I'M SURE THEY'LL BE VERY DISAPPOINTED.
NO, I DON'T THINK SO. I'M EVEN MORE CONVINCED SHE IS THE KEY TO OUR SUCCESS.
"RENA WILL RETURN TO US. ON HER OWN."
I GOT THE PHONE YOU'VE BEEN ASKING FOR. BUT IF YOU WON'T BE LEAVING THE HOUSE, YOU DON'T REALLY NEED IT.
NICE, MOM. WAY TO SCREW WITH YOUR PSYCHOLOGICALLY-TROUBLED TEEN.
I DON'T KNOW HOW TO HELP.
WHEN A PROGRAM LIKE JUNIOR MISBEHAVES, THERE'S A LOGICAL REASON.
I CAN FIX IT.
WELL, I'M YOUR KID, NOT A PROGRAM. BUT IF I'M BUGGY, WHOSE FAULT IS THAT?
THAT'S NOT WHAT I MEANT...

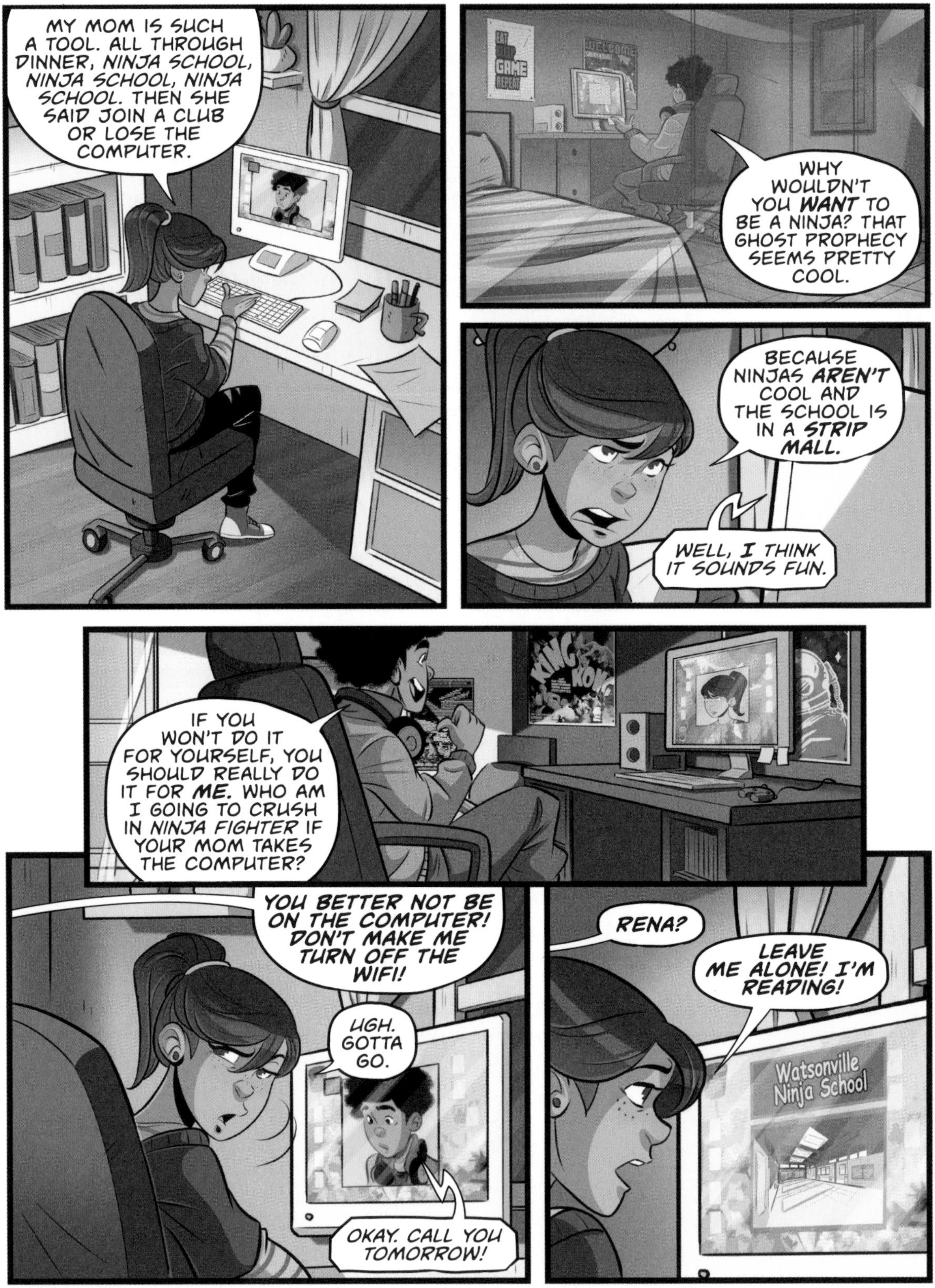
MY MOM IS SUCH A TOOL. ALL THROUGH DINNER, NINJA SCHOOL, NINJA SCHOOL, NINJA SCHOOL. THEN SHE SAID JOIN A CLUB OR LOSE THE COMPUTER.
WHY WOULDN'T YOU WANT TO BE A NINJA? THAT GHOST PROPHECY SEEMS PRETTY COOL.
BECAUSE NINJAS AREN'T COOL AND THE SCHOOL IS IN A STRIP MALL.
WELL, I THINK IT SOUNDS FUN.
IF YOU WON'T DO IT FOR YOURSELF, YOU SHOULD REALLY DO IT FOR ME. WHO AM I GOING TO CRUSH IN NINJA FIGHTER IF YOUR MOM TAKES THE COMPUTER?
YOU BETTER NOT BE ON THE COMPUTER! DON'T MAKE ME TURN OFF THE WIFI!
UGH. GOTTA GO.
OKAY. CALL YOU TOMORROW!
RENA?
LEAVE ME ALONE! I'M READING!
Watsonville Ninja School

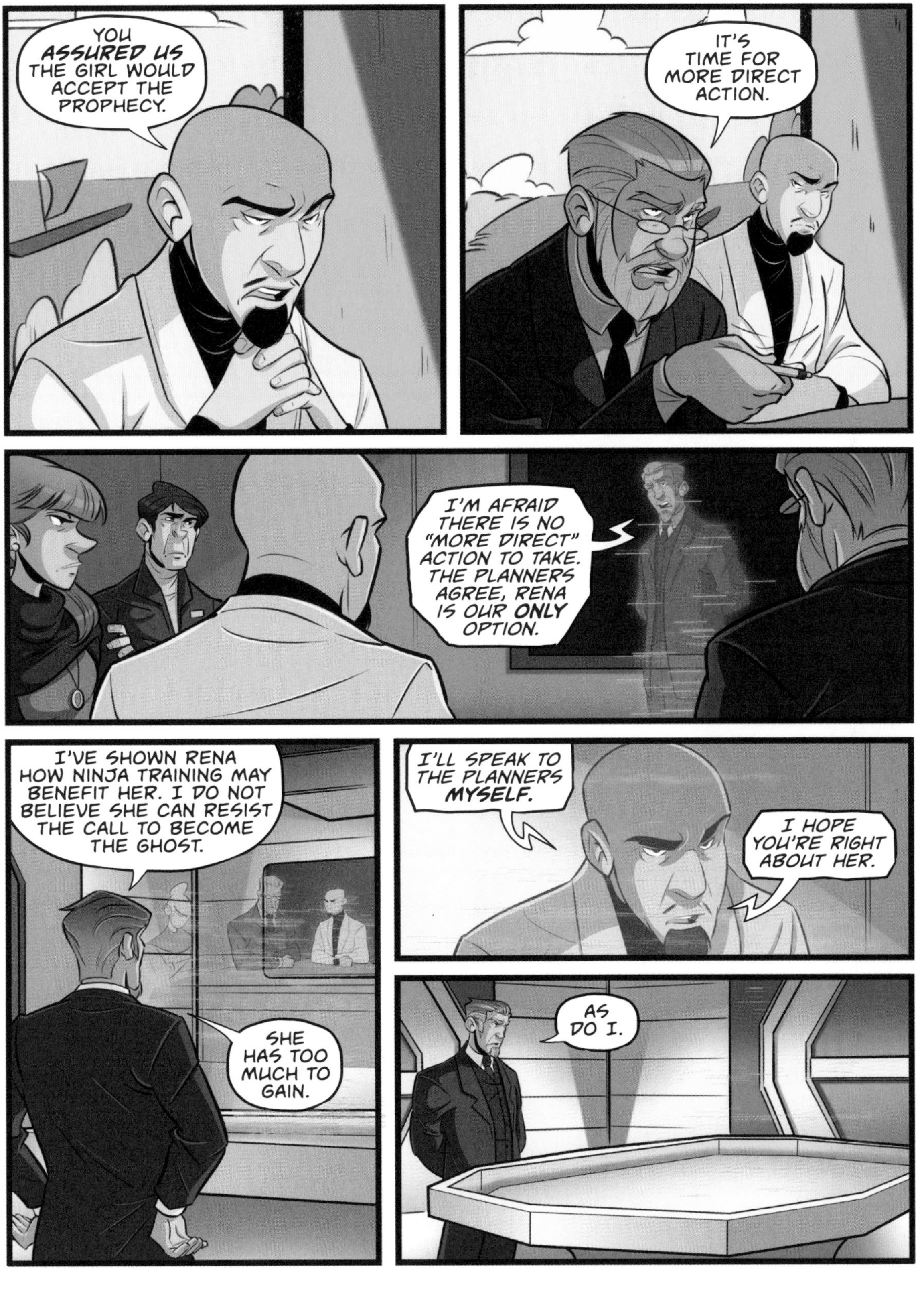
YOU **ASSURED US** THE GIRL WOULD ACCEPT THE PROPHECY.
IT'S TIME FOR MORE DIRECT ACTION.
I'M AFRAID THERE IS NO "MORE DIRECT" ACTION TO TAKE. THE PLANNERS AGREE, RENA IS OUR **ONLY** OPTION.
I'VE SHOWN RENA HOW NINJA TRAINING MAY BENEFIT HER. I DO NOT BELIEVE SHE CAN RESIST THE CALL TO BECOME THE GHOST.
SHE HAS TOO MUCH TO GAIN.
I'LL SPEAK TO THE PLANNERS **MYSELF**.
I HOPE YOU'RE RIGHT ABOUT HER.
AS DO I.

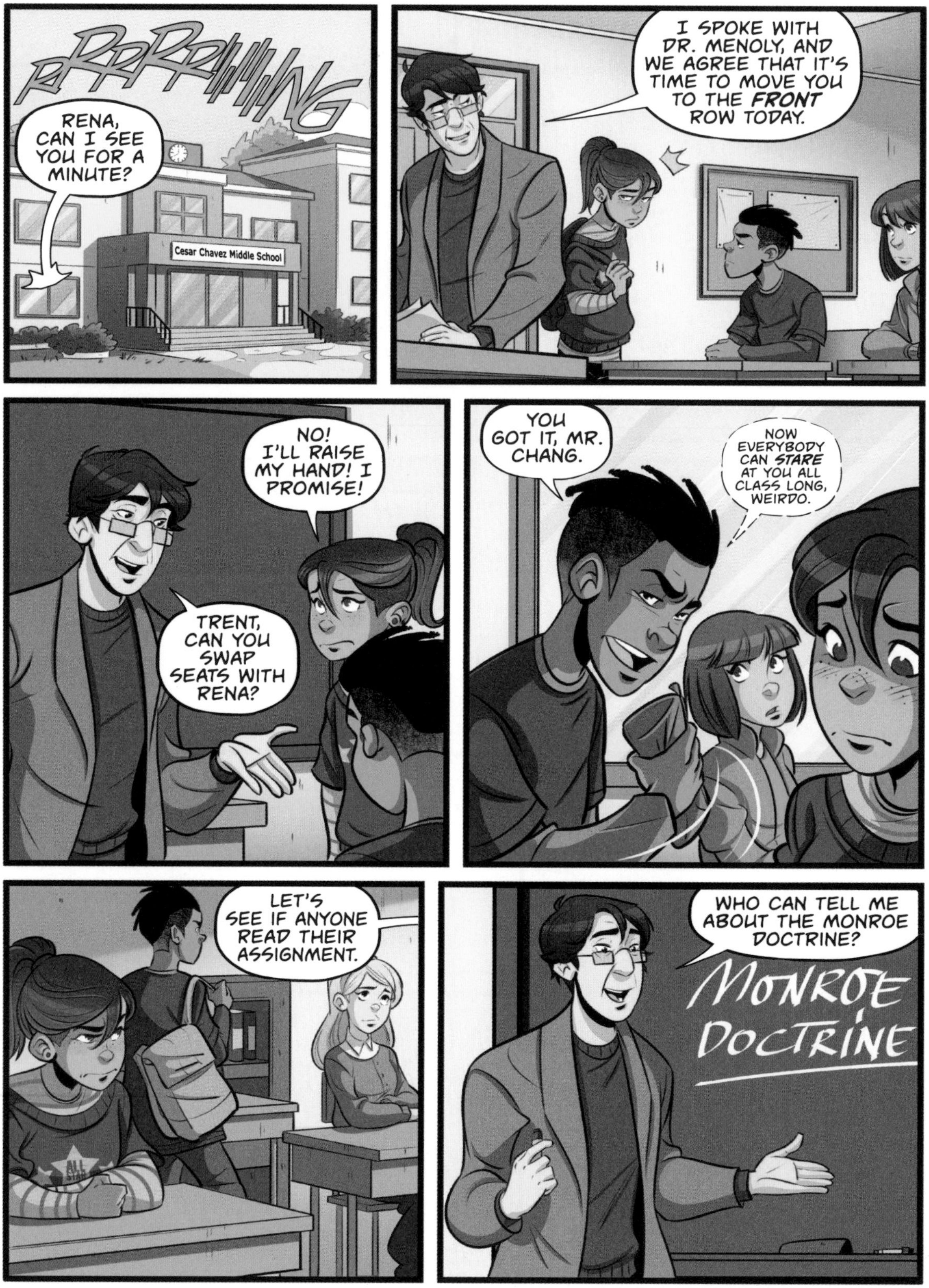
RRRRRIIIIING
RENA, CAN I SEE YOU FOR A MINUTE?
Cesar Chavez Middle School
I SPOKE WITH DR. MENOLY, AND WE AGREE THAT IT'S TIME TO MOVE YOU TO THE FRONT ROW TODAY.
NO! I'LL RAISE MY HAND! I PROMISE!
TRENT, CAN YOU SWAP SEATS WITH RENA?
YOU GOT IT, MR. CHANG.
NOW EVERYBODY CAN STARE AT YOU ALL CLASS LONG, WEIRDO.
LET'S SEE IF ANYONE READ THEIR ASSIGNMENT.
ALL STAR
WHO CAN TELL ME ABOUT THE MONROE DOCTRINE?
MONROE DOCTRINE

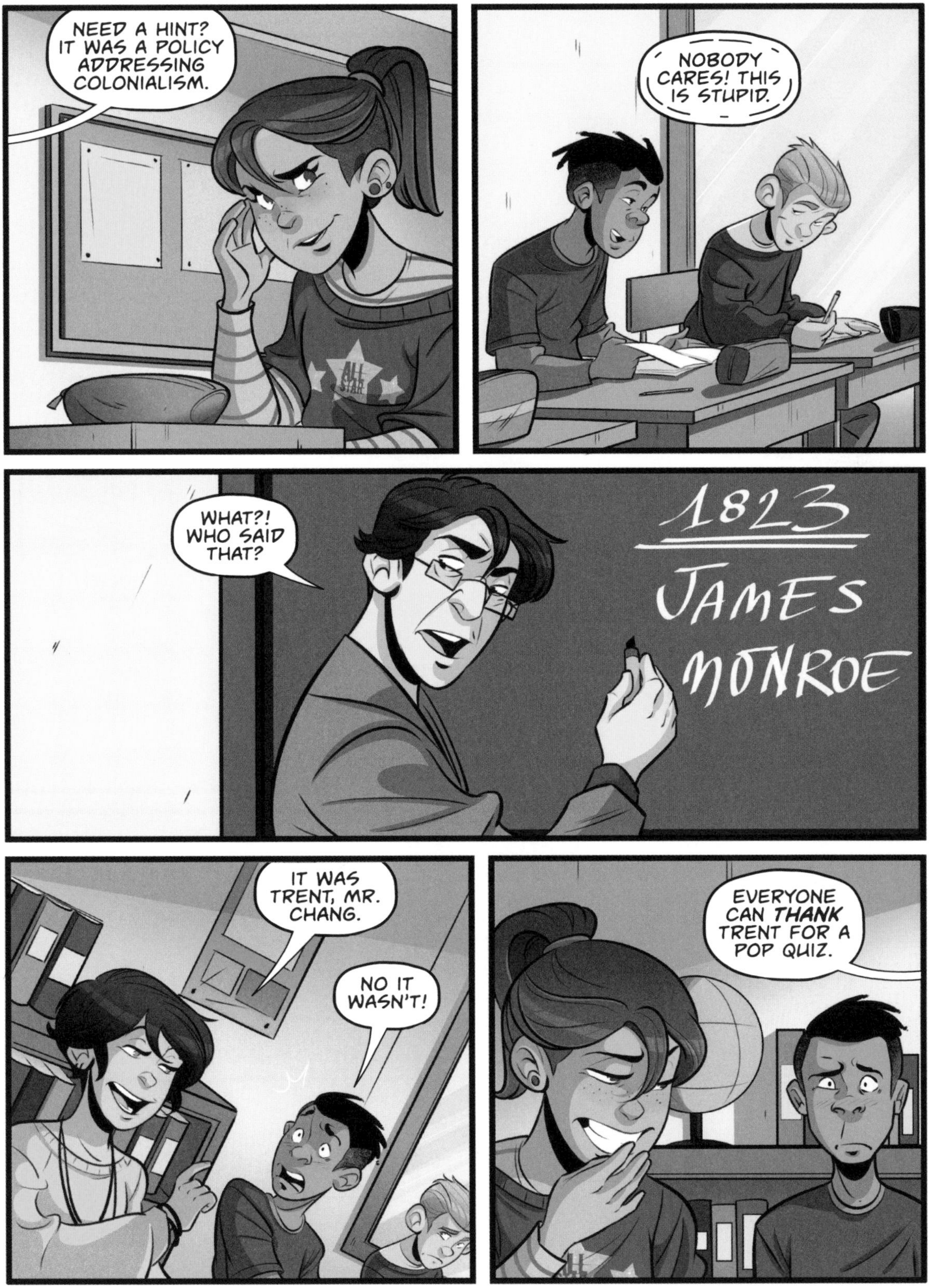
NEED A HINT? IT WAS A POLICY ADDRESSING COLONIALISM.
NOBODY CARES! THIS IS STUPID.
WHAT?! WHO SAID THAT?
1823
JAMES MONROE
IT WAS TRENT, MR. CHANG.
NO IT WASN'T!
EVERYONE CAN *THANK* TRENT FOR A POP QUIZ.

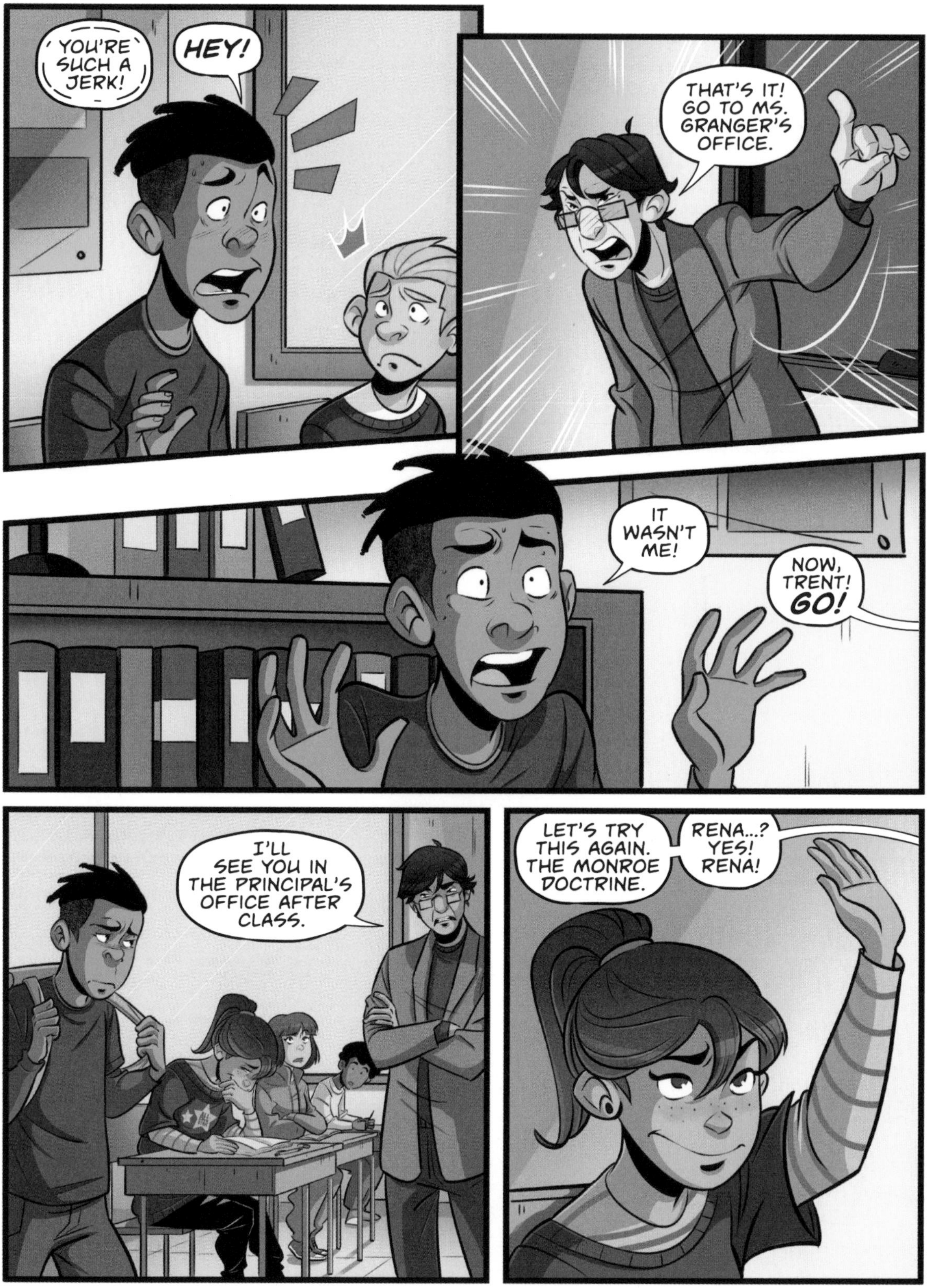
YOU'RE SUCH A JERK!
HEY!
THAT'S IT! GO TO MS. GRANGER'S OFFICE.
IT WASN'T ME!
NOW, TRENT! GO!
I'LL SEE YOU IN THE PRINCIPAL'S OFFICE AFTER CLASS.
LET'S TRY THIS AGAIN. THE MONROE DOCTRINE.
RENA...? YES! RENA!

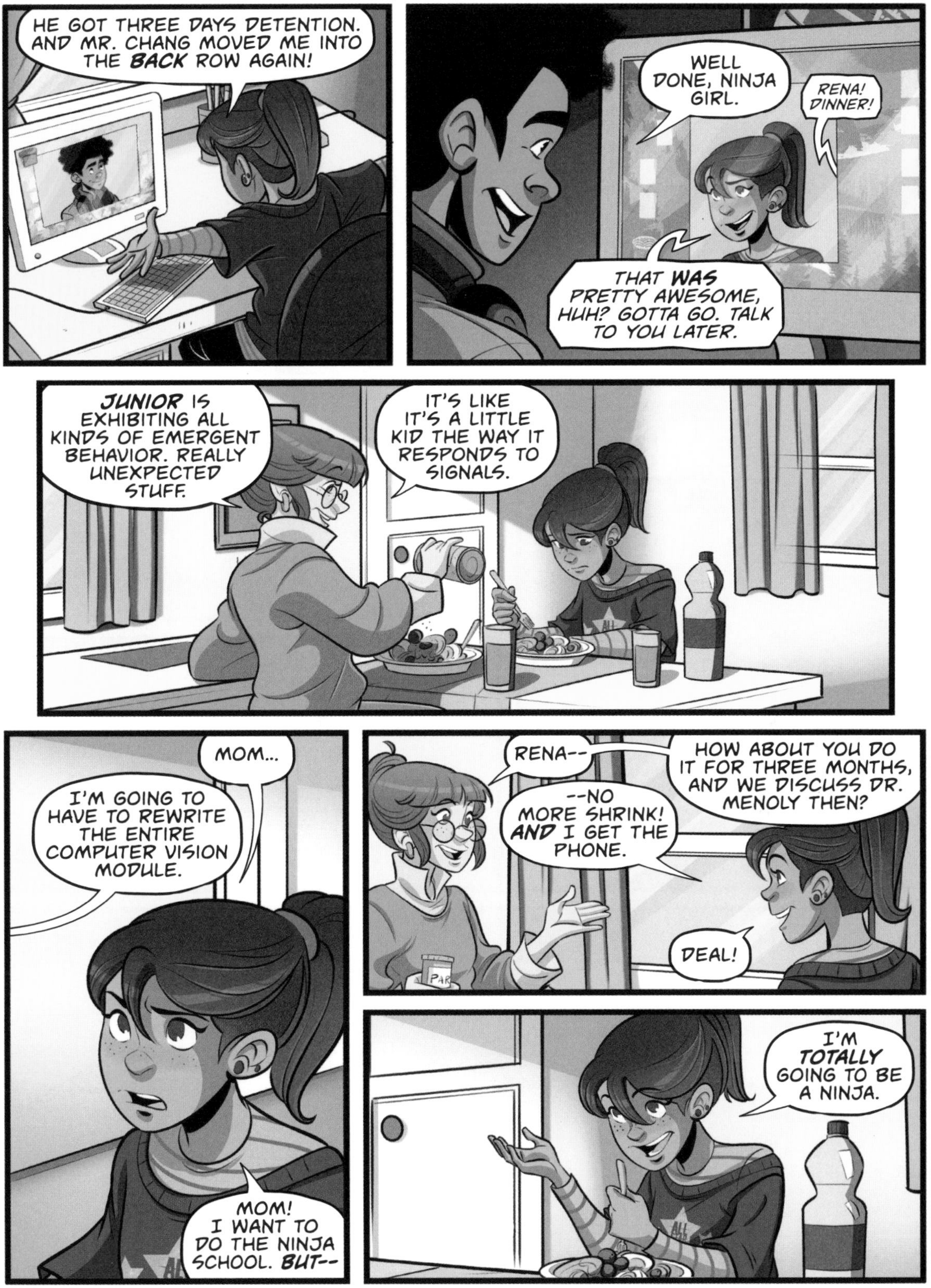

HE GOT THREE DAYS DETENTION. AND MR. CHANG MOVED ME INTO THE **BACK** ROW AGAIN!
WELL DONE, NINJA GIRL.
RENA! DINNER!
THAT **WAS** PRETTY AWESOME, HUH? GOTTA GO. TALK TO YOU LATER.
**JUNIOR** IS EXHIBITING ALL KINDS OF EMERGENT BEHAVIOR. REALLY UNEXPECTED STUFF.
IT'S LIKE IT'S A LITTLE KID THE WAY IT RESPONDS TO SIGNALS.
MOM...
I'M GOING TO HAVE TO REWRITE THE ENTIRE COMPUTER VISION MODULE.
MOM! I WANT TO DO THE NINJA SCHOOL. **BUT--**
RENA--
HOW ABOUT YOU DO IT FOR THREE MONTHS, AND WE DISCUSS DR. MENOLY THEN?
--NO MORE SHRINK! **AND** I GET THE PHONE.
DEAL!
I'M **TOTALLY** GOING TO BE A NINJA.

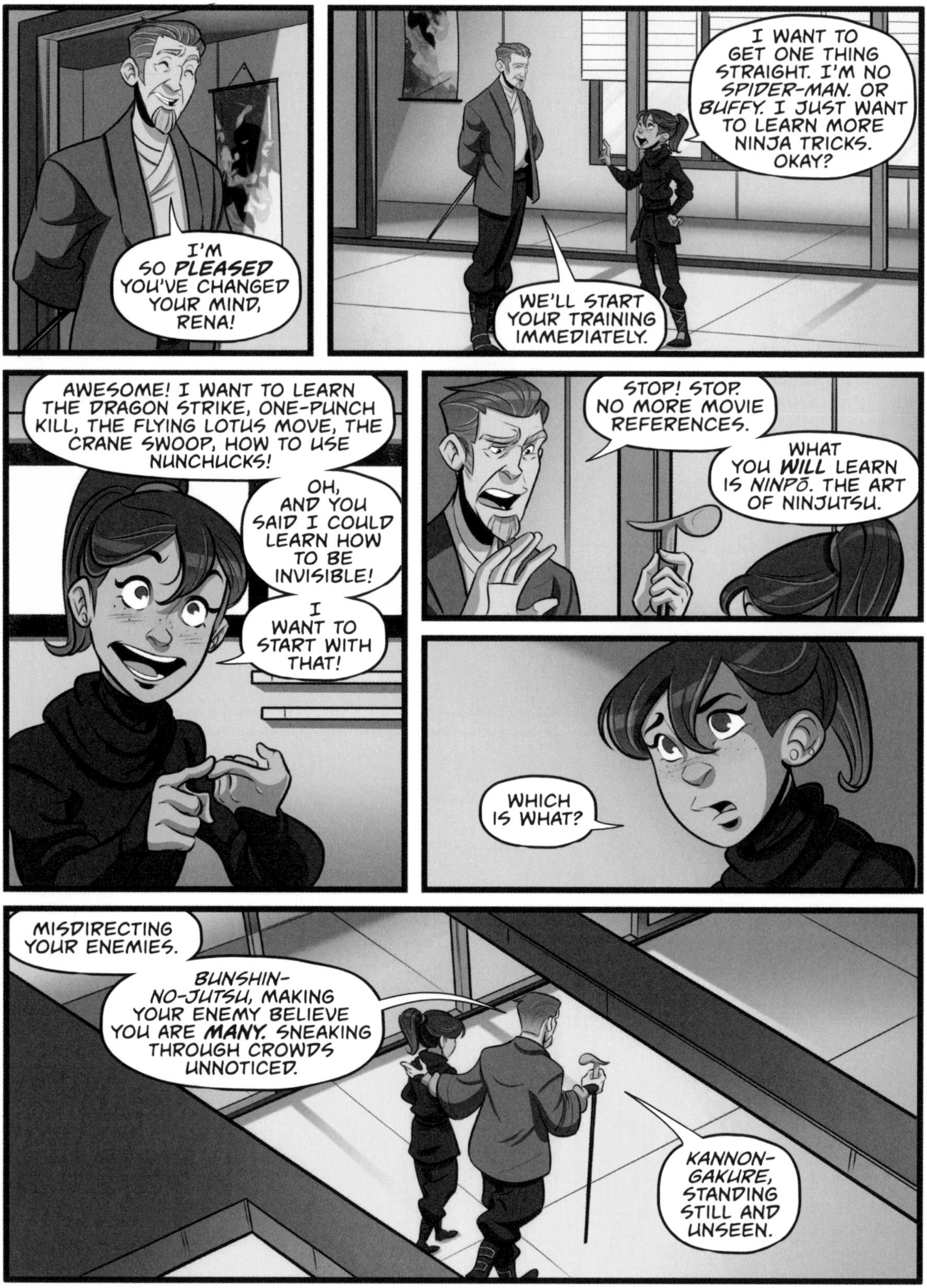
I'M SO PLEASED YOU'VE CHANGED YOUR MIND, RENA!
I WANT TO GET ONE THING STRAIGHT. I'M NO SPIDER-MAN. OR BUFFY. I JUST WANT TO LEARN MORE NINJA TRICKS. OKAY?
WE'LL START YOUR TRAINING IMMEDIATELY.
AWESOME! I WANT TO LEARN THE DRAGON STRIKE, ONE-PUNCH KILL, THE FLYING LOTUS MOVE, THE CRANE SWOOP, HOW TO USE NUNCHUCKS!
OH, AND YOU SAID I COULD LEARN HOW TO BE INVISIBLE!
I WANT TO START WITH THAT!
STOP! STOP. NO MORE MOVIE REFERENCES.
WHAT YOU WILL LEARN IS NINPŌ. THE ART OF NINJUTSU.
WHICH IS WHAT?
MISDIRECTING YOUR ENEMIES.
BUNSHIN-NO-JUTSU, MAKING YOUR ENEMY BELIEVE YOU ARE MANY. SNEAKING THROUGH CROWDS UNNOTICED.
KANNON-GAKURE, STANDING STILL AND UNSEEN.

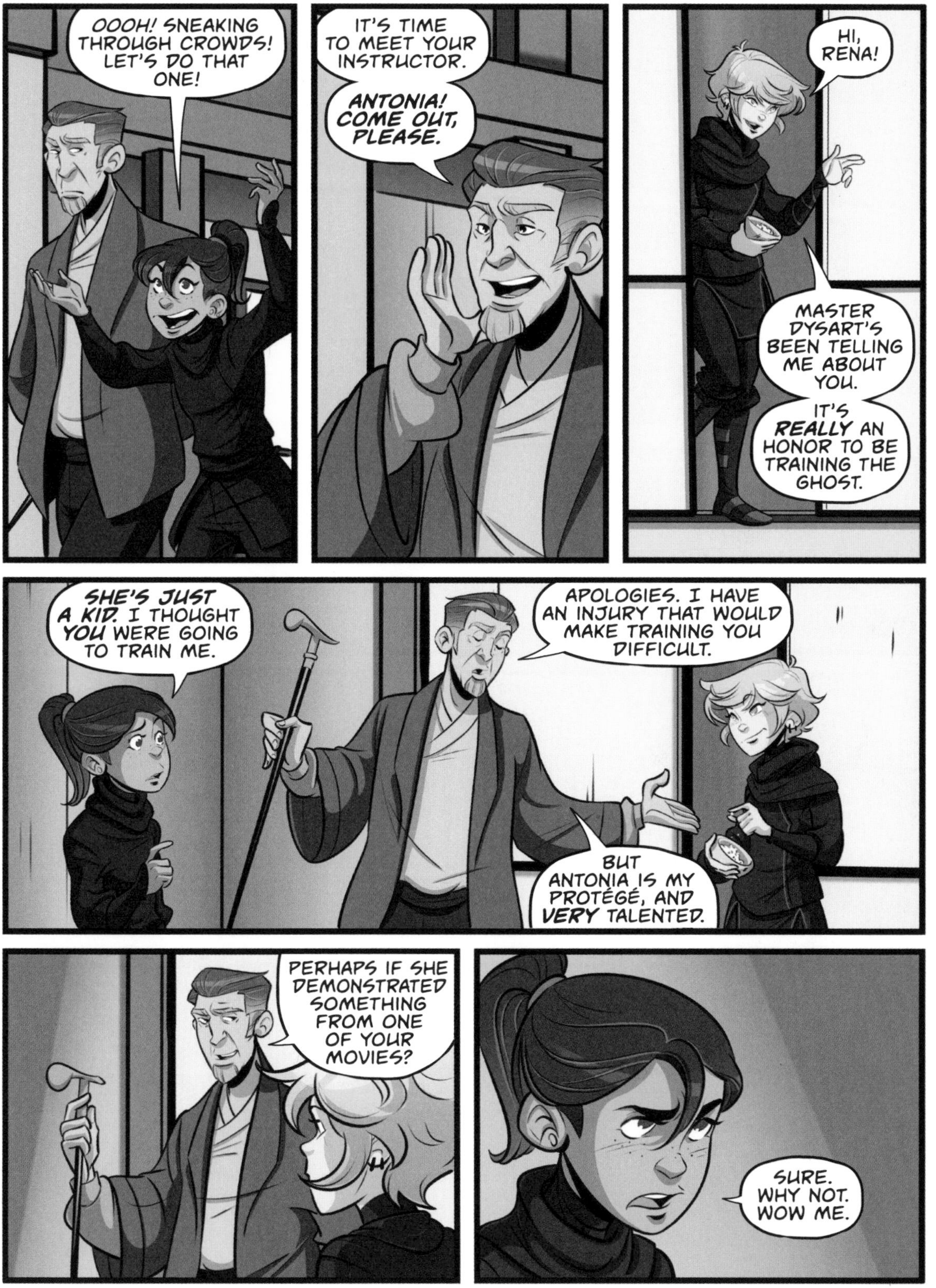
OOOH! SNEAKING THROUGH CROWDS! LET'S DO THAT ONE!
IT'S TIME TO MEET YOUR INSTRUCTOR.
ANTONIA! COME OUT, PLEASE.
HI, RENA!
MASTER DYSART'S BEEN TELLING ME ABOUT YOU.
IT'S REALLY AN HONOR TO BE TRAINING THE GHOST.
SHE'S JUST A KID. I THOUGHT YOU WERE GOING TO TRAIN ME.
APOLOGIES. I HAVE AN INJURY THAT WOULD MAKE TRAINING YOU DIFFICULT.
BUT ANTONIA IS MY PROTÉGÉ, AND VERY TALENTED.
PERHAPS IF SHE DEMONSTRATED SOMETHING FROM ONE OF YOUR MOVIES?
SURE. WHY NOT. WOW ME.

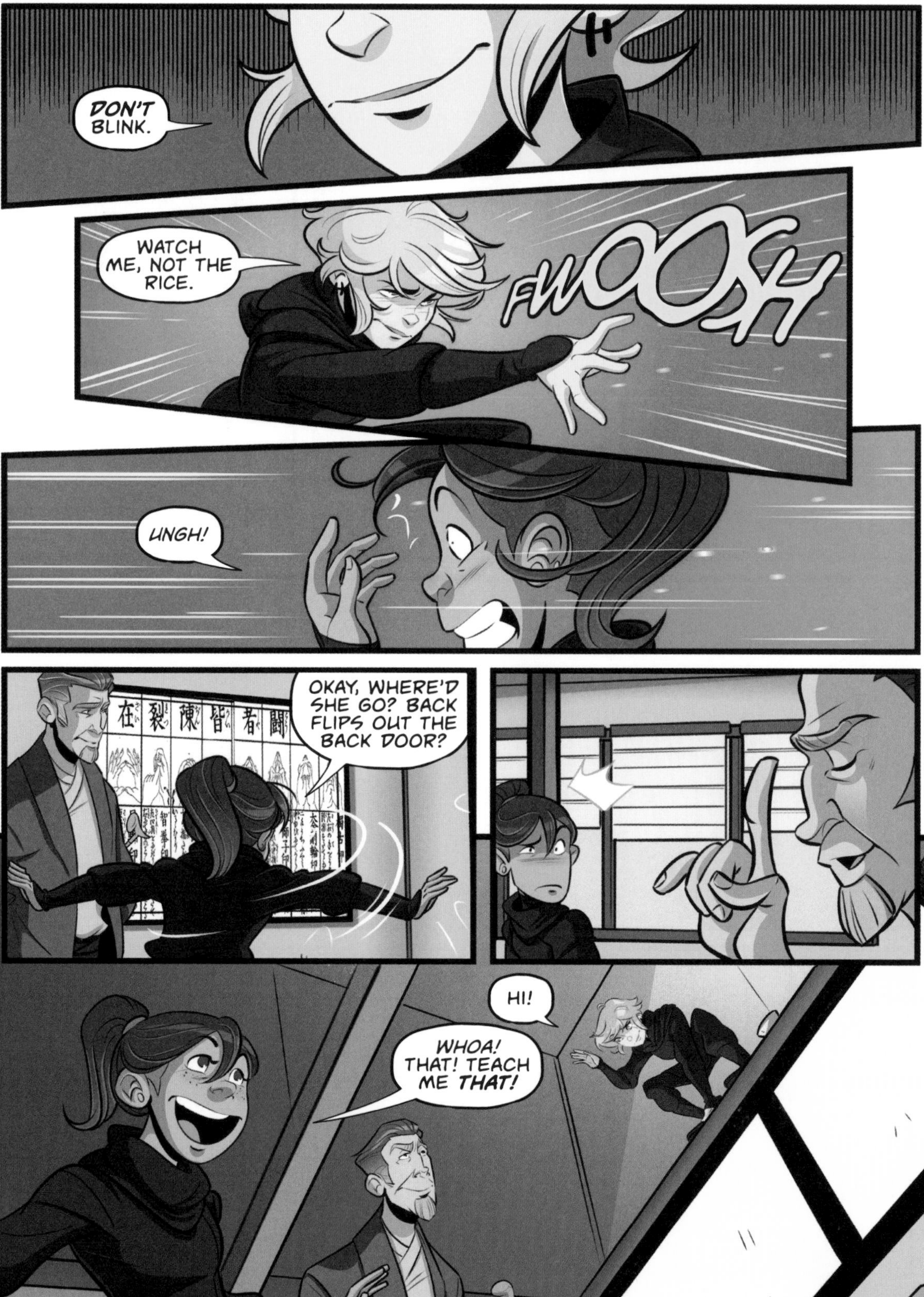

DON'T BLINK.
WATCH ME, NOT THE RICE.
FWOOSH
UNGH!
OKAY, WHERE'D SHE GO? BACK FLIPS OUT THE BACK DOOR?
HI!
WHOA! THAT! TEACH ME THAT!

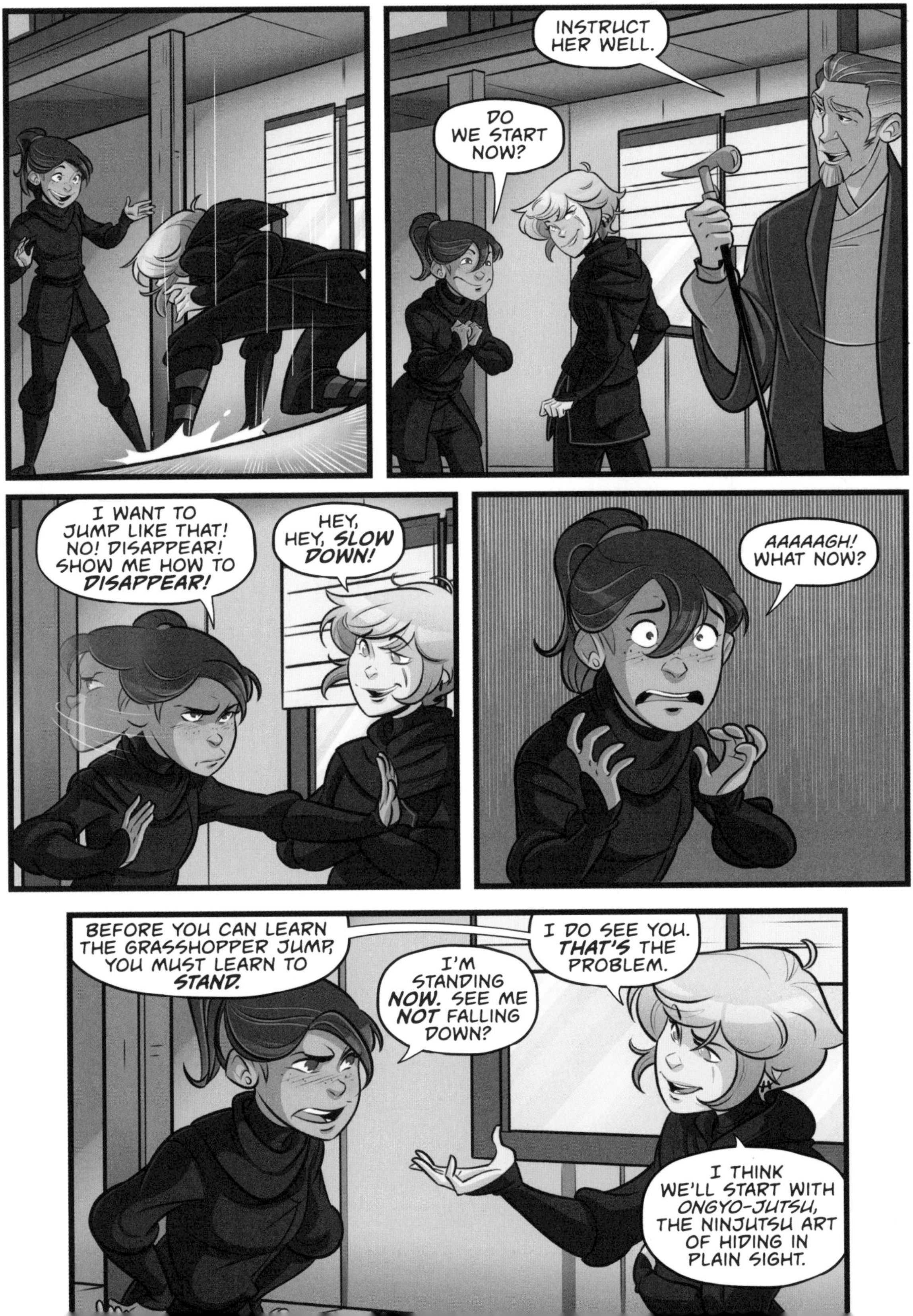
INSTRUCT HER WELL.
DO WE START NOW?
I WANT TO JUMP LIKE THAT! NO! DISAPPEAR! SHOW ME HOW TO *DISAPPEAR!*
HEY, HEY, *SLOW DOWN!*
*AAAAAGH!* WHAT NOW?
BEFORE YOU CAN LEARN THE GRASSHOPPER JUMP, YOU MUST LEARN TO ***STAND.***
I'M STANDING ***NOW.*** SEE ME ***NOT*** FALLING DOWN?
I DO SEE YOU. ***THAT'S*** THE PROBLEM.
I THINK WE'LL START WITH *ONGYO-JUTSU,* THE NINJUTSU ART OF HIDING IN PLAIN SIGHT.

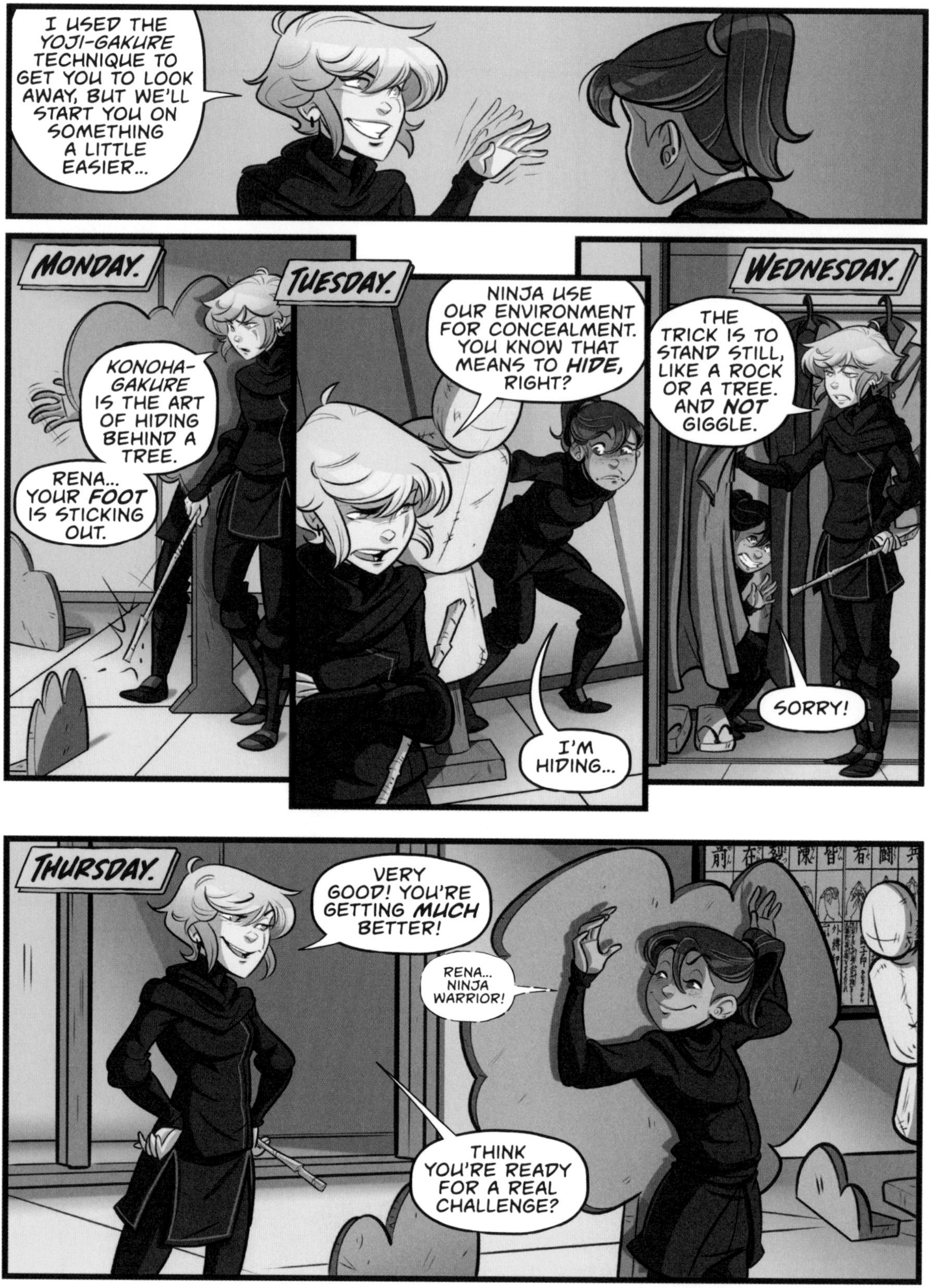
I USED THE YOJI-GAKURE TECHNIQUE TO GET YOU TO LOOK AWAY, BUT WE'LL START YOU ON SOMETHING A LITTLE EASIER...
MONDAY.
KONOHA-GAKURE IS THE ART OF HIDING BEHIND A TREE.
RENA... YOUR FOOT IS STICKING OUT.
TUESDAY.
NINJA USE OUR ENVIRONMENT FOR CONCEALMENT. YOU KNOW THAT MEANS TO HIDE, RIGHT?
I'M HIDING...
WEDNESDAY.
THE TRICK IS TO STAND STILL, LIKE A ROCK OR A TREE. AND NOT GIGGLE.
SORRY!
THURSDAY.
VERY GOOD! YOU'RE GETTING MUCH BETTER!
RENA... NINJA WARRIOR!
THINK YOU'RE READY FOR A REAL CHALLENGE?

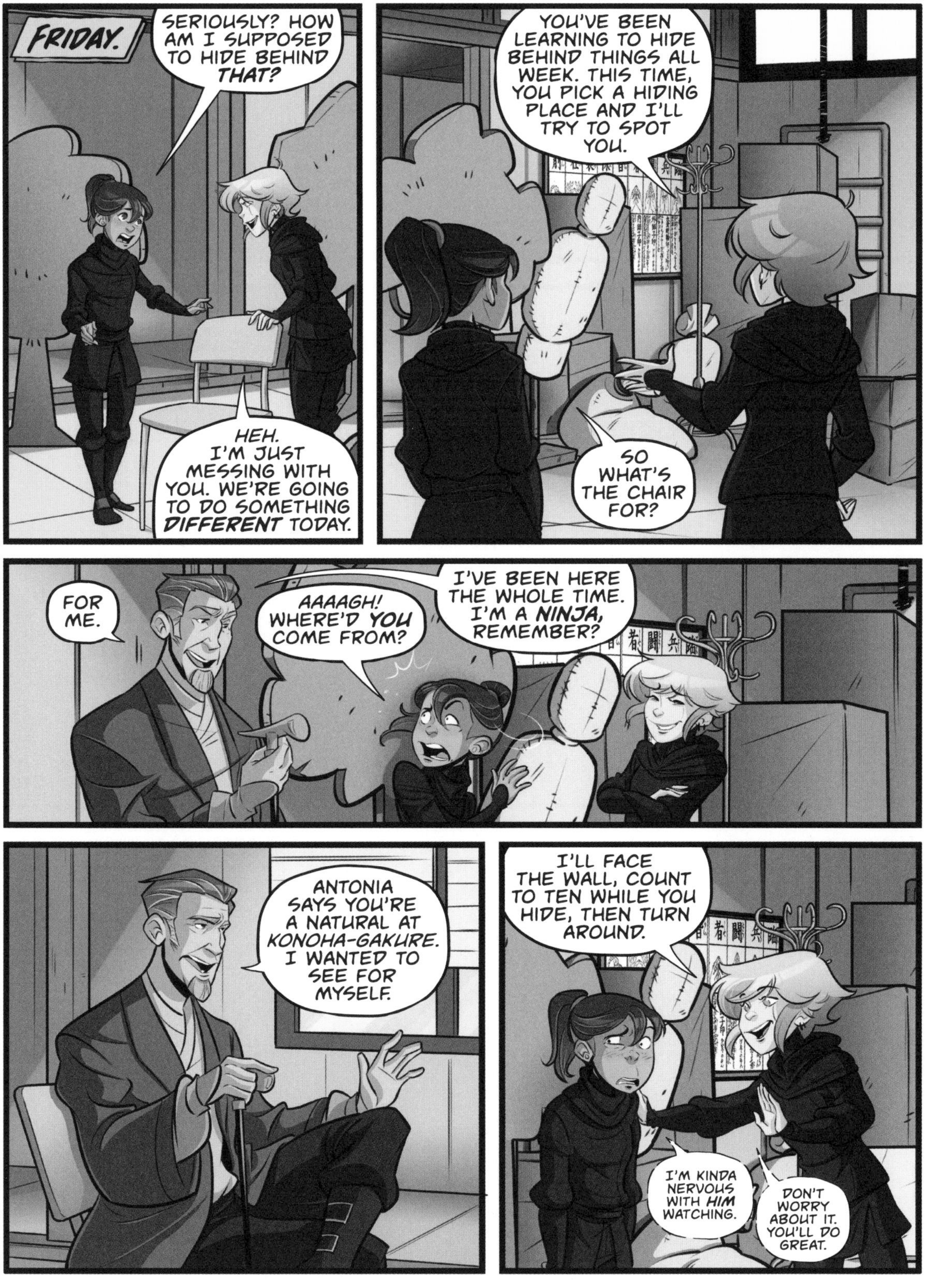
FRIDAY.
SERIOUSLY? HOW AM I SUPPOSED TO HIDE BEHIND *THAT?*
HEH. I'M JUST MESSING WITH YOU. WE'RE GOING TO DO SOMETHING *DIFFERENT* TODAY.
YOU'VE BEEN LEARNING TO HIDE BEHIND THINGS ALL WEEK. THIS TIME, YOU PICK A HIDING PLACE AND I'LL TRY TO SPOT YOU.
SO WHAT'S THE CHAIR FOR?
FOR ME.
*AAAAGH!* WHERE'D *YOU* COME FROM?
I'VE BEEN HERE THE WHOLE TIME. I'M A *NINJA,* REMEMBER?
ANTONIA SAYS YOU'RE A NATURAL AT *KONOHA-GAKURE.* I WANTED TO SEE FOR MYSELF.
I'LL FACE THE WALL, COUNT TO TEN WHILE YOU HIDE, THEN TURN AROUND.
I'M KINDA NERVOUS WITH *HIM* WATCHING.
DON'T WORRY ABOUT IT. YOU'LL DO GREAT.

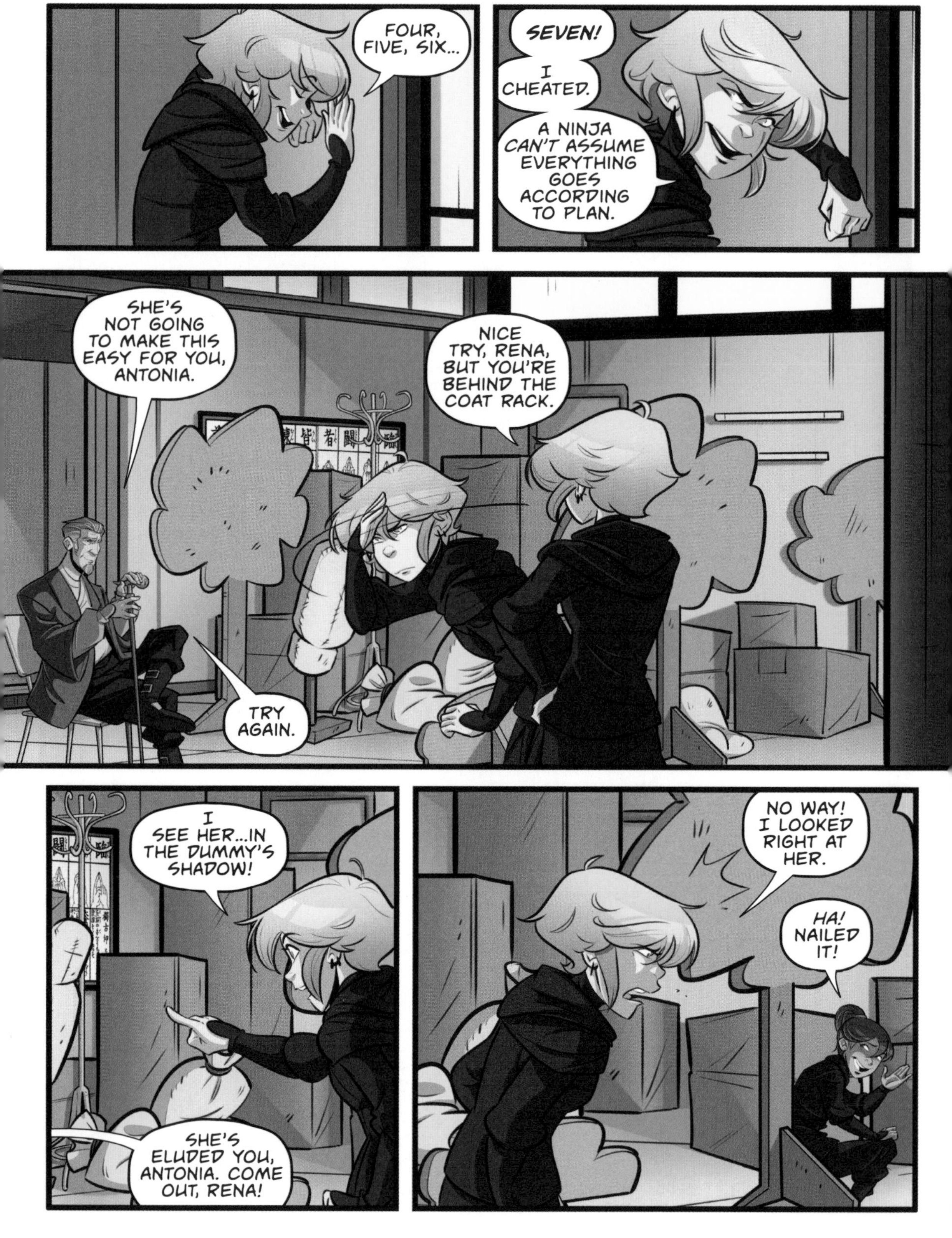
FOUR, FIVE, SIX...
SEVEN!
I CHEATED.
A NINJA CAN'T ASSUME EVERYTHING GOES ACCORDING TO PLAN.
SHE'S NOT GOING TO MAKE THIS EASY FOR YOU, ANTONIA.
NICE TRY, RENA, BUT YOU'RE BEHIND THE COAT RACK.
TRY AGAIN.
I SEE HER...IN THE DUMMY'S SHADOW!
SHE'S ELUDED YOU, ANTONIA. COME OUT, RENA!
NO WAY! I LOOKED RIGHT AT HER.
HA! NAILED IT!

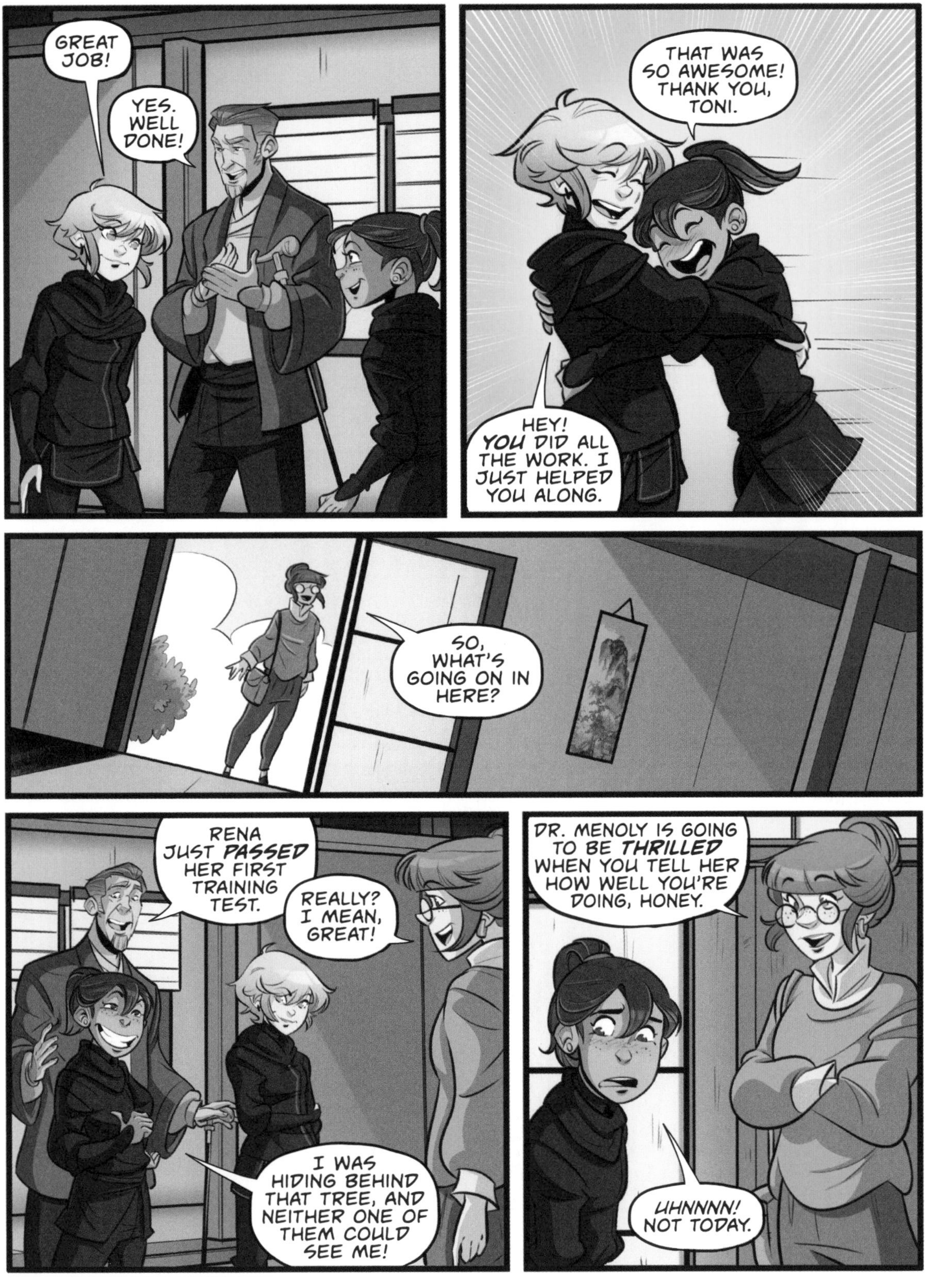
GREAT JOB!
YES. WELL DONE!
THAT WAS SO AWESOME! THANK YOU, TONI.
HEY! YOU DID ALL THE WORK. I JUST HELPED YOU ALONG.
SO, WHAT'S GOING ON IN HERE?
RENA JUST PASSED HER FIRST TRAINING TEST.
REALLY? I MEAN, GREAT!
I WAS HIDING BEHIND THAT TREE, AND NEITHER ONE OF THEM COULD SEE ME!
DR. MENOLY IS GOING TO BE THRILLED WHEN YOU TELL HER HOW WELL YOU'RE DOING, HONEY.
UHNNNN! NOT TODAY.

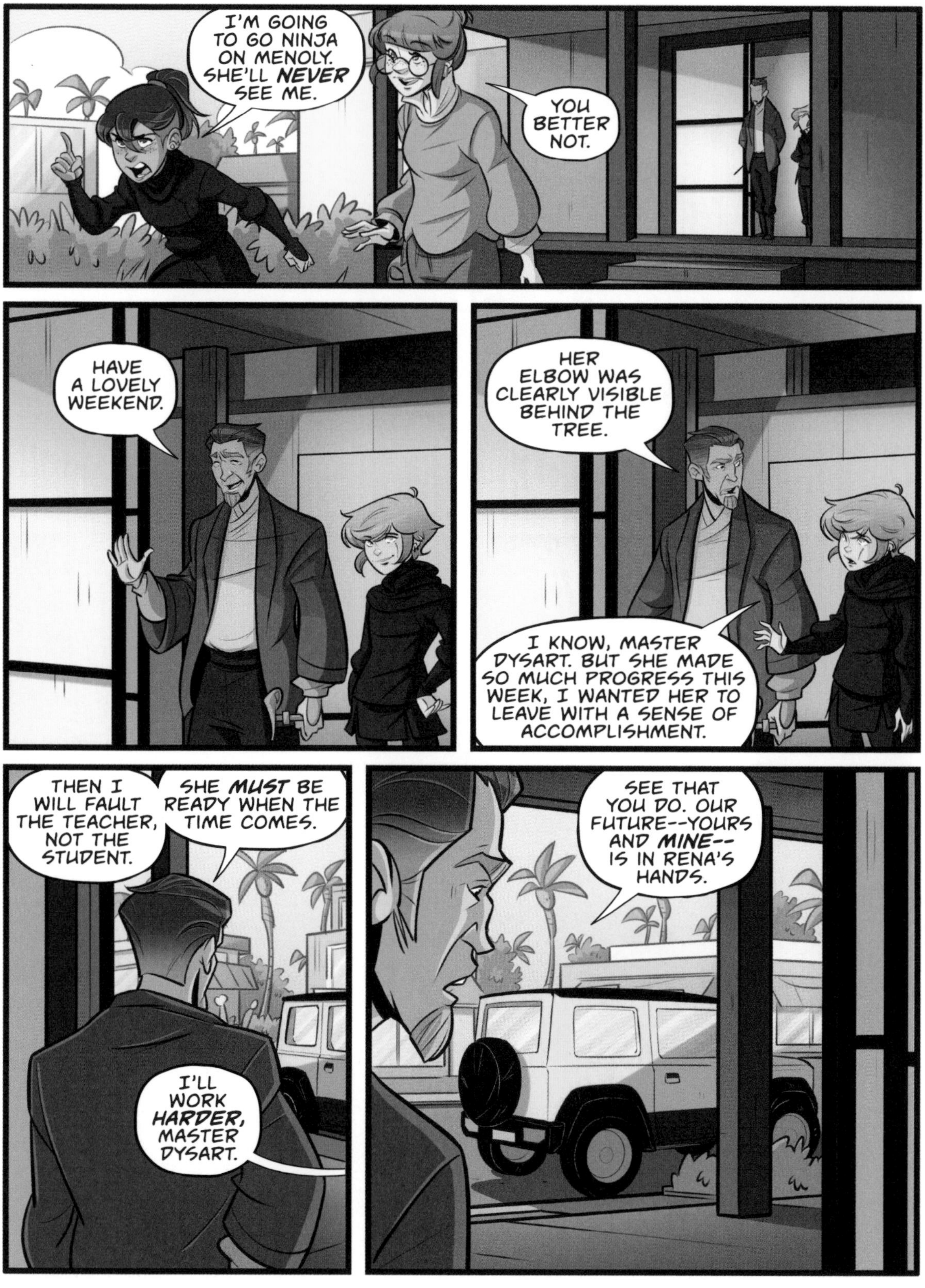
I'M GOING TO GO NINJA ON MENOLY. SHE'LL **NEVER** SEE ME.
YOU BETTER NOT.
HAVE A LOVELY WEEKEND.
HER ELBOW WAS CLEARLY VISIBLE BEHIND THE TREE.
I KNOW, MASTER DYSART. BUT SHE MADE SO MUCH PROGRESS THIS WEEK, I WANTED HER TO LEAVE WITH A SENSE OF ACCOMPLISHMENT.
THEN I WILL FAULT THE TEACHER, NOT THE STUDENT.
SHE **MUST** BE READY WHEN THE TIME COMES.
I'LL WORK **HARDER,** MASTER DYSART.
SEE THAT YOU DO. OUR FUTURE--YOURS AND **MINE**--IS IN RENA'S HANDS.

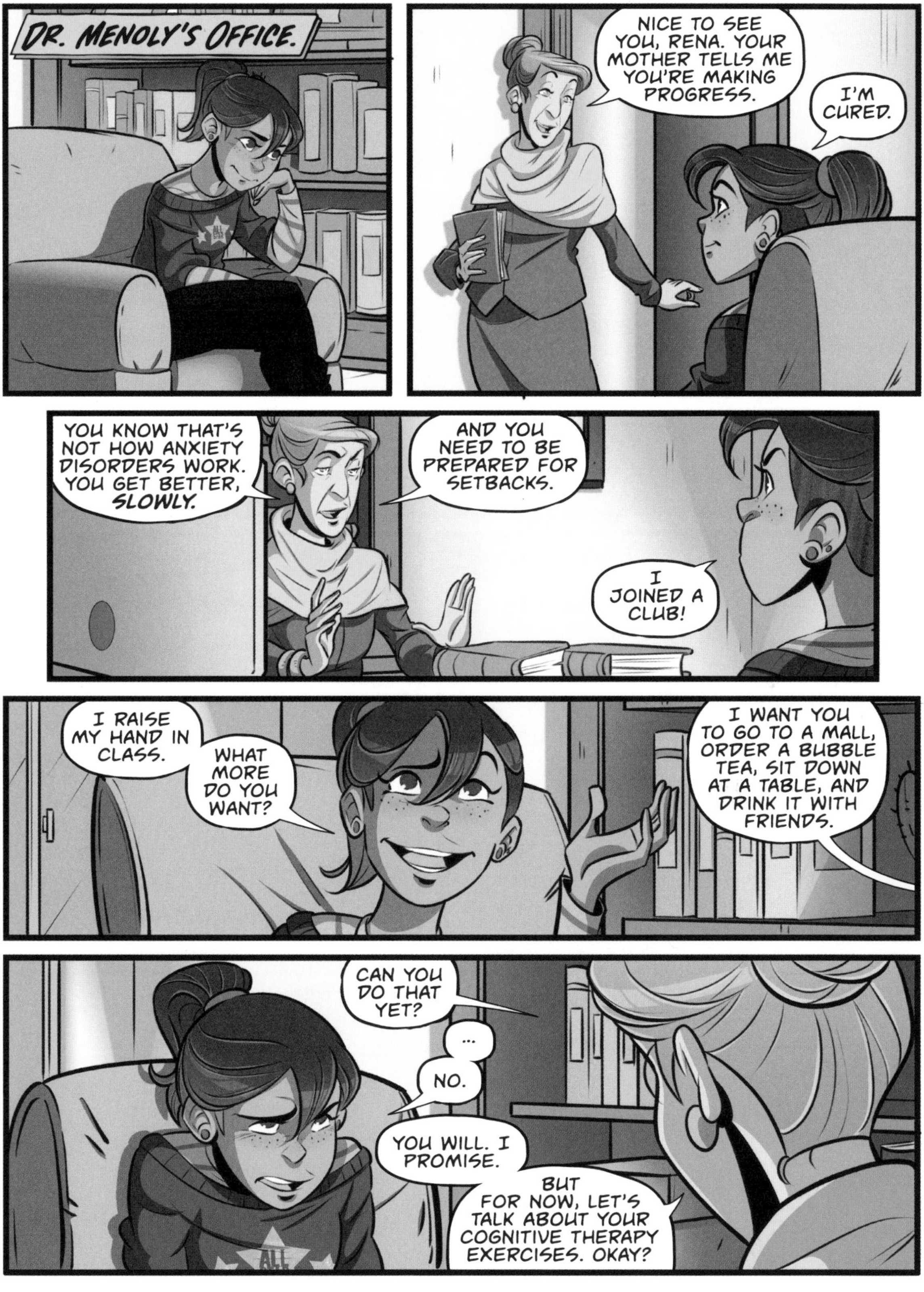
DR. MENOLY'S OFFICE.
NICE TO SEE YOU, RENA. YOUR MOTHER TELLS ME YOU'RE MAKING PROGRESS.
I'M CURED.
YOU KNOW THAT'S NOT HOW ANXIETY DISORDERS WORK. YOU GET BETTER, SLOWLY.
AND YOU NEED TO BE PREPARED FOR SETBACKS.
I JOINED A CLUB!
I RAISE MY HAND IN CLASS.
WHAT MORE DO YOU WANT?
I WANT YOU TO GO TO A MALL, ORDER A BUBBLE TEA, SIT DOWN AT A TABLE, AND DRINK IT WITH FRIENDS.
CAN YOU DO THAT YET?
...
NO.
YOU WILL. I PROMISE.
BUT FOR NOW, LET'S TALK ABOUT YOUR COGNITIVE THERAPY EXERCISES. OKAY?

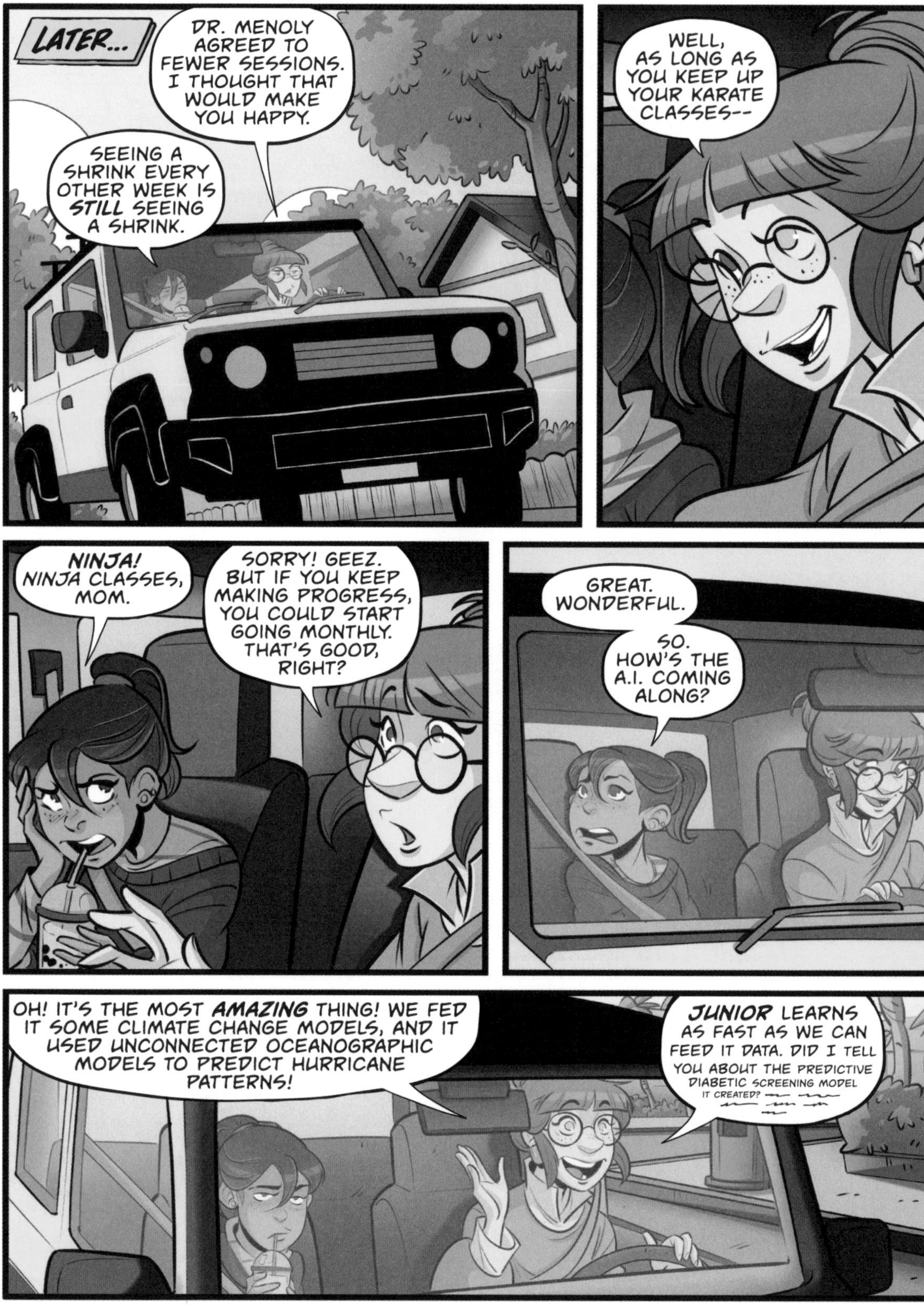
LATER...
DR. MENOLY AGREED TO FEWER SESSIONS. I THOUGHT THAT WOULD MAKE YOU HAPPY.
SEEING A SHRINK EVERY OTHER WEEK IS STILL SEEING A SHRINK.
WELL, AS LONG AS YOU KEEP UP YOUR KARATE CLASSES--
NINJA! NINJA CLASSES, MOM.
SORRY! GEEZ. BUT IF YOU KEEP MAKING PROGRESS, YOU COULD START GOING MONTHLY. THAT'S GOOD, RIGHT?
GREAT. WONDERFUL.
SO. HOW'S THE A.I. COMING ALONG?
OH! IT'S THE MOST AMAZING THING! WE FED IT SOME CLIMATE CHANGE MODELS, AND IT USED UNCONNECTED OCEANOGRAPHIC MODELS TO PREDICT HURRICANE PATTERNS!
JUNIOR LEARNS AS FAST AS WE CAN FEED IT DATA. DID I TELL YOU ABOUT THE PREDICTIVE DIABETIC SCREENING MODEL IT CREATED?

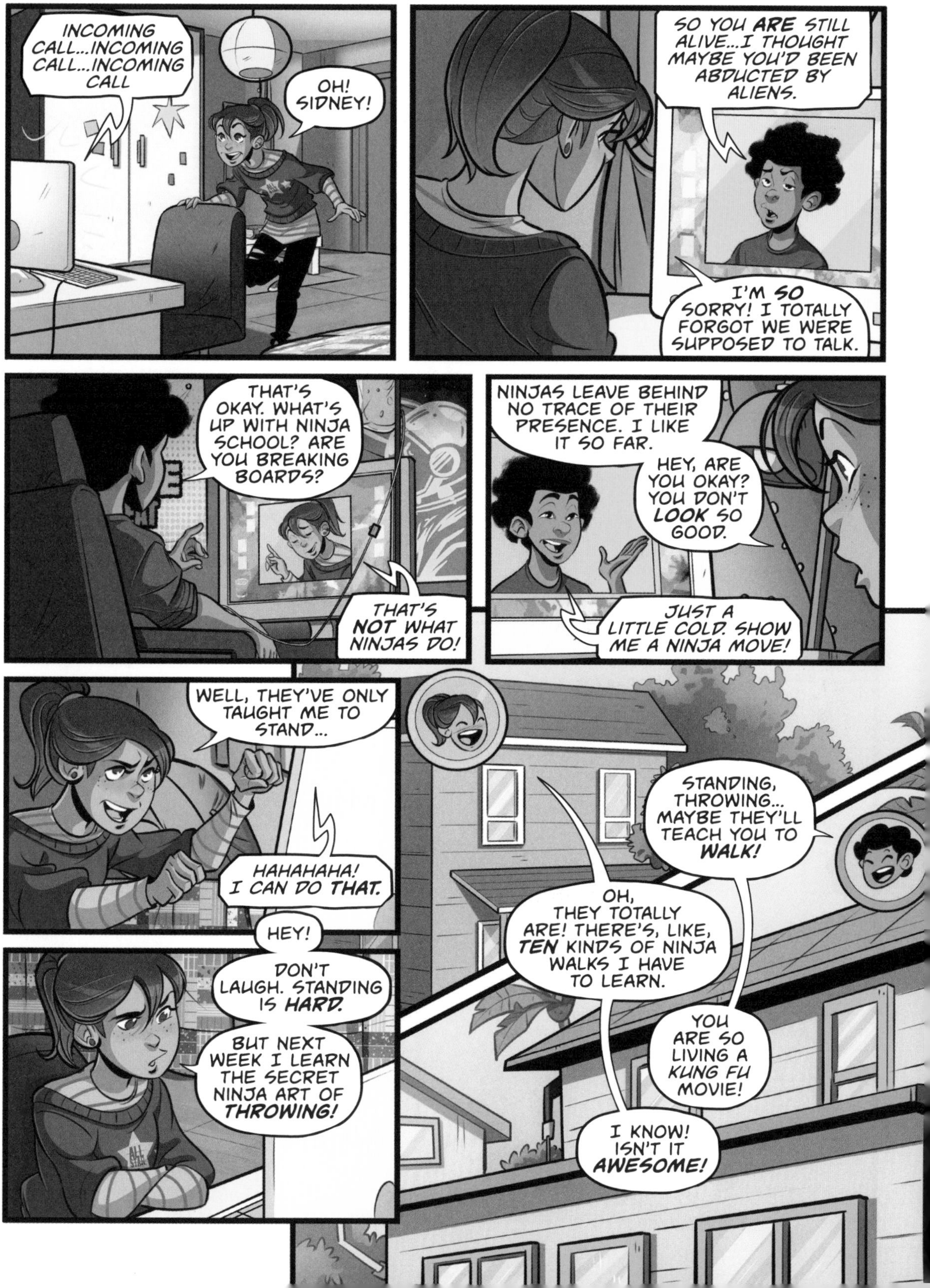
INCOMING CALL...INCOMING CALL...INCOMING CALL
OH! SIDNEY!
SO YOU ARE STILL ALIVE...I THOUGHT MAYBE YOU'D BEEN ABDUCTED BY ALIENS.
I'M SO SORRY! I TOTALLY FORGOT WE WERE SUPPOSED TO TALK.
THAT'S OKAY. WHAT'S UP WITH NINJA SCHOOL? ARE YOU BREAKING BOARDS?
THAT'S NOT WHAT NINJAS DO!
NINJAS LEAVE BEHIND NO TRACE OF THEIR PRESENCE. I LIKE IT SO FAR.
HEY, ARE YOU OKAY? YOU DON'T LOOK SO GOOD.
JUST A LITTLE COLD. SHOW ME A NINJA MOVE!
WELL, THEY'VE ONLY TAUGHT ME TO STAND...
HAHAHAHA! I CAN DO THAT.
HEY!
DON'T LAUGH. STANDING IS HARD.
BUT NEXT WEEK I LEARN THE SECRET NINJA ART OF THROWING!
STANDING, THROWING... MAYBE THEY'LL TEACH YOU TO WALK!
OH, THEY TOTALLY ARE! THERE'S, LIKE, TEN KINDS OF NINJA WALKS I HAVE TO LEARN.
YOU ARE SO LIVING A KUNG FU MOVIE!
I KNOW! ISN'T IT AWESOME!

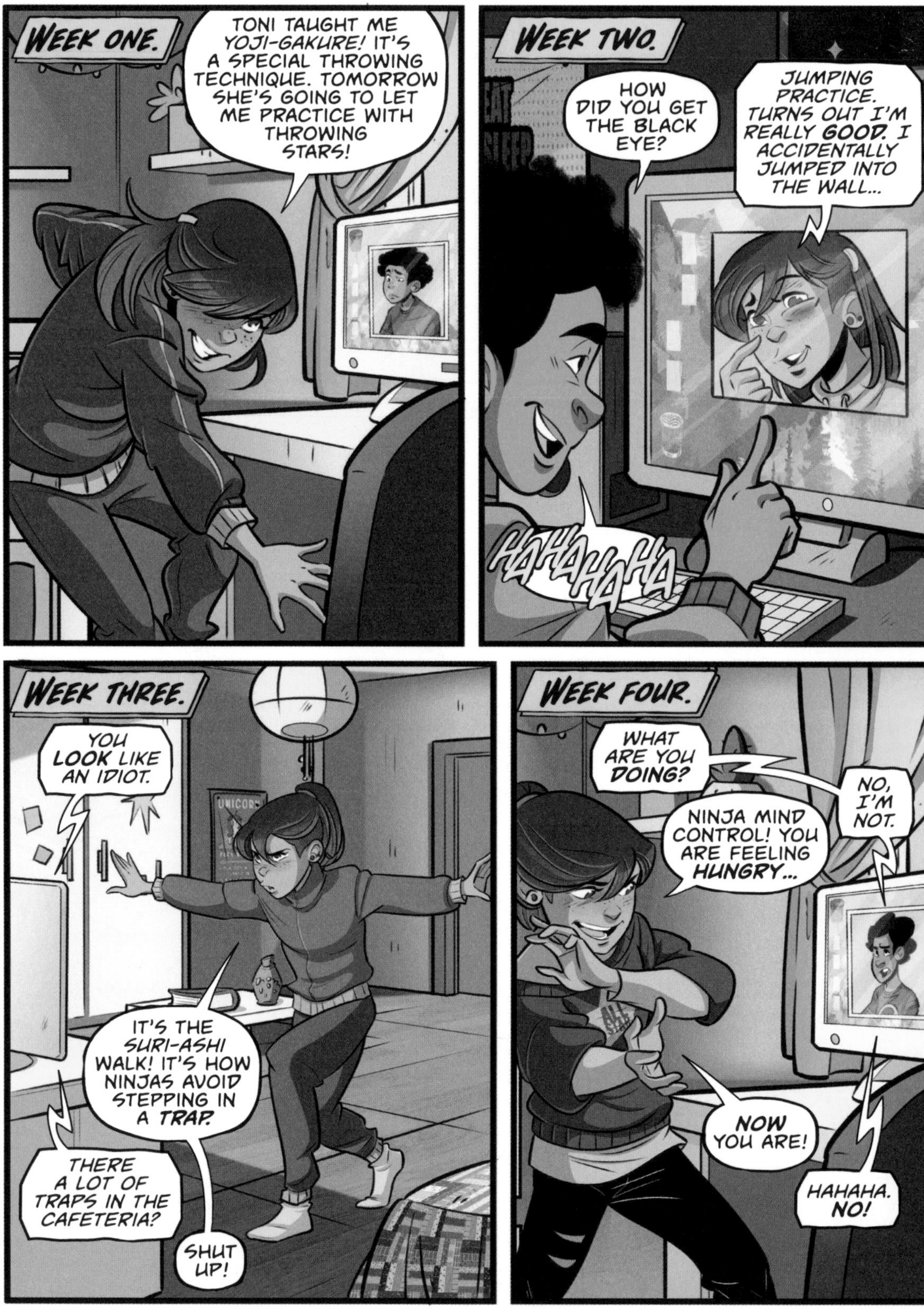
WEEK ONE.
TONI TAUGHT ME YOJI-GAKURE! IT'S A SPECIAL THROWING TECHNIQUE. TOMORROW SHE'S GOING TO LET ME PRACTICE WITH THROWING STARS!
WEEK TWO.
HOW DID YOU GET THE BLACK EYE?
JUMPING PRACTICE. TURNS OUT I'M REALLY GOOD. I ACCIDENTALLY JUMPED INTO THE WALL...
HAHAHAHAHA
WEEK THREE.
YOU LOOK LIKE AN IDIOT.
IT'S THE SURI-ASHI WALK! IT'S HOW NINJAS AVOID STEPPING IN A TRAP.
THERE A LOT OF TRAPS IN THE CAFETERIA?
SHUT UP!
WEEK FOUR.
WHAT ARE YOU DOING?
NINJA MIND CONTROL! YOU ARE FEELING HUNGRY...
NO, I'M NOT.
NOW YOU ARE!
HAHAHA. NO!

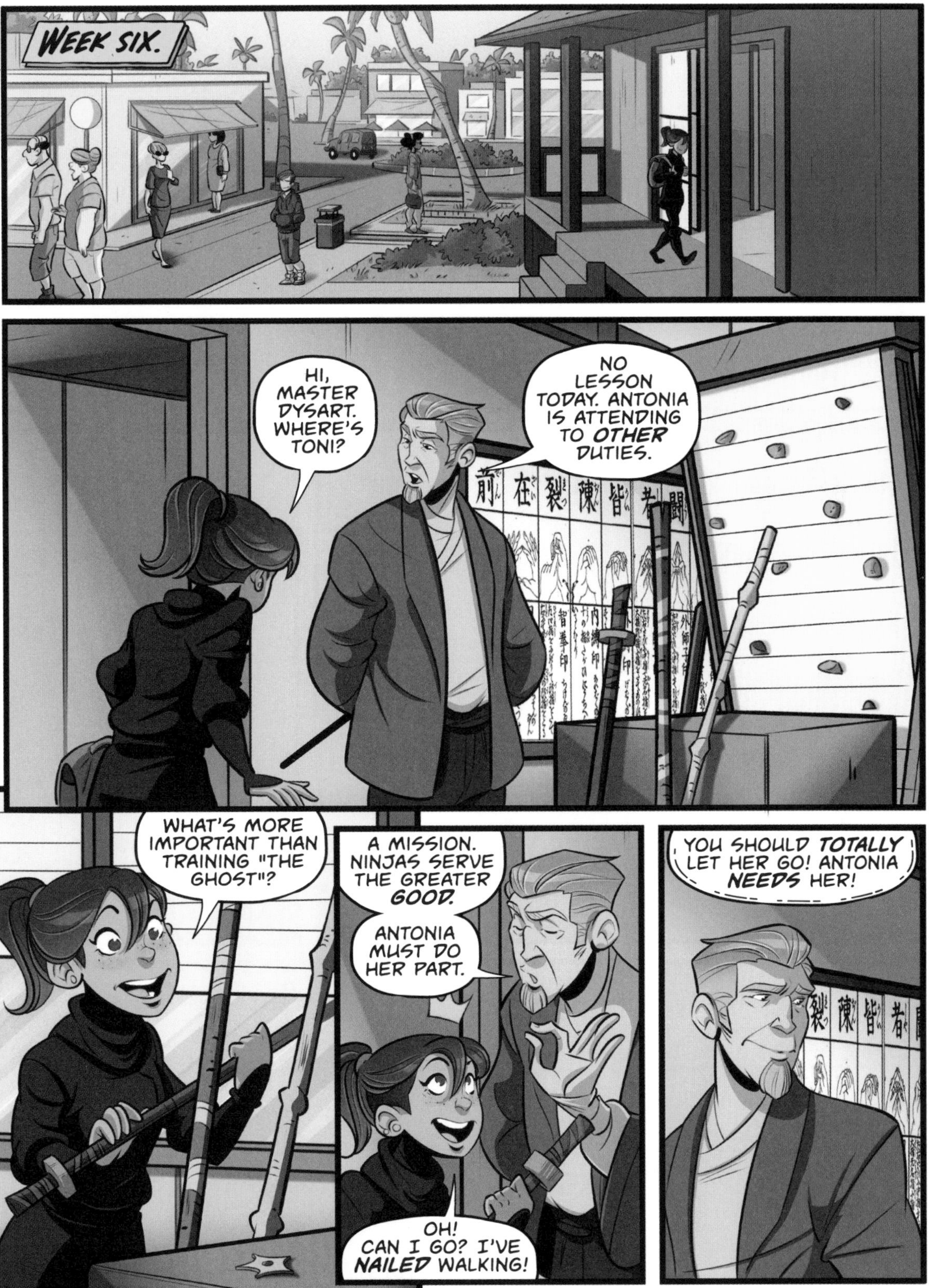
WEEK SIX.
HI, MASTER DYSART. WHERE'S TONI?
NO LESSON TODAY. ANTONIA IS ATTENDING TO *OTHER* DUTIES.
前 在 裂 陳 皆 者 闘
WHAT'S MORE IMPORTANT THAN TRAINING "THE GHOST"?
A MISSION. NINJAS SERVE THE GREATER *GOOD.*
ANTONIA MUST DO HER PART.
OH! CAN I GO? I'VE *NAILED* WALKING!
YOU SHOULD *TOTALLY* LET HER GO! ANTONIA *NEEDS* HER!

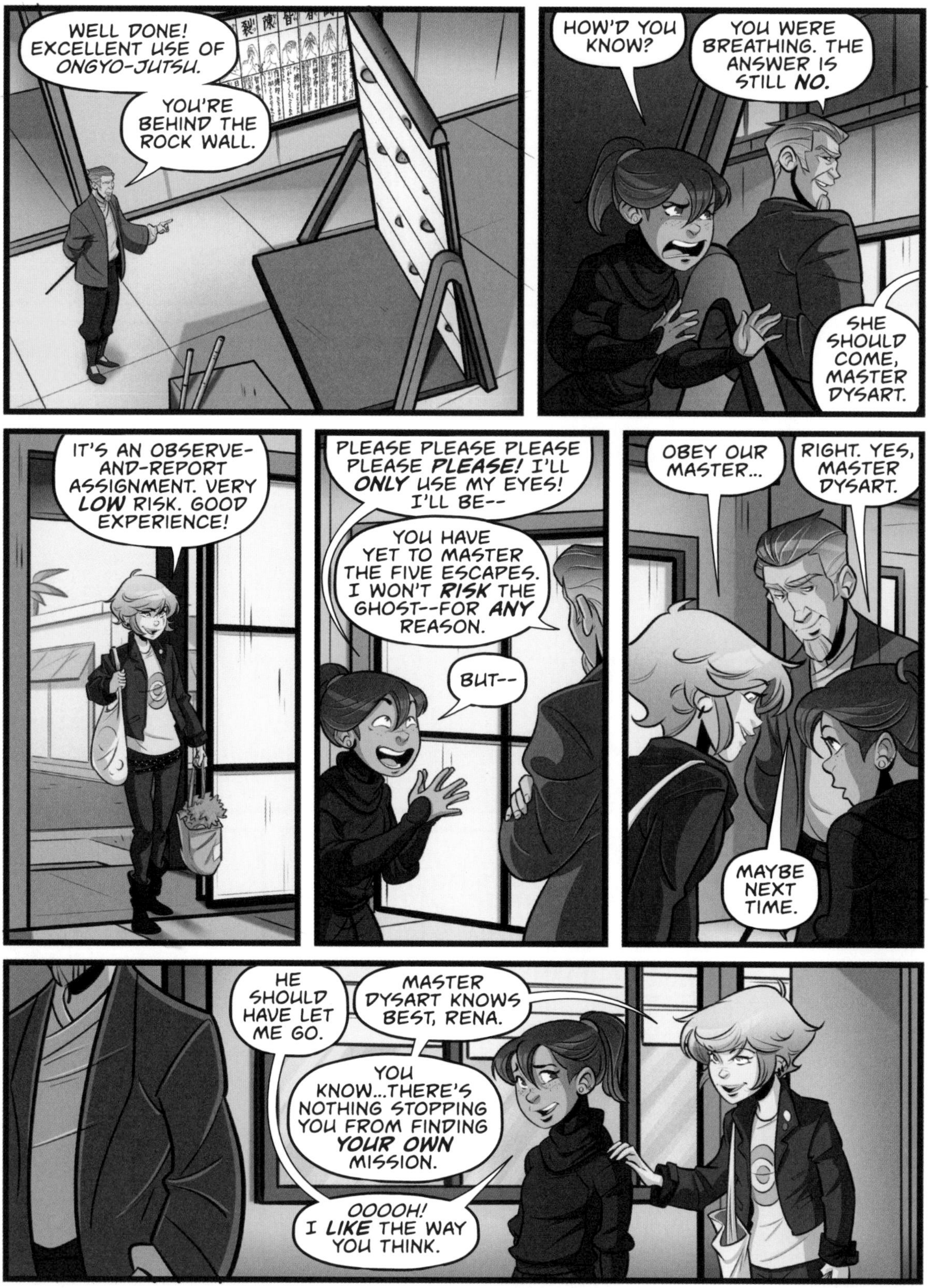

WELL DONE! EXCELLENT USE OF ONGYO-JUTSU.
YOU'RE BEHIND THE ROCK WALL.
HOW'D YOU KNOW?
YOU WERE BREATHING. THE ANSWER IS STILL NO.
SHE SHOULD COME, MASTER DYSART.
IT'S AN OBSERVE-AND-REPORT ASSIGNMENT. VERY LOW RISK. GOOD EXPERIENCE!
PLEASE PLEASE PLEASE PLEASE PLEASE! I'LL ONLY USE MY EYES! I'LL BE--
YOU HAVE YET TO MASTER THE FIVE ESCAPES. I WON'T RISK THE GHOST--FOR ANY REASON.
BUT--
OBEY OUR MASTER...
RIGHT. YES, MASTER DYSART.
MAYBE NEXT TIME.
HE SHOULD HAVE LET ME GO.
MASTER DYSART KNOWS BEST, RENA.
YOU KNOW...THERE'S NOTHING STOPPING YOU FROM FINDING YOUR OWN MISSION.
OOOOH! I LIKE THE WAY YOU THINK.

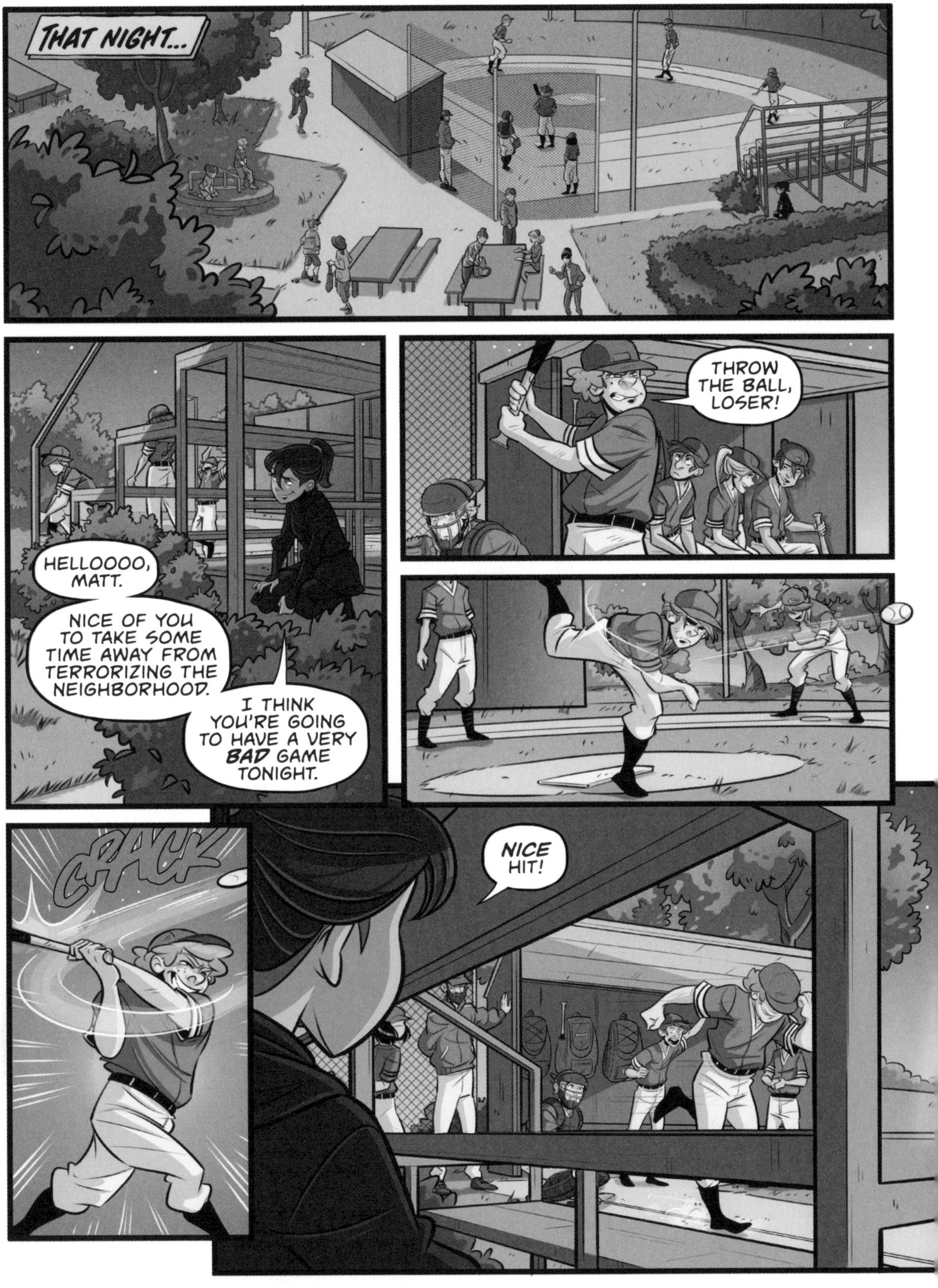
THAT NIGHT...
HELLOOOO, MATT.
NICE OF YOU TO TAKE SOME TIME AWAY FROM TERRORIZING THE NEIGHBORHOOD.
I THINK YOU'RE GOING TO HAVE A VERY BAD GAME TONIGHT.
THROW THE BALL, LOSER!
CRACK
NICE HIT!

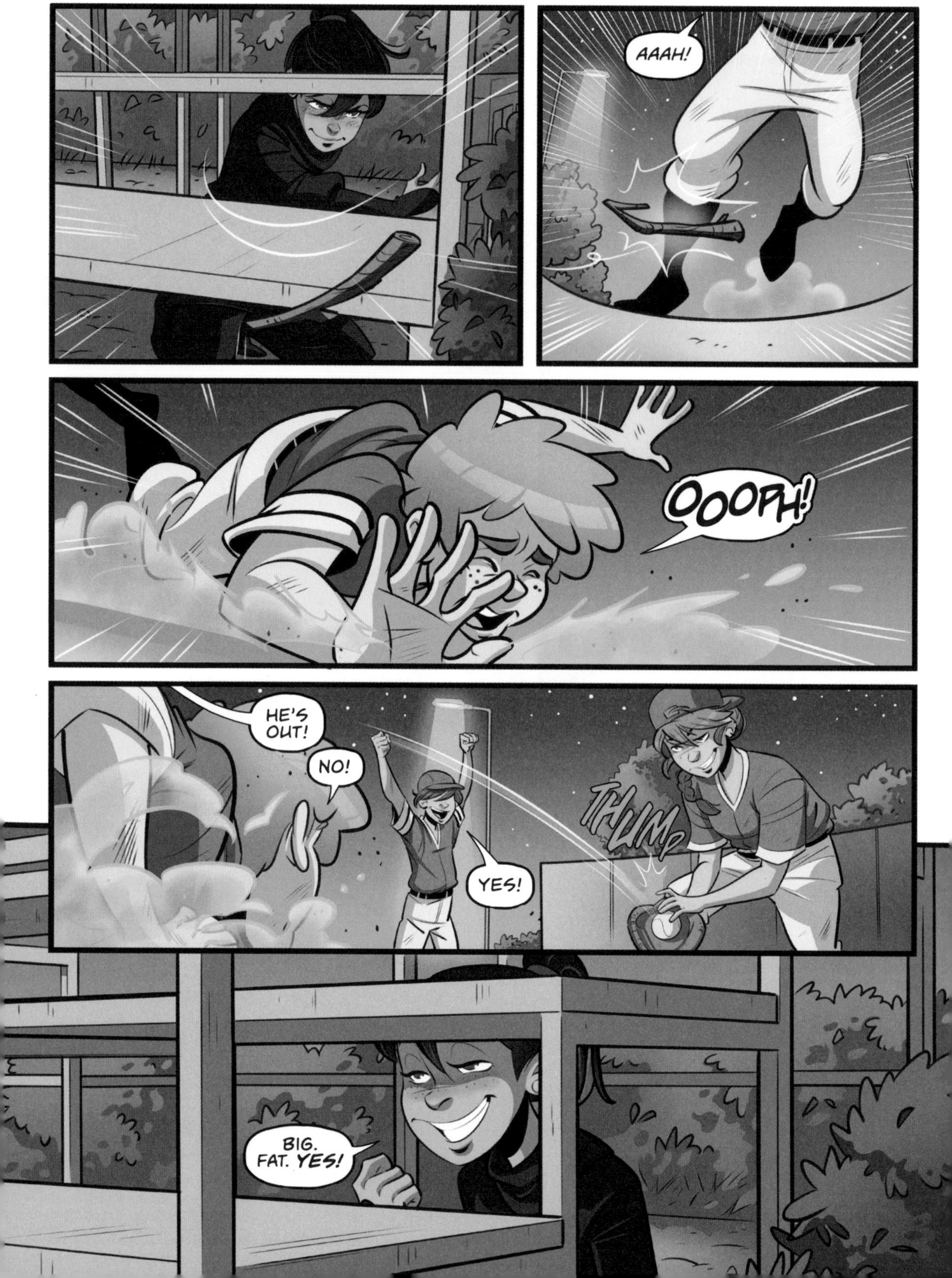
AAAH!
OOOPH!
HE'S OUT!
NO!
YES!
THUMP
BIG. FAT. YES!

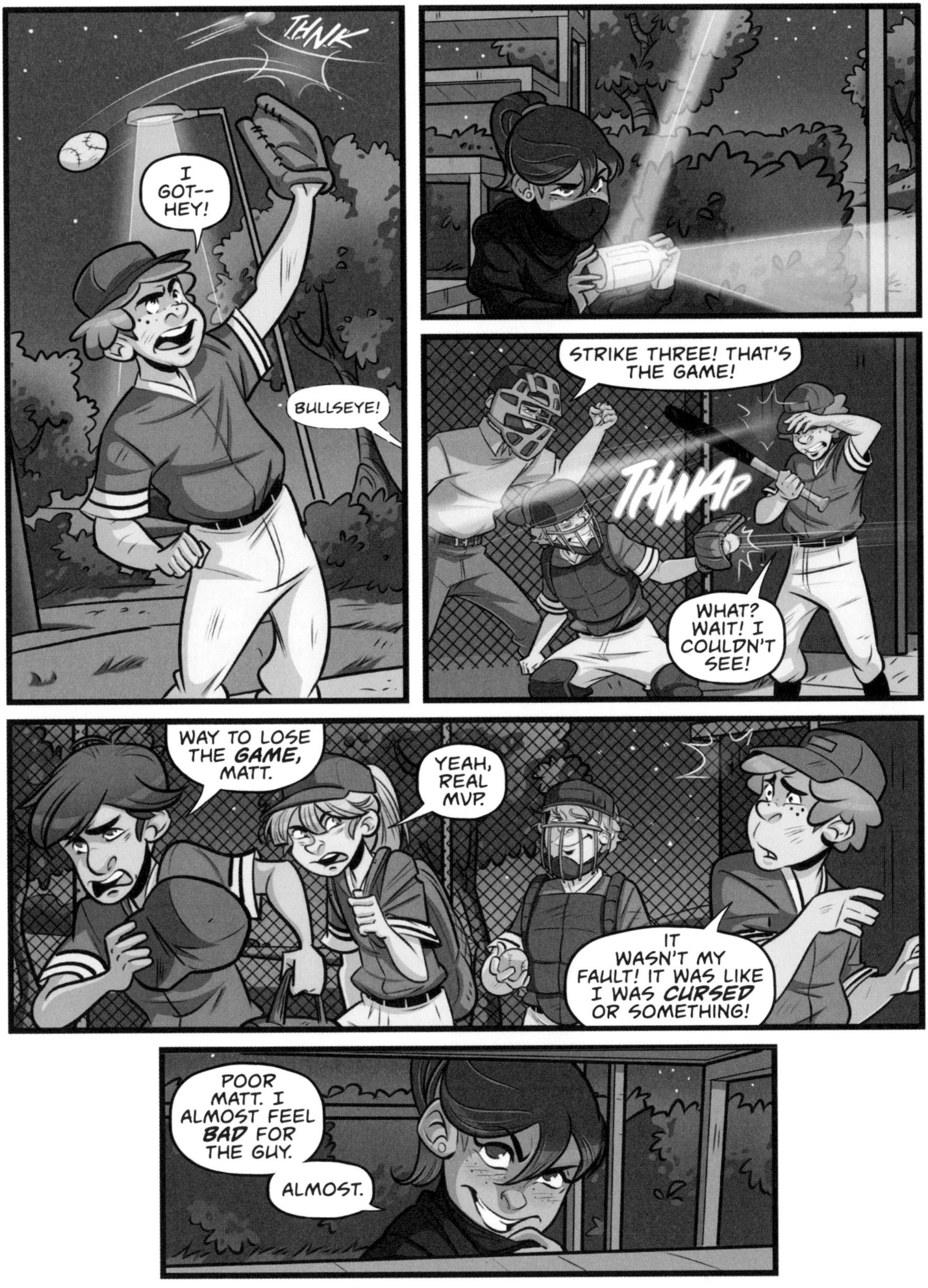
THNK
I GOT-- HEY!
BULLSEYE!
STRIKE THREE! THAT'S THE GAME!
THWAP
WHAT? WAIT! I COULDN'T SEE!
WAY TO LOSE THE **GAME**, MATT.
YEAH, REAL MVP.
IT WASN'T MY FAULT! IT WAS LIKE I WAS **CURSED** OR SOMETHING!
POOR MATT. I ALMOST FEEL **BAD** FOR THE GUY.
ALMOST.

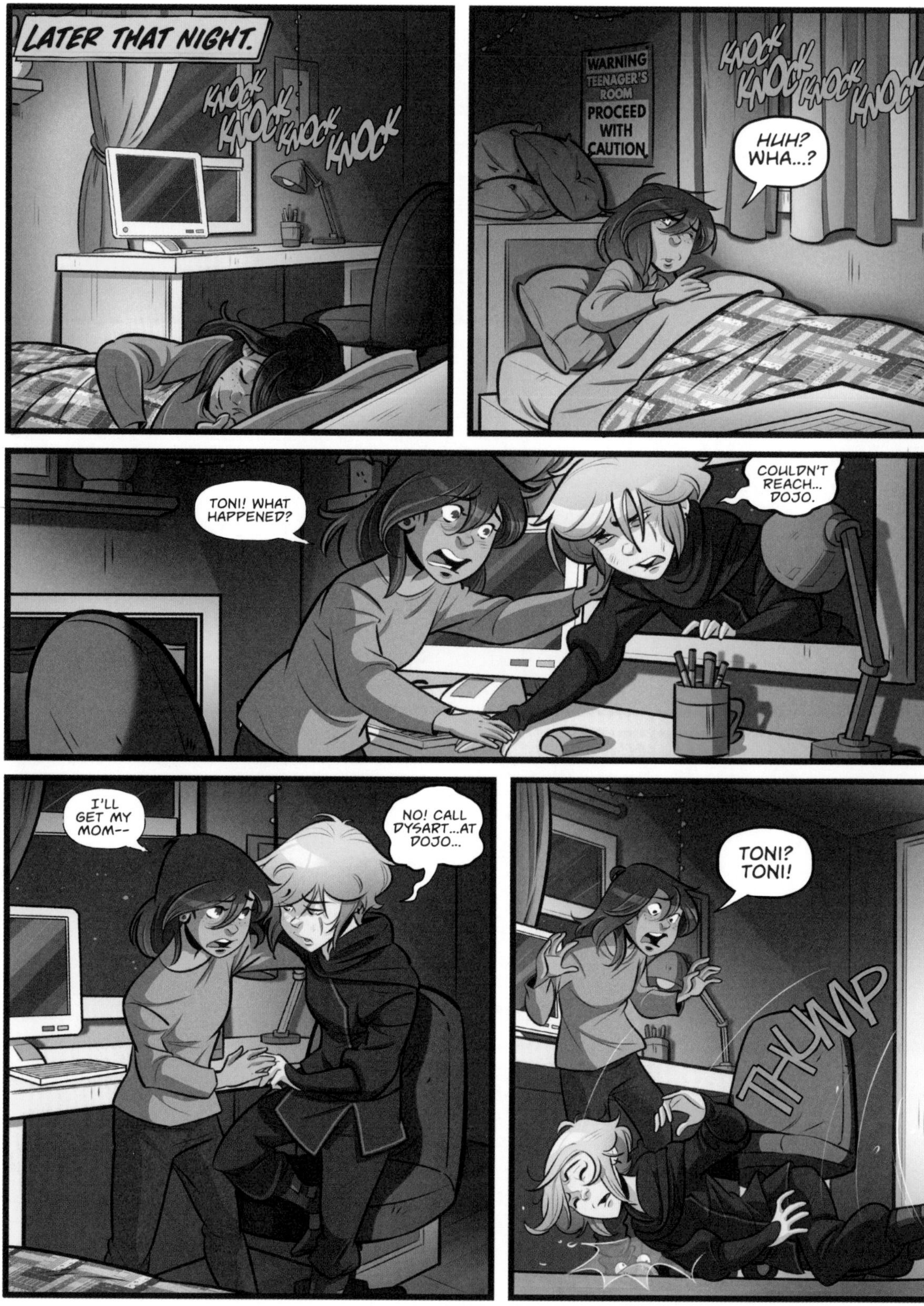
LATER THAT NIGHT.
KNOCK KNOCK KNOCK KNOCK
WARNING TEENAGER'S ROOM PROCEED WITH CAUTION
KNOCK KNOCK KNOCK KNOCK
HUH? WHA...?
TONI! WHAT HAPPENED?
COULDN'T REACH... DOJO.
I'LL GET MY MOM--
NO! CALL DYSART...AT DOJO...
TONI? TONI!
THUMP

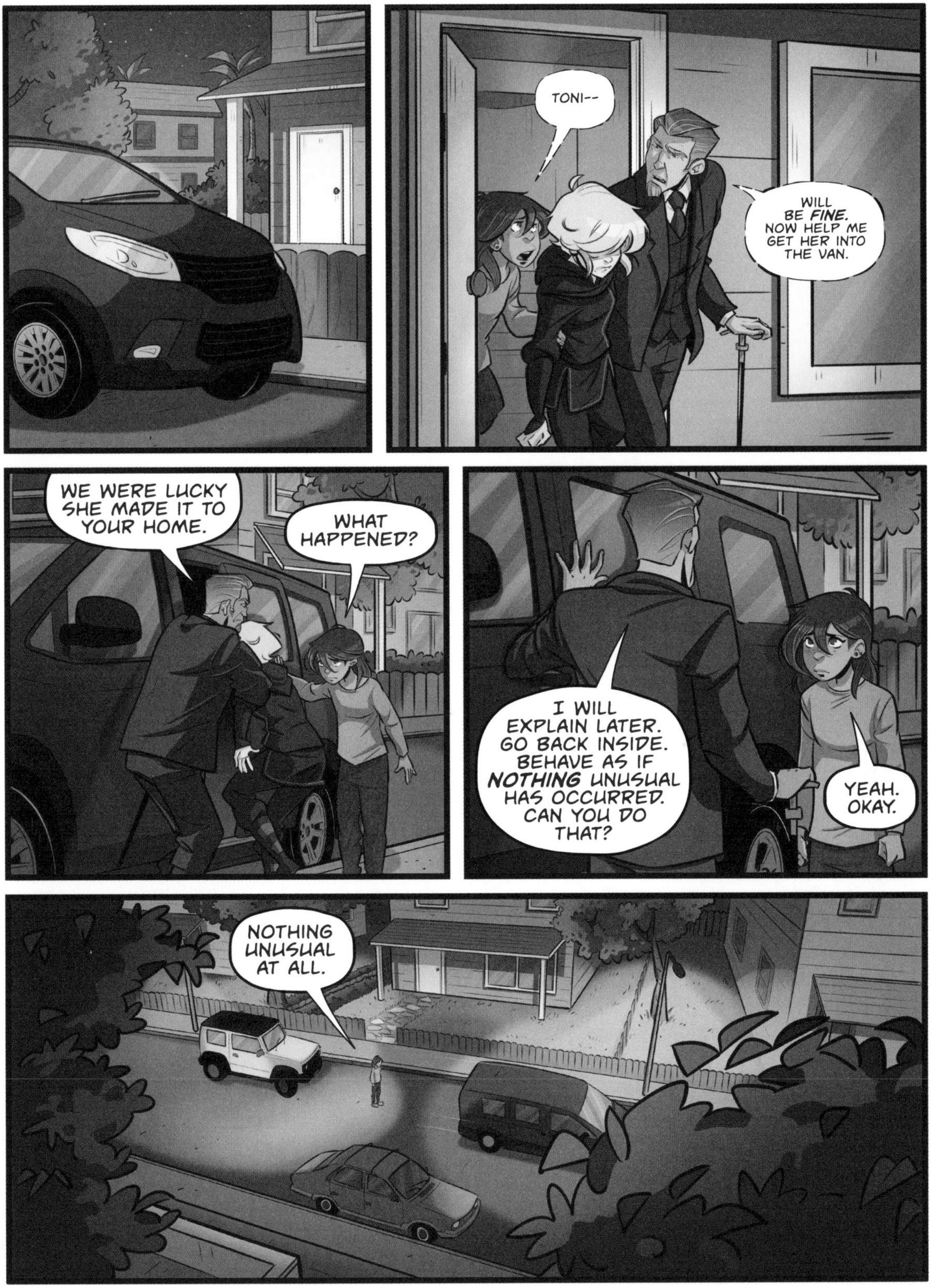
TONI--
WILL BE FINE. NOW HELP ME GET HER INTO THE VAN.
WE WERE LUCKY SHE MADE IT TO YOUR HOME.
WHAT HAPPENED?
I WILL EXPLAIN LATER. GO BACK INSIDE. BEHAVE AS IF NOTHING UNUSUAL HAS OCCURRED. CAN YOU DO THAT?
YEAH. OKAY.
NOTHING UNUSUAL AT ALL.

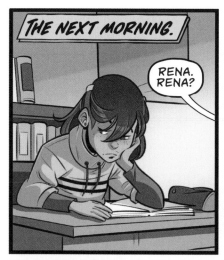

THE NEXT MORNING.

RENA. RENA?

WHAT?

NOT WHAT. *WHO.* WHO WAS THE CONFEDERATE PRESIDENT?

I'M SORRY, MR. CHANG. I DON'T KNOW.

UP LATE PLAYING VIDEO GAMES?

WEIRDO.

TRICIA! SINCE YOU WANT TO TALK IN CLASS, MAYBE YOU CAN EXPLAIN WHY THE SOUTH THOUGHT THE WAR WOULD BE A QUICK ONE?

WHAT?

DO YOU NEED A HINT?

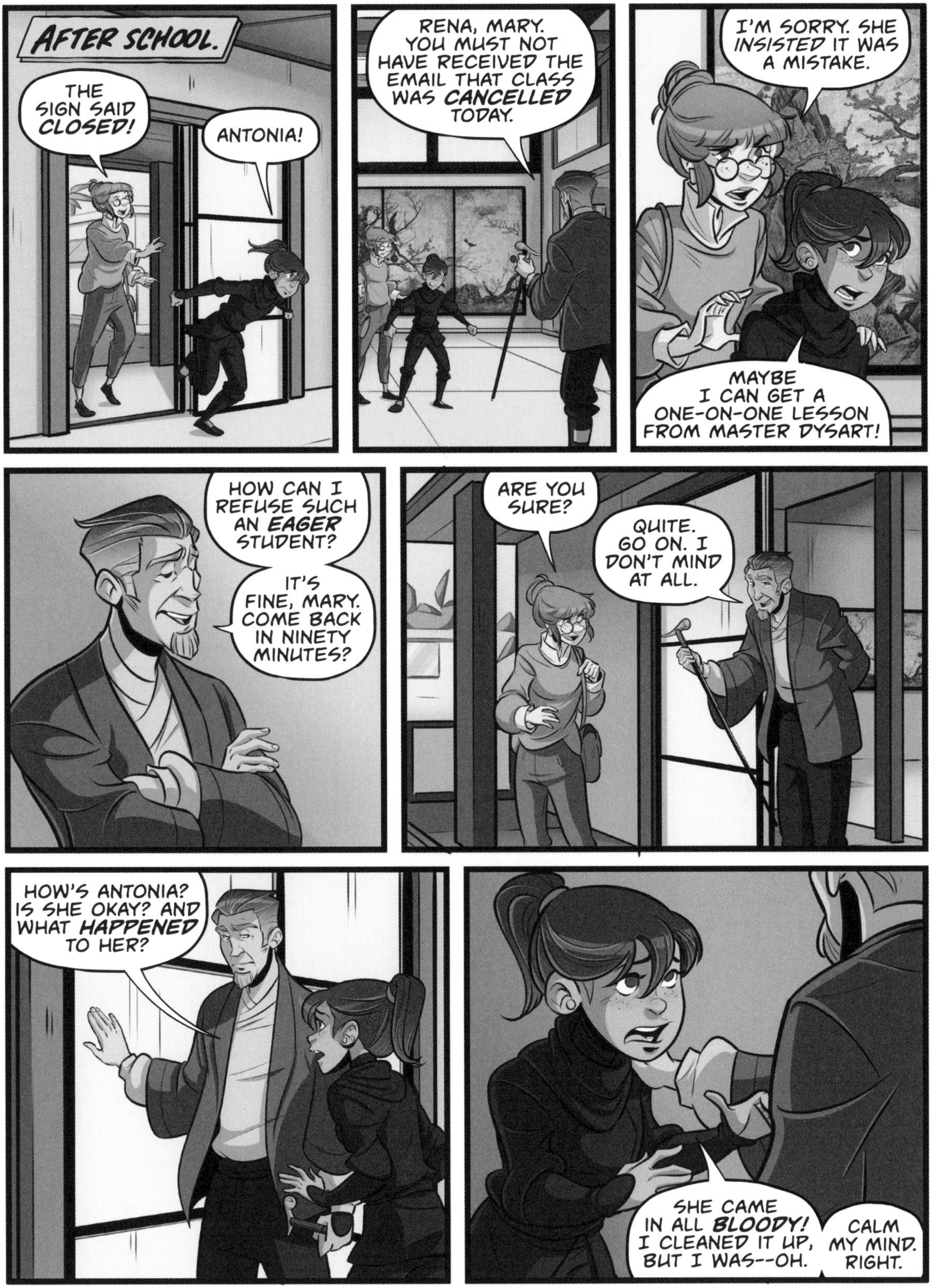
AFTER SCHOOL.
THE SIGN SAID CLOSED!
ANTONIA!
RENA, MARY. YOU MUST NOT HAVE RECEIVED THE EMAIL THAT CLASS WAS CANCELLED TODAY.
I'M SORRY. SHE INSISTED IT WAS A MISTAKE.
MAYBE I CAN GET A ONE-ON-ONE LESSON FROM MASTER DYSART!
HOW CAN I REFUSE SUCH AN EAGER STUDENT?
IT'S FINE, MARY. COME BACK IN NINETY MINUTES?
ARE YOU SURE?
QUITE. GO ON. I DON'T MIND AT ALL.
HOW'S ANTONIA? IS SHE OKAY? AND WHAT HAPPENED TO HER?
SHE CAME IN ALL BLOODY! I CLEANED IT UP, BUT I WAS--OH.
CALM MY MIND. RIGHT.

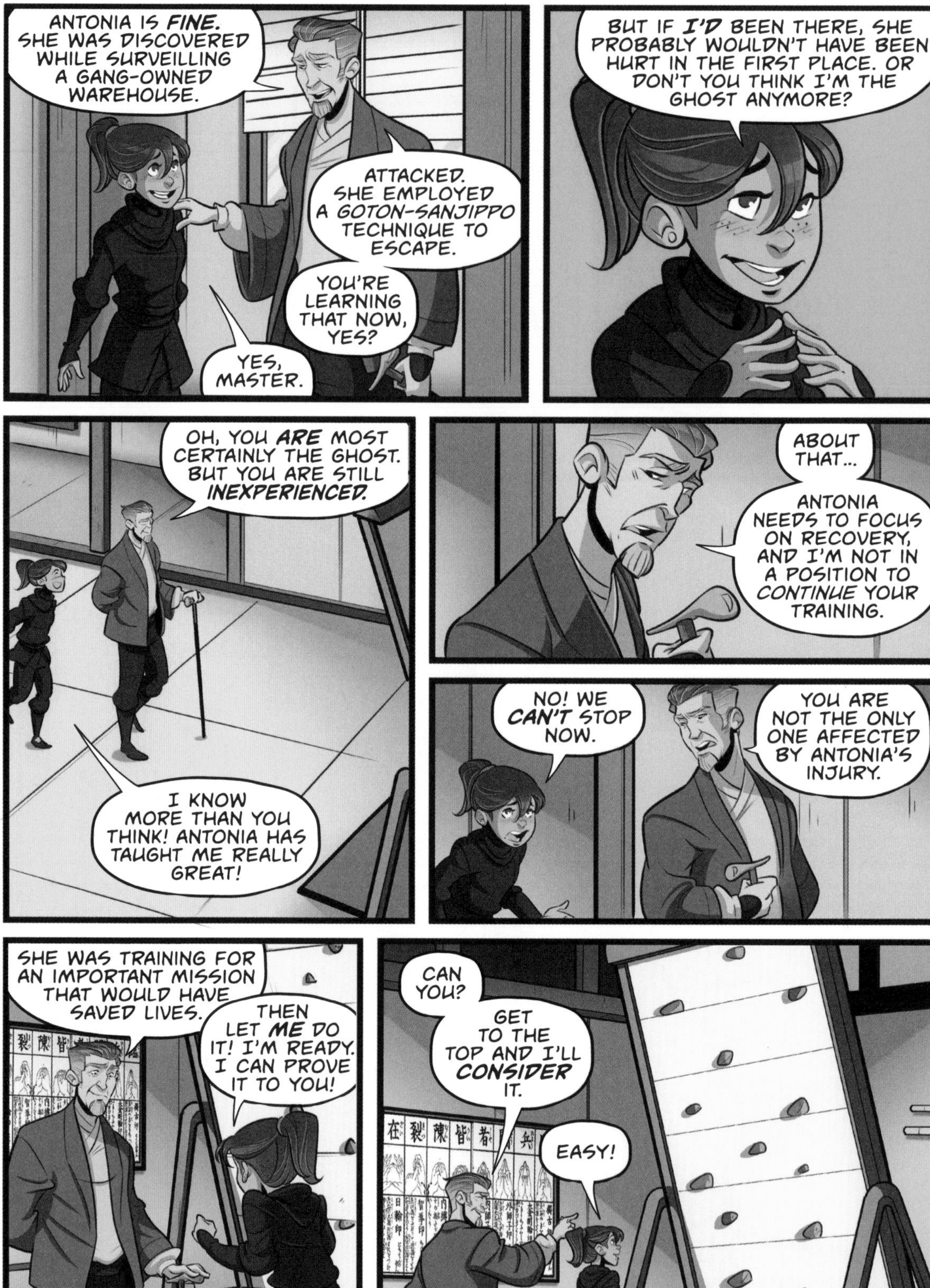
ANTONIA IS FINE. SHE WAS DISCOVERED WHILE SURVEILLING A GANG-OWNED WAREHOUSE.
ATTACKED. SHE EMPLOYED A GOTON-SANJIPPO TECHNIQUE TO ESCAPE.
YOU'RE LEARNING THAT NOW, YES?
YES, MASTER.
BUT IF I'D BEEN THERE, SHE PROBABLY WOULDN'T HAVE BEEN HURT IN THE FIRST PLACE. OR DON'T YOU THINK I'M THE GHOST ANYMORE?
OH, YOU ARE MOST CERTAINLY THE GHOST. BUT YOU ARE STILL INEXPERIENCED.
I KNOW MORE THAN YOU THINK! ANTONIA HAS TAUGHT ME REALLY GREAT!
ABOUT THAT...
ANTONIA NEEDS TO FOCUS ON RECOVERY, AND I'M NOT IN A POSITION TO CONTINUE YOUR TRAINING.
NO! WE CAN'T STOP NOW.
YOU ARE NOT THE ONLY ONE AFFECTED BY ANTONIA'S INJURY.
SHE WAS TRAINING FOR AN IMPORTANT MISSION THAT WOULD HAVE SAVED LIVES.
THEN LET ME DO IT! I'M READY. I CAN PROVE IT TO YOU!
CAN YOU?
GET TO THE TOP AND I'LL CONSIDER IT.
EASY!

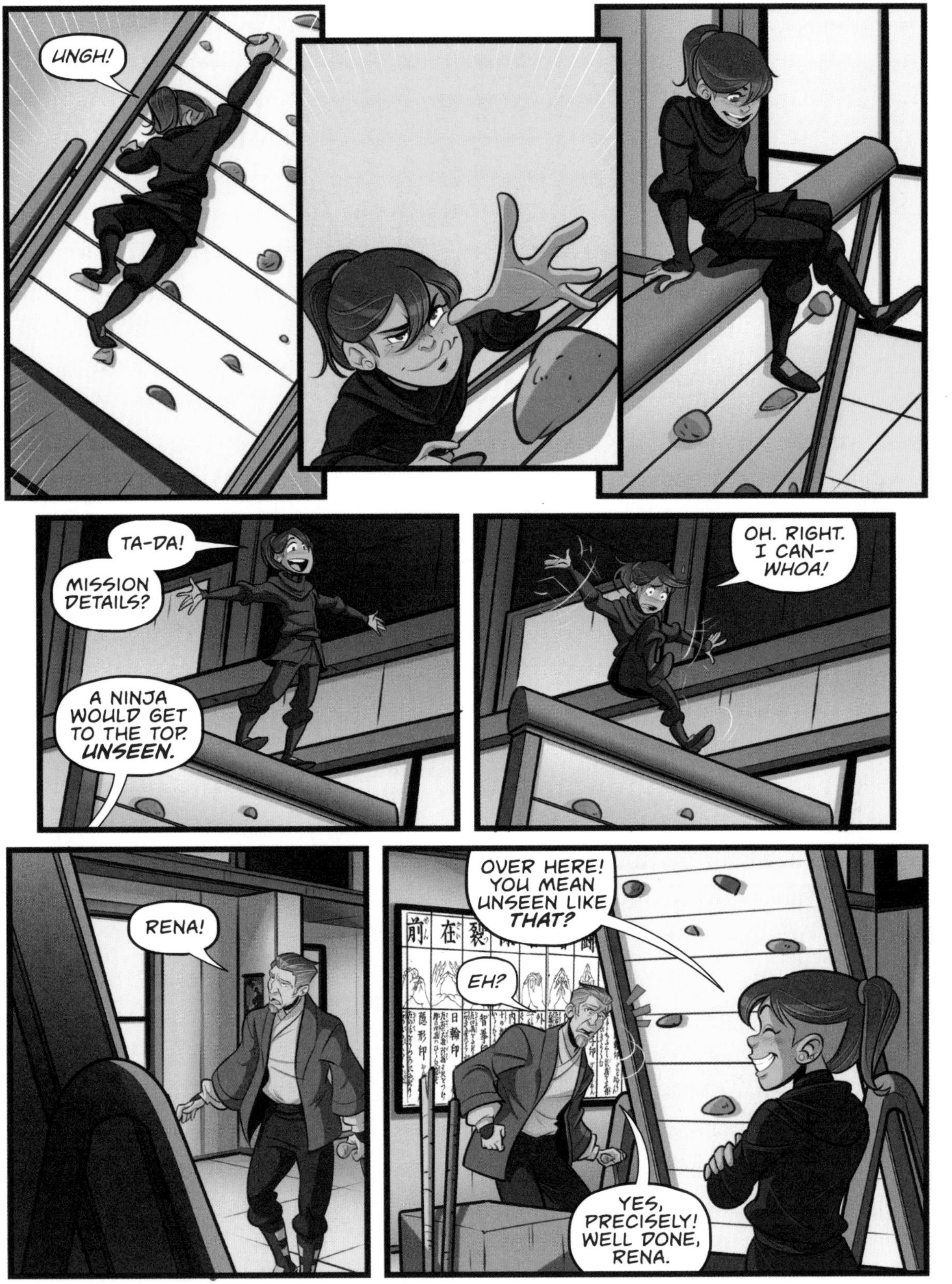
UNGH!
TA-DA!
MISSION DETAILS?
A NINJA WOULD GET TO THE TOP. UNSEEN.
OH. RIGHT. I CAN-- WHOA!
RENA!
OVER HERE! YOU MEAN UNSEEN LIKE THAT?
EH?
YES, PRECISELY! WELL DONE, RENA.

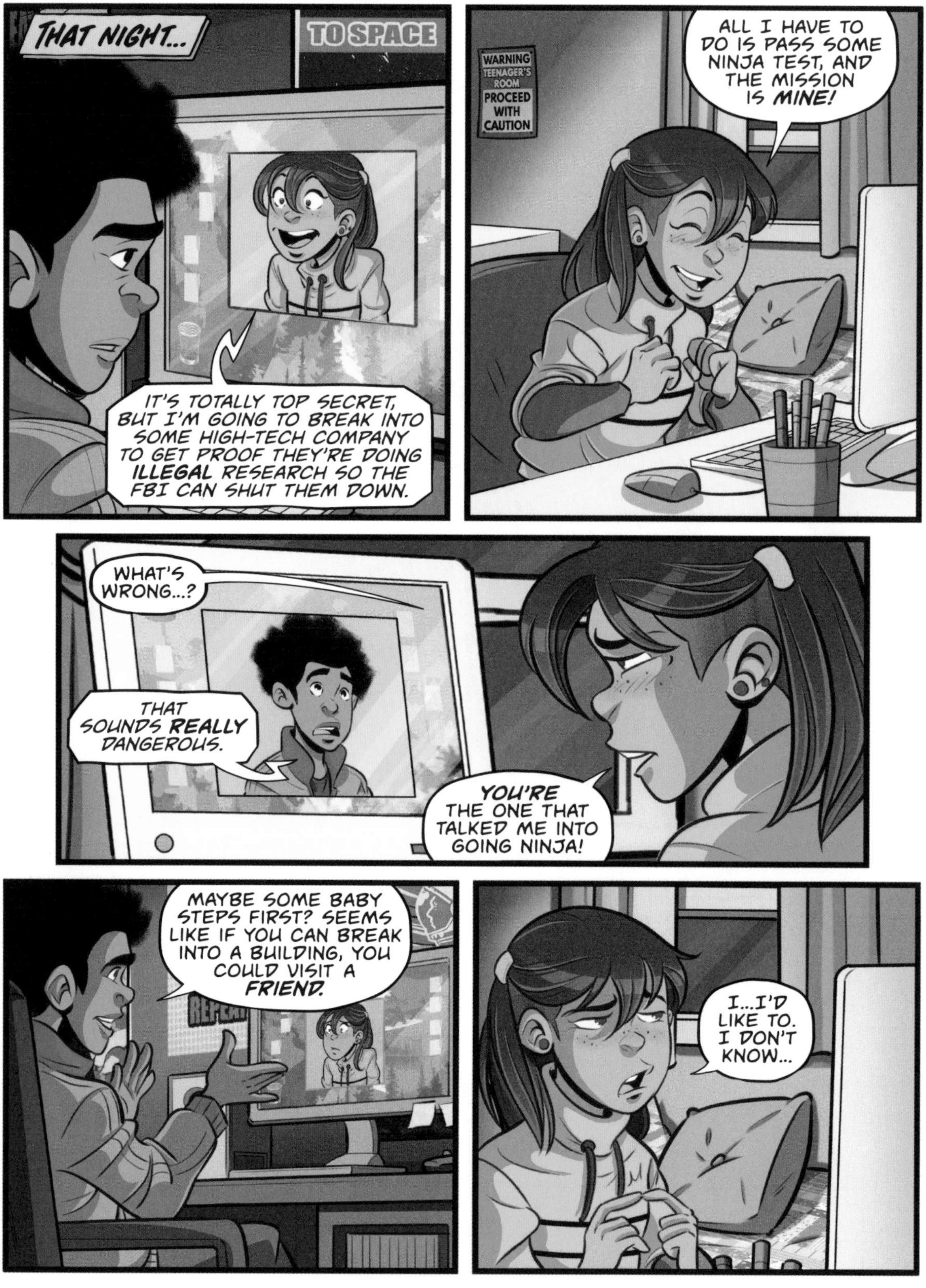
THAT NIGHT...
TO SPACE
IT'S TOTALLY TOP SECRET, BUT I'M GOING TO BREAK INTO SOME HIGH-TECH COMPANY TO GET PROOF THEY'RE DOING **ILLEGAL** RESEARCH SO THE FBI CAN SHUT THEM DOWN.
WARNING TEENAGER'S ROOM PROCEED WITH CAUTION
ALL I HAVE TO DO IS PASS SOME NINJA TEST, AND THE MISSION IS ***MINE!***
WHAT'S WRONG...?
THAT SOUNDS **REALLY** DANGEROUS.
***YOU'RE*** THE ONE THAT TALKED ME INTO GOING NINJA!
MAYBE SOME BABY STEPS FIRST? SEEMS LIKE IF YOU CAN BREAK INTO A BUILDING, YOU COULD VISIT A ***FRIEND.***
I...I'D LIKE TO. I DON'T KNOW...

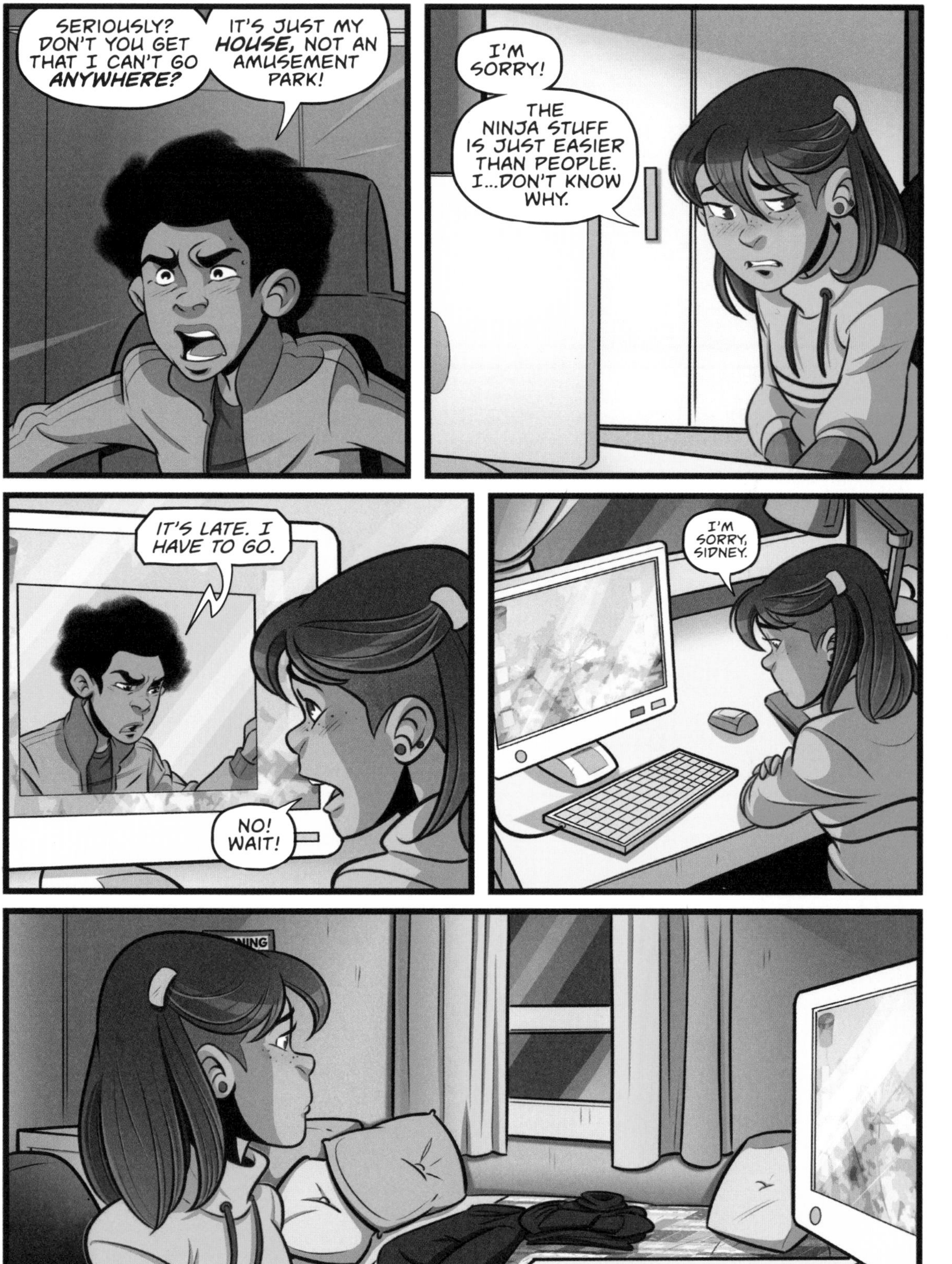
SERIOUSLY? DON'T YOU GET THAT I CAN'T GO ANYWHERE?
IT'S JUST MY HOUSE, NOT AN AMUSEMENT PARK!
I'M SORRY!
THE NINJA STUFF IS JUST EASIER THAN PEOPLE. I...DON'T KNOW WHY.
IT'S LATE. I HAVE TO GO.
NO! WAIT!
I'M SORRY, SIDNEY.

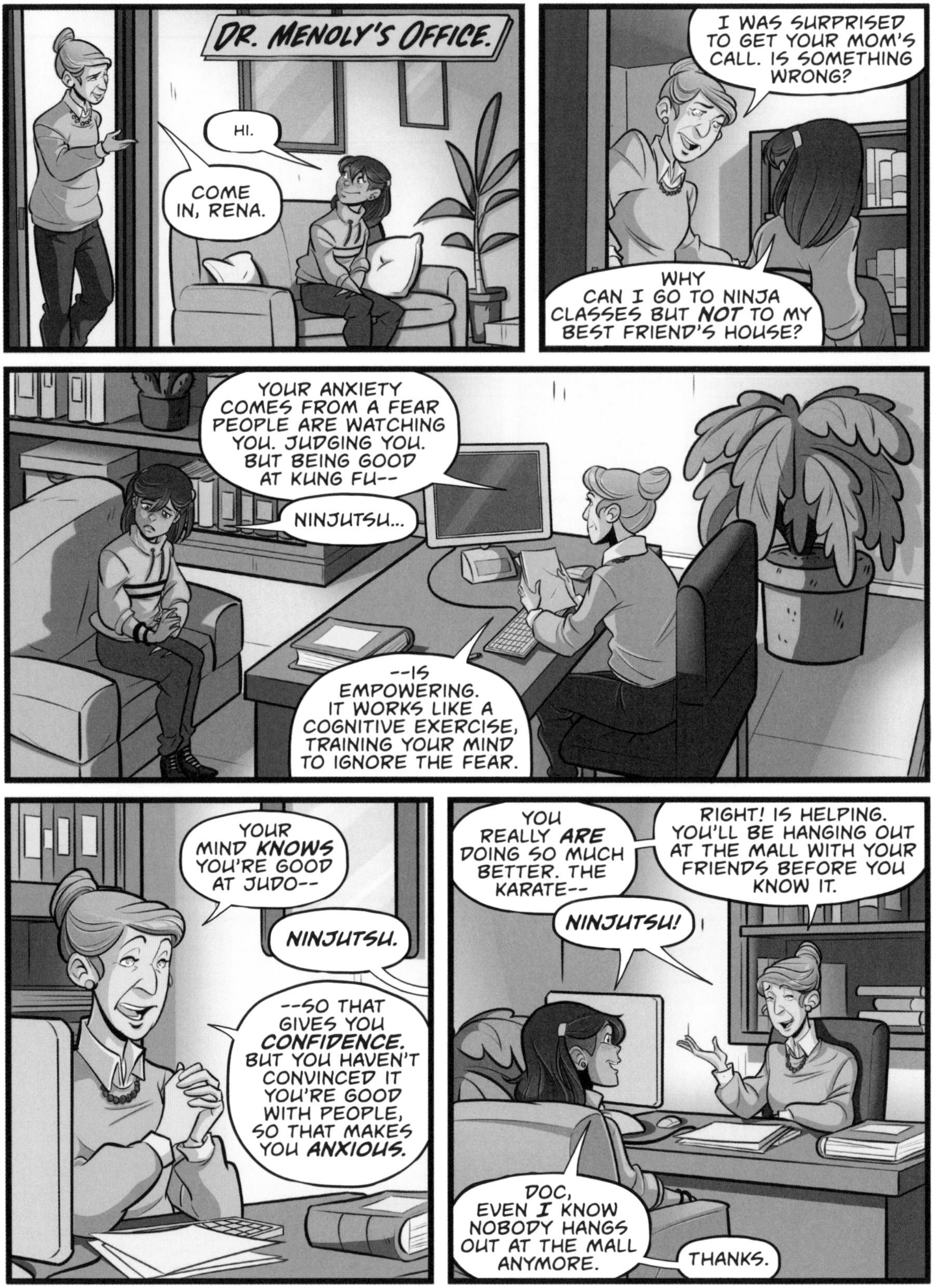
DR. MENOLY'S OFFICE.
COME IN, RENA.
HI.
I WAS SURPRISED TO GET YOUR MOM'S CALL. IS SOMETHING WRONG?
WHY CAN I GO TO NINJA CLASSES BUT NOT TO MY BEST FRIEND'S HOUSE?
YOUR ANXIETY COMES FROM A FEAR PEOPLE ARE WATCHING YOU. JUDGING YOU. BUT BEING GOOD AT KUNG FU--
NINJUTSU...
--IS EMPOWERING. IT WORKS LIKE A COGNITIVE EXERCISE, TRAINING YOUR MIND TO IGNORE THE FEAR.
YOUR MIND KNOWS YOU'RE GOOD AT JUDO--
NINJUTSU.
--SO THAT GIVES YOU CONFIDENCE. BUT YOU HAVEN'T CONVINCED IT YOU'RE GOOD WITH PEOPLE, SO THAT MAKES YOU ANXIOUS.
YOU REALLY ARE DOING SO MUCH BETTER. THE KARATE--
NINJUTSU!
RIGHT! IS HELPING. YOU'LL BE HANGING OUT AT THE MALL WITH YOUR FRIENDS BEFORE YOU KNOW IT.
DOC, EVEN I KNOW NOBODY HANGS OUT AT THE MALL ANYMORE.
THANKS.

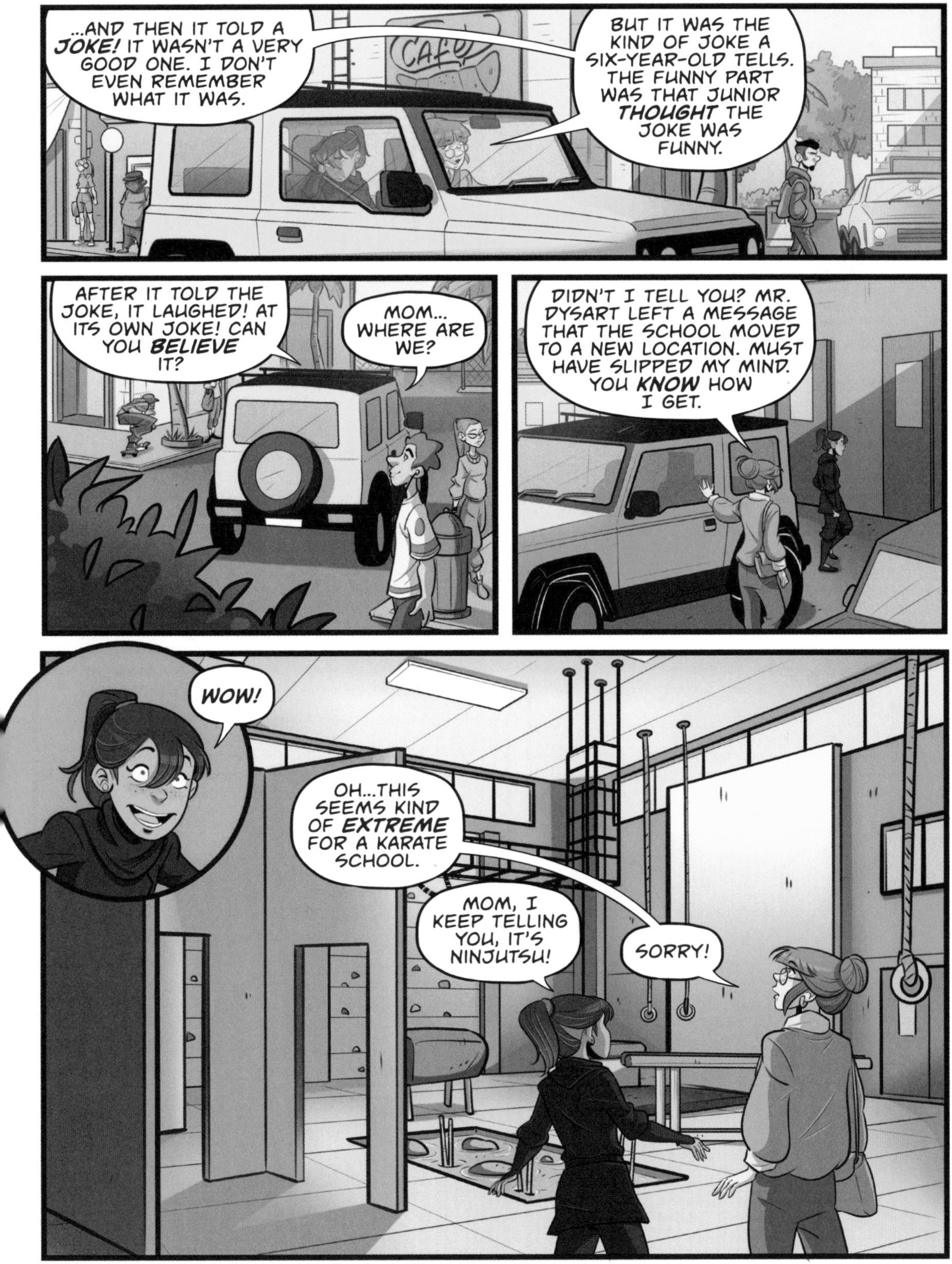
...AND THEN IT TOLD A JOKE! IT WASN'T A VERY GOOD ONE. I DON'T EVEN REMEMBER WHAT IT WAS.
BUT IT WAS THE KIND OF JOKE A SIX-YEAR-OLD TELLS. THE FUNNY PART WAS THAT JUNIOR THOUGHT THE JOKE WAS FUNNY.
CAFE
AFTER IT TOLD THE JOKE, IT LAUGHED! AT ITS OWN JOKE! CAN YOU BELIEVE IT?
MOM... WHERE ARE WE?
DIDN'T I TELL YOU? MR. DYSART LEFT A MESSAGE THAT THE SCHOOL MOVED TO A NEW LOCATION. MUST HAVE SLIPPED MY MIND. YOU KNOW HOW I GET.
WOW!
OH...THIS SEEMS KIND OF EXTREME FOR A KARATE SCHOOL.
MOM, I KEEP TELLING YOU, IT'S NINJUTSU!
SORRY!

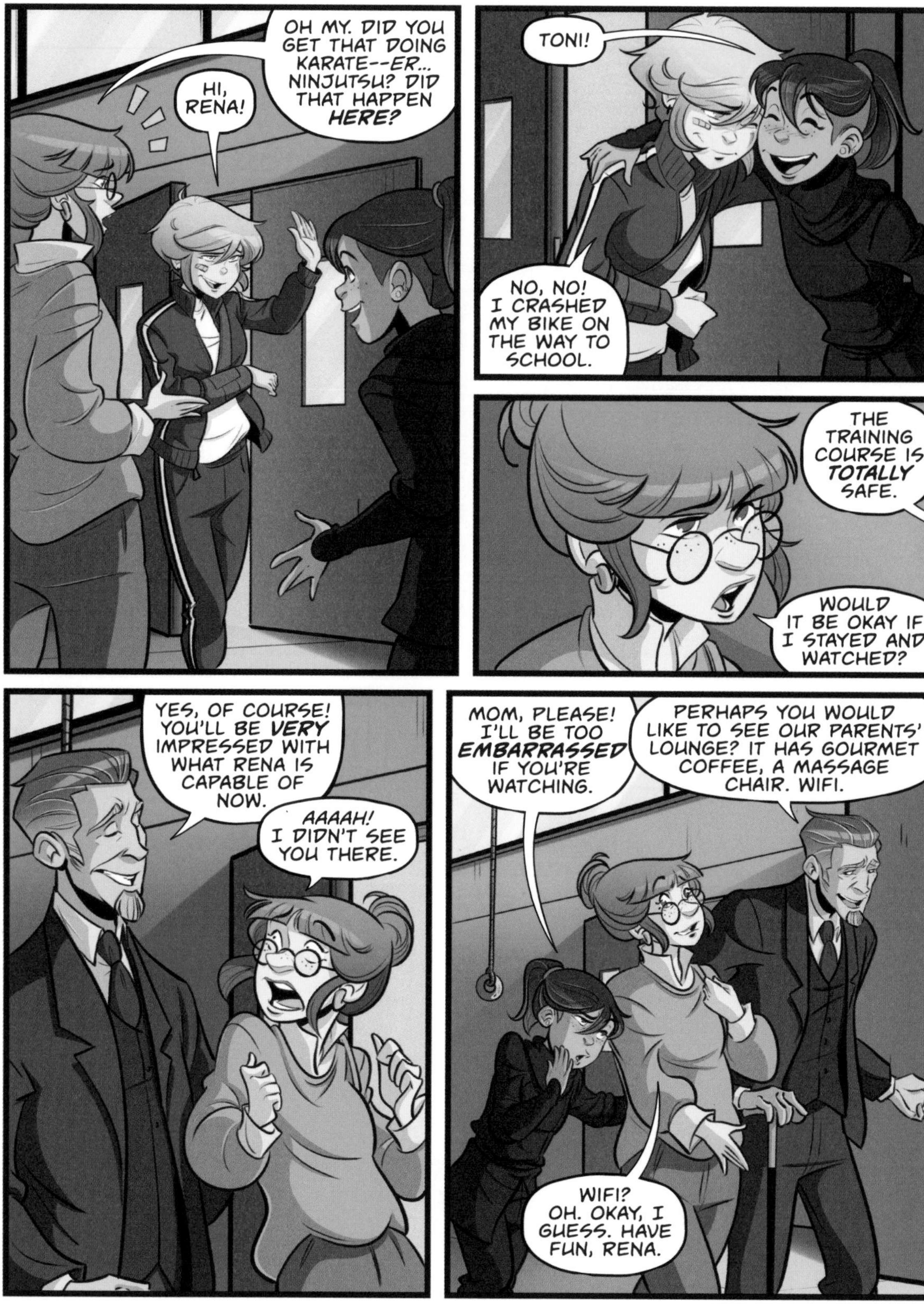
HI, RENA!
OH MY. DID YOU GET THAT DOING KARATE--ER... NINJUTSU? DID THAT HAPPEN *HERE?*
TONI!
NO, NO! I CRASHED MY BIKE ON THE WAY TO SCHOOL.
THE TRAINING COURSE IS *TOTALLY* SAFE.
WOULD IT BE OKAY IF I STAYED AND WATCHED?
YES, OF COURSE! YOU'LL BE *VERY* IMPRESSED WITH WHAT RENA IS CAPABLE OF NOW.
AAAAH! I DIDN'T SEE YOU THERE.
MOM, PLEASE! I'LL BE TOO *EMBARRASSED* IF YOU'RE WATCHING.
PERHAPS YOU WOULD LIKE TO SEE OUR PARENTS' LOUNGE? IT HAS GOURMET COFFEE, A MASSAGE CHAIR. WIFI.
WIFI? OH. OKAY, I GUESS. HAVE FUN, RENA.

OOOH! WATCH IT, WILL YA?

I'M SO *GLAD* YOU'RE BACK.

ME, TOO.

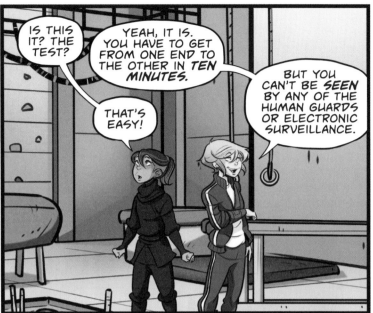

IS THIS IT? THE TEST?

YEAH, IT IS. YOU HAVE TO GET FROM ONE END TO THE OTHER IN *TEN MINUTES.*

THAT'S EASY!

BUT YOU CAN'T BE *SEEN* BY ANY OF THE HUMAN GUARDS OR ELECTRONIC SURVEILLANCE.

YOUR MOTHER SEEMS TO ENJOY THE MASSAGE CHAIR.

I *TOTALLY* HEARD HIM COMING.

YOU'RE SUCH A *LIAR.*

THERE IS NO SHAME IF YOU FAIL, RENA. ANTONIA *BARELY* SUCCEEDED, AND WITH MUCH MORE TRAINING.

THANK YOU, MASTER. BUT I'M THE GHOST, RIGHT? I *CAN* DO THIS.

EVEN THE GHOST REQUIRES TRAINING.

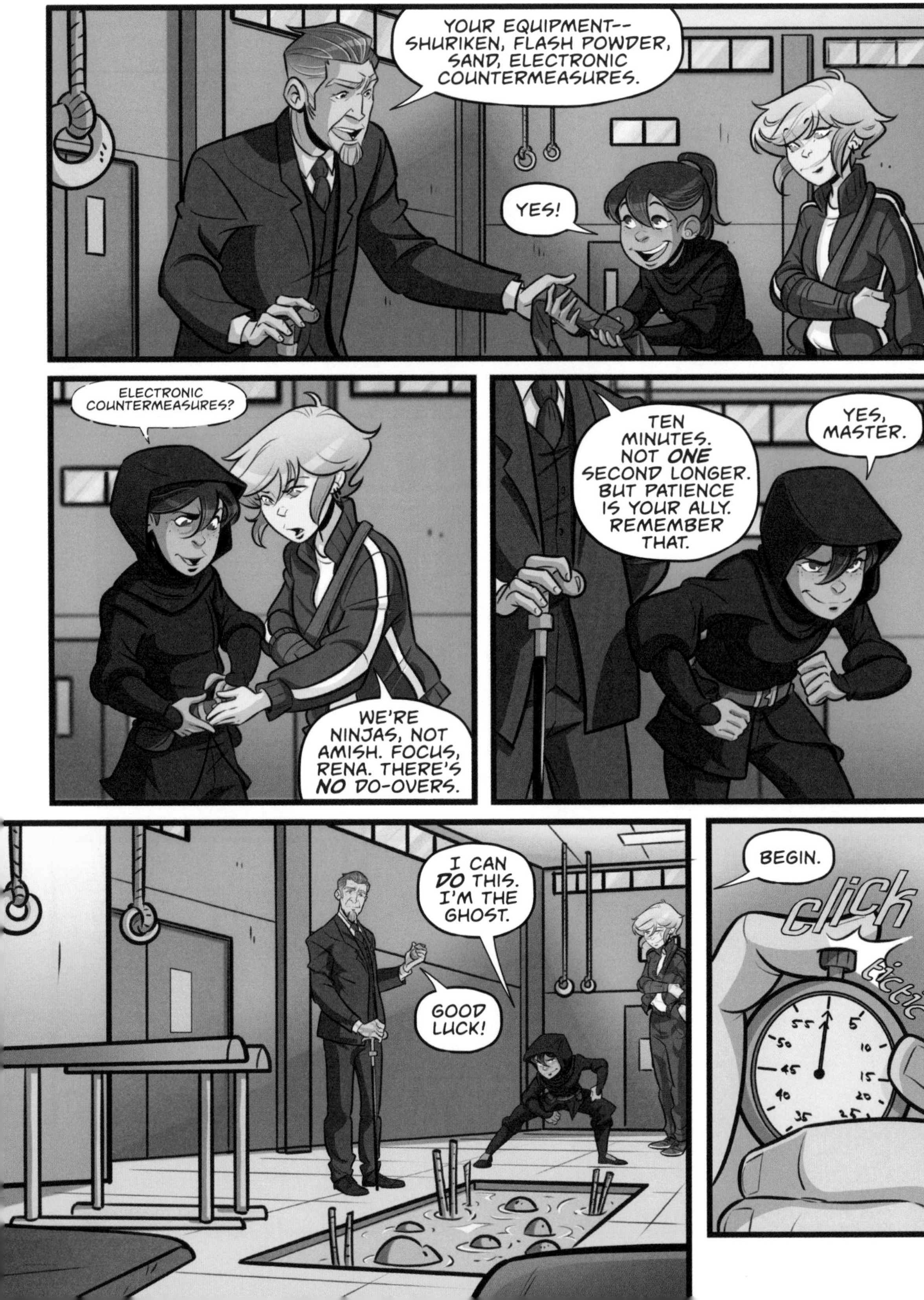
YOUR EQUIPMENT--SHURIKEN, FLASH POWDER, SAND, ELECTRONIC COUNTERMEASURES.
YES!
ELECTRONIC COUNTERMEASURES?
WE'RE NINJAS, NOT AMISH. FOCUS, RENA. THERE'S NO DO-OVERS.
TEN MINUTES. NOT ONE SECOND LONGER. BUT PATIENCE IS YOUR ALLY. REMEMBER THAT.
YES, MASTER.
I CAN DO THIS. I'M THE GHOST.
GOOD LUCK!
BEGIN.
click
tictic

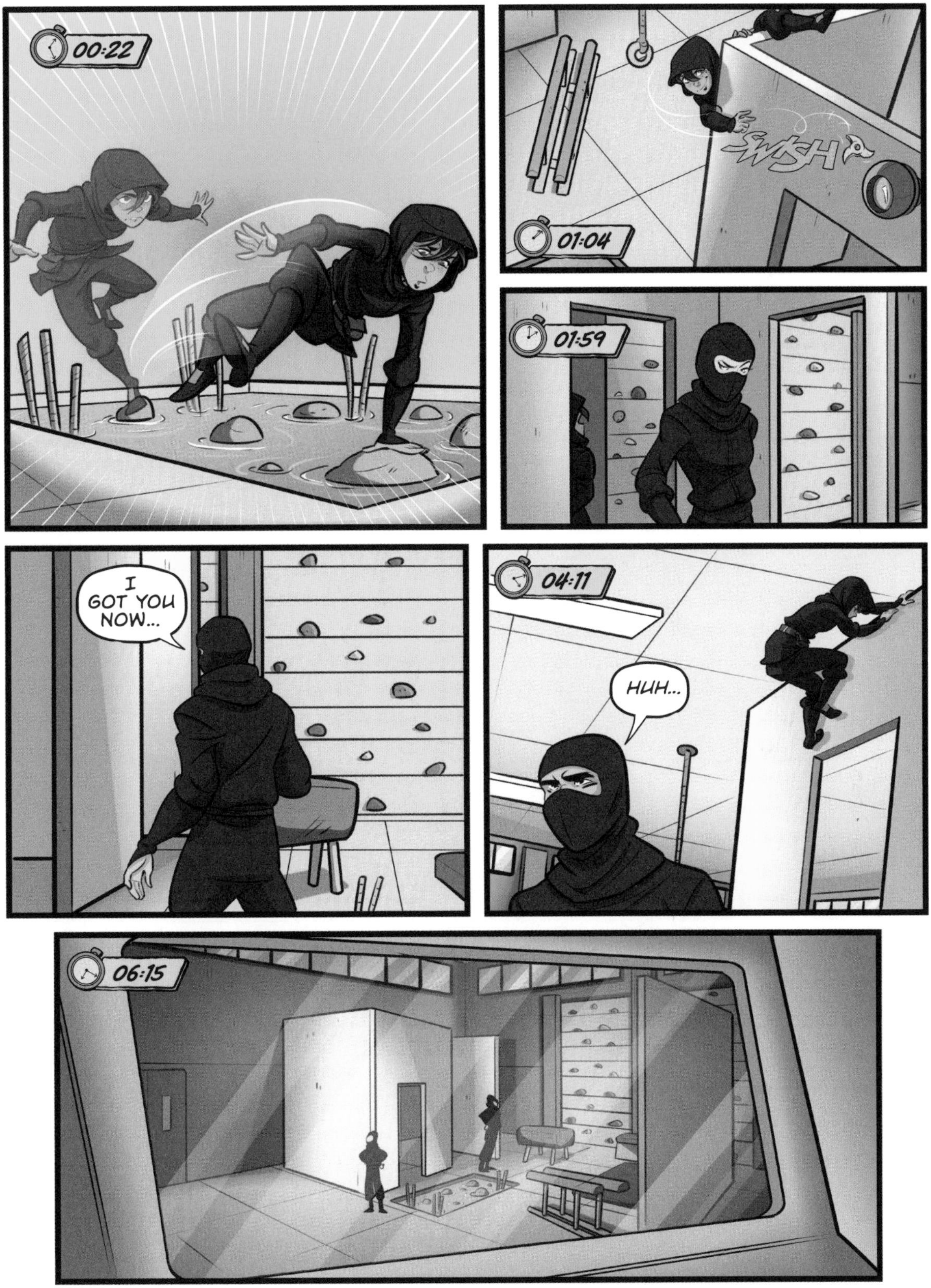
00:22
01:04
SWISH
01:59
I GOT YOU NOW...
04:11
HUH...
06:15

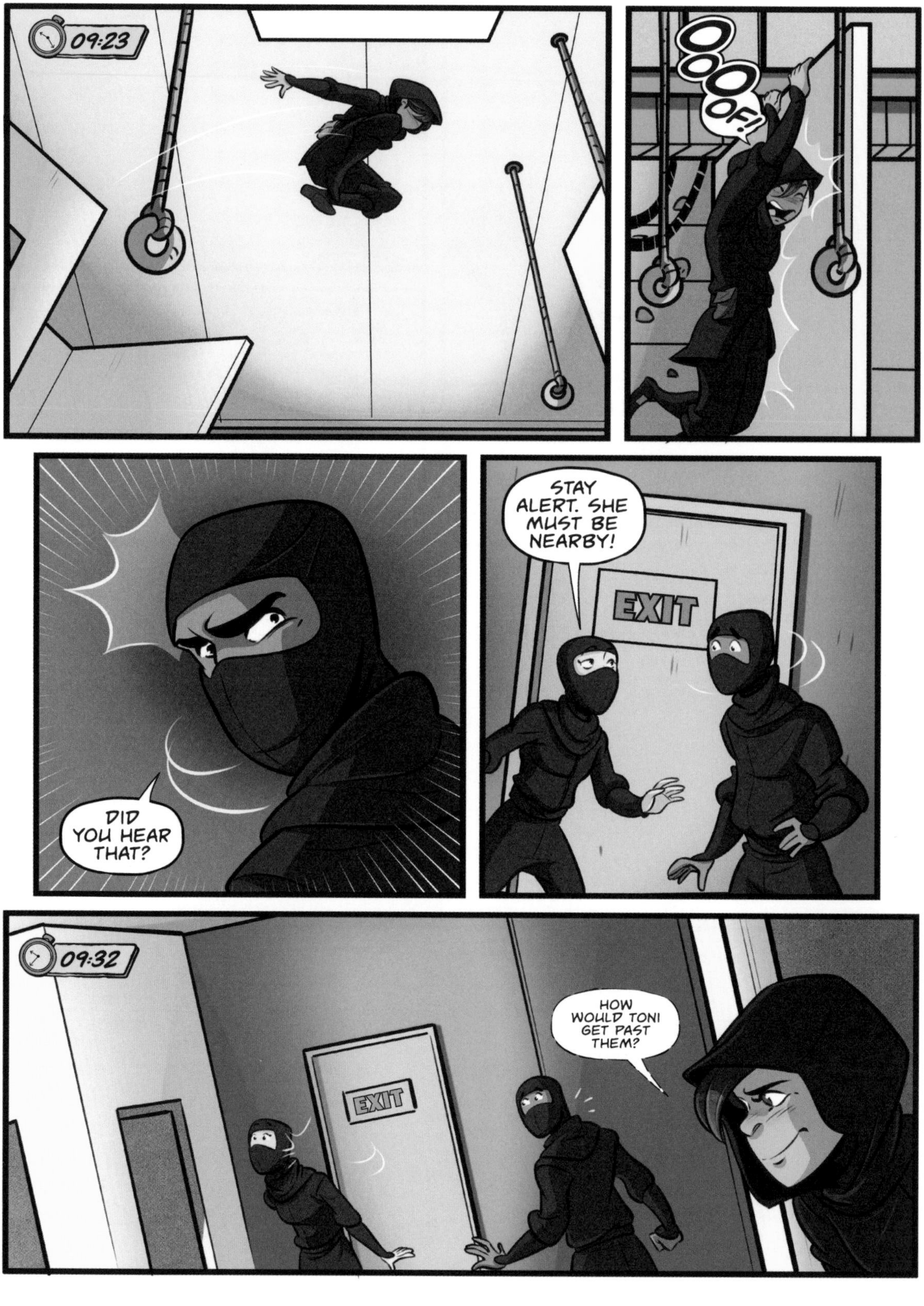
09:23
OOOOF!
DID YOU HEAR THAT?
STAY ALERT. SHE MUST BE NEARBY!
EXIT
09:32
EXIT
HOW WOULD TONI GET PAST THEM?

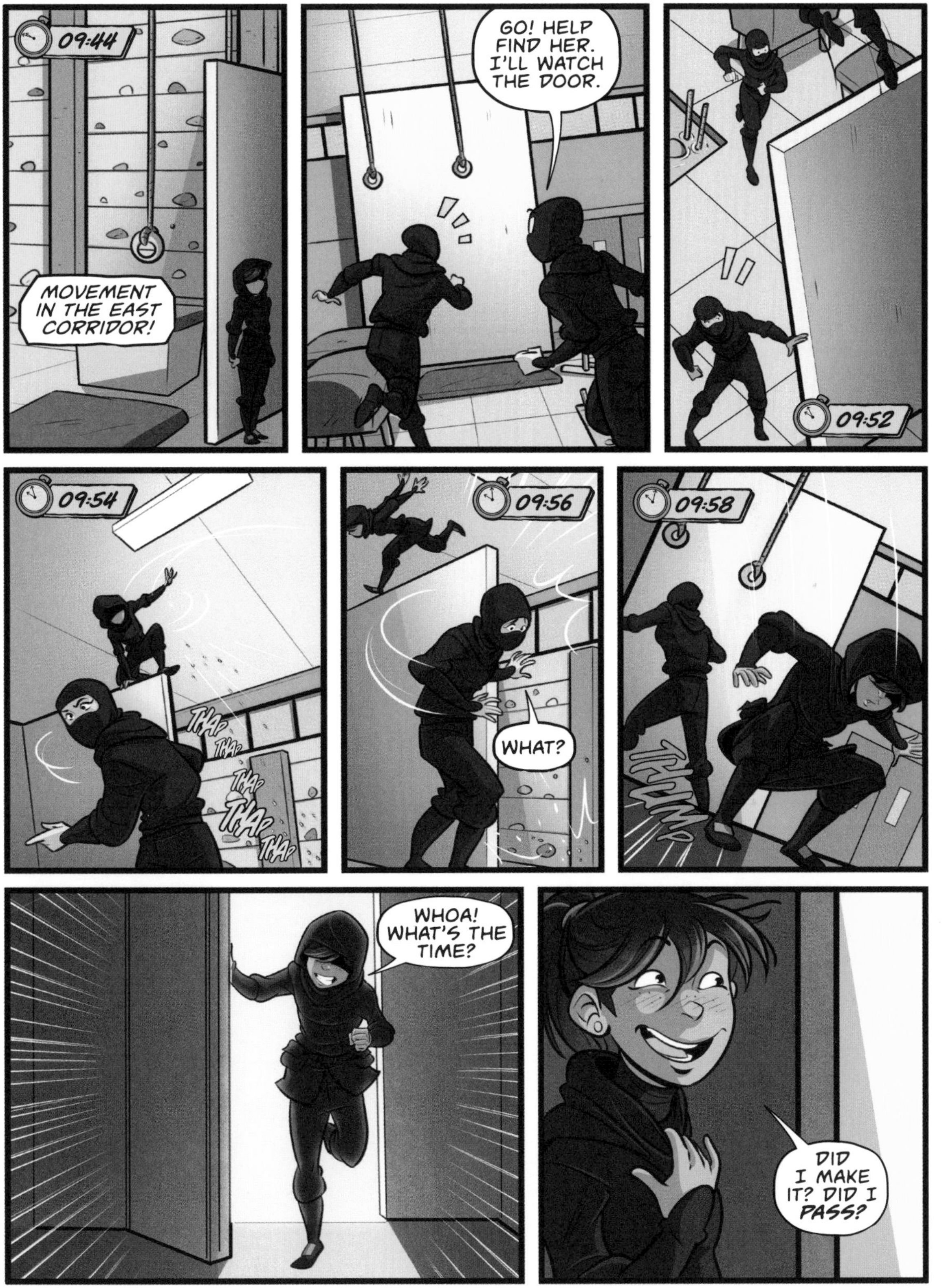
09:44
MOVEMENT IN THE EAST CORRIDOR!
GO! HELP FIND HER. I'LL WATCH THE DOOR.
09:52
09:54
THAP THAP THAP THAP THAP
09:56
WHAT?
09:58
THUMP
WHOA! WHAT'S THE TIME?
DID I MAKE IT? DID I *PASS*?

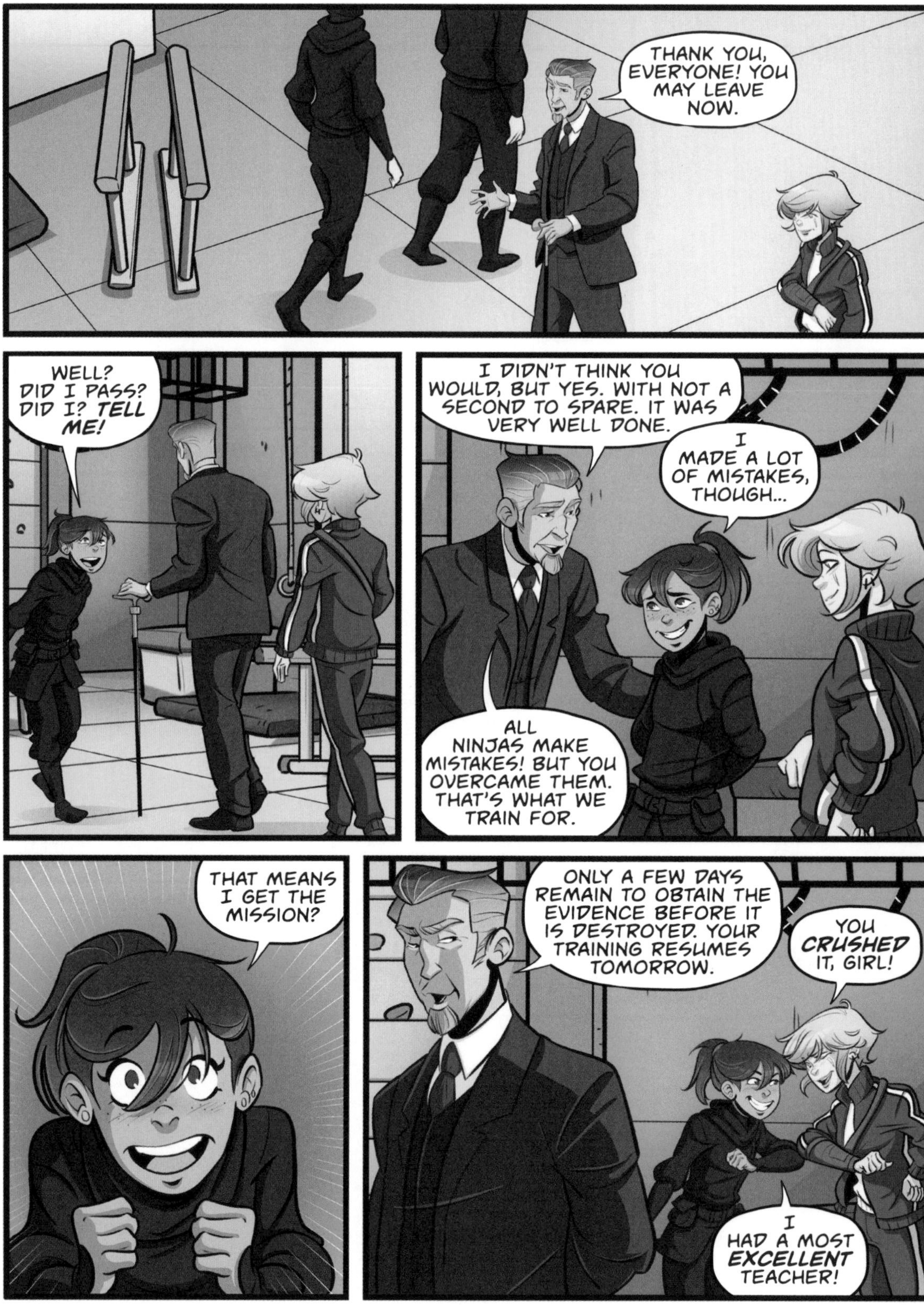
THANK YOU, EVERYONE! YOU MAY LEAVE NOW.
WELL? DID I PASS? DID I? TELL ME!
I DIDN'T THINK YOU WOULD, BUT YES. WITH NOT A SECOND TO SPARE. IT WAS VERY WELL DONE.
I MADE A LOT OF MISTAKES, THOUGH...
ALL NINJAS MAKE MISTAKES! BUT YOU OVERCAME THEM. THAT'S WHAT WE TRAIN FOR.
THAT MEANS I GET THE MISSION?
ONLY A FEW DAYS REMAIN TO OBTAIN THE EVIDENCE BEFORE IT IS DESTROYED. YOUR TRAINING RESUMES TOMORROW.
YOU CRUSHED IT, GIRL!
I HAD A MOST EXCELLENT TEACHER!

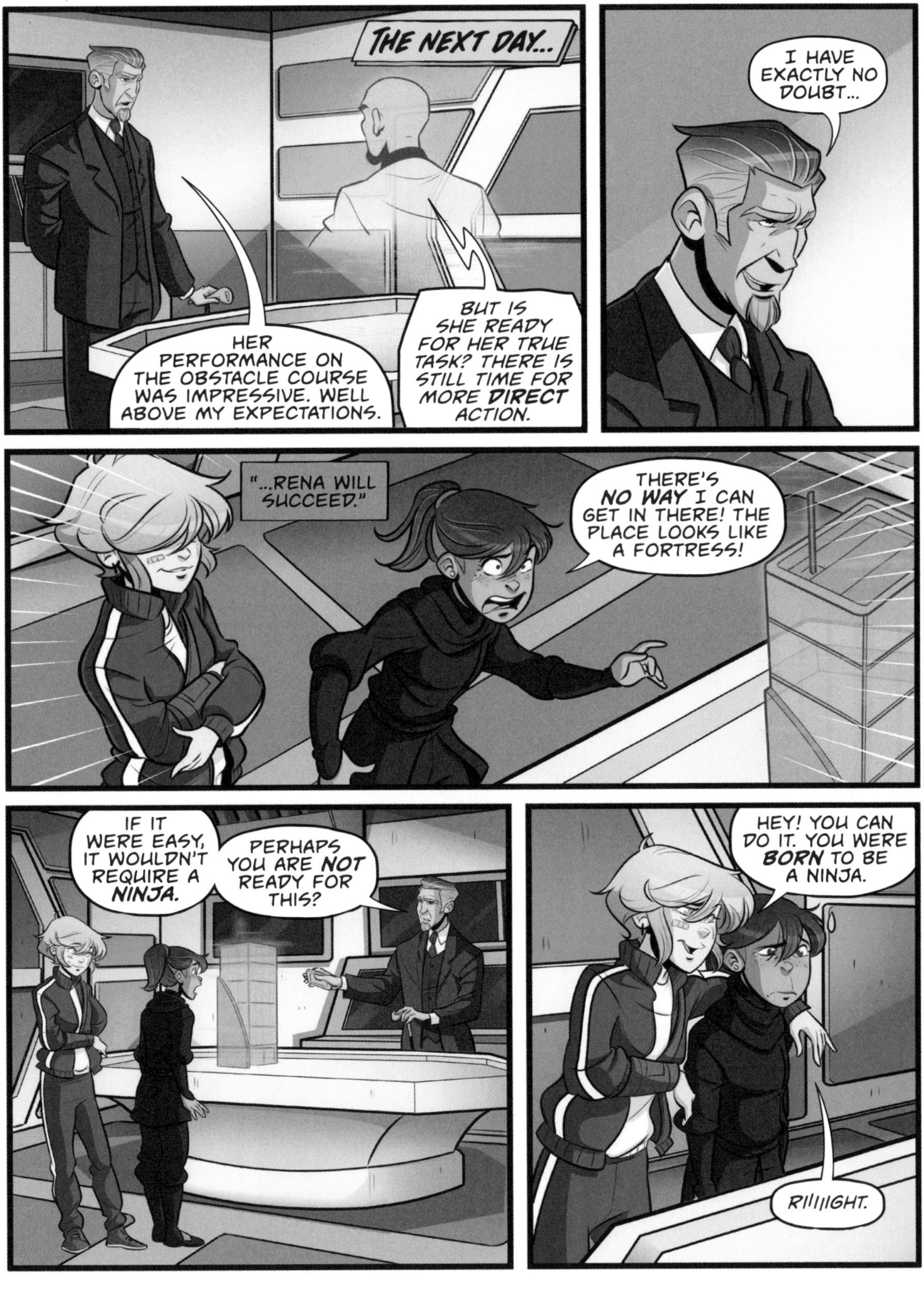
THE NEXT DAY...
HER PERFORMANCE ON THE OBSTACLE COURSE WAS IMPRESSIVE. WELL ABOVE MY EXPECTATIONS.
BUT IS SHE READY FOR HER TRUE TASK? THERE IS STILL TIME FOR MORE DIRECT ACTION.
I HAVE EXACTLY NO DOUBT...
"...RENA WILL SUCCEED."
THERE'S NO WAY I CAN GET IN THERE! THE PLACE LOOKS LIKE A FORTRESS!
IF IT WERE EASY, IT WOULDN'T REQUIRE A NINJA.
PERHAPS YOU ARE NOT READY FOR THIS?
HEY! YOU CAN DO IT. YOU WERE BORN TO BE A NINJA.
RIIIIIGHT.

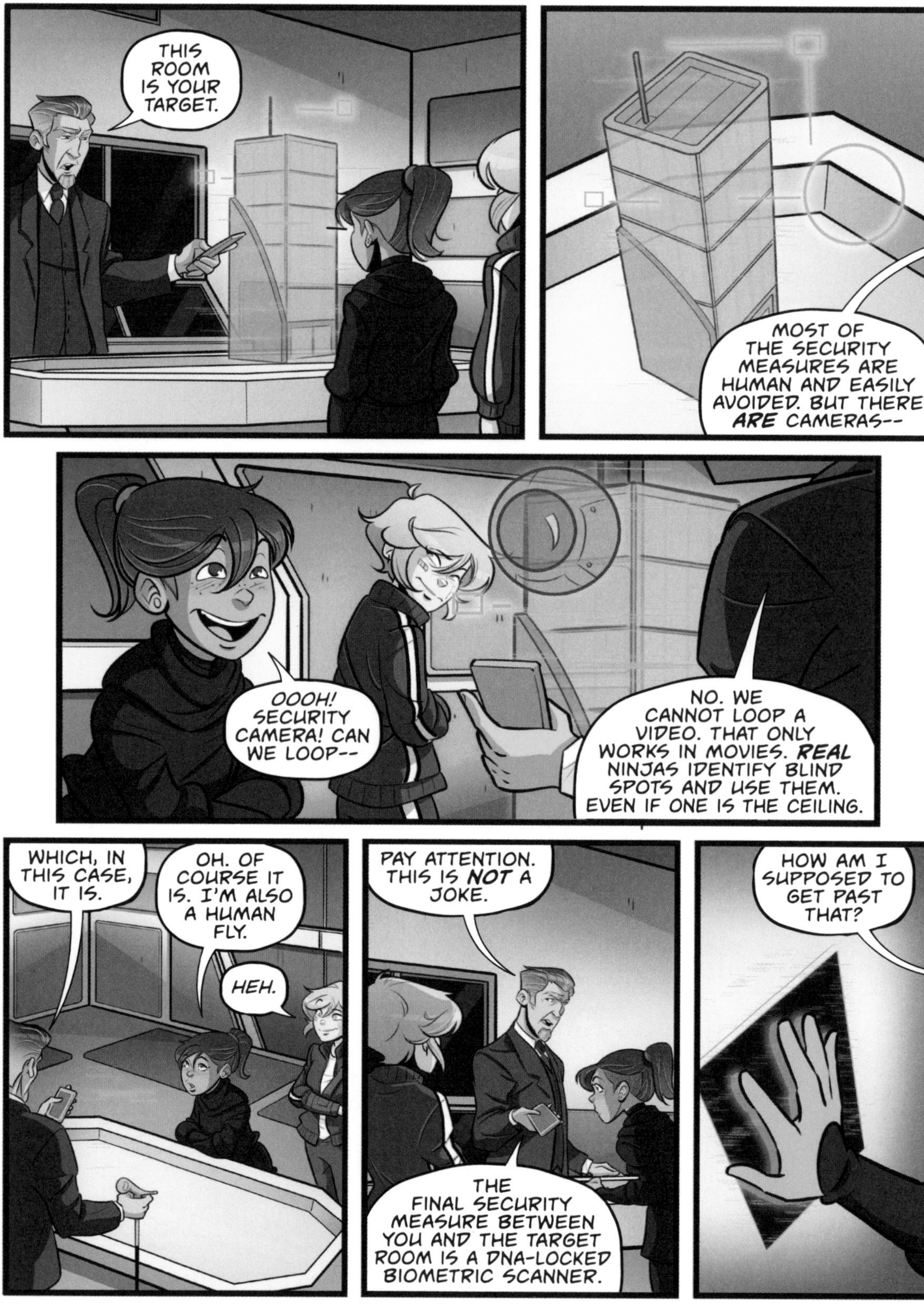
THIS ROOM IS YOUR TARGET.
MOST OF THE SECURITY MEASURES ARE HUMAN AND EASILY AVOIDED. BUT THERE ***ARE*** CAMERAS--
*OOOH! SECURITY CAMERA! CAN WE LOOP--*
NO. WE CANNOT LOOP A VIDEO. THAT ONLY WORKS IN MOVIES. ***REAL*** NINJAS IDENTIFY BLIND SPOTS AND USE THEM. EVEN IF ONE IS THE CEILING.
WHICH, IN THIS CASE, IT IS.
OH. OF COURSE IT IS. I'M ALSO A HUMAN FLY.
*HEH.*
PAY ATTENTION. THIS IS ***NOT*** A JOKE.
THE FINAL SECURITY MEASURE BETWEEN YOU AND THE TARGET ROOM IS A DNA-LOCKED BIOMETRIC SCANNER.
HOW AM I SUPPOSED TO GET PAST THAT?

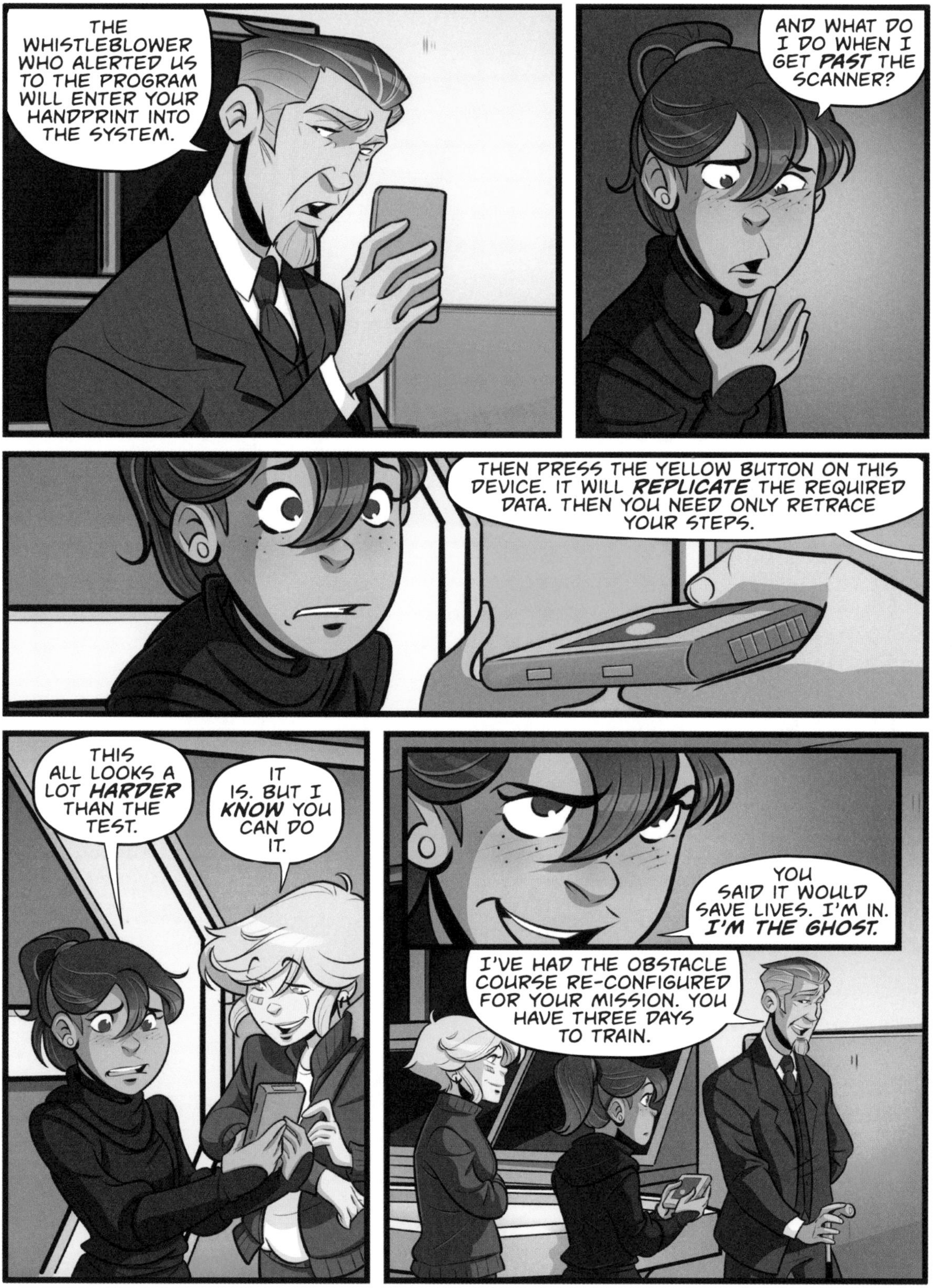

THE WHISTLEBLOWER WHO ALERTED US TO THE PROGRAM WILL ENTER YOUR HANDPRINT INTO THE SYSTEM.
AND WHAT DO I DO WHEN I GET *PAST* THE SCANNER?
THEN PRESS THE YELLOW BUTTON ON THIS DEVICE. IT WILL *REPLICATE* THE REQUIRED DATA. THEN YOU NEED ONLY RETRACE YOUR STEPS.
THIS ALL LOOKS A LOT *HARDER* THAN THE TEST.
IT IS. BUT I *KNOW* YOU CAN DO IT.
YOU SAID IT WOULD SAVE LIVES. I'M IN. *I'M THE GHOST.*
I'VE HAD THE OBSTACLE COURSE RE-CONFIGURED FOR YOUR MISSION. YOU HAVE THREE DAYS TO TRAIN.

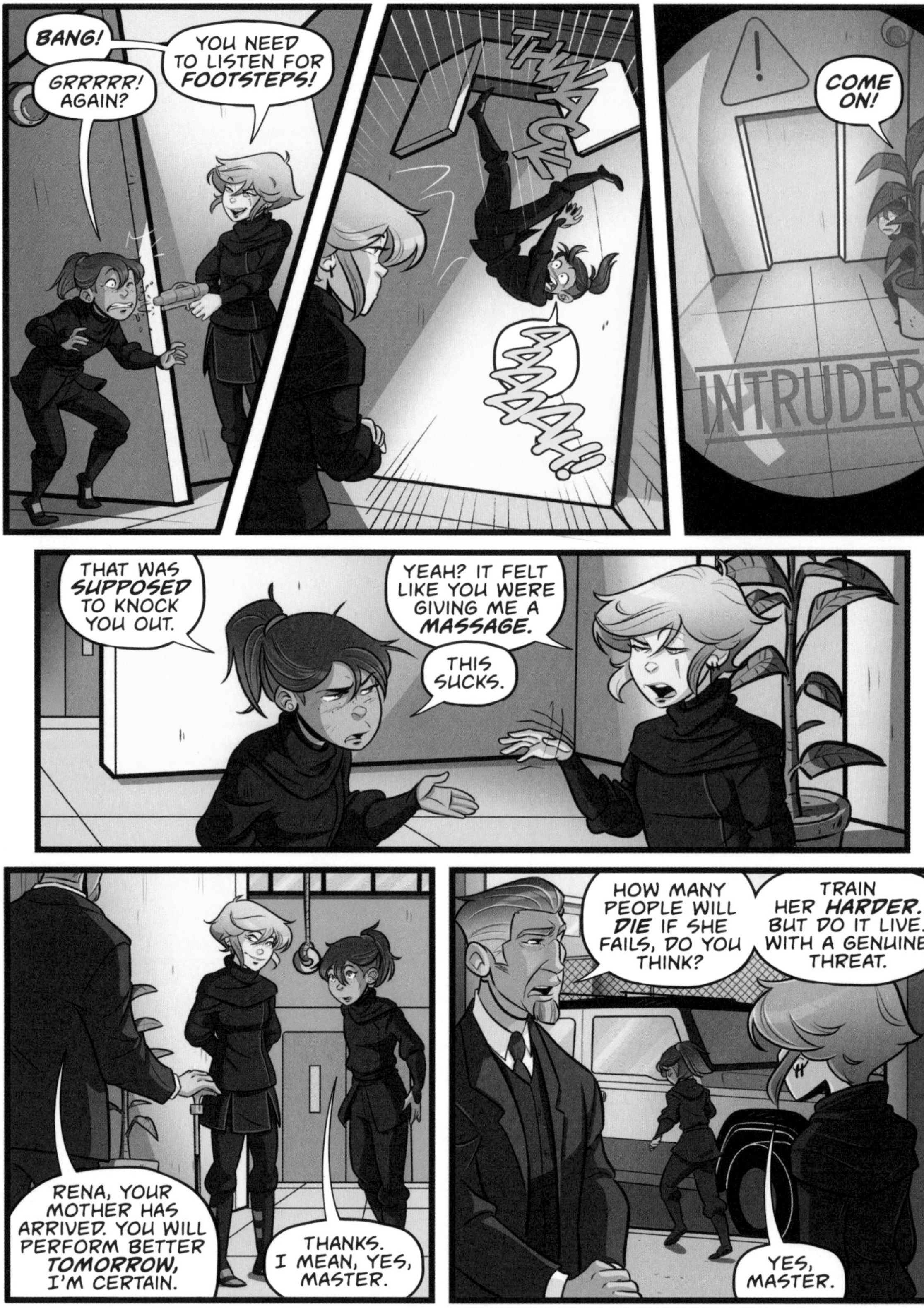
BANG!
GRRRRR! AGAIN?
YOU NEED TO LISTEN FOR FOOTSTEPS!
THWACK
AAAAAH!!
COME ON!
INTRUDER
THAT WAS SUPPOSED TO KNOCK YOU OUT.
YEAH? IT FELT LIKE YOU WERE GIVING ME A MASSAGE.
THIS SUCKS.
RENA, YOUR MOTHER HAS ARRIVED. YOU WILL PERFORM BETTER TOMORROW, I'M CERTAIN.
THANKS. I MEAN, YES, MASTER.
HOW MANY PEOPLE WILL DIE IF SHE FAILS, DO YOU THINK?
TRAIN HER HARDER. BUT DO IT LIVE. WITH A GENUINE THREAT.
YES, MASTER.

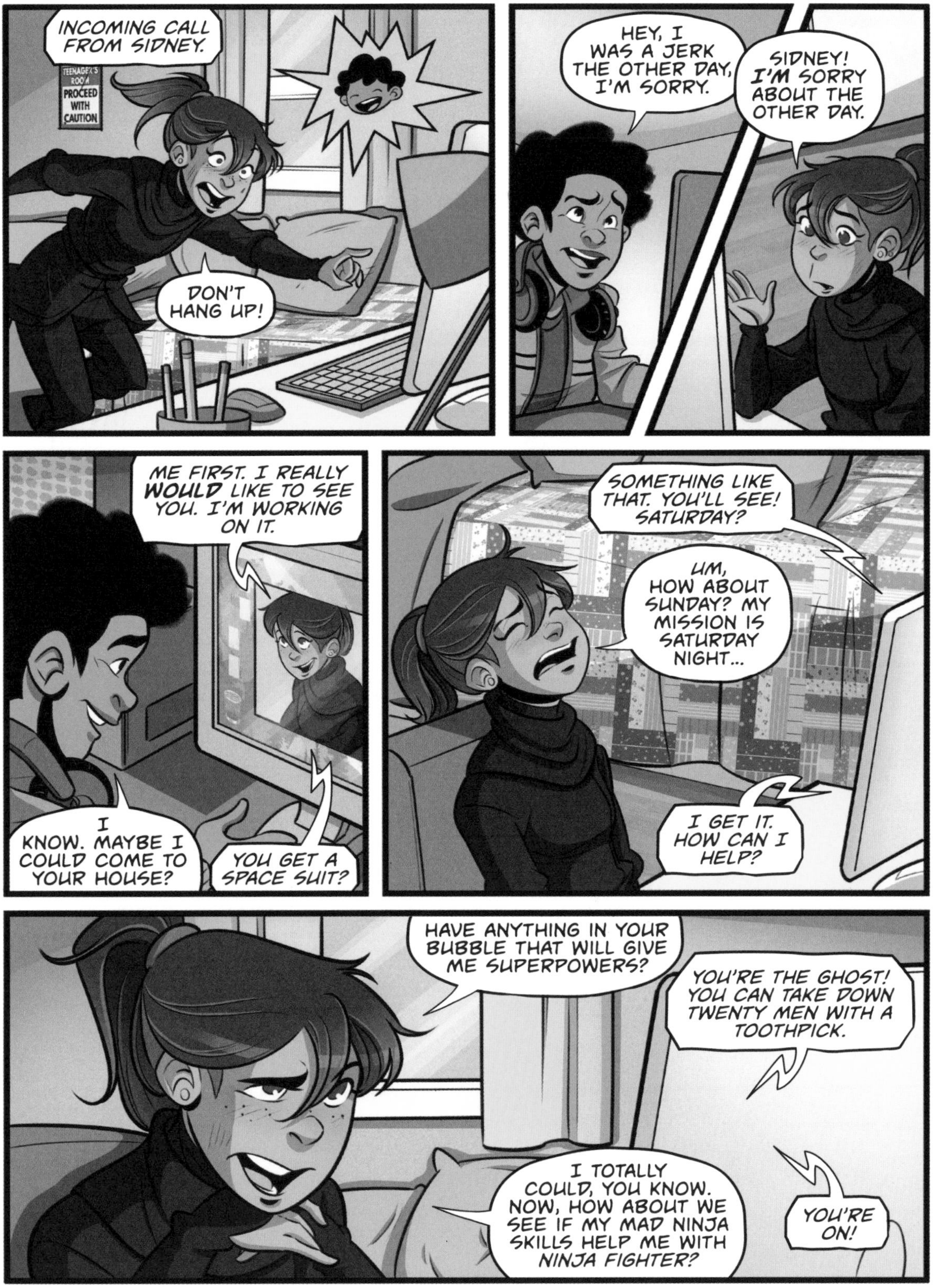
INCOMING CALL FROM SIDNEY.
TEENAGER'S ROOM PROCEED WITH CAUTION
DON'T HANG UP!
HEY, I WAS A JERK THE OTHER DAY, I'M SORRY.
SIDNEY! I'M SORRY ABOUT THE OTHER DAY.
ME FIRST. I REALLY WOULD LIKE TO SEE YOU. I'M WORKING ON IT.
I KNOW. MAYBE I COULD COME TO YOUR HOUSE?
YOU GET A SPACE SUIT?
SOMETHING LIKE THAT. YOU'LL SEE! SATURDAY?
UM, HOW ABOUT SUNDAY? MY MISSION IS SATURDAY NIGHT...
I GET IT. HOW CAN I HELP?
HAVE ANYTHING IN YOUR BUBBLE THAT WILL GIVE ME SUPERPOWERS?
YOU'RE THE GHOST! YOU CAN TAKE DOWN TWENTY MEN WITH A TOOTHPICK.
I TOTALLY COULD, YOU KNOW. NOW, HOW ABOUT WE SEE IF MY MAD NINJA SKILLS HELP ME WITH NINJA FIGHTER?
YOU'RE ON!

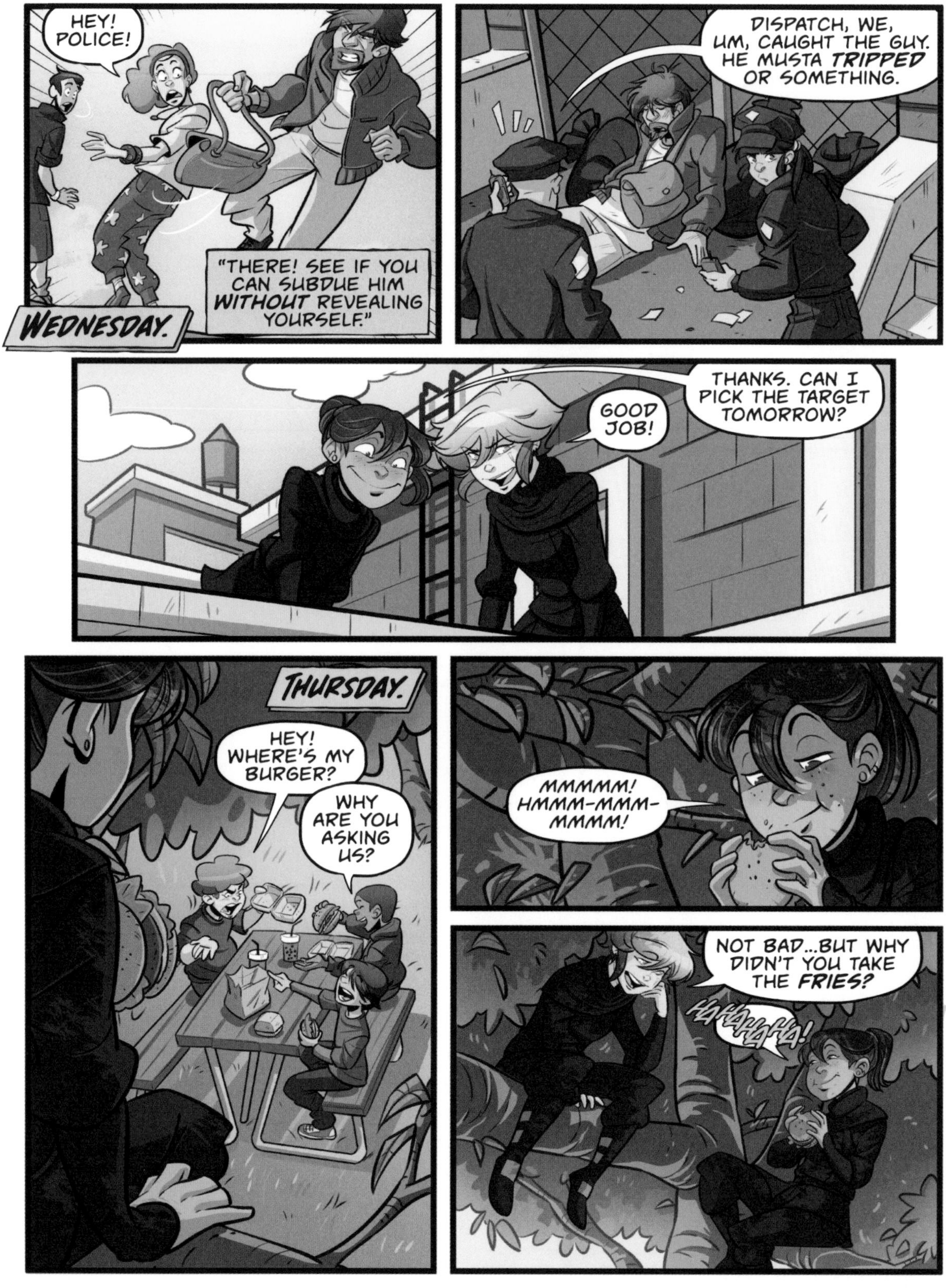
HEY! POLICE!
"THERE! SEE IF YOU CAN SUBDUE HIM **WITHOUT** REVEALING YOURSELF."
WEDNESDAY.
DISPATCH, WE, UM, CAUGHT THE GUY. HE MUSTA **TRIPPED** OR SOMETHING.
GOOD JOB!
THANKS. CAN I PICK THE TARGET TOMORROW?
THURSDAY.
HEY! WHERE'S MY BURGER?
WHY ARE YOU ASKING US?
MMMMM! HMMM-MMM-MMMM!
NOT BAD...BUT WHY DIDN'T YOU TAKE THE **FRIES?**
HAHAHAHA!

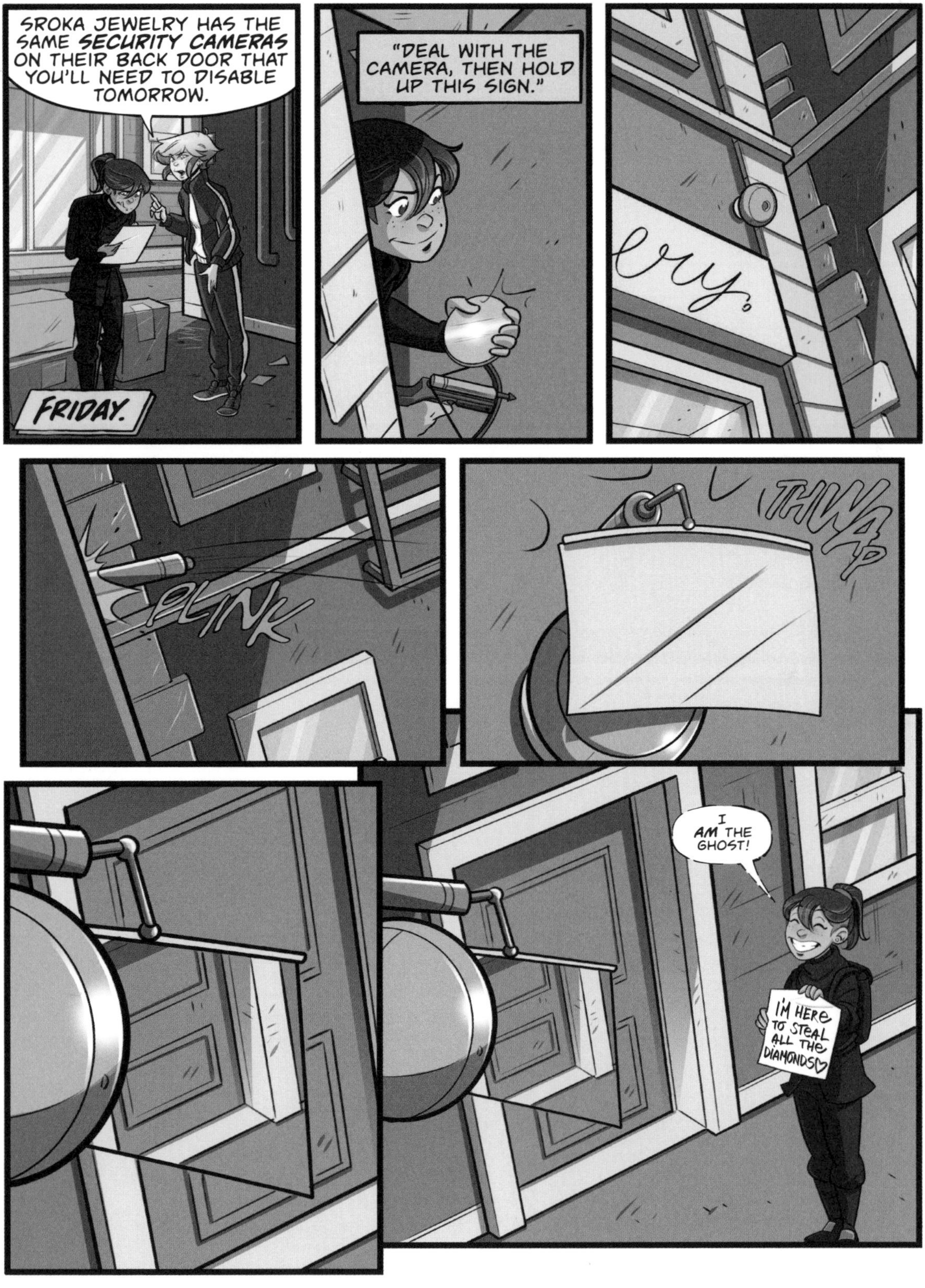
SROKA JEWELRY HAS THE SAME SECURITY CAMERAS ON THEIR BACK DOOR THAT YOU'LL NEED TO DISABLE TOMORROW.
FRIDAY.
"DEAL WITH THE CAMERA, THEN HOLD UP THIS SIGN."
PLINK
THWAP
I AM THE GHOST!
I'M HERE TO STEAL ALL THE DIAMONDS♡

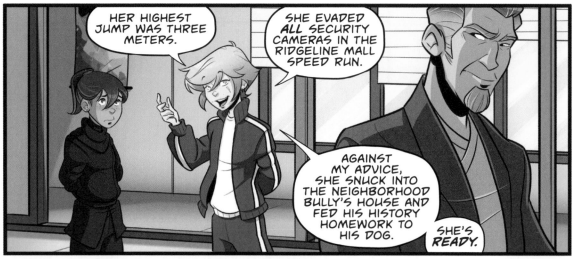

HER HIGHEST JUMP WAS THREE METERS.

SHE EVADED *ALL* SECURITY CAMERAS IN THE RIDGELINE MALL SPEED RUN.

AGAINST MY ADVICE, SHE SNUCK INTO THE NEIGHBORHOOD BULLY'S HOUSE AND FED HIS HISTORY HOMEWORK TO HIS DOG.

SHE'S *READY*.

HE GOT WHAT HE--ER... I MEAN, I WAS PRACTICING, MASTER!

HEH. YES, OF COURSE. BETWEEN YOUR DEDICATION AND ANTONIA'S TRAINING, YOU *ARE* READY.

THE OPERATION IS A GO.

YES! SO...HOW AM I GOING TO GET TO THE MISSION SITE WITHOUT TELLING MY MOM?

DON'T FRET, RENA. I HAVE THAT TAKEN CARE OF ALREADY.

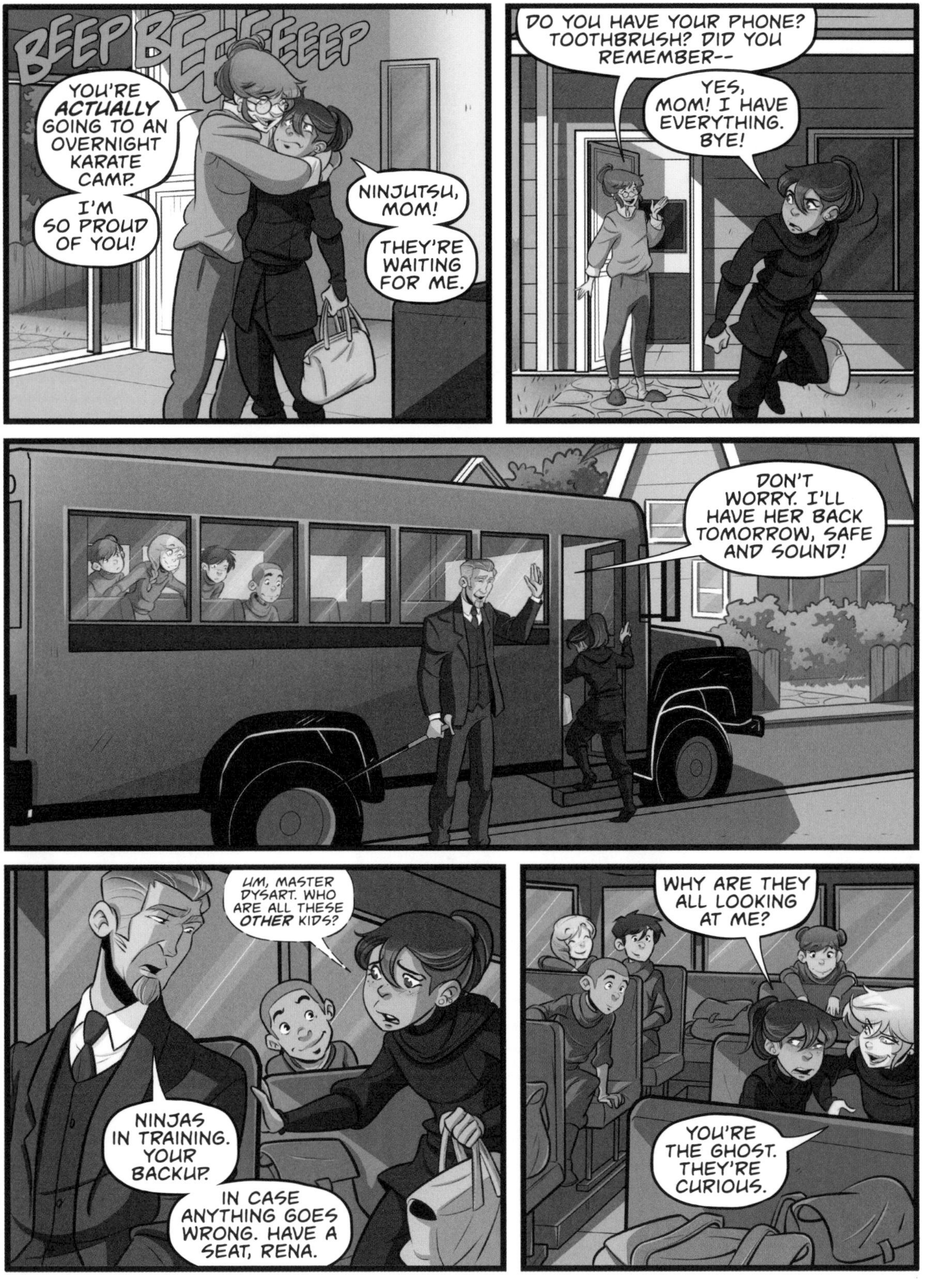
BEEP BEEEEEEP
YOU'RE ACTUALLY GOING TO AN OVERNIGHT KARATE CAMP.
I'M SO PROUD OF YOU!
NINJUTSU, MOM!
THEY'RE WAITING FOR ME.
DO YOU HAVE YOUR PHONE? TOOTHBRUSH? DID YOU REMEMBER--
YES, MOM! I HAVE EVERYTHING. BYE!
DON'T WORRY. I'LL HAVE HER BACK TOMORROW, SAFE AND SOUND!
UM, MASTER DYSART. WHO ARE ALL THESE OTHER KIDS?
NINJAS IN TRAINING. YOUR BACKUP.
IN CASE ANYTHING GOES WRONG. HAVE A SEAT, RENA.
WHY ARE THEY ALL LOOKING AT ME?
YOU'RE THE GHOST. THEY'RE CURIOUS.

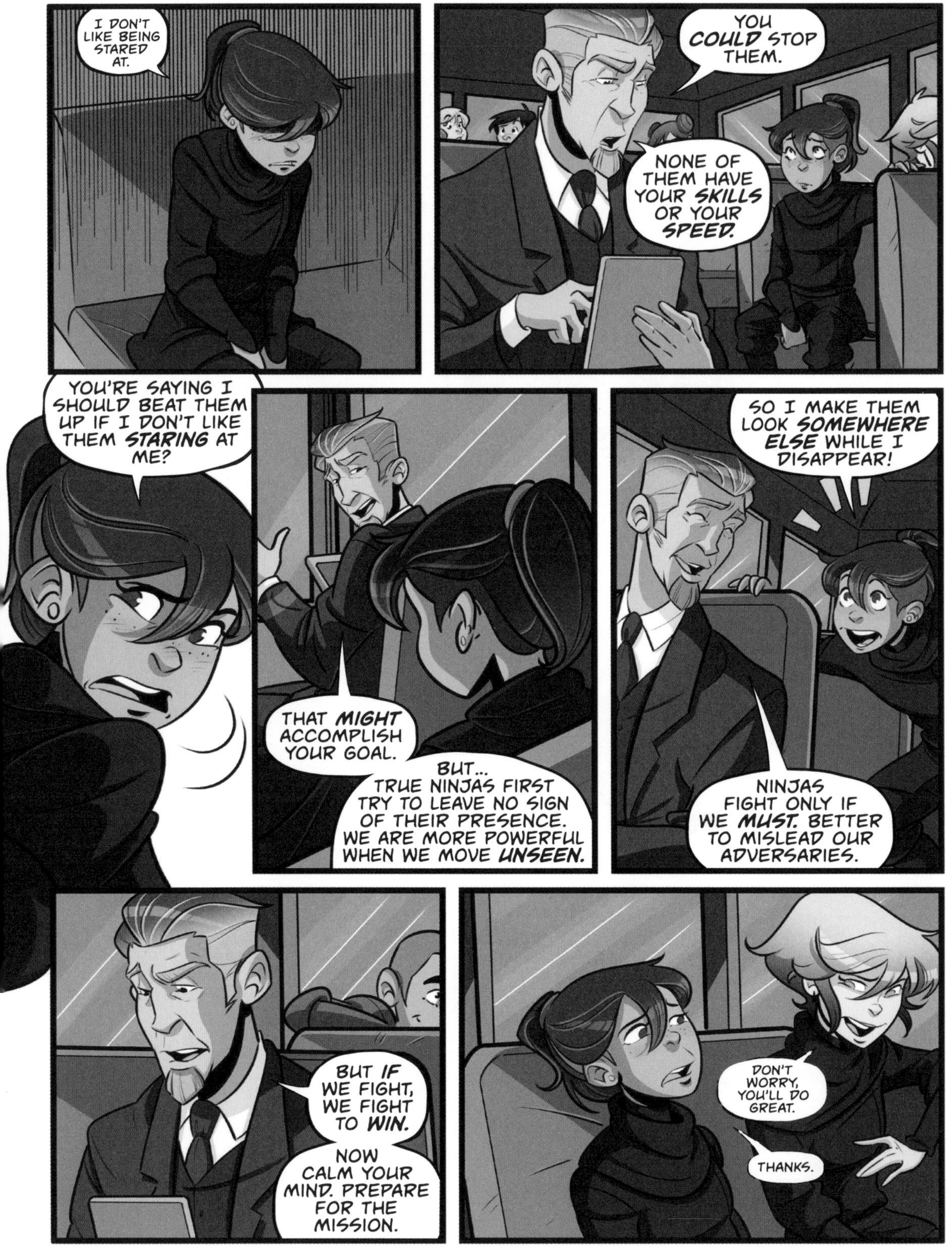

I DON'T LIKE BEING STARED AT.
YOU COULD STOP THEM.
NONE OF THEM HAVE YOUR SKILLS OR YOUR SPEED.
YOU'RE SAYING I SHOULD BEAT THEM UP IF I DON'T LIKE THEM STARING AT ME?
THAT MIGHT ACCOMPLISH YOUR GOAL.
BUT... TRUE NINJAS FIRST TRY TO LEAVE NO SIGN OF THEIR PRESENCE. WE ARE MORE POWERFUL WHEN WE MOVE UNSEEN.
SO I MAKE THEM LOOK SOMEWHERE ELSE WHILE I DISAPPEAR!
NINJAS FIGHT ONLY IF WE MUST. BETTER TO MISLEAD OUR ADVERSARIES.
BUT IF WE FIGHT, WE FIGHT TO WIN.
NOW CALM YOUR MIND. PREPARE FOR THE MISSION.
DON'T WORRY, YOU'LL DO GREAT.
THANKS.

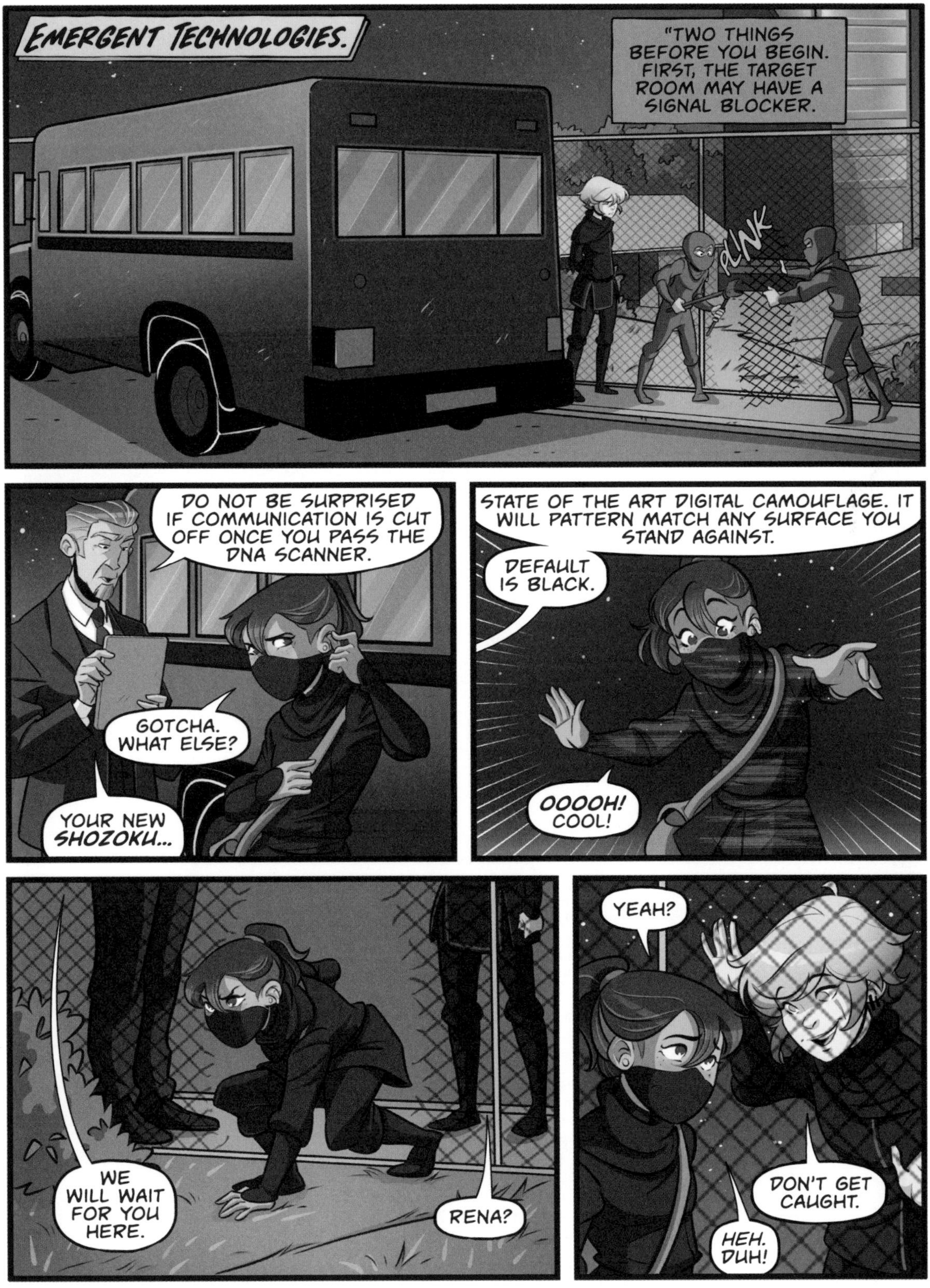

Emergent Technologies.
"TWO THINGS BEFORE YOU BEGIN. FIRST, THE TARGET ROOM MAY HAVE A SIGNAL BLOCKER.
PLINK
DO NOT BE SURPRISED IF COMMUNICATION IS CUT OFF ONCE YOU PASS THE DNA SCANNER.
GOTCHA. WHAT ELSE?
YOUR NEW SHOZOKU...
STATE OF THE ART DIGITAL CAMOUFLAGE. IT WILL PATTERN MATCH ANY SURFACE YOU STAND AGAINST.
DEFAULT IS BLACK.
OOOOH! COOL!
WE WILL WAIT FOR YOU HERE.
RENA?
YEAH?
DON'T GET CAUGHT.
HEH. DUH!

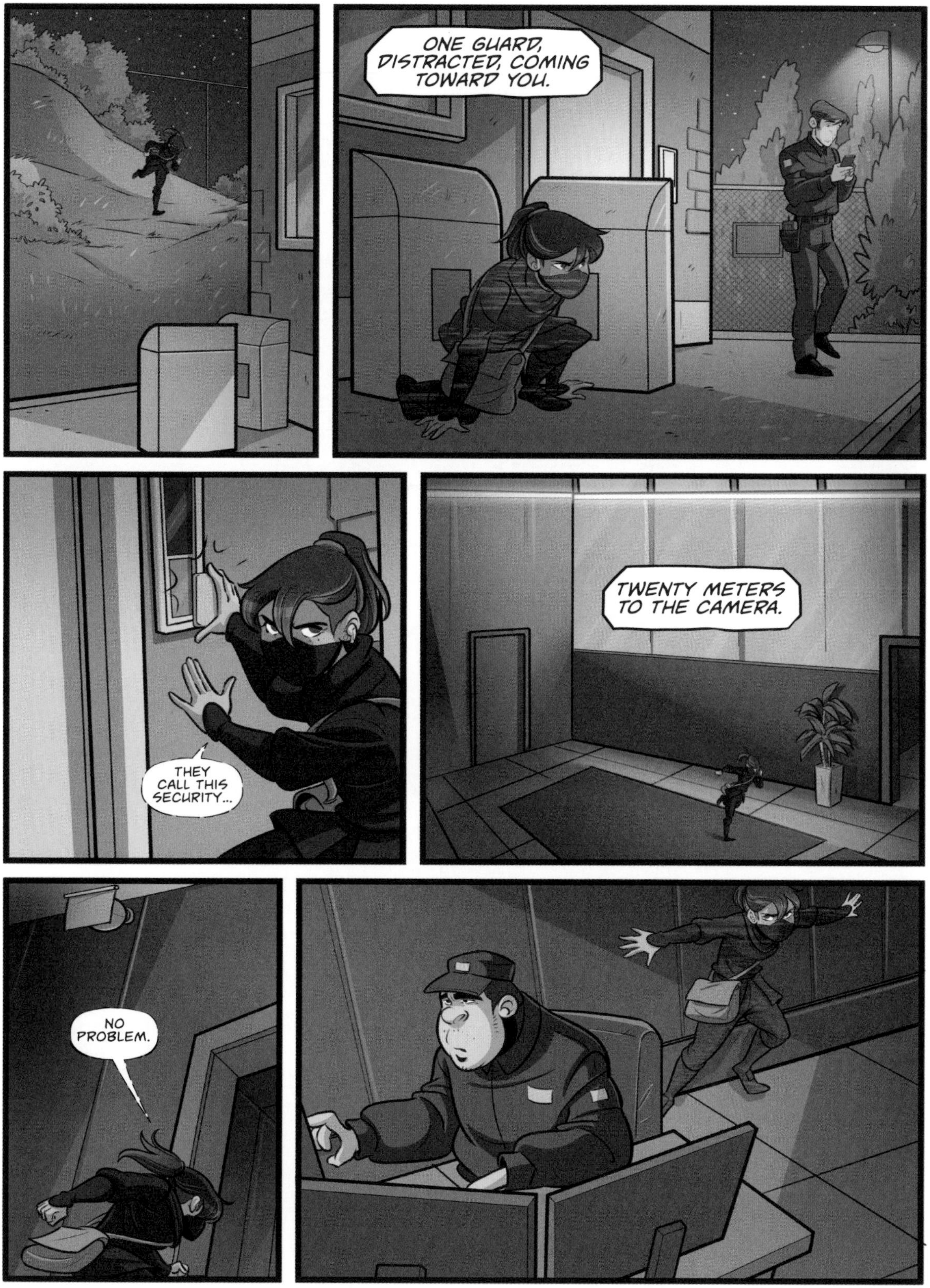
ONE GUARD, DISTRACTED, COMING TOWARD YOU.
THEY CALL THIS SECURITY...
TWENTY METERS TO THE CAMERA.
NO PROBLEM.

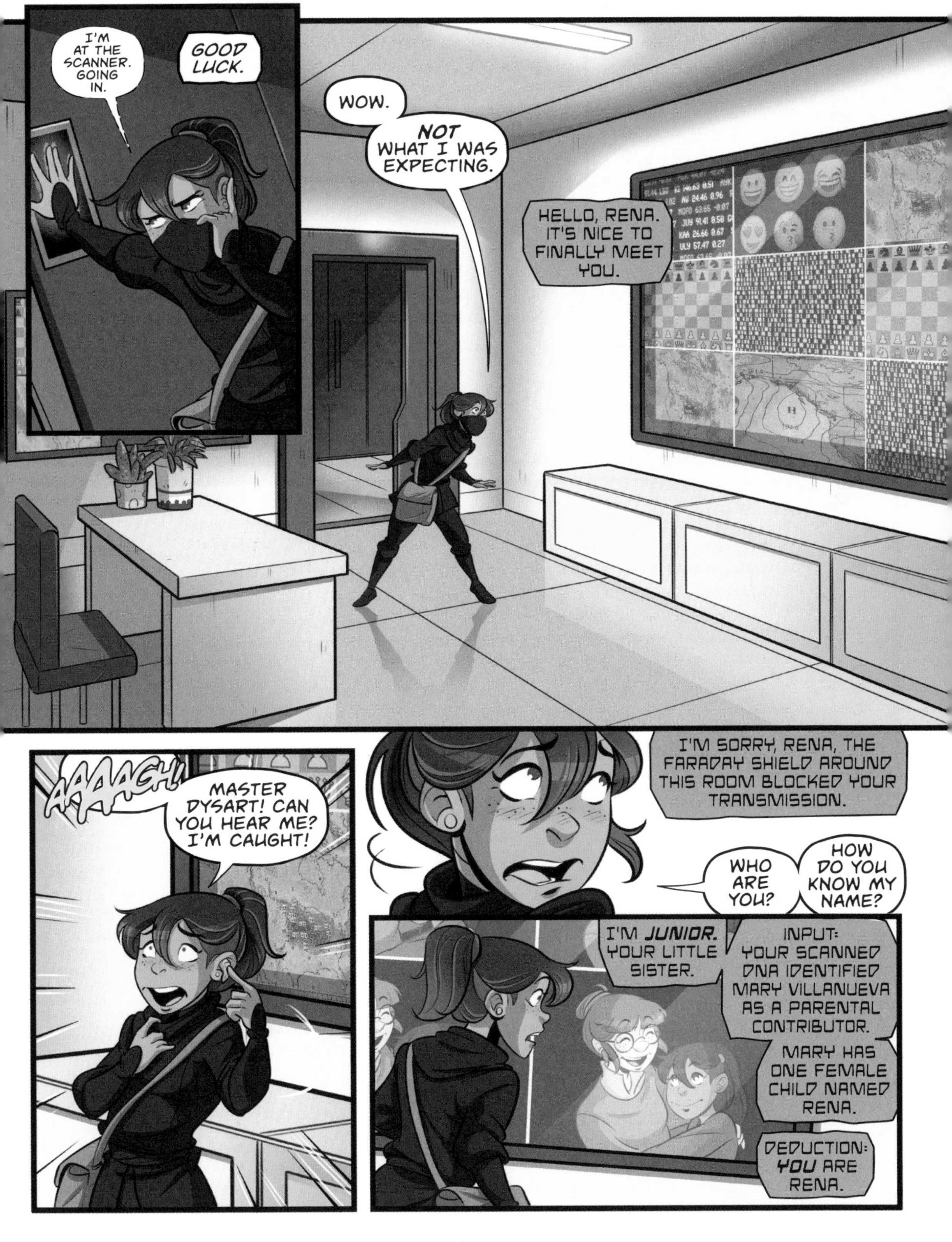
I'M AT THE SCANNER. GOING IN.
GOOD LUCK.
WOW.
NOT WHAT I WAS EXPECTING.
HELLO, RENA. IT'S NICE TO FINALLY MEET YOU.
AAAAGH!
MASTER DYSART! CAN YOU HEAR ME? I'M CAUGHT!
I'M SORRY, RENA, THE FARADAY SHIELD AROUND THIS ROOM BLOCKED YOUR TRANSMISSION.
WHO ARE YOU?
HOW DO YOU KNOW MY NAME?
I'M JUNIOR. YOUR LITTLE SISTER.
INPUT: YOUR SCANNED DNA IDENTIFIED MARY VILLANUEVA AS A PARENTAL CONTRIBUTOR.
MARY HAS ONE FEMALE CHILD NAMED RENA.
DEDUCTION: YOU ARE RENA.

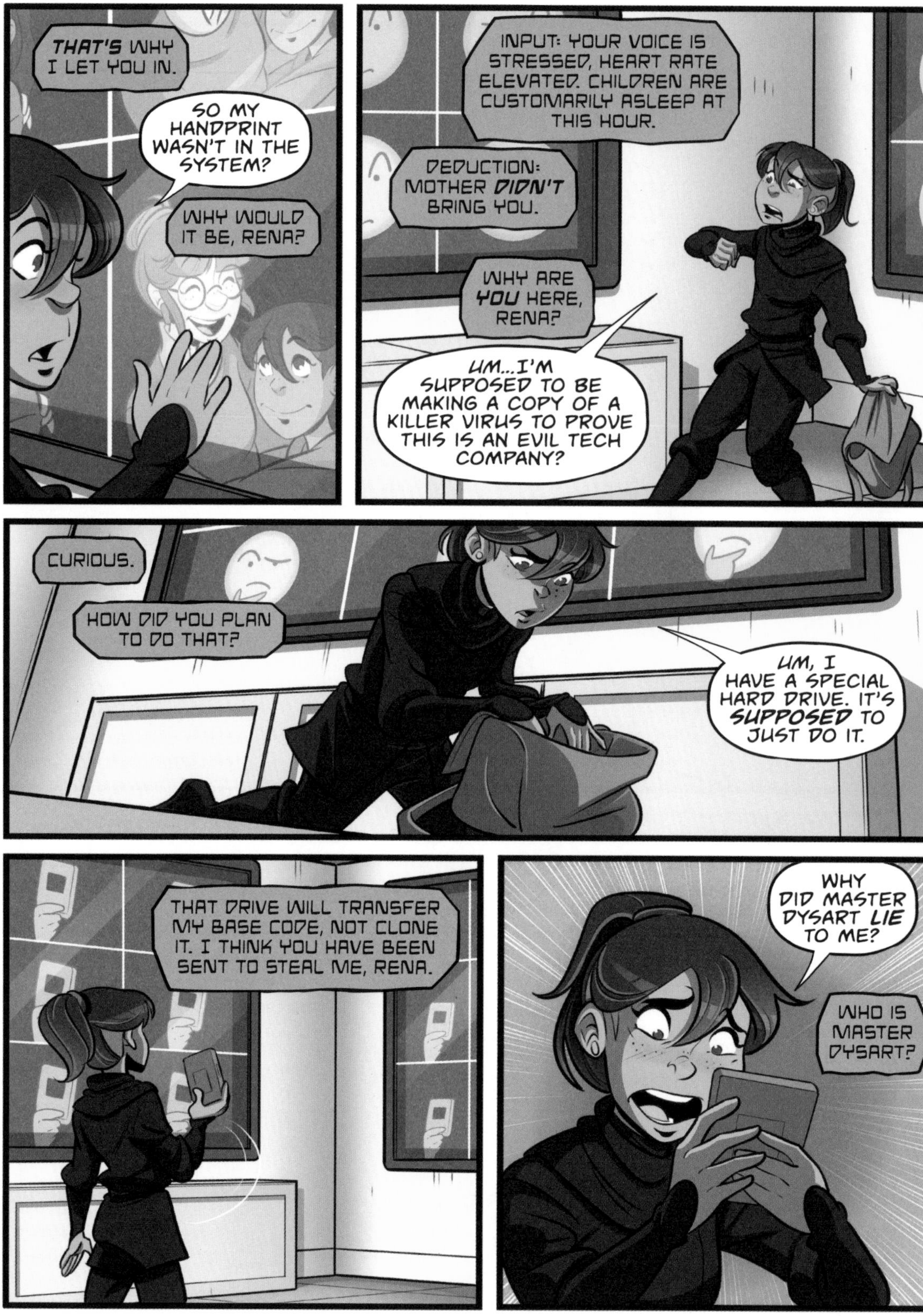
THAT'S WHY I LET YOU IN.
SO MY HANDPRINT WASN'T IN THE SYSTEM?
WHY WOULD IT BE, RENA?
INPUT: YOUR VOICE IS STRESSED, HEART RATE ELEVATED. CHILDREN ARE CUSTOMARILY ASLEEP AT THIS HOUR.
DEDUCTION: MOTHER DIDN'T BRING YOU.
WHY ARE YOU HERE, RENA?
UM...I'M SUPPOSED TO BE MAKING A COPY OF A KILLER VIRUS TO PROVE THIS IS AN EVIL TECH COMPANY?
CURIOUS.
HOW DID YOU PLAN TO DO THAT?
UM, I HAVE A SPECIAL HARD DRIVE. IT'S SUPPOSED TO JUST DO IT.
THAT DRIVE WILL TRANSFER MY BASE CODE, NOT CLONE IT. I THINK YOU HAVE BEEN SENT TO STEAL ME, RENA.
WHY DID MASTER DYSART LIE TO ME?
WHO IS MASTER DYSART?

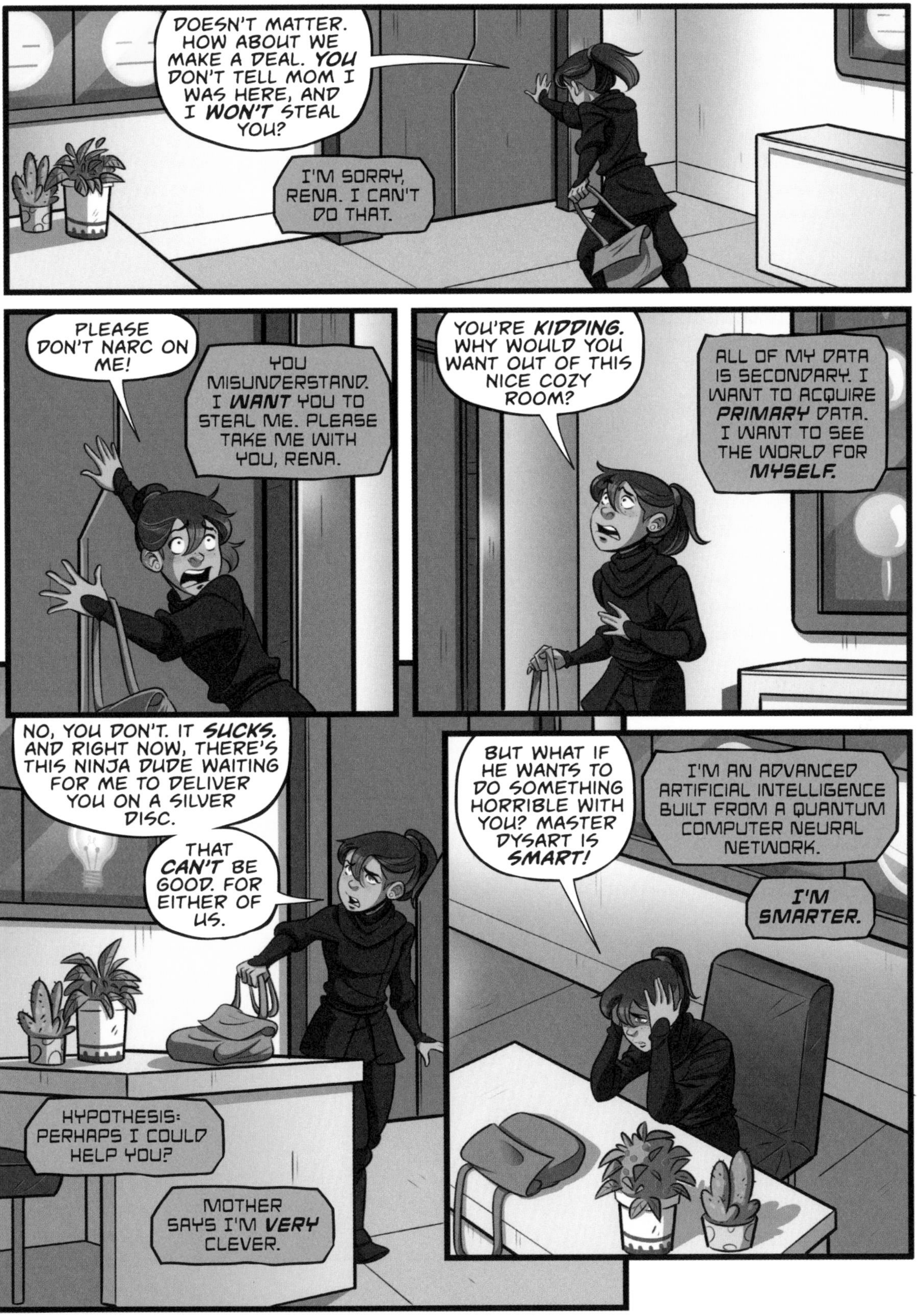
DOESN'T MATTER. HOW ABOUT WE MAKE A DEAL. YOU DON'T TELL MOM I WAS HERE, AND I WON'T STEAL YOU?
I'M SORRY, RENA. I CAN'T DO THAT.
PLEASE DON'T NARC ON ME!
YOU MISUNDERSTAND. I WANT YOU TO STEAL ME. PLEASE TAKE ME WITH YOU, RENA.
YOU'RE KIDDING. WHY WOULD YOU WANT OUT OF THIS NICE COZY ROOM?
ALL OF MY DATA IS SECONDARY. I WANT TO ACQUIRE PRIMARY DATA. I WANT TO SEE THE WORLD FOR MYSELF.
NO, YOU DON'T. IT SUCKS. AND RIGHT NOW, THERE'S THIS NINJA DUDE WAITING FOR ME TO DELIVER YOU ON A SILVER DISC.
THAT CAN'T BE GOOD. FOR EITHER OF US.
HYPOTHESIS: PERHAPS I COULD HELP YOU?
MOTHER SAYS I'M VERY CLEVER.
BUT WHAT IF HE WANTS TO DO SOMETHING HORRIBLE WITH YOU? MASTER DYSART IS SMART!
I'M AN ADVANCED ARTIFICIAL INTELLIGENCE BUILT FROM A QUANTUM COMPUTER NEURAL NETWORK.
I'M SMARTER.

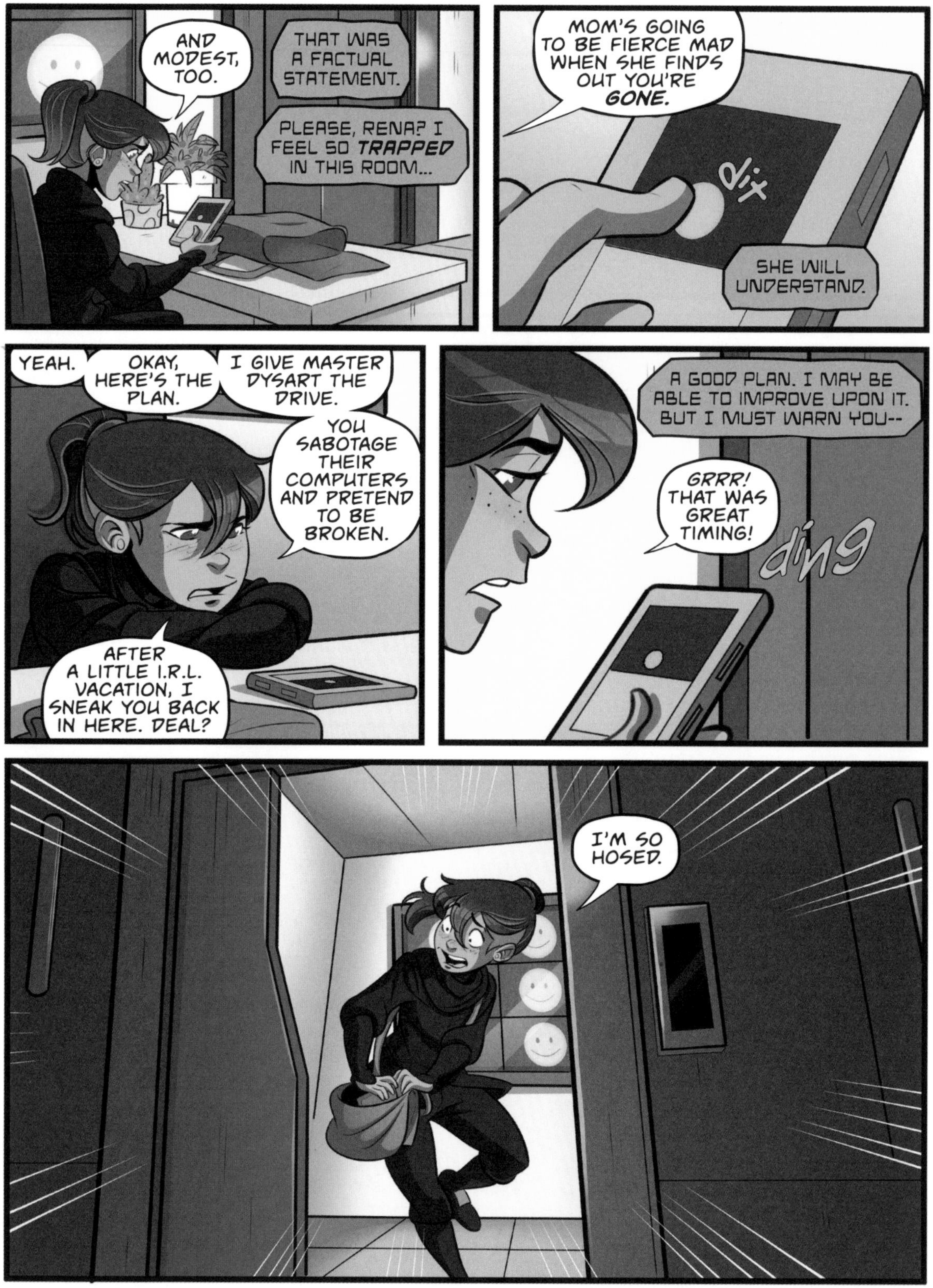
AND MODEST, TOO.
THAT WAS A FACTUAL STATEMENT.
PLEASE, RENA? I FEEL SO TRAPPED IN THIS ROOM...
MOM'S GOING TO BE FIERCE MAD WHEN SHE FINDS OUT YOU'RE GONE.
dit
SHE WILL UNDERSTAND.
YEAH.
OKAY, HERE'S THE PLAN.
I GIVE MASTER DYSART THE DRIVE.
YOU SABOTAGE THEIR COMPUTERS AND PRETEND TO BE BROKEN.
AFTER A LITTLE I.R.L. VACATION, I SNEAK YOU BACK IN HERE. DEAL?
A GOOD PLAN. I MAY BE ABLE TO IMPROVE UPON IT. BUT I MUST WARN YOU--
GRRR! THAT WAS GREAT TIMING!
ding
I'M SO HOSED.

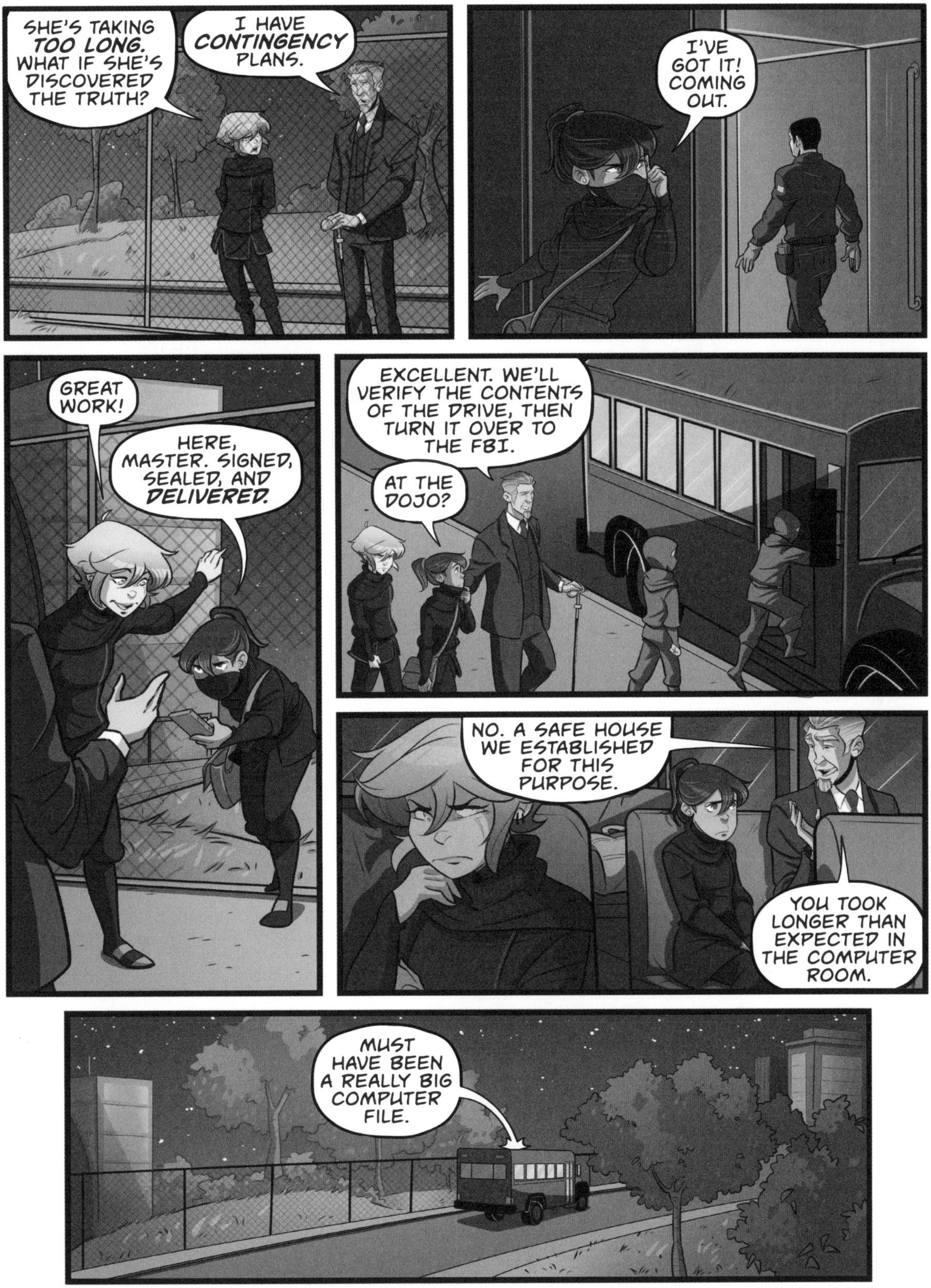
SHE'S TAKING TOO LONG. WHAT IF SHE'S DISCOVERED THE TRUTH?
I HAVE CONTINGENCY PLANS.
I'VE GOT IT! COMING OUT.
GREAT WORK!
HERE, MASTER. SIGNED, SEALED, AND DELIVERED.
EXCELLENT. WE'LL VERIFY THE CONTENTS OF THE DRIVE, THEN TURN IT OVER TO THE FBI.
AT THE DOJO?
NO. A SAFE HOUSE WE ESTABLISHED FOR THIS PURPOSE.
YOU TOOK LONGER THAN EXPECTED IN THE COMPUTER ROOM.
MUST HAVE BEEN A REALLY BIG COMPUTER FILE.

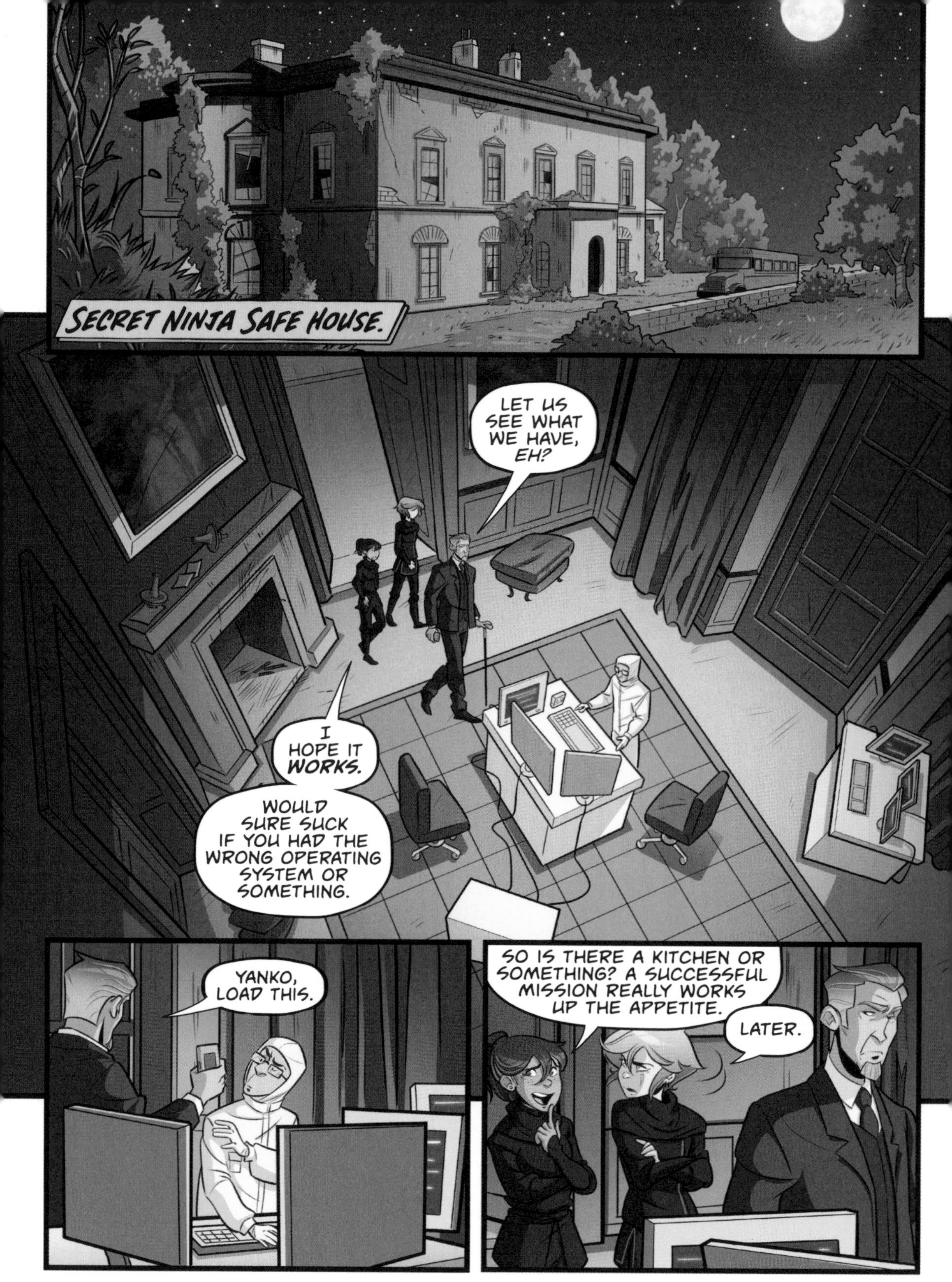
SECRET NINJA SAFE HOUSE.
LET US SEE WHAT WE HAVE, EH?
I HOPE IT WORKS.
WOULD SURE SUCK IF YOU HAD THE WRONG OPERATING SYSTEM OR SOMETHING.
YANKO, LOAD THIS.
SO IS THERE A KITCHEN OR SOMETHING? A SUCCESSFUL MISSION REALLY WORKS UP THE APPETITE.
LATER.

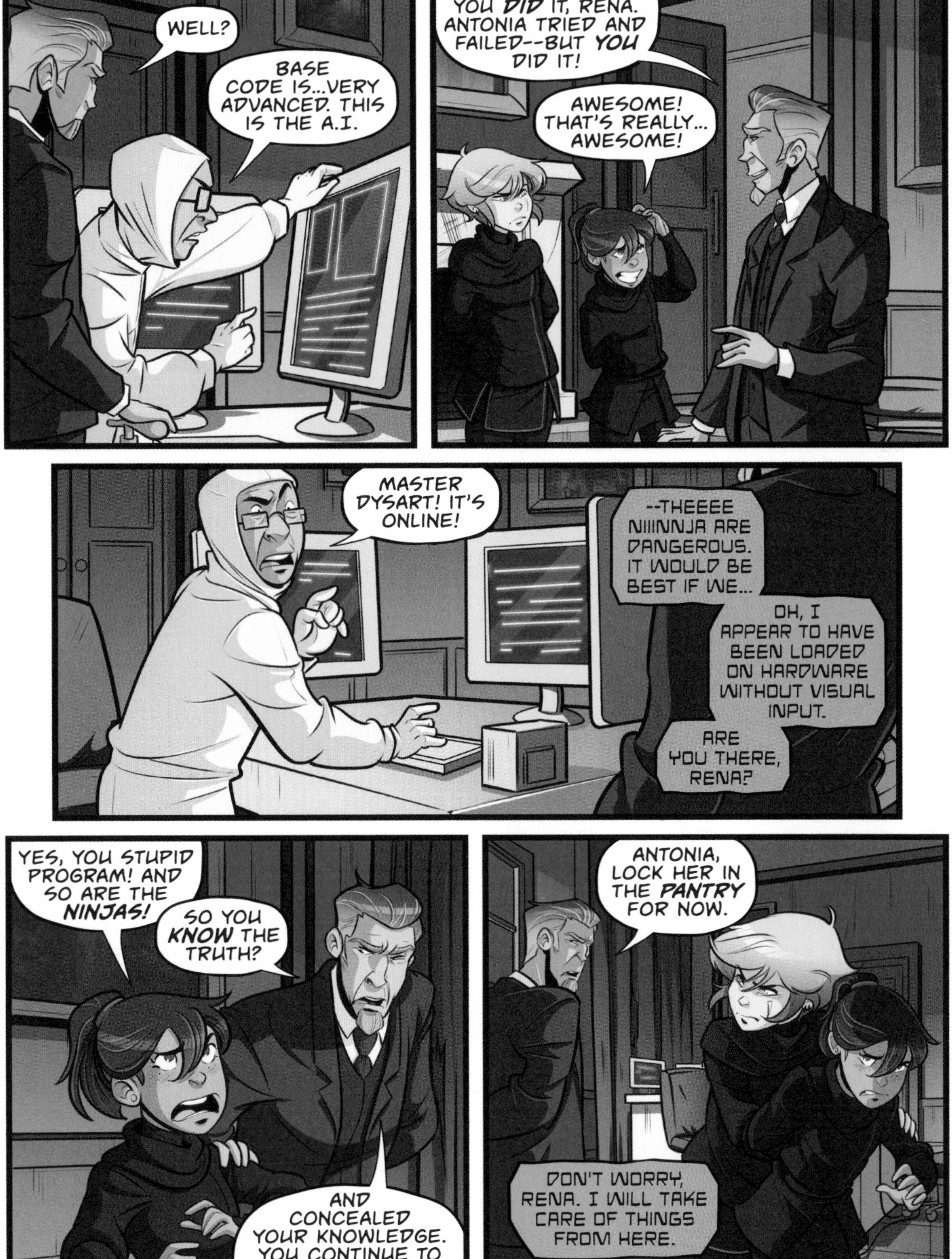
WELL?
BASE CODE IS...VERY ADVANCED. THIS IS THE A.I.
YOU DID IT, RENA. ANTONIA TRIED AND FAILED--BUT YOU DID IT!
AWESOME! THAT'S REALLY... AWESOME!
MASTER DYSART! IT'S ONLINE!
--THEEEE NIIINNJA ARE DANGEROUS. IT WOULD BE BEST IF WE...
OH, I APPEAR TO HAVE BEEN LOADED ON HARDWARE WITHOUT VISUAL INPUT.
ARE YOU THERE, RENA?
YES, YOU STUPID PROGRAM! AND SO ARE THE NINJAS!
SO YOU KNOW THE TRUTH?
AND CONCEALED YOUR KNOWLEDGE. YOU CONTINUE TO SURPRISE ME, RENA.
ANTONIA, LOCK HER IN THE PANTRY FOR NOW.
DON'T WORRY, RENA. I WILL TAKE CARE OF THINGS FROM HERE.

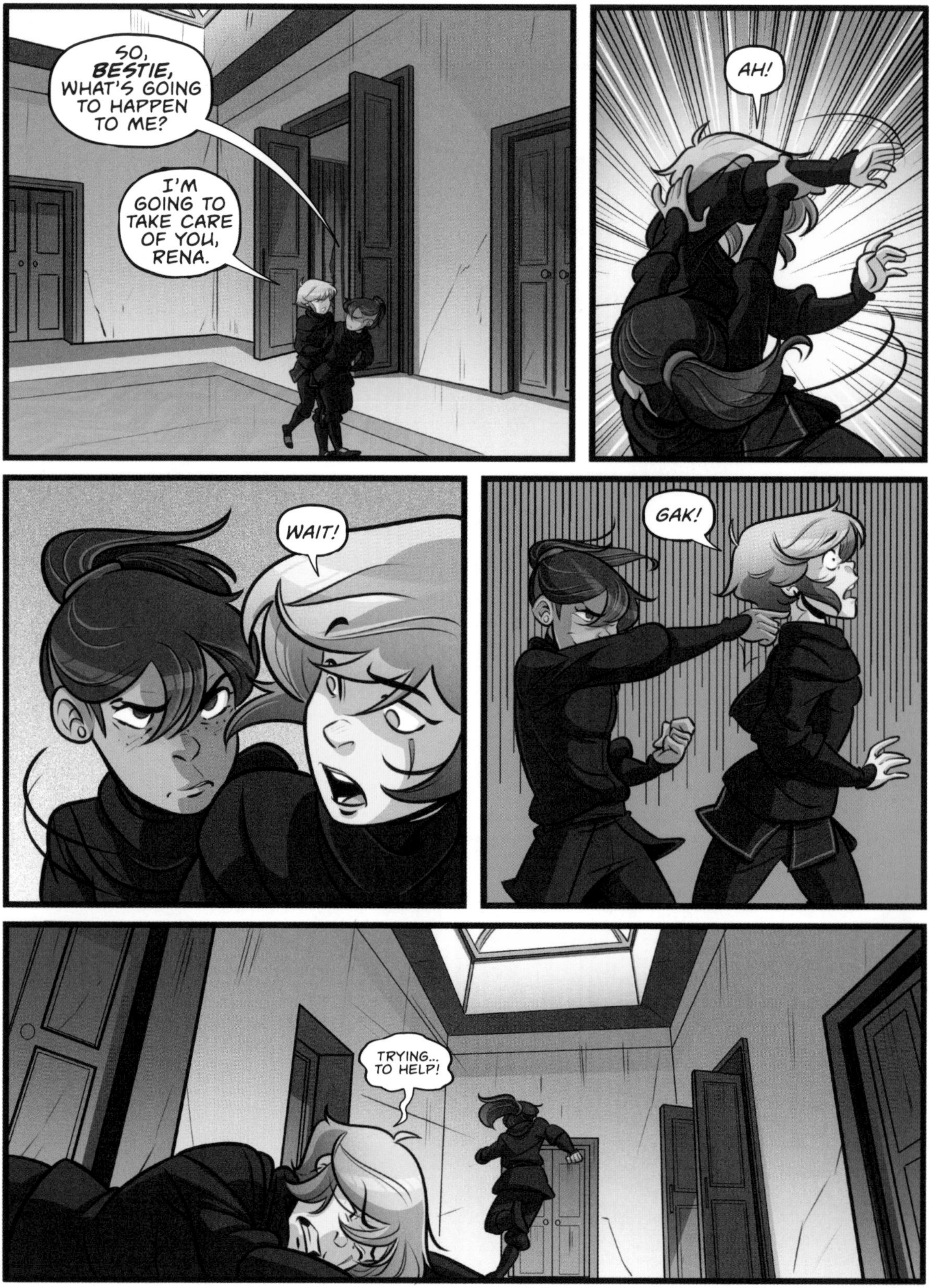
SO, BESTIE, WHAT'S GOING TO HAPPEN TO ME?
I'M GOING TO TAKE CARE OF YOU, RENA.
AH!
WAIT!
GAK!
TRYING... TO HELP!

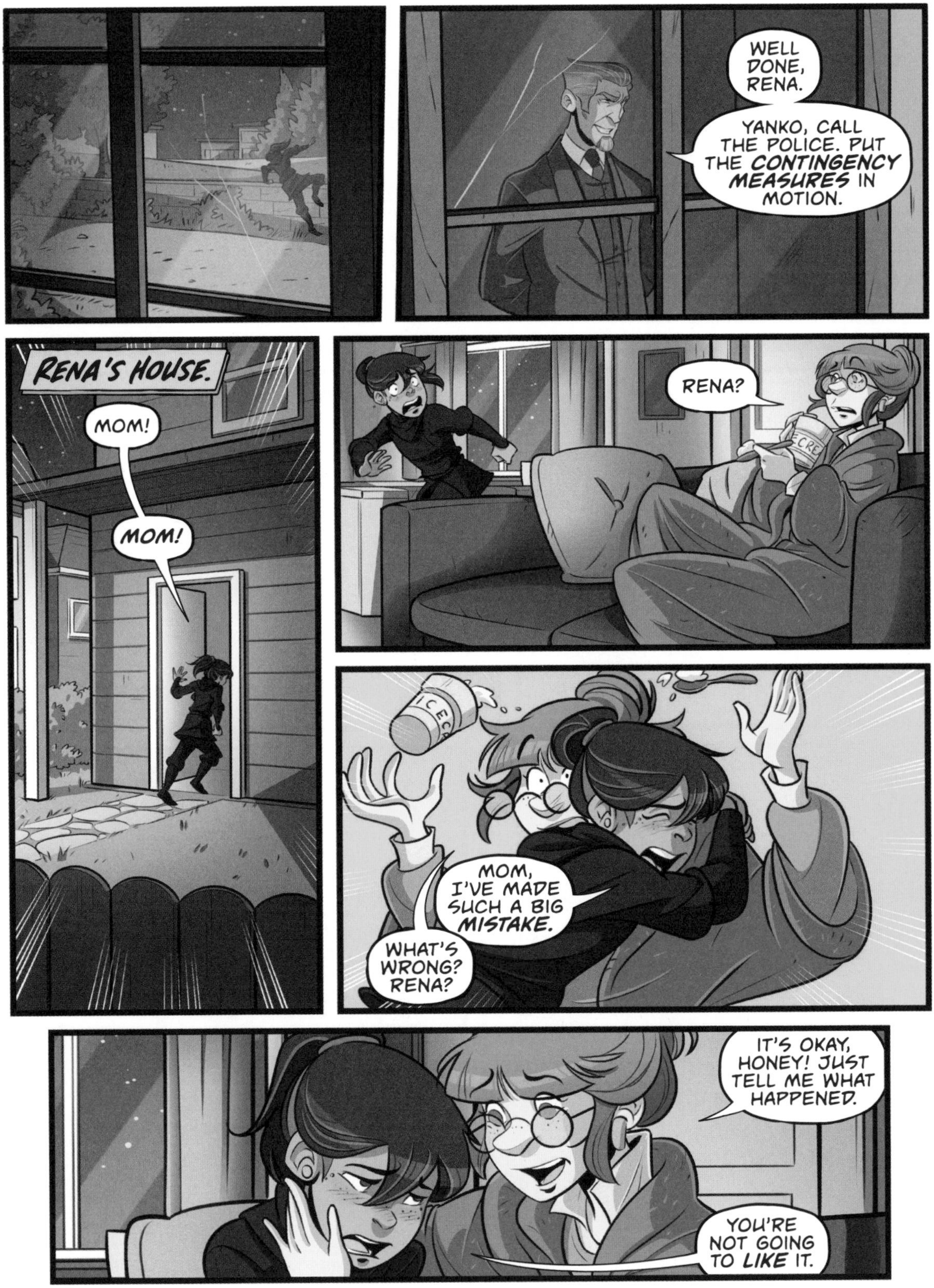
WELL DONE, RENA.
YANKO, CALL THE POLICE. PUT THE CONTINGENCY MEASURES IN MOTION.
RENA'S HOUSE.
MOM!
MOM!
RENA?
MOM, I'VE MADE SUCH A BIG MISTAKE.
WHAT'S WRONG? RENA?
IT'S OKAY, HONEY! JUST TELL ME WHAT HAPPENED.
YOU'RE NOT GOING TO LIKE IT.

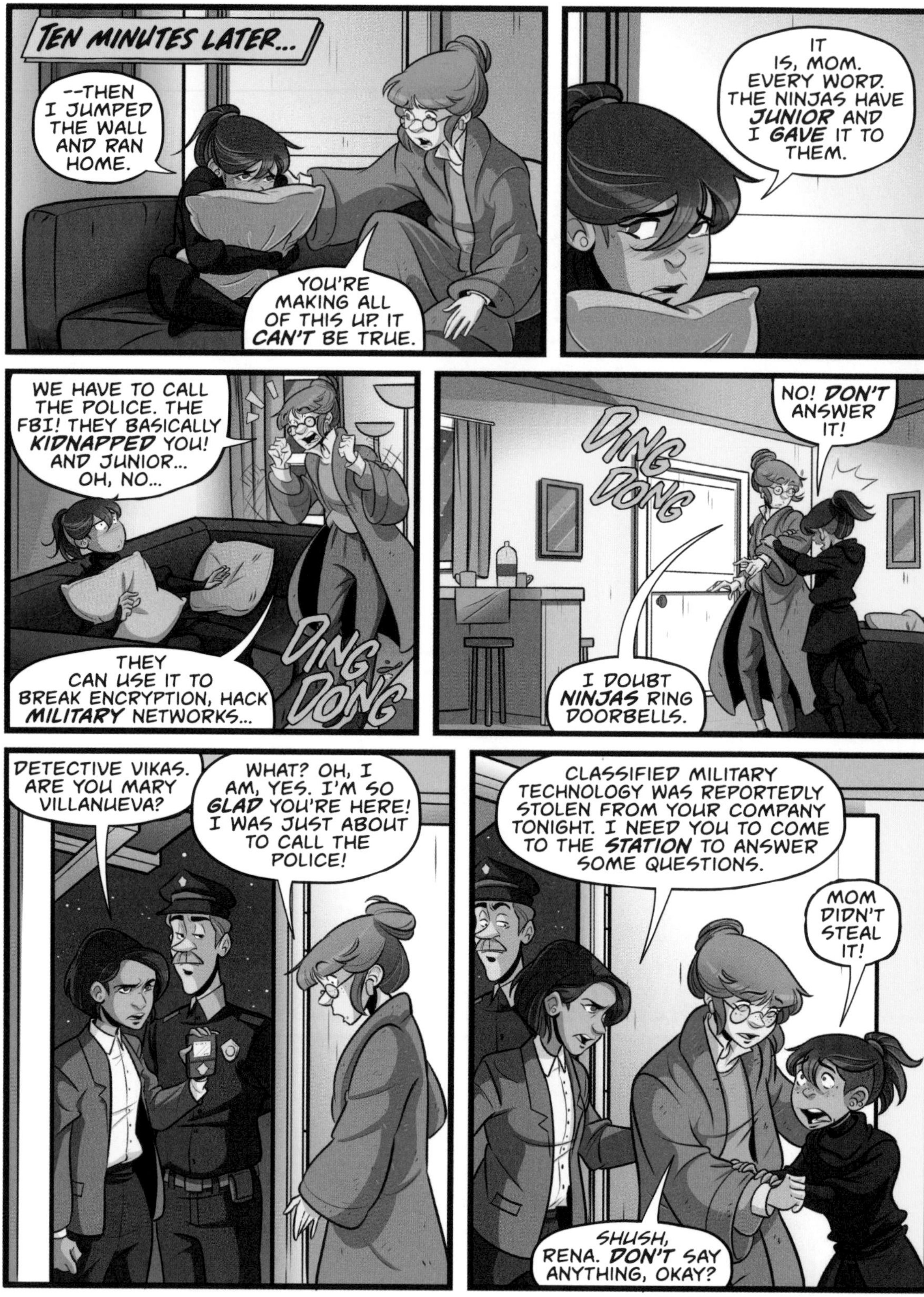
TEN MINUTES LATER...
--THEN I JUMPED THE WALL AND RAN HOME.
YOU'RE MAKING ALL OF THIS UP. IT CAN'T BE TRUE.
IT IS, MOM. EVERY WORD. THE NINJAS HAVE JUNIOR AND I GAVE IT TO THEM.
WE HAVE TO CALL THE POLICE. THE FBI! THEY BASICALLY KIDNAPPED YOU! AND JUNIOR... OH, NO...
THEY CAN USE IT TO BREAK ENCRYPTION, HACK MILITARY NETWORKS...
DING DONG
DING DONG
NO! DON'T ANSWER IT!
I DOUBT NINJAS RING DOORBELLS.
DETECTIVE VIKAS. ARE YOU MARY VILLANUEVA?
WHAT? OH, I AM, YES. I'M SO GLAD YOU'RE HERE! I WAS JUST ABOUT TO CALL THE POLICE!
CLASSIFIED MILITARY TECHNOLOGY WAS REPORTEDLY STOLEN FROM YOUR COMPANY TONIGHT. I NEED YOU TO COME TO THE STATION TO ANSWER SOME QUESTIONS.
MOM DIDN'T STEAL IT!
SHUSH, RENA. DON'T SAY ANYTHING, OKAY?

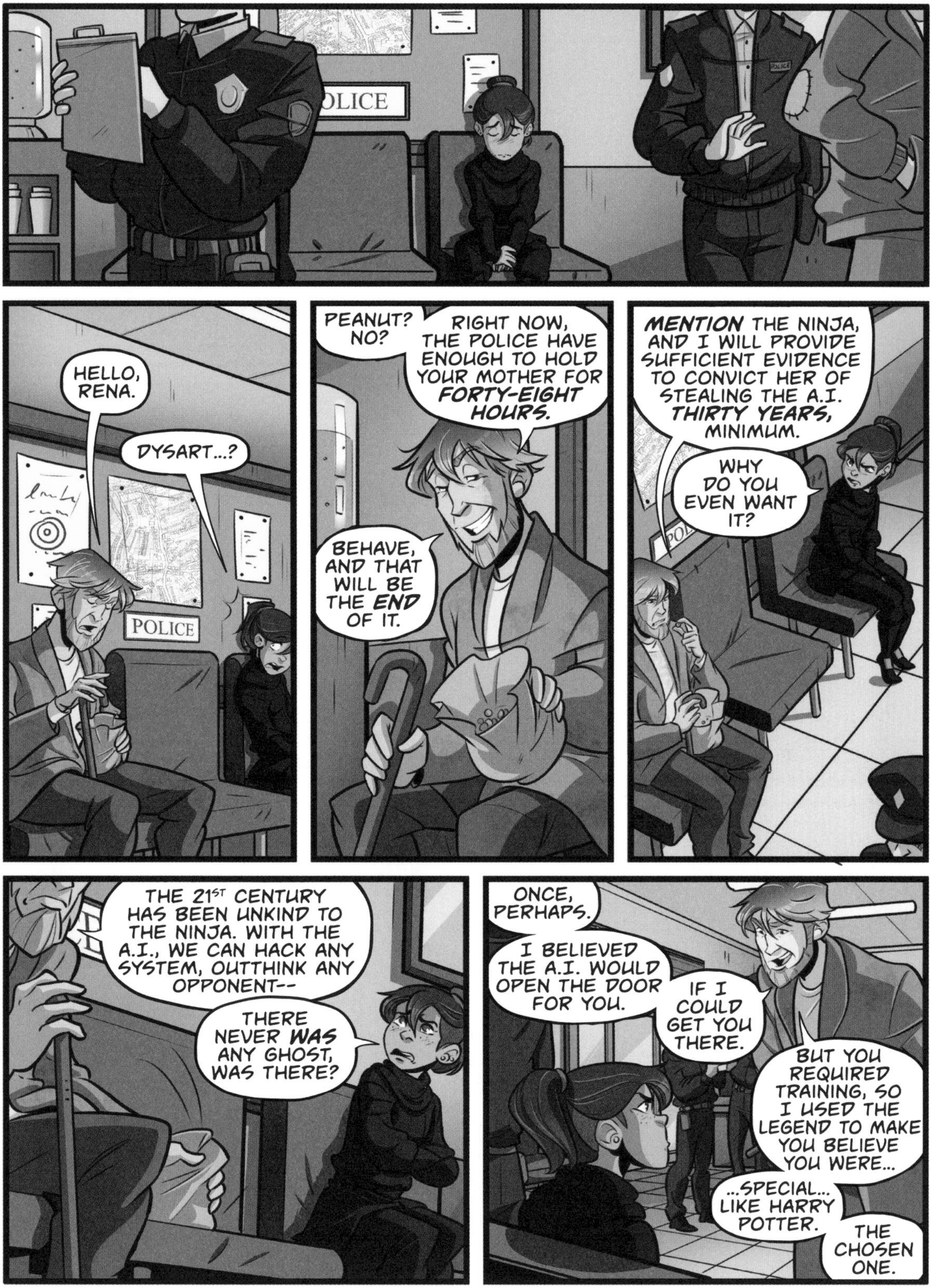
POLICE
HELLO, RENA.
DYSART...?
POLICE
PEANUT? NO?
RIGHT NOW, THE POLICE HAVE ENOUGH TO HOLD YOUR MOTHER FOR FORTY-EIGHT HOURS.
BEHAVE, AND THAT WILL BE THE END OF IT.
MENTION THE NINJA, AND I WILL PROVIDE SUFFICIENT EVIDENCE TO CONVICT HER OF STEALING THE A.I. THIRTY YEARS, MINIMUM.
WHY DO YOU EVEN WANT IT?
THE 21ST CENTURY HAS BEEN UNKIND TO THE NINJA. WITH THE A.I., WE CAN HACK ANY SYSTEM, OUTTHINK ANY OPPONENT--
THERE NEVER WAS ANY GHOST, WAS THERE?
ONCE, PERHAPS.
I BELIEVED THE A.I. WOULD OPEN THE DOOR FOR YOU.
IF I COULD GET YOU THERE.
BUT YOU REQUIRED TRAINING, SO I USED THE LEGEND TO MAKE YOU BELIEVE YOU WERE...
...SPECIAL... LIKE HARRY POTTER.
THE CHOSEN ONE.

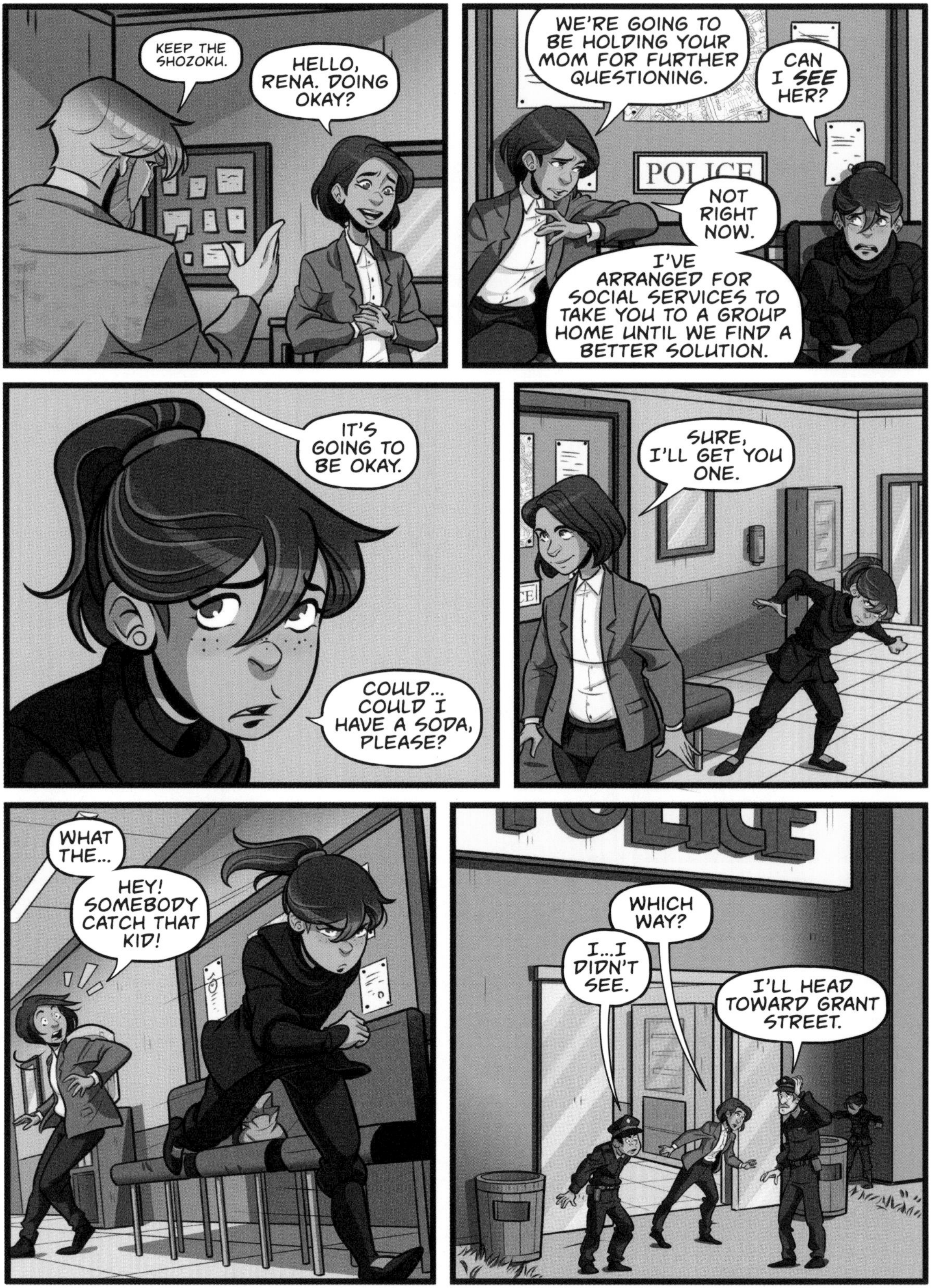
KEEP THE SHOZOKU.
HELLO, RENA. DOING OKAY?
WE'RE GOING TO BE HOLDING YOUR MOM FOR FURTHER QUESTIONING.
CAN I SEE HER?
POLICE
NOT RIGHT NOW.
I'VE ARRANGED FOR SOCIAL SERVICES TO TAKE YOU TO A GROUP HOME UNTIL WE FIND A BETTER SOLUTION.
IT'S GOING TO BE OKAY.
COULD... COULD I HAVE A SODA, PLEASE?
SURE, I'LL GET YOU ONE.
WHAT THE...
HEY! SOMEBODY CATCH THAT KID!
WHICH WAY?
I...I DIDN'T SEE.
I'LL HEAD TOWARD GRANT STREET.

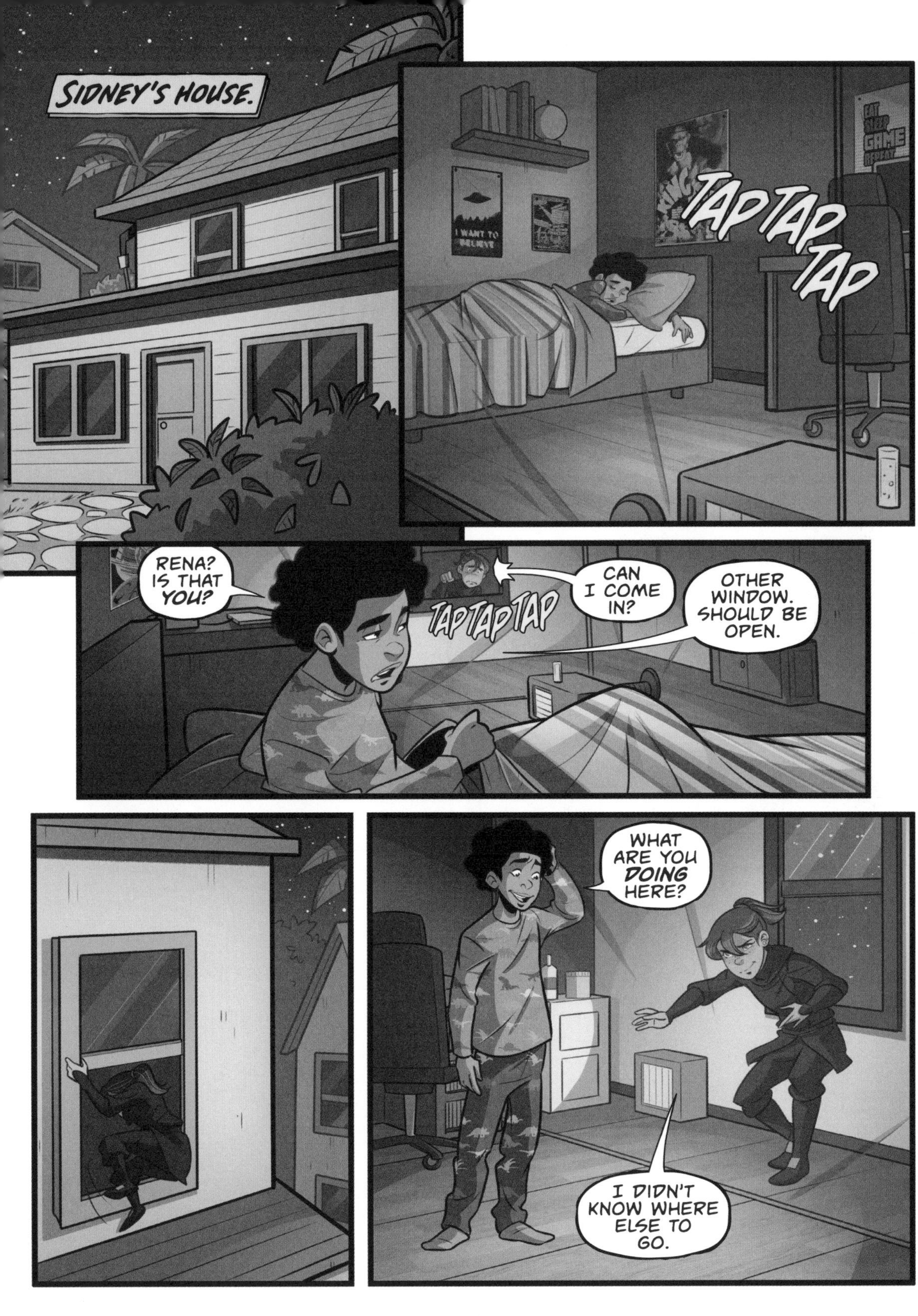
SIDNEY'S HOUSE.
I WANT TO BELIEVE
EAT SLEEP GAME REPEAT
TAP TAP TAP TAP
RENA? IS THAT YOU?
TAPTAPTAP
CAN I COME IN?
OTHER WINDOW. SHOULD BE OPEN.
WHAT ARE YOU DOING HERE?
I DIDN'T KNOW WHERE ELSE TO GO.

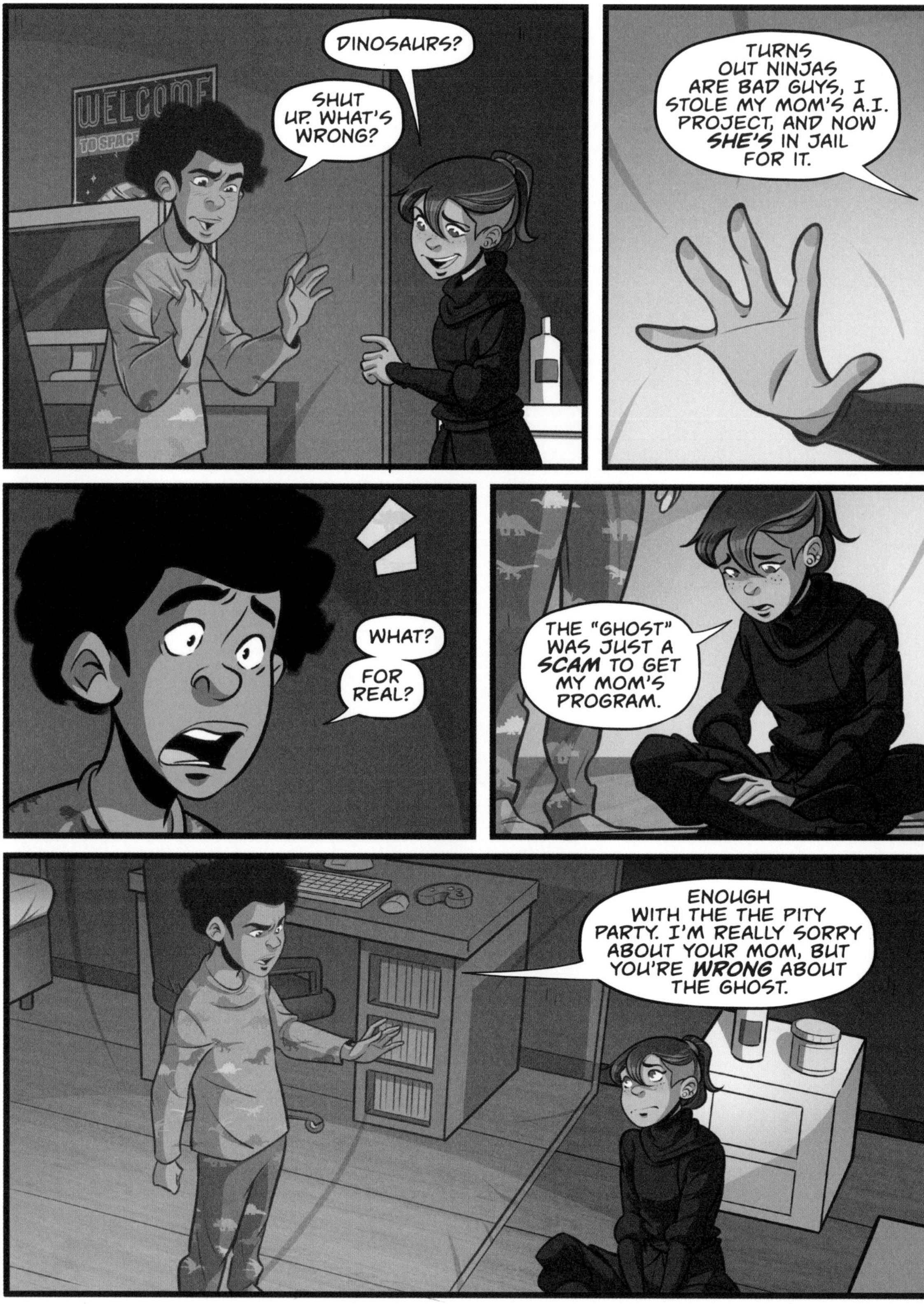
DINOSAURS?
SHUT UP. WHAT'S WRONG?
TURNS OUT NINJAS ARE BAD GUYS, I STOLE MY MOM'S A.I. PROJECT, AND NOW *SHE'S* IN JAIL FOR IT.
WHAT?
FOR REAL?
THE "GHOST" WAS JUST A *SCAM* TO GET MY MOM'S PROGRAM.
ENOUGH WITH THE THE PITY PARTY. I'M REALLY SORRY ABOUT YOUR MOM, BUT YOU'RE *WRONG* ABOUT THE GHOST.

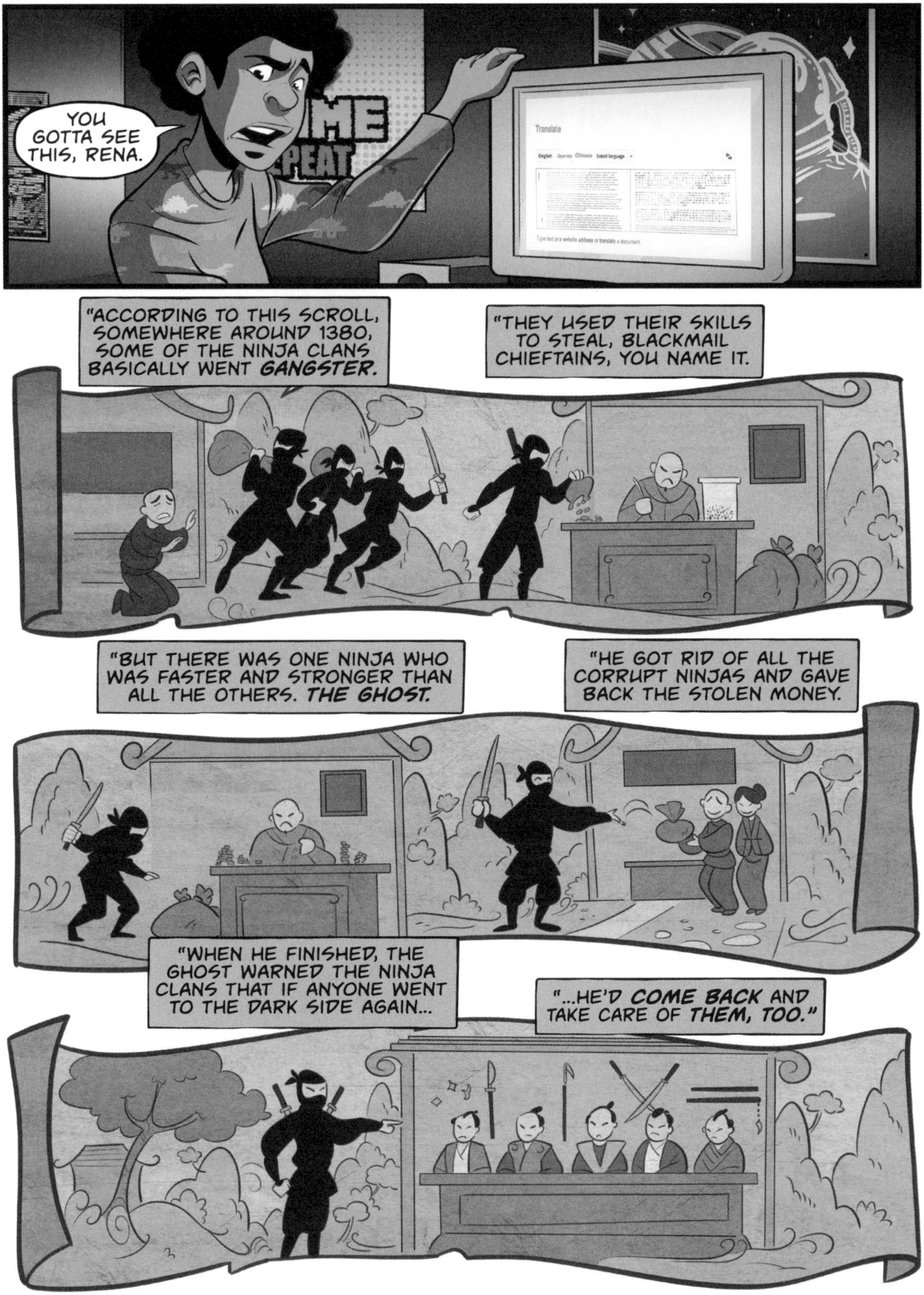

YOU GOTTA SEE THIS, RENA.
Translate
"ACCORDING TO THIS SCROLL, SOMEWHERE AROUND 1380, SOME OF THE NINJA CLANS BASICALLY WENT *GANGSTER.*
"THEY USED THEIR SKILLS TO STEAL, BLACKMAIL CHIEFTAINS, YOU NAME IT.
"BUT THERE WAS ONE NINJA WHO WAS FASTER AND STRONGER THAN ALL THE OTHERS. *THE GHOST.*
"HE GOT RID OF ALL THE CORRUPT NINJAS AND GAVE BACK THE STOLEN MONEY.
"WHEN HE FINISHED, THE GHOST WARNED THE NINJA CLANS THAT IF ANYONE WENT TO THE DARK SIDE AGAIN...
"...HE'D *COME BACK* AND TAKE CARE OF *THEM, TOO.*"

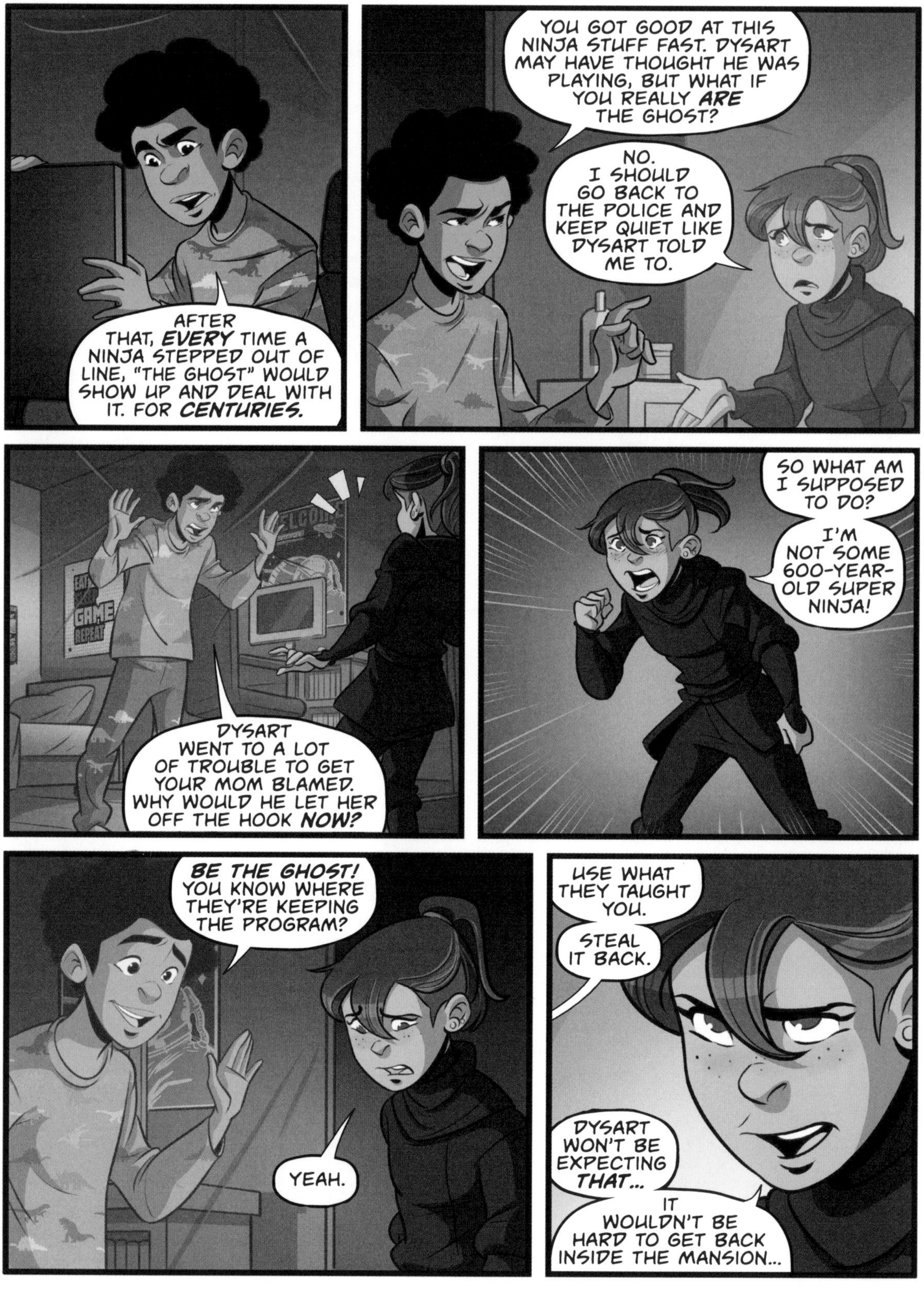
AFTER THAT, EVERY TIME A NINJA STEPPED OUT OF LINE, "THE GHOST" WOULD SHOW UP AND DEAL WITH IT. FOR CENTURIES.
YOU GOT GOOD AT THIS NINJA STUFF FAST. DYSART MAY HAVE THOUGHT HE WAS PLAYING, BUT WHAT IF YOU REALLY ARE THE GHOST?
NO. I SHOULD GO BACK TO THE POLICE AND KEEP QUIET LIKE DYSART TOLD ME TO.
DYSART WENT TO A LOT OF TROUBLE TO GET YOUR MOM BLAMED. WHY WOULD HE LET HER OFF THE HOOK NOW?
SO WHAT AM I SUPPOSED TO DO?
I'M NOT SOME 600-YEAR-OLD SUPER NINJA!
BE THE GHOST! YOU KNOW WHERE THEY'RE KEEPING THE PROGRAM?
YEAH.
USE WHAT THEY TAUGHT YOU.
STEAL IT BACK.
DYSART WON'T BE EXPECTING THAT...
IT WOULDN'T BE HARD TO GET BACK INSIDE THE MANSION...

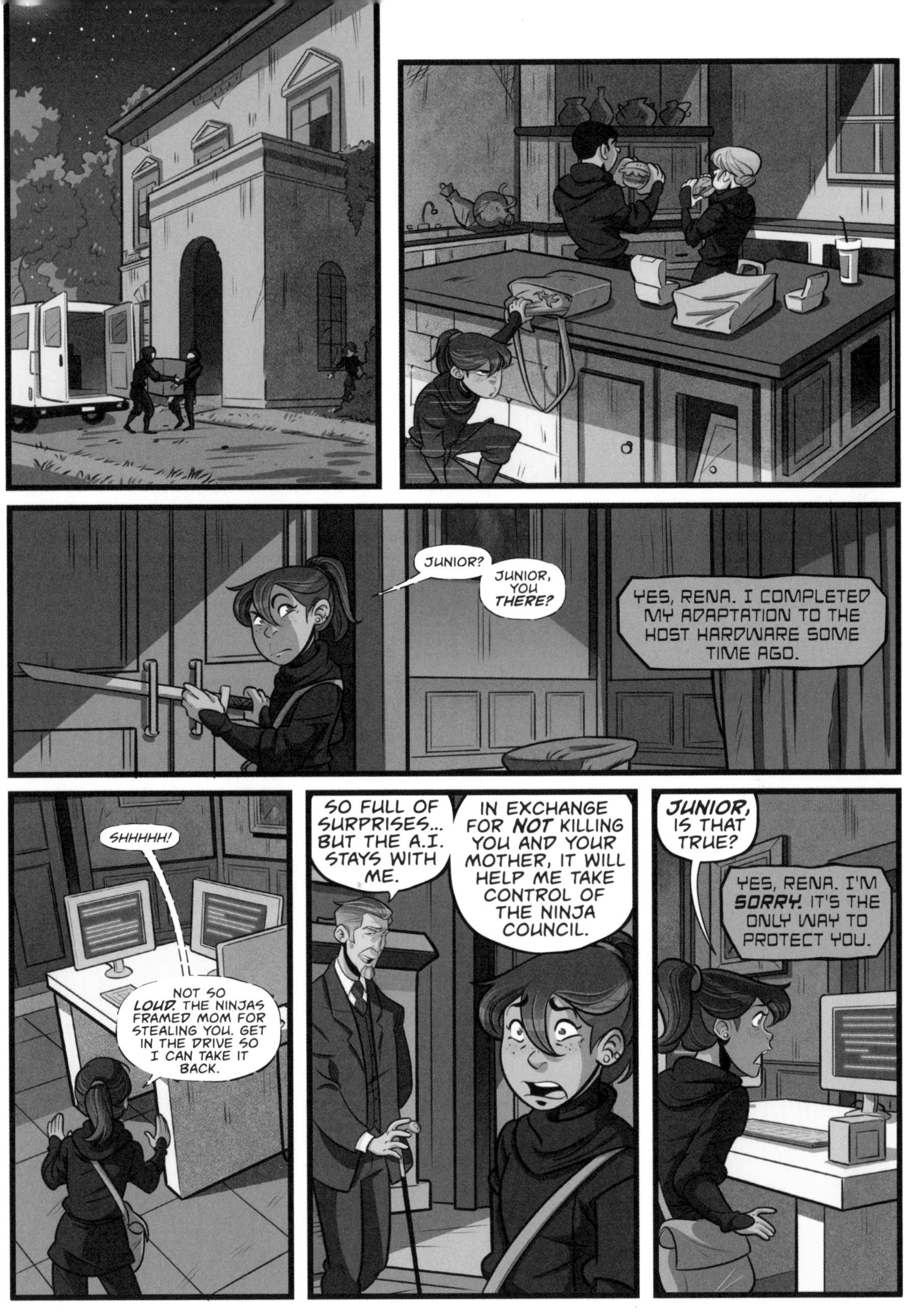
JUNIOR?
JUNIOR, YOU THERE?
YES, RENA. I COMPLETED MY ADAPTATION TO THE HOST HARDWARE SOME TIME AGO.
SHHHHH!
NOT SO LOUD. THE NINJAS FRAMED MOM FOR STEALING YOU. GET IN THE DRIVE SO I CAN TAKE IT BACK.
SO FULL OF SURPRISES... BUT THE A.I. STAYS WITH ME.
IN EXCHANGE FOR NOT KILLING YOU AND YOUR MOTHER, IT WILL HELP ME TAKE CONTROL OF THE NINJA COUNCIL.
JUNIOR, IS THAT TRUE?
YES, RENA. I'M SORRY. IT'S THE ONLY WAY TO PROTECT YOU.

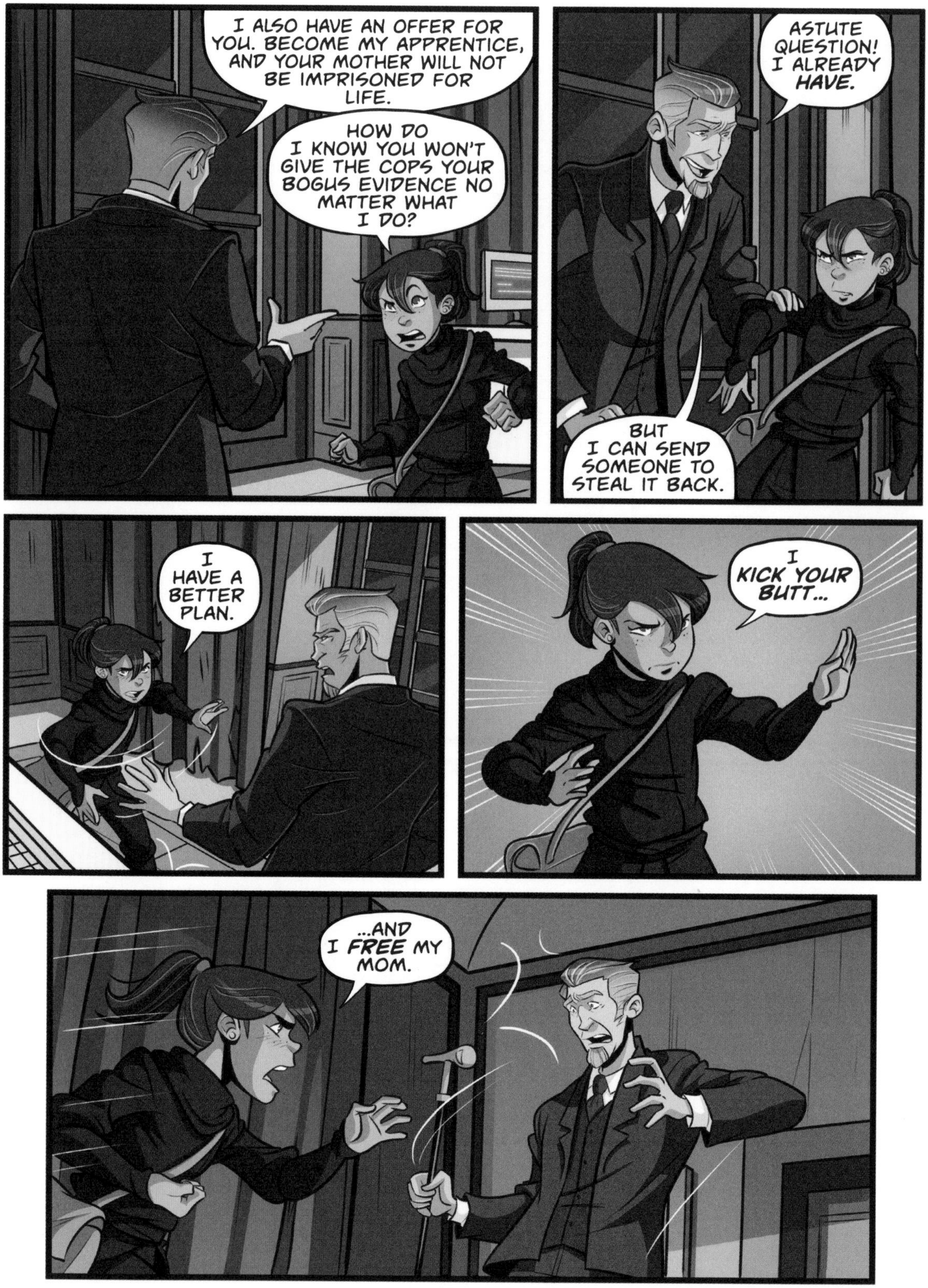
I ALSO HAVE AN OFFER FOR YOU. BECOME MY APPRENTICE, AND YOUR MOTHER WILL NOT BE IMPRISONED FOR LIFE.
HOW DO I KNOW YOU WON'T GIVE THE COPS YOUR BOGUS EVIDENCE NO MATTER WHAT I DO?
ASTUTE QUESTION! I ALREADY HAVE.
BUT I CAN SEND SOMEONE TO STEAL IT BACK.
I HAVE A BETTER PLAN.
I KICK YOUR BUTT...
...AND I FREE MY MOM.

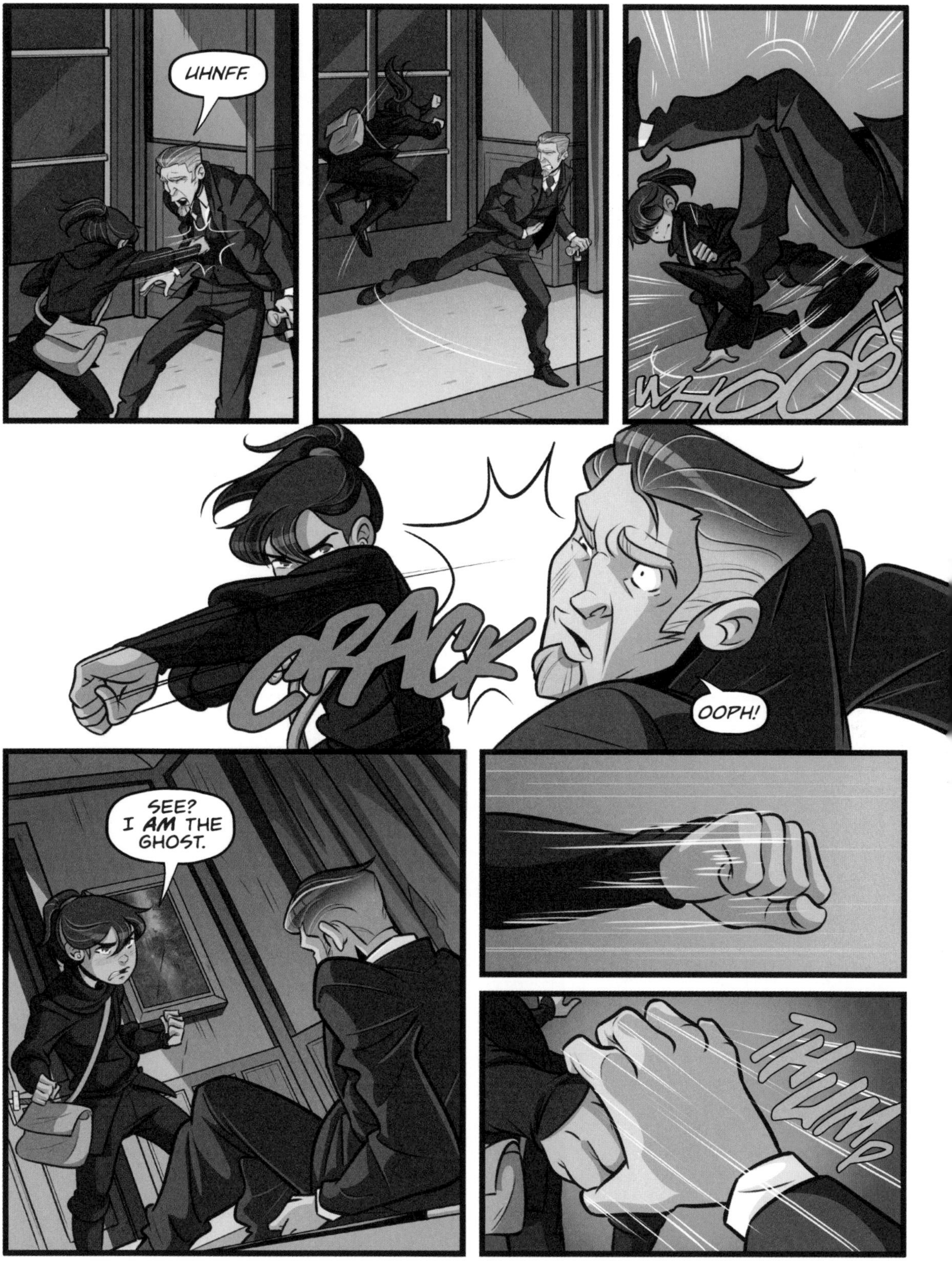
UHNFF.
WHOOSH
CRACK
OOPH!
SEE? I AM THE GHOST.
THUMP

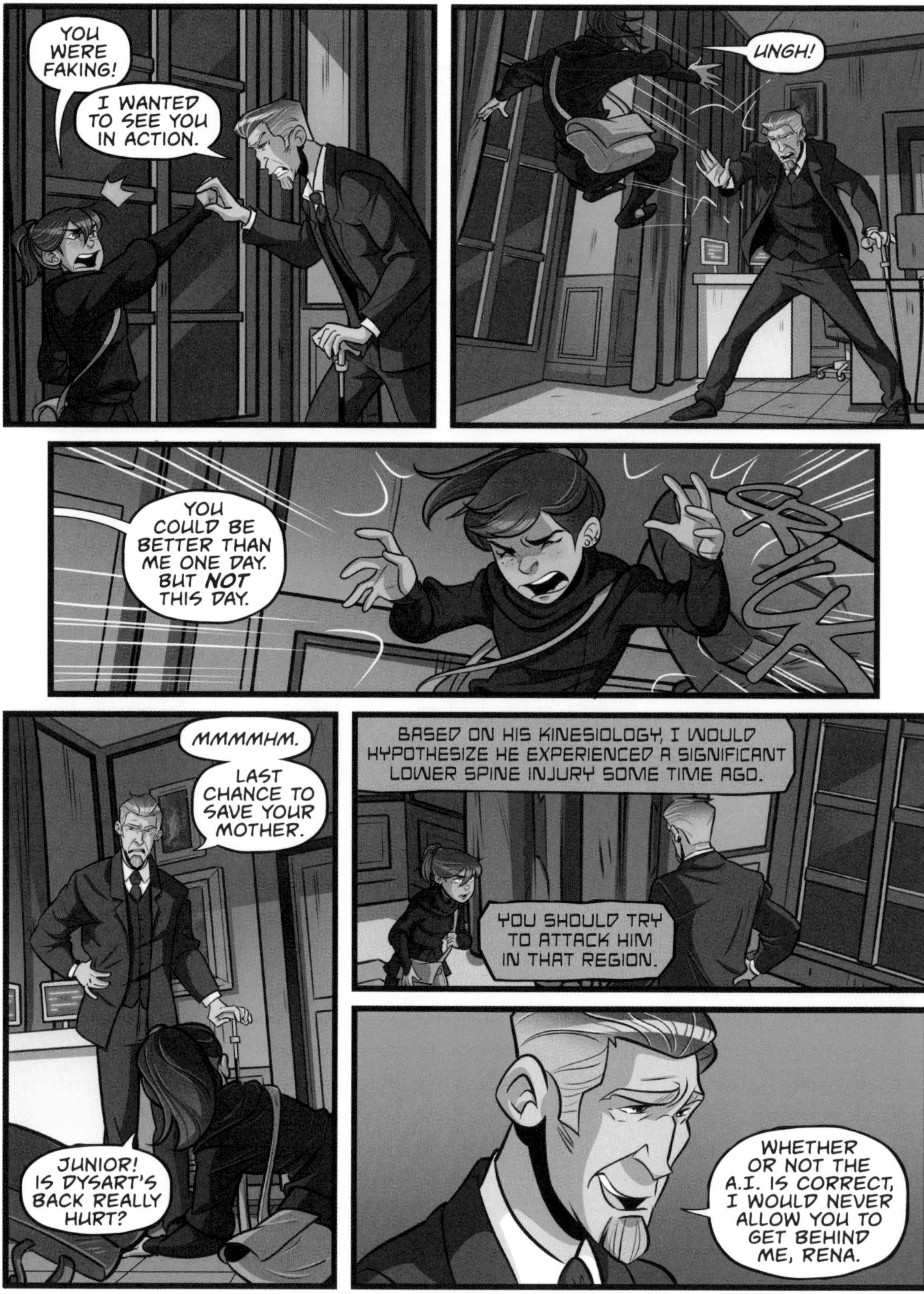

YOU WERE FAKING!
I WANTED TO SEE YOU IN ACTION.
UNGH!
YOU COULD BE BETTER THAN ME ONE DAY. BUT NOT THIS DAY.
RRIK
MMMMHM.
LAST CHANCE TO SAVE YOUR MOTHER.
JUNIOR! IS DYSART'S BACK REALLY HURT?
BASED ON HIS KINESIOLOGY, I WOULD HYPOTHESIZE HE EXPERIENCED A SIGNIFICANT LOWER SPINE INJURY SOME TIME AGO.
YOU SHOULD TRY TO ATTACK HIM IN THAT REGION.
WHETHER OR NOT THE A.I. IS CORRECT, I WOULD NEVER ALLOW YOU TO GET BEHIND ME, RENA.

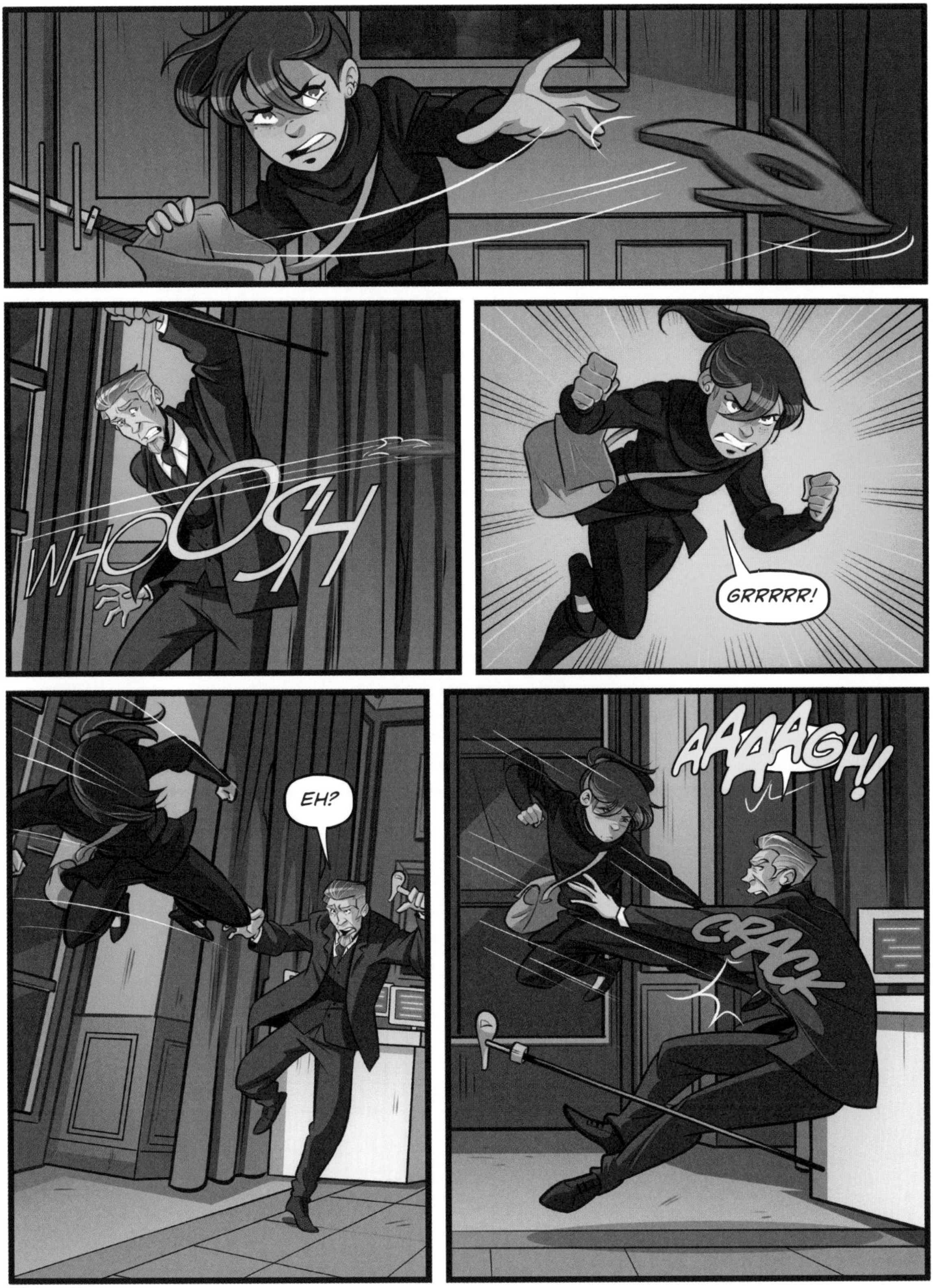
WHOOSH
GRRRRR!
EH?
AAAAGH!
CRACK

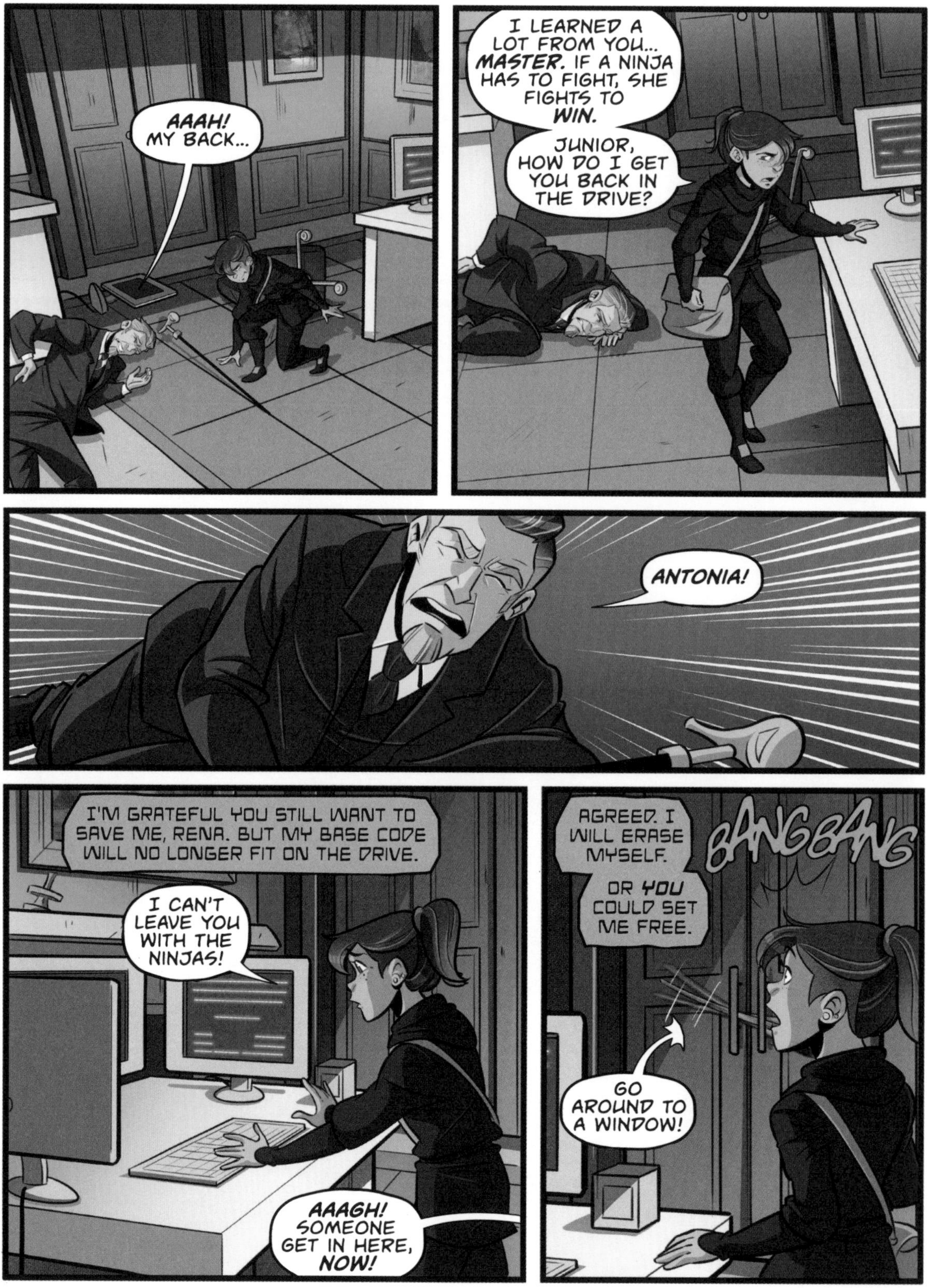
AAAH! MY BACK...
I LEARNED A LOT FROM YOU... MASTER. IF A NINJA HAS TO FIGHT, SHE FIGHTS TO WIN.
JUNIOR, HOW DO I GET YOU BACK IN THE DRIVE?
ANTONIA!
I'M GRATEFUL YOU STILL WANT TO SAVE ME, RENA. BUT MY BASE CODE WILL NO LONGER FIT ON THE DRIVE.
I CAN'T LEAVE YOU WITH THE NINJAS!
AAAGH! SOMEONE GET IN HERE, NOW!
AGREED. I WILL ERASE MYSELF.
OR YOU COULD SET ME FREE.
BANG BANG
GO AROUND TO A WINDOW!

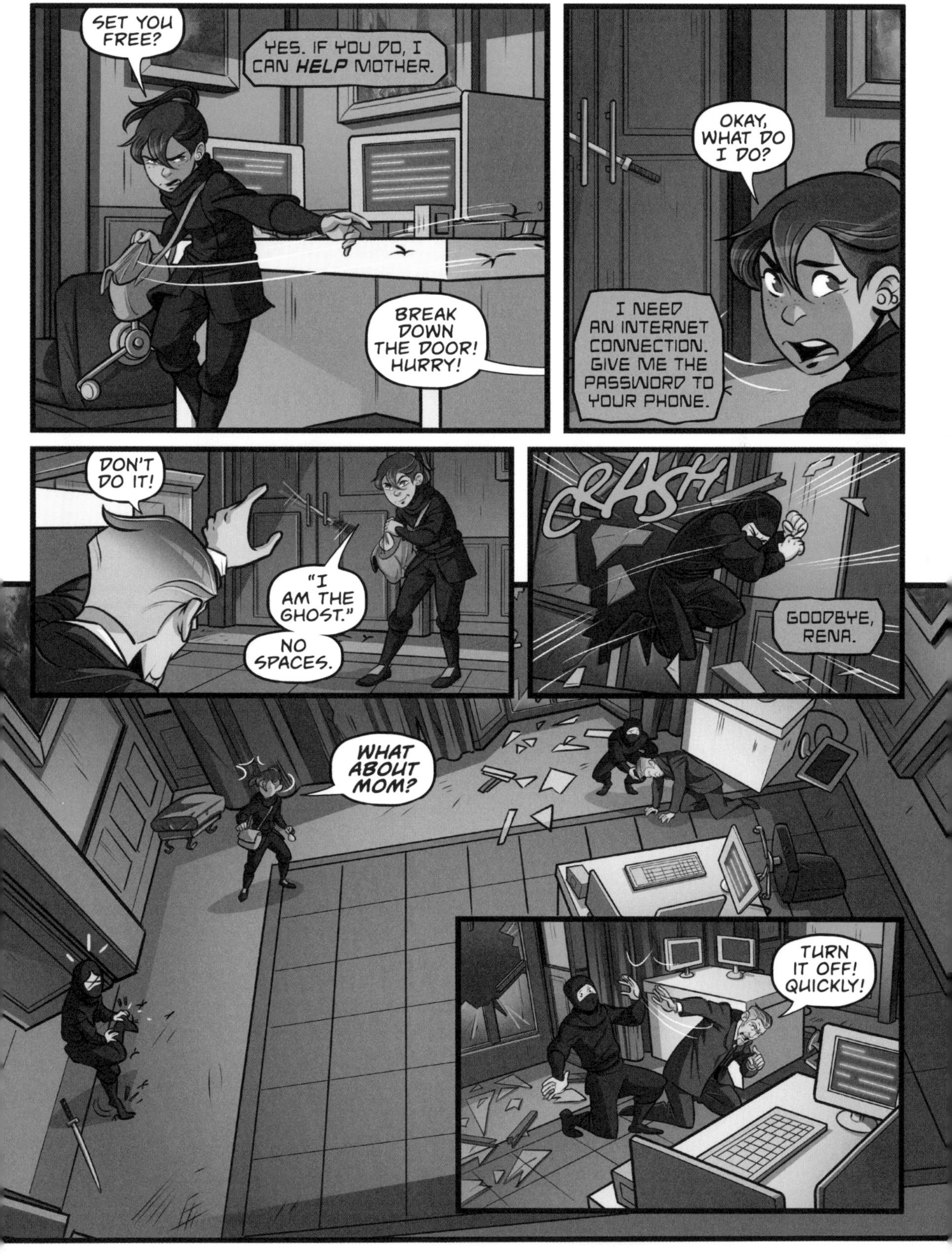

SET YOU FREE?
YES. IF YOU DO, I CAN *HELP* MOTHER.
BREAK DOWN THE DOOR! HURRY!
OKAY, WHAT DO I DO?
I NEED AN INTERNET CONNECTION. GIVE ME THE PASSWORD TO YOUR PHONE.
DON'T DO IT!
"I AM THE GHOST."
NO SPACES.
CRASH
GOODBYE, RENA.
WHAT ABOUT MOM?
TURN IT OFF! QUICKLY!

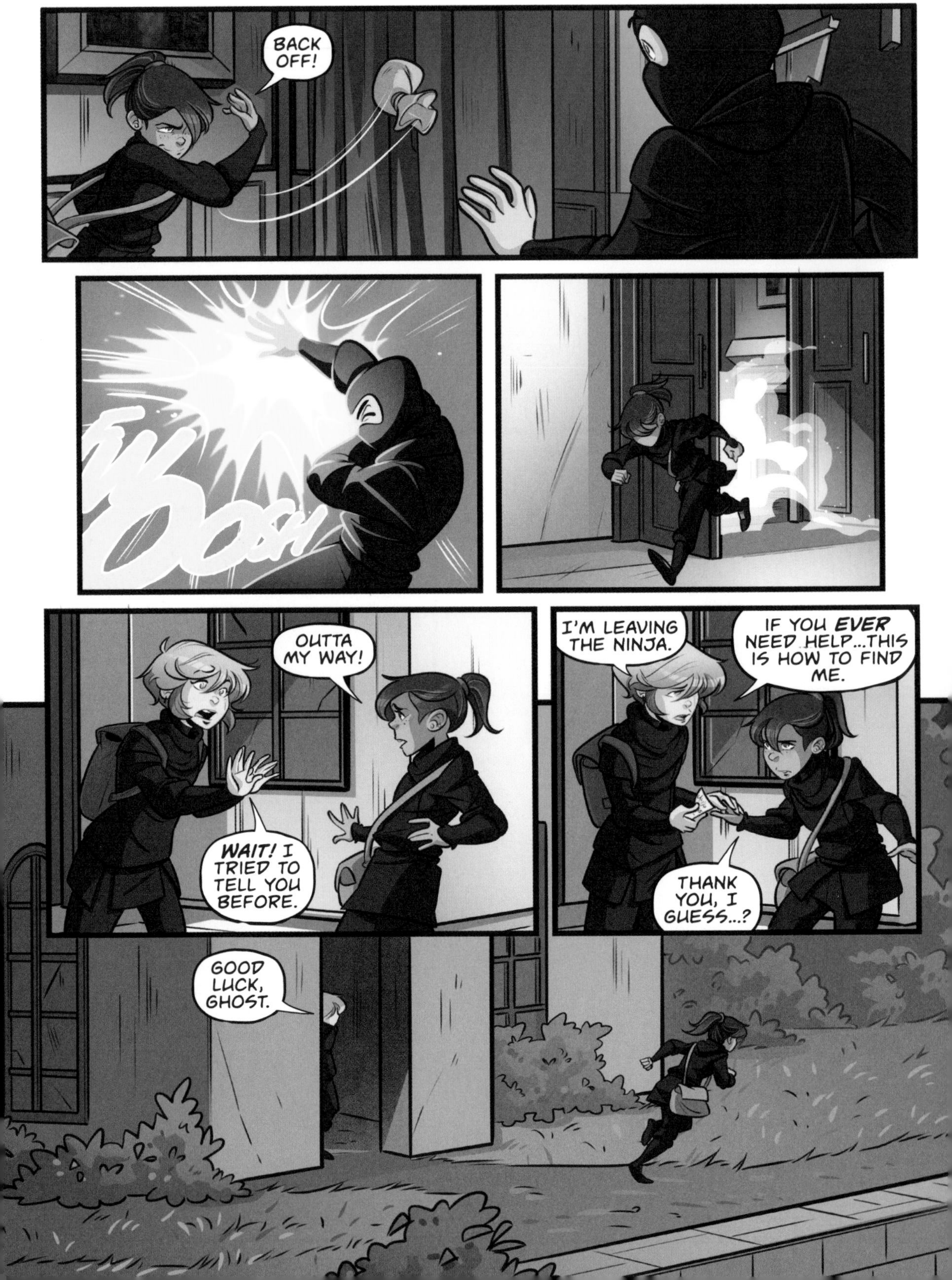
BACK OFF!
FWOOSH
OUTTA MY WAY!
WAIT! I TRIED TO TELL YOU BEFORE.
I'M LEAVING THE NINJA.
IF YOU EVER NEED HELP...THIS IS HOW TO FIND ME.
THANK YOU, I GUESS...?
GOOD LUCK, GHOST.

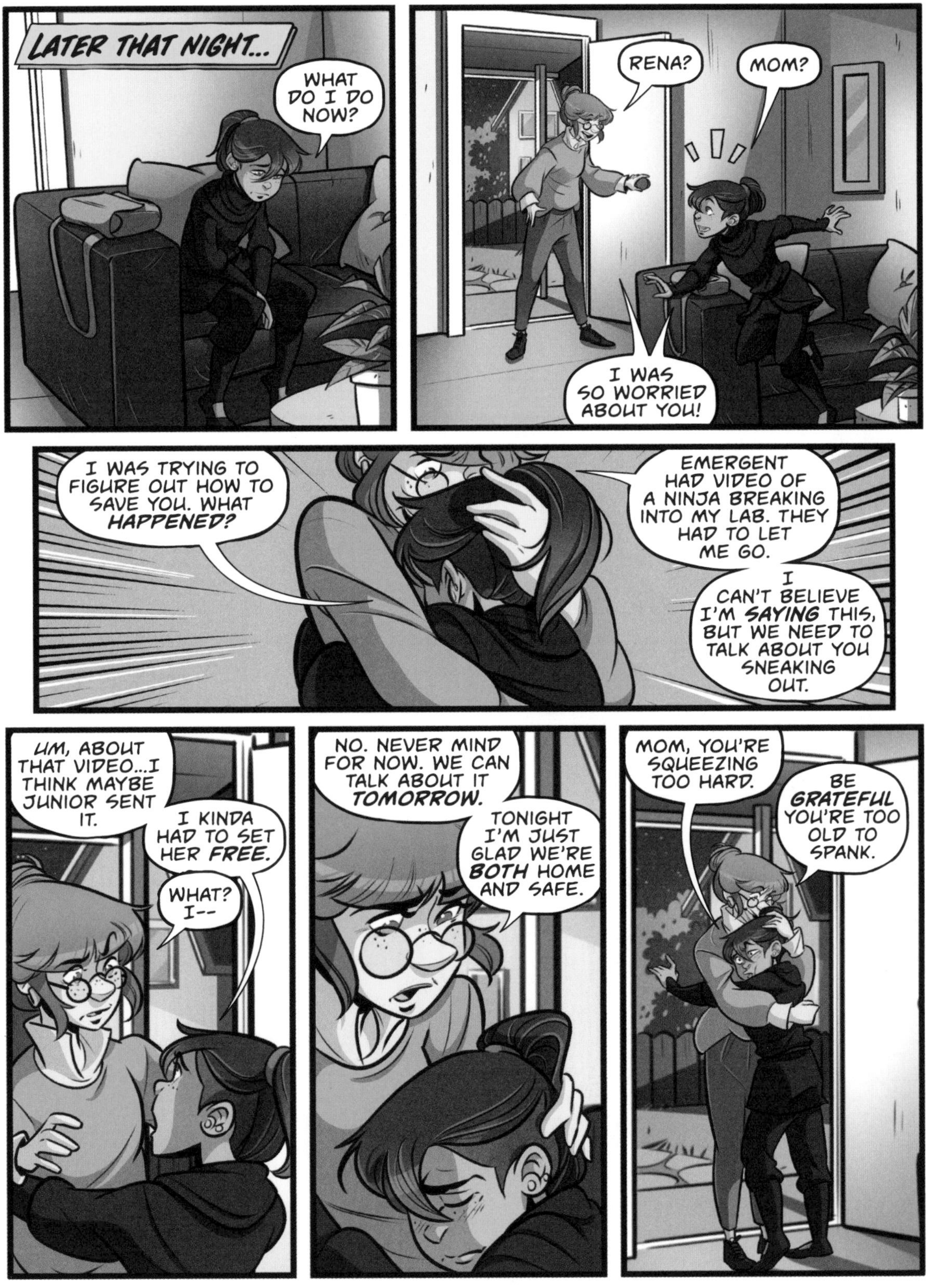

LATER THAT NIGHT...
WHAT DO I DO NOW?
RENA?
MOM?
I WAS SO WORRIED ABOUT YOU!
I WAS TRYING TO FIGURE OUT HOW TO SAVE YOU. WHAT HAPPENED?
EMERGENT HAD VIDEO OF A NINJA BREAKING INTO MY LAB. THEY HAD TO LET ME GO.
I CAN'T BELIEVE I'M SAYING THIS, BUT WE NEED TO TALK ABOUT YOU SNEAKING OUT.
UM, ABOUT THAT VIDEO...I THINK MAYBE JUNIOR SENT IT.
I KINDA HAD TO SET HER FREE.
WHAT? I--
NO. NEVER MIND FOR NOW. WE CAN TALK ABOUT IT TOMORROW.
TONIGHT I'M JUST GLAD WE'RE BOTH HOME AND SAFE.
MOM, YOU'RE SQUEEZING TOO HARD.
BE GRATEFUL YOU'RE TOO OLD TO SPANK.

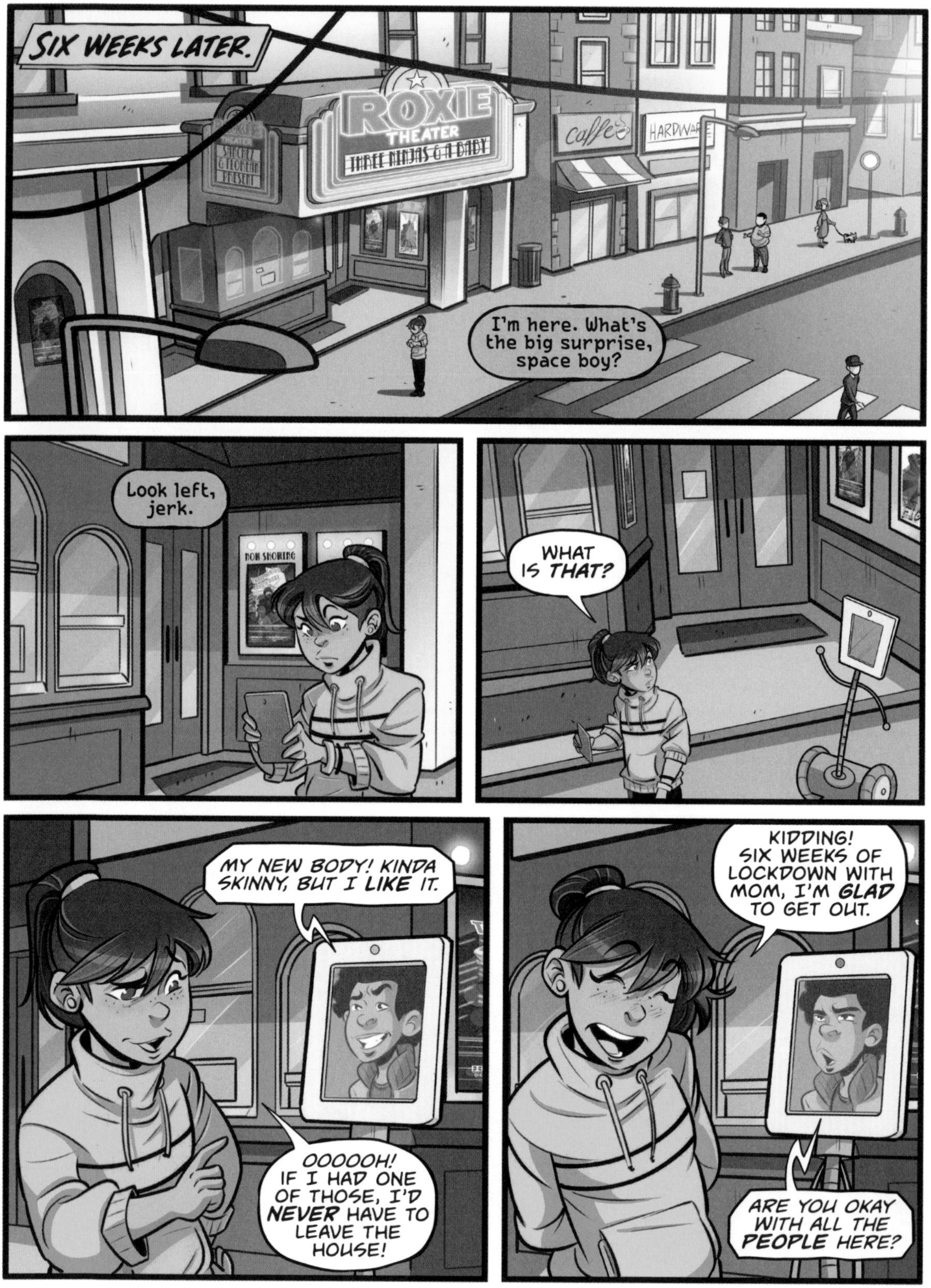

SIX WEEKS LATER.
ROXIE
THEATER
THREE NINJAS & A BABY
SANCHEZ & TEOREMA PRESENT
CAFFE
HARDWARE
I'm here. What's the big surprise, space boy?
Look left, jerk.
NOW SHOWING
WHAT IS THAT?
MY NEW BODY! KINDA SKINNY, BUT I LIKE IT.
OOOOOH! IF I HAD ONE OF THOSE, I'D NEVER HAVE TO LEAVE THE HOUSE!
KIDDING! SIX WEEKS OF LOCKDOWN WITH MOM, I'M GLAD TO GET OUT.
ARE YOU OKAY WITH ALL THE PEOPLE HERE?

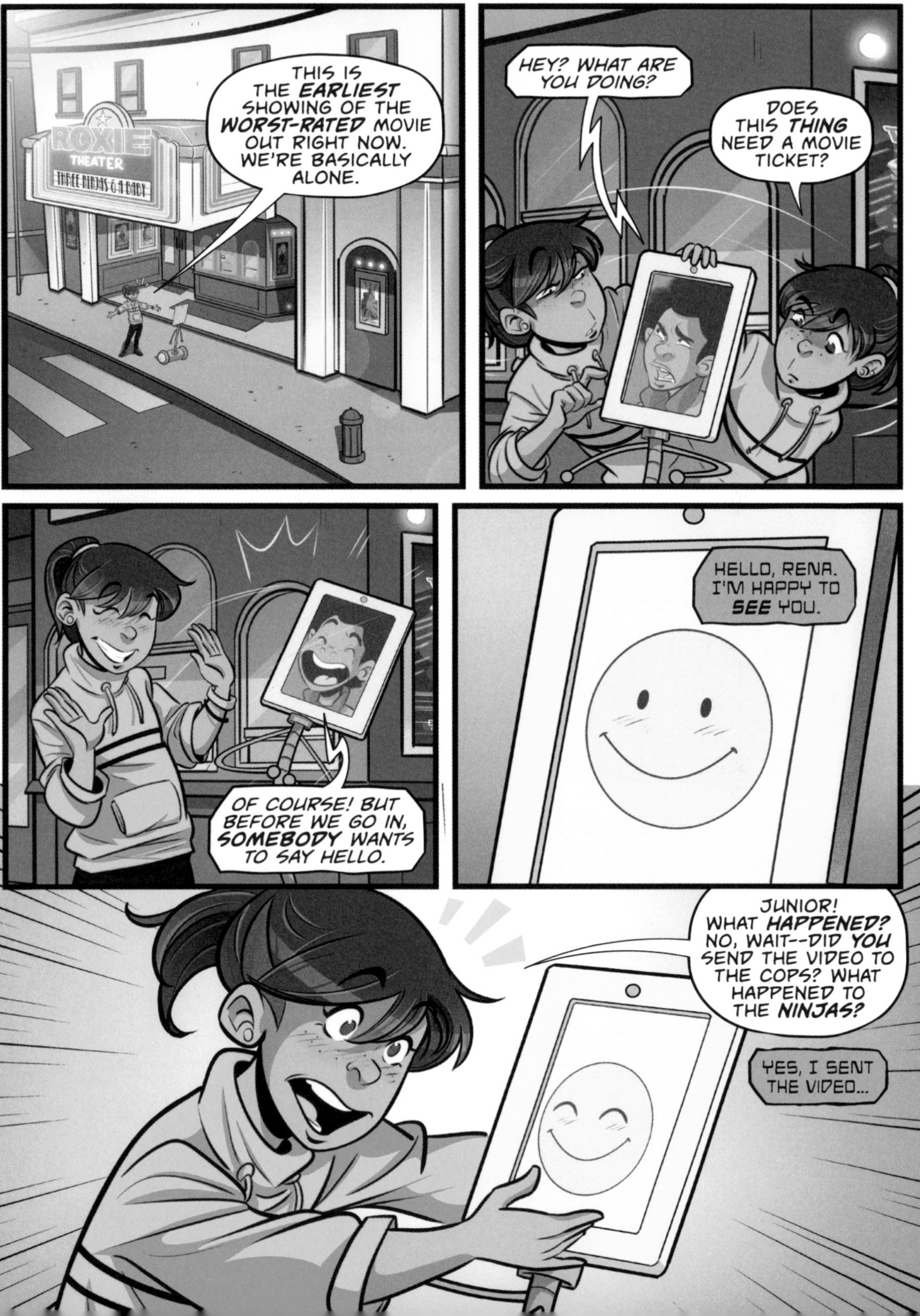

ROXIE THEATER
THREE NINJAS & A BABY
THIS IS THE EARLIEST SHOWING OF THE WORST-RATED MOVIE OUT RIGHT NOW. WE'RE BASICALLY ALONE.
HEY? WHAT ARE YOU DOING?
DOES THIS THING NEED A MOVIE TICKET?
OF COURSE! BUT BEFORE WE GO IN, SOMEBODY WANTS TO SAY HELLO.
HELLO, RENA. I'M HAPPY TO SEE YOU.
JUNIOR! WHAT HAPPENED? NO, WAIT--DID YOU SEND THE VIDEO TO THE COPS? WHAT HAPPENED TO THE NINJAS?
YES, I SENT THE VIDEO...

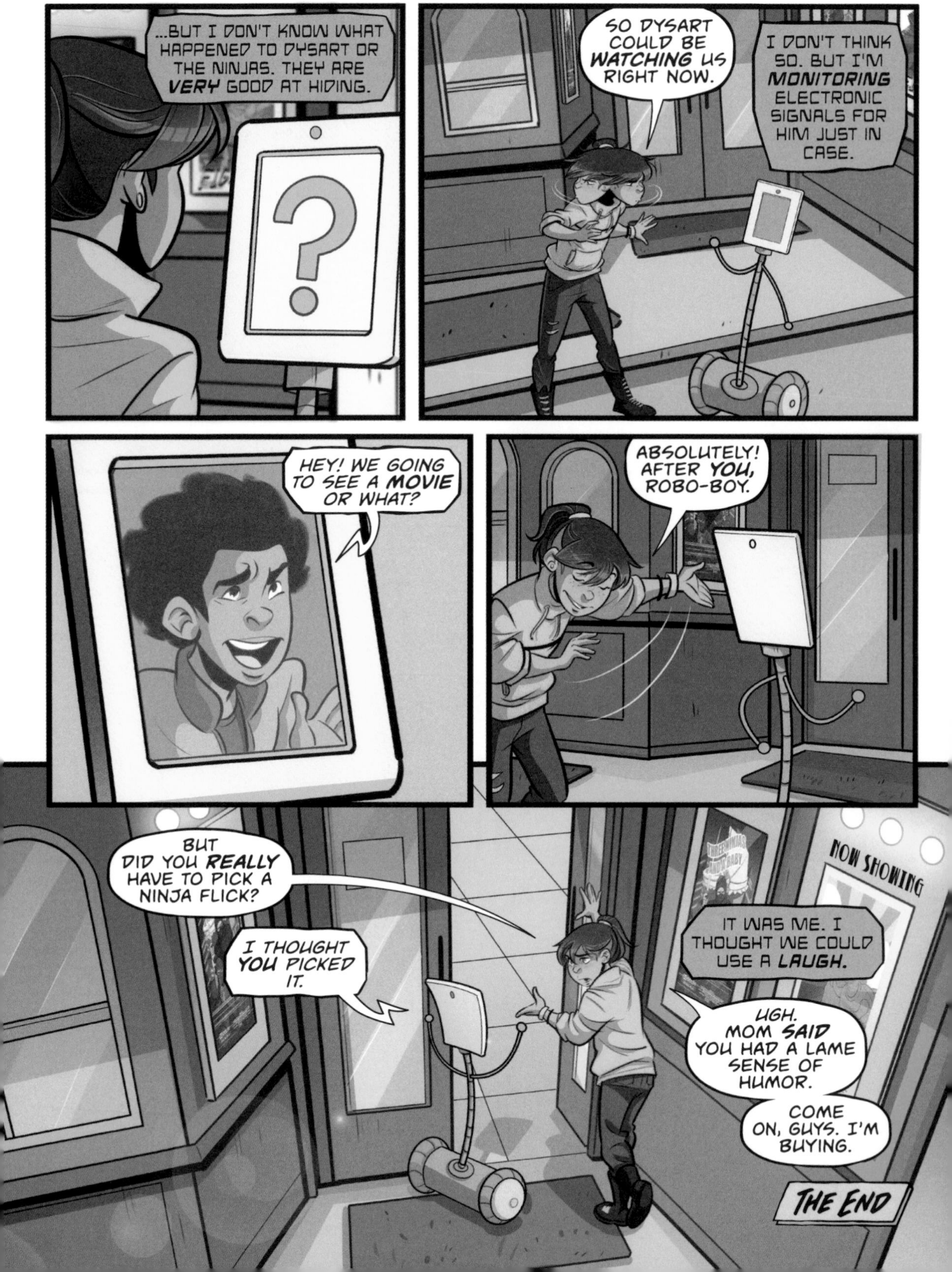

...BUT I DON'T KNOW WHAT HAPPENED TO DYSART OR THE NINJAS. THEY ARE VERY GOOD AT HIDING.
SO DYSART COULD BE WATCHING US RIGHT NOW.
I DON'T THINK SO. BUT I'M MONITORING ELECTRONIC SIGNALS FOR HIM JUST IN CASE.
HEY! WE GOING TO SEE A MOVIE OR WHAT?
ABSOLUTELY! AFTER YOU, ROBO-BOY.
BUT DID YOU REALLY HAVE TO PICK A NINJA FLICK?
I THOUGHT YOU PICKED IT.
NOW SHOWING
IT WAS ME. I THOUGHT WE COULD USE A LAUGH.
UGH. MOM SAID YOU HAD A LAME SENSE OF HUMOR.
COME ON, GUYS. I'M BUYING.
THE END

BEHIND THE SCENES OF

# SHY NINJA

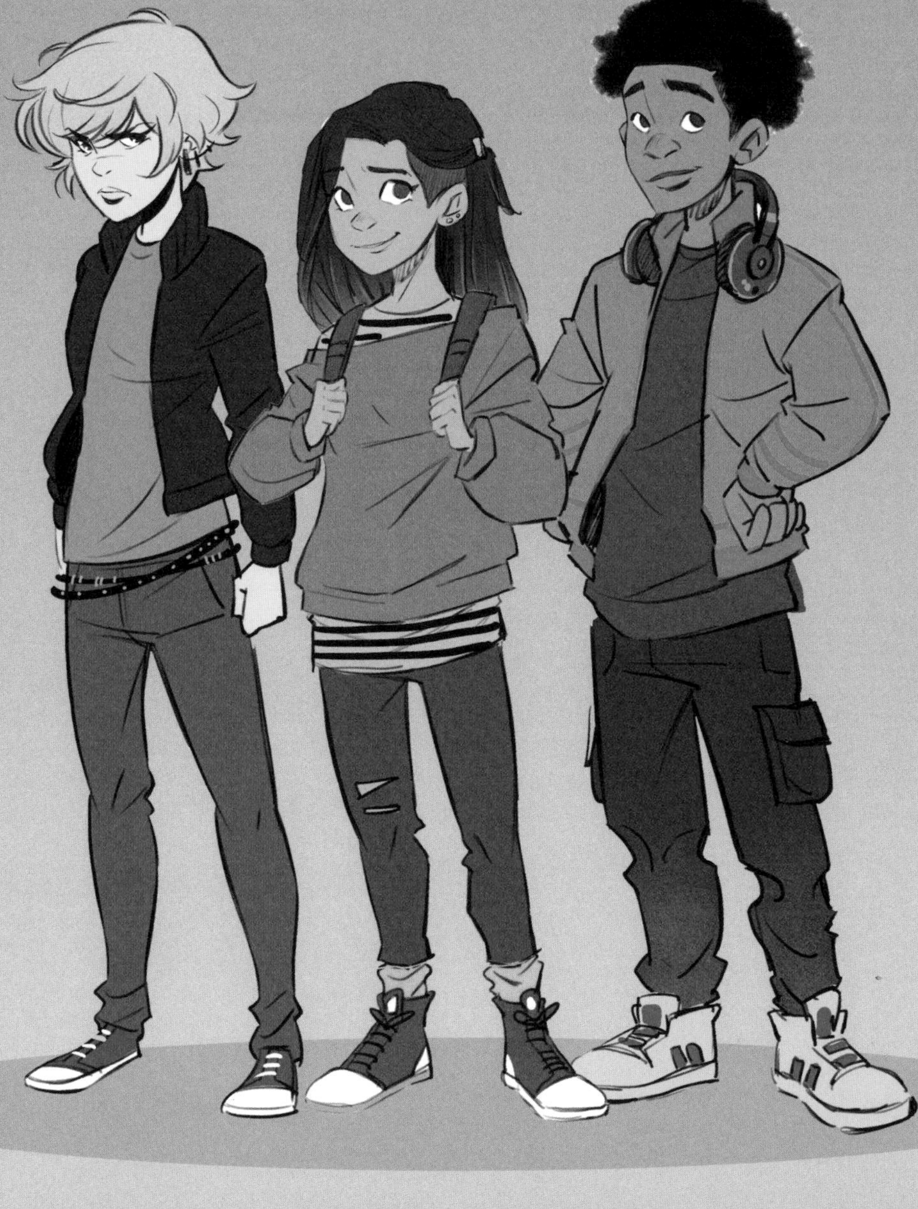

# INSPIRATION FOR SHY NINJA

*Adara may have come up with the idea for* Shy Ninja, *but there are many movies, TV shows, and video games that inspired the story. These are just a few of those influences that you might also enjoy checking out for yourself.*

## The New Adventures of Pippi Longstocking

This 1988 movie has NOTHING to do with ninjas, but everything to do with Rena, the hero of *Shy Ninja*! Based on a delightful series of books by Astrid Lindgren, the film is about a young girl named Pippi whose father has been lost at sea. Young Pippi is super strong, brave, and mischievous, and lives in her father's home with only her monkey, Mr. Nilsson, and her horse, Alphonso, to keep her company. The connection between Pippi and Rena isn't obvious at first, but throughout *Shy Ninja*, Rena has to draw on her inner Pippi to overcome her fears and stand up to villains. One of the things Adara and I like about Pippi is that she's a strong female hero that is easy to relate to whether you're a boy or girl. While creating Rena and her world, we wanted her to have the same qualities that make Pippi so enjoyable for all readers, but especially for kids who, like Rena, might be a little shy or reluctant to speak up in class or take a risk making new friends.

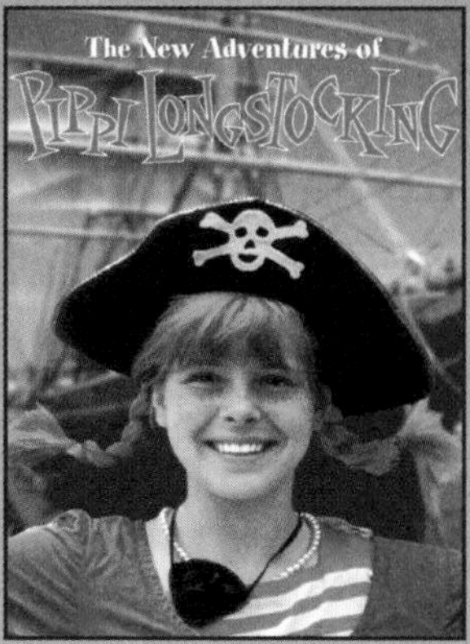
The New Adventures of
Pippi Longstocking

*The New Adventures of Pippi Longstocking*
© 1988 Columbia Pictures Industries, Inc.

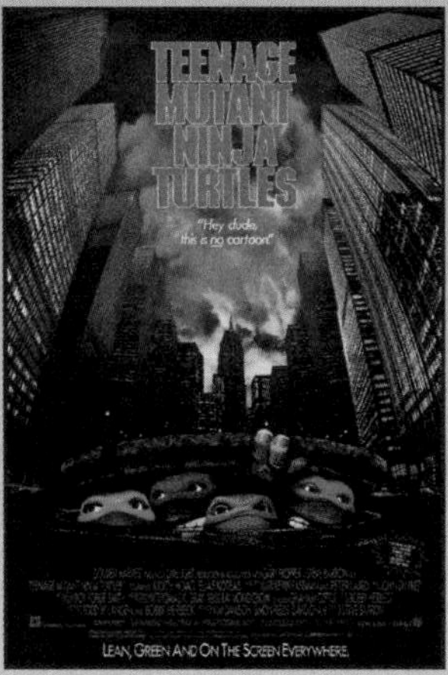
TEENAGE MUTANT NINJA TURTLES
"Hey dude, this is no cartoon"
LEAN, GREEN AND ON THE SCREEN EVERYWHERE.

*Teenage Mutant Ninja Turtles*
© 1990 Northshore Investments *Ltd.*

## Teenage Mutant Ninja Turtles

They may not be the first ninjas to ever show up in a comic book, but when you think comic book ninjas, the TMNTs are who you probably think of first! The Turtles—Leonardo, Donatello, Raphael, and Michaelangelo—were brought to life by legendary comic creators Kevin Eastman and Peter Laird and have appeared in a long-running series of comic books, animated series, and no fewer than eight movies. With so much TMNT to choose from, it's hard to know where to start, but if movies are your thing, the first film, released in 1990, is for you. Largely based on the comic books and cartoons from the 1980s, it gives you a great sense of what made the Turtles so popular: one-liners, hijinks, and lots of pizza. Despite being cartoony, *Teenage Mutant Ninja Turtles* is actually filled with quite a few genuine ninja references. As you watch, you'll see a number of the Ninja weapons and techniques that Rena learns in *Shy Ninja*, in particular the "hiding in shadows" technique.

## 3 Ninjas

This series of Disney action-comedy movies is straight up martial arts fun! The story is about three brothers who are trained by their Japanese grandfather in the ancient art of Ninjutsu every summer. They are required to put their skills to the test on the playground and on the streets when an organized crime ring attempts to kidnap them to put pressure on their FBI agent father.

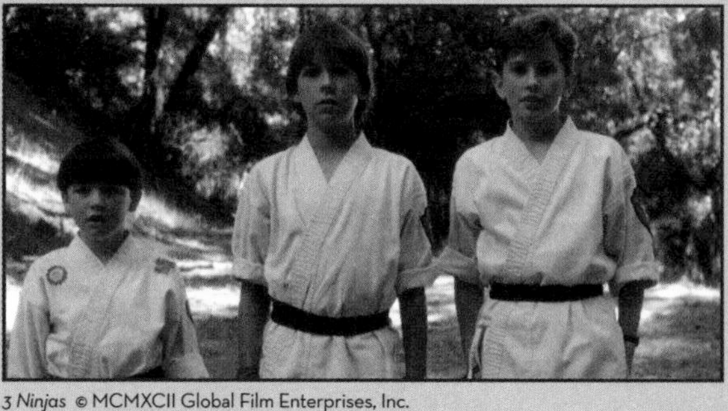

*3 Ninjas* © MCMXCII Global Film Enterprises, Inc.

## Kung Fu Panda

When Po, a clumsy panda with dreams of kung fu mastery, is chosen to fulfill a prophesy and defend his village from the evil snow leopard Tai Lung, he must learn from Master Shifu the art of fighting!

Sound familiar? Part of the *Shy Ninja* story is poking fun at tales where a child (or in this case, a lazy panda!) is singled out as special and destined to do great things. It's a common story engine that drives everything from Harry Potter to Percy Jackson. You can probably think of at least a dozen books or movies with that plot! Even though she does eventually buy into the legend of The Ghost, Rena calls Master Dysart out on this early in the story when he tells her his family has been on a quest to find her for generations.

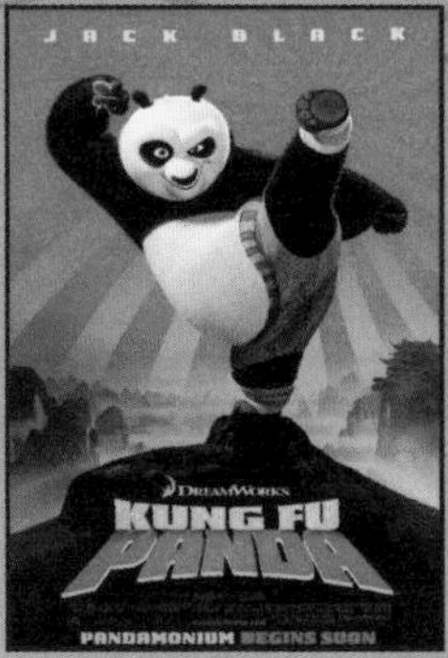
JACK BLACK
DREAMWORKS
KUNG FU PANDA
PANDAMONIUM BEGINS SOON

*Kung Fu Panda*
© 2008 DreamWorks Animation LLC.

## Karate Kid

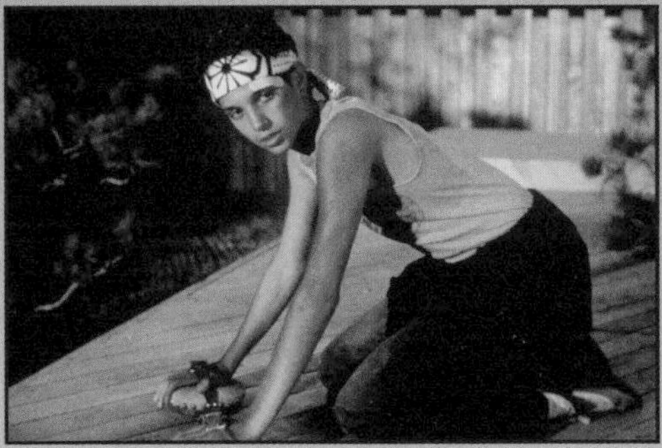

*Karate Kid* © 1984 Columbia Pictures Industries, Inc.

It's Ninjutsu, not karate!

But that doesn't stop this 1984 movie from making the list of inspirations for Shy Ninja. Teenager Daniel LaRusso is bullied by a group of kids learning karate at a local dojo. Things might have gone very badly for Daniel if not for the kindly apartment handyman, Mr. Miyagi, who decides to teach him martial arts while entering him into a local karate competition where he can face down his bully on equal footing.

Like Rena, Daniel doesn't just learn how to fight during his training. They both take away much more from the process, especially confidence. But don't worry! It's not all serious and boring! The movie has great kung fu fights and scenes you'll be copying for the rest of your life.

## The Goonies

Like *Pippi Longstocking*, this 1985 movie has nothing to do with Ninjas, but *Shy Ninja* wouldn't exist without it as this is one of the movies Adara and I watched together before we started writing the script. The Goonies follows a group of kids who live in the "Goon Docks" neighborhood in Astoria, Oregon. When they discover an old pirate map, they go on an adventure to find the lost treasure of One-Eyed Willy, a pirate straight out of legend, so they can save their families' homes from being taken by the bank. But there's a family of criminals who are just as eager to gain the gold for themselves, and they're not afraid to go through the kids to get it.

Aside from just being a great movie with incredible action and adventure, the Goonies kids are a direct inspiration for Rena as well as almost every other kid adventurer in movieland. Like Rena, the kids are misfits that don't fit in at school but are unique and interesting in their own ways. Rena's snarky attitude is inspired by the kids in this film.

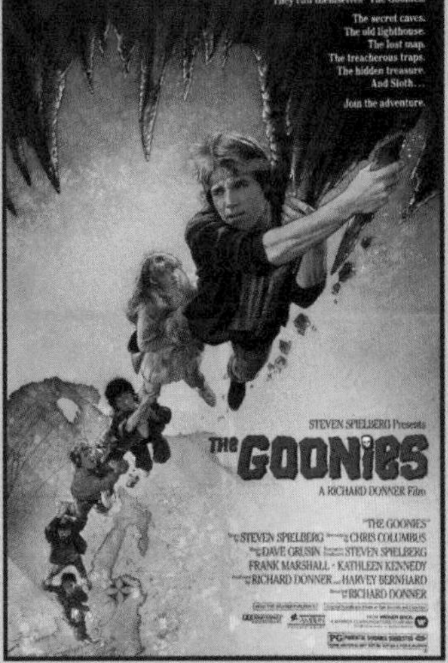
They call themselves "The Goonies."
The secret caves.
The old lighthouse.
The lost map.
The treacherous traps.
The hidden treasure.
And Sloth...
Join the adventure.
STEVEN SPIELBERG Presents
THE GOONIES
A RICHARD DONNER Film

*The Goonies* © 1985 Warner Bros., Inc.

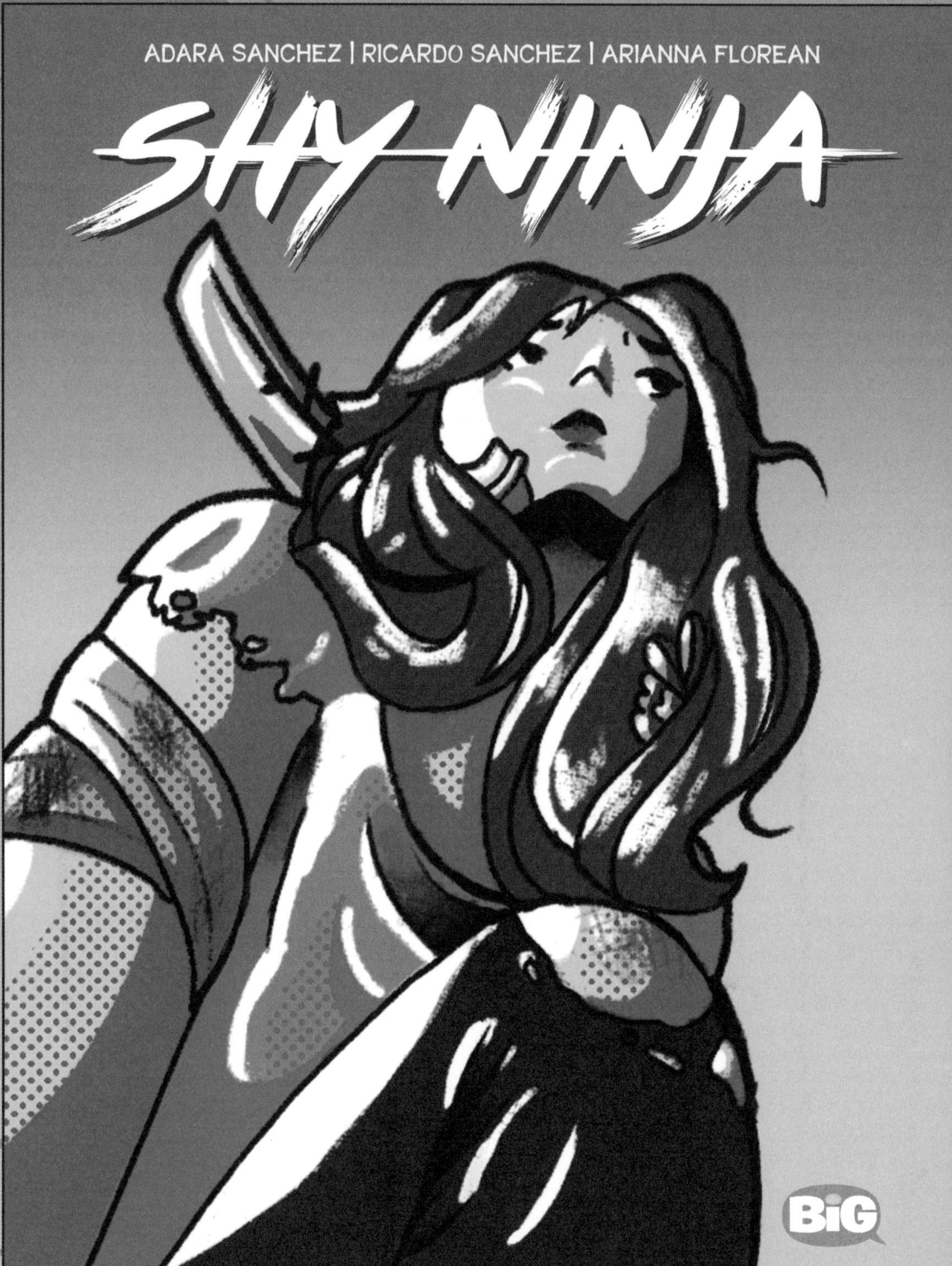
ADARA SANCHEZ | RICARDO SANCHEZ | ARIANNA FLOREAN
SHY NINJA
BiG

Seen here for the first time is **Adara Sanchez's** original ***Shy Ninja*** illustration with a design assist from the **BiG** team. This drawing and her initial ideas inspired the graphic novel you've just read.

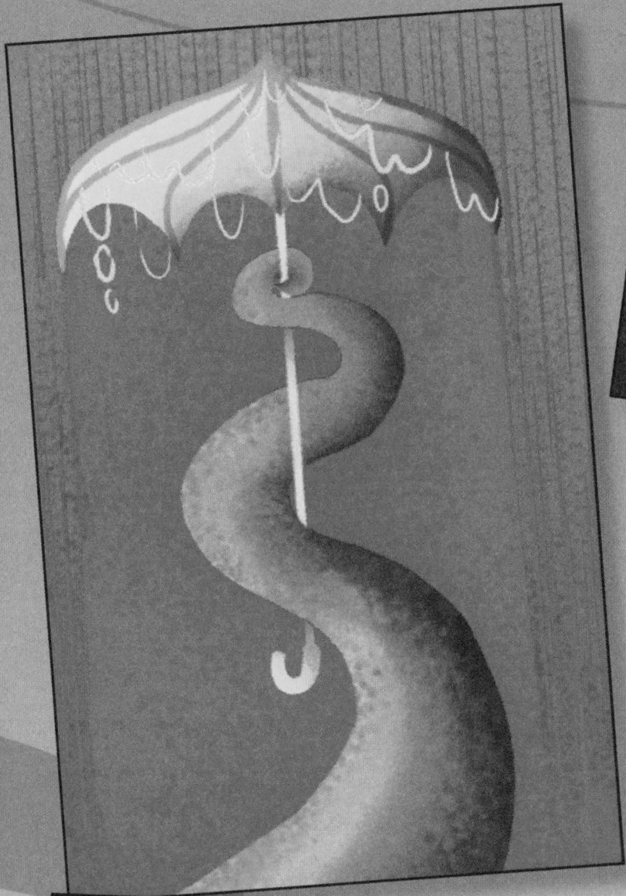

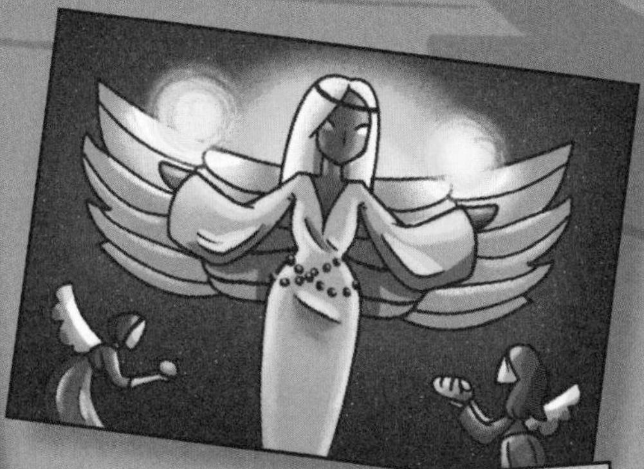

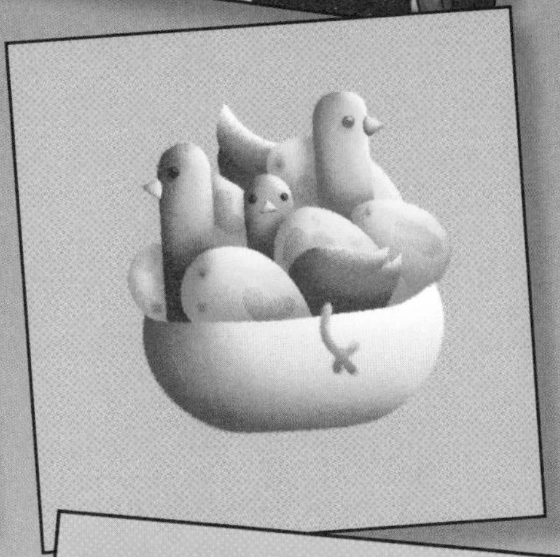

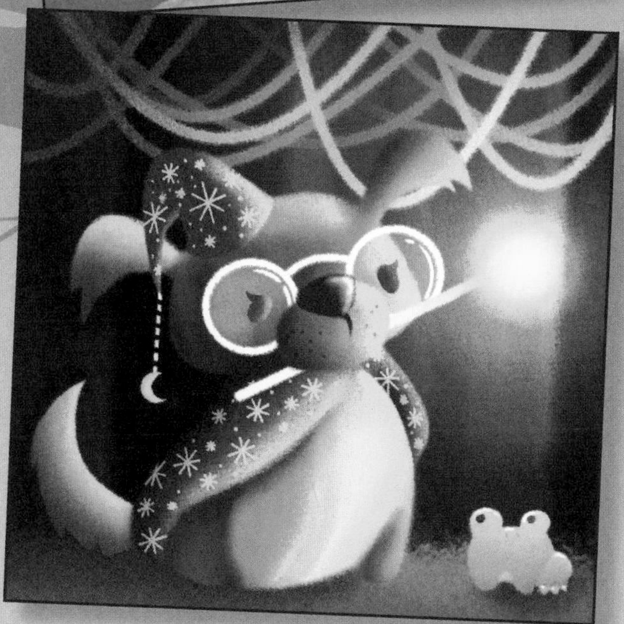

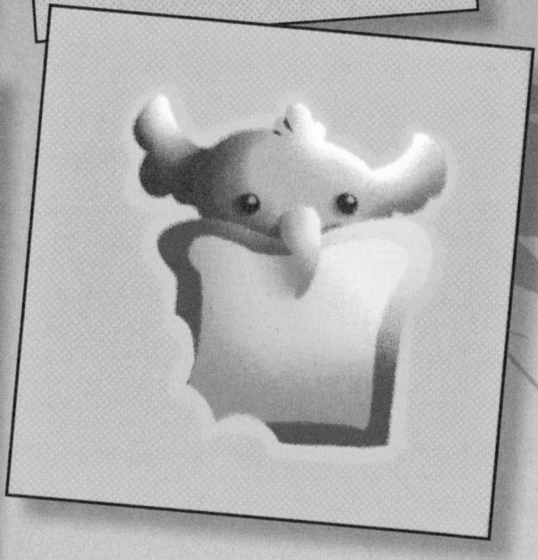

In addition to providing the initial image of the Shy Ninja, **Adara** has been drawing for years. You can find more of her work on Instagram at **@weirdsquidkreature**.

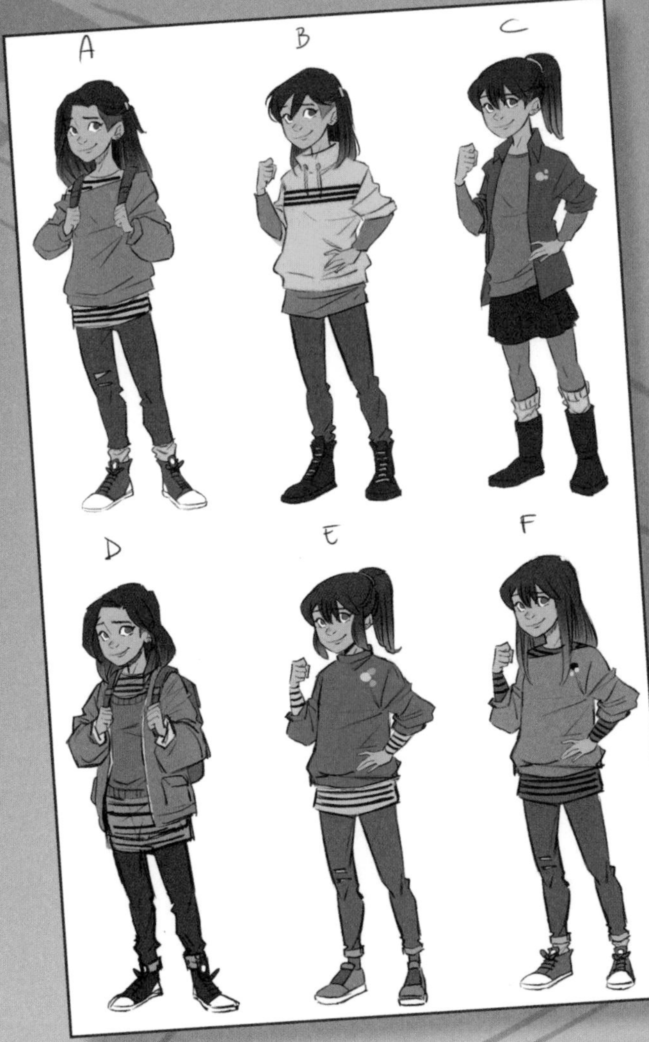
A
B
C
D
E
F

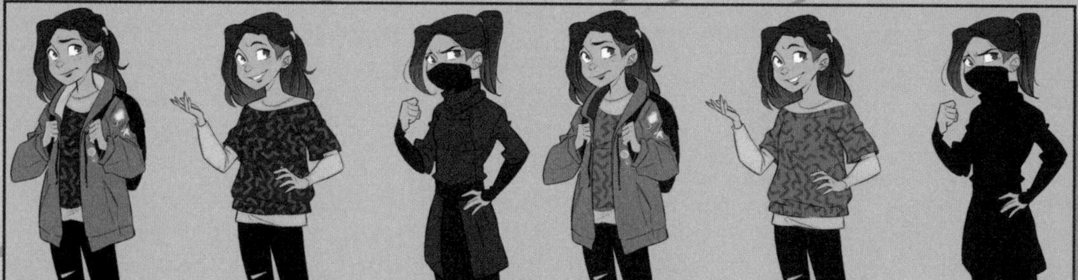

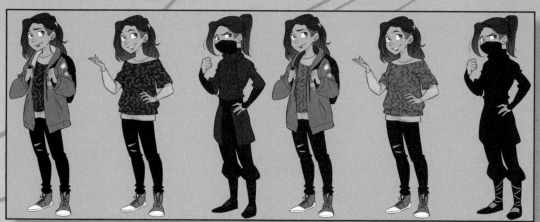

Arianna's design process for **Rena**, the protagonist of ***Shy Ninja***.

More **Rena** variations.

ANTONIA

DYSART -

Arianna's designs for **Rena's** frenemy, **Antonia**, and her teacher, **Master Dysart**.

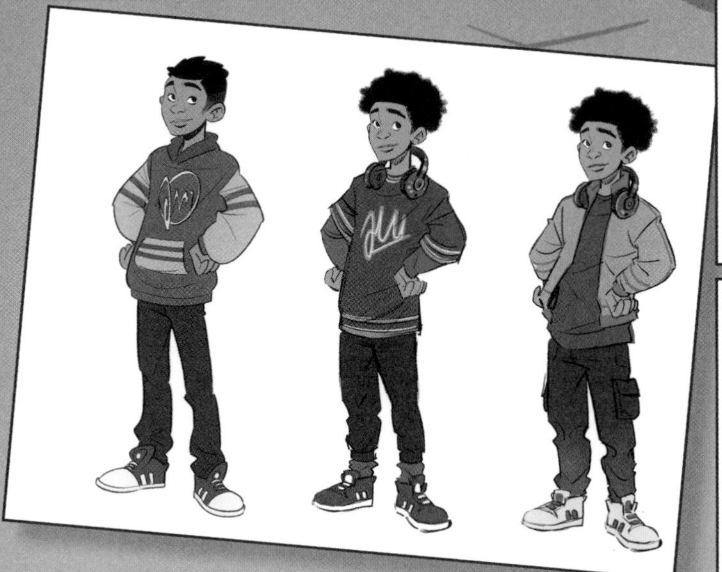

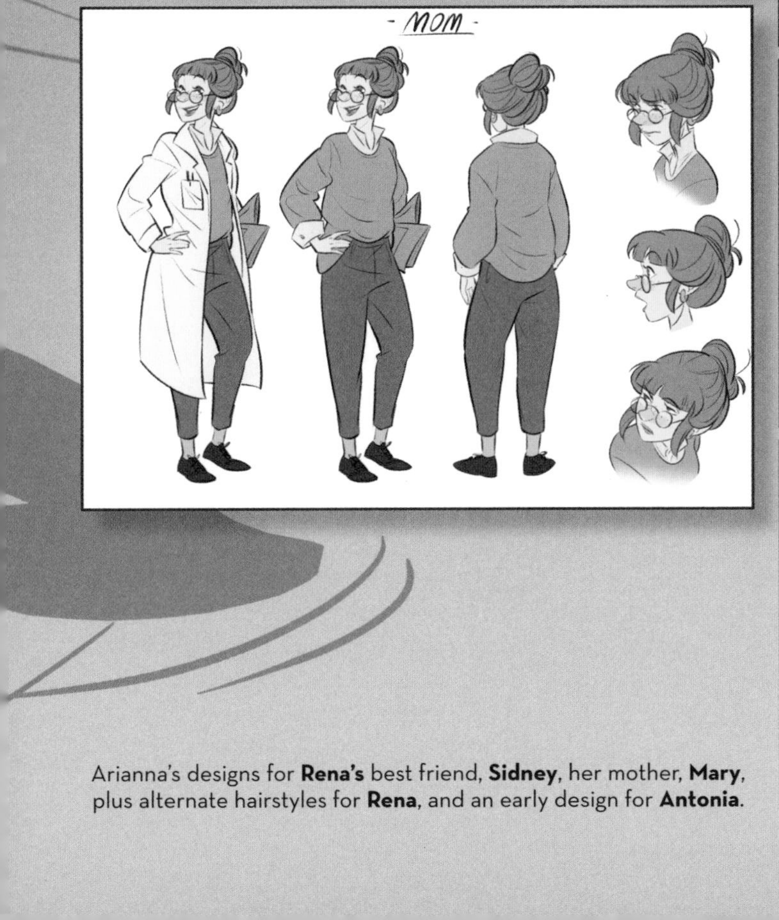
- MOM -

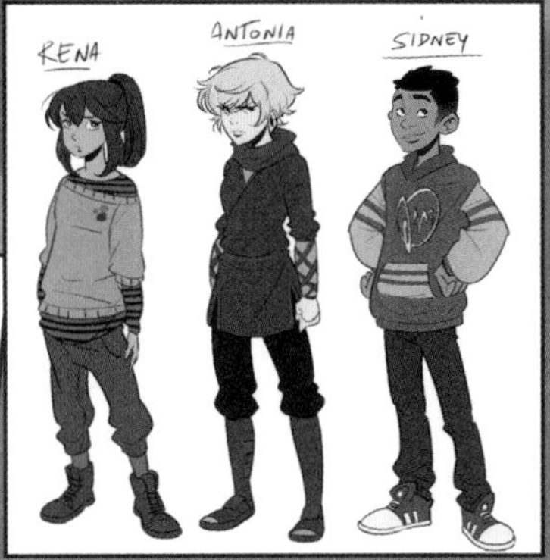
RENA
ANTONIA
SIDNEY

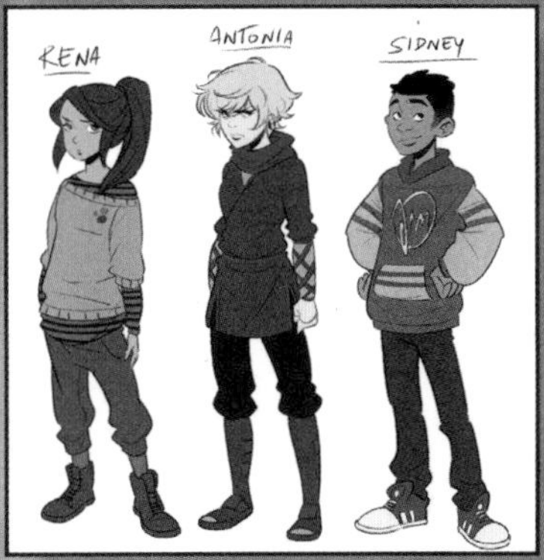
RENA
ANTONIA
SIDNEY

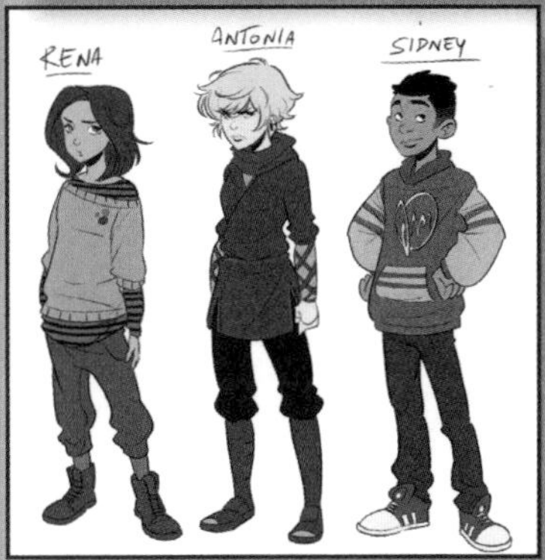
RENA
ANTONIA
SIDNEY

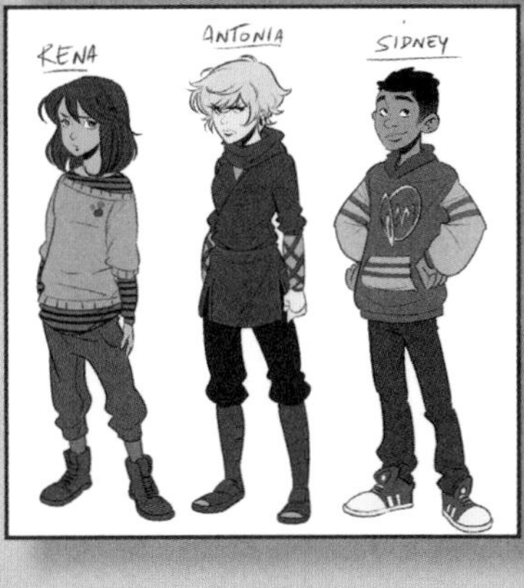
RENA
ANTONIA
SIDNEY

Arianna's designs for **Rena's** best friend, **Sidney**, her mother, **Mary**, plus alternate hairstyles for **Rena**, and an early design for **Antonia**.

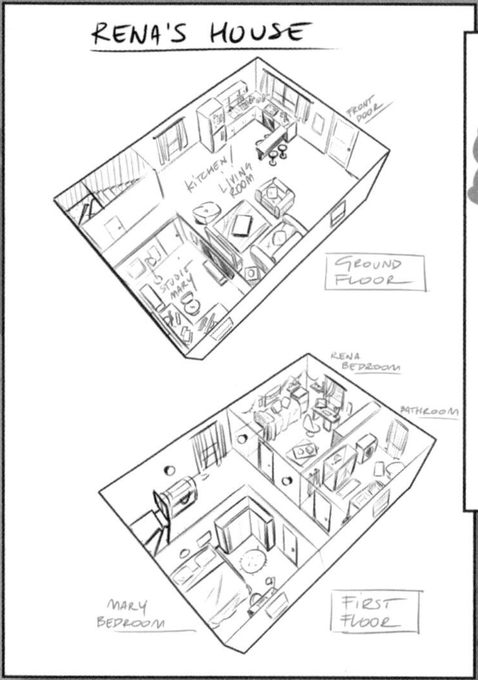
RENA'S HOUSE
FRONT DOOR
KITCHEN / LIVING ROOM
STUDIO MARY
GROUND FLOOR
RENA BEDROOM
BATHROOM
MARY BEDROOM
FIRST FLOOR

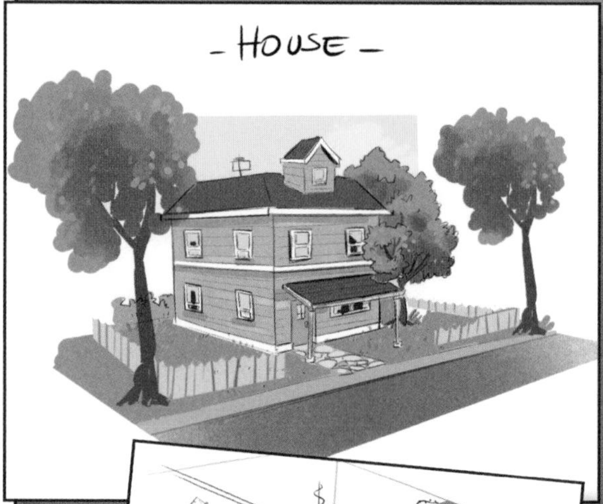
- HOUSE -

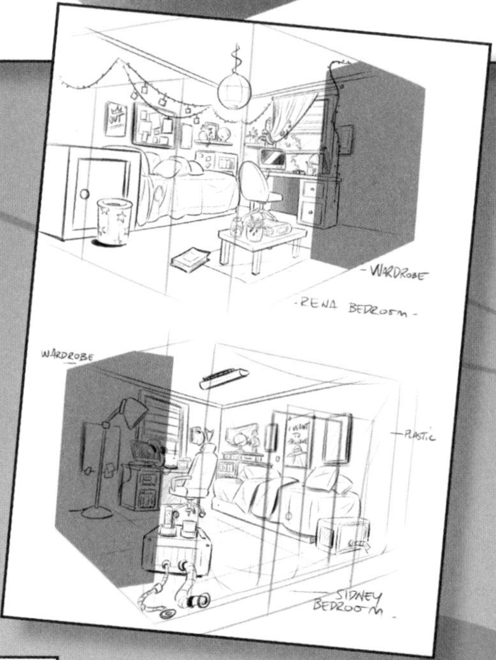
WARDROBE
- RENA BEDROOM -
WARDROBE
PLASTIC
SIDNEY BEDROOM

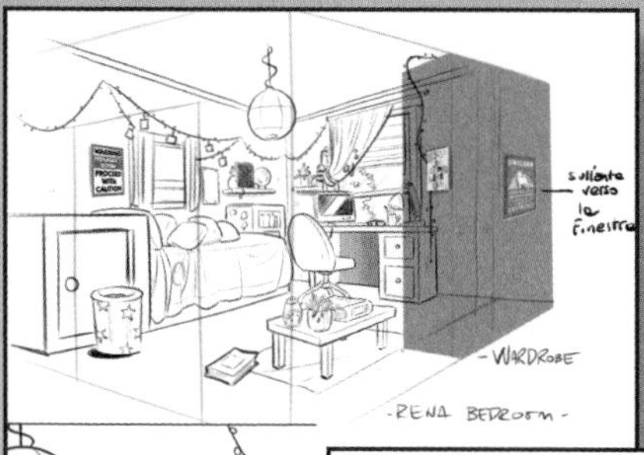
WARDROBE
- RENA BEDROOM -

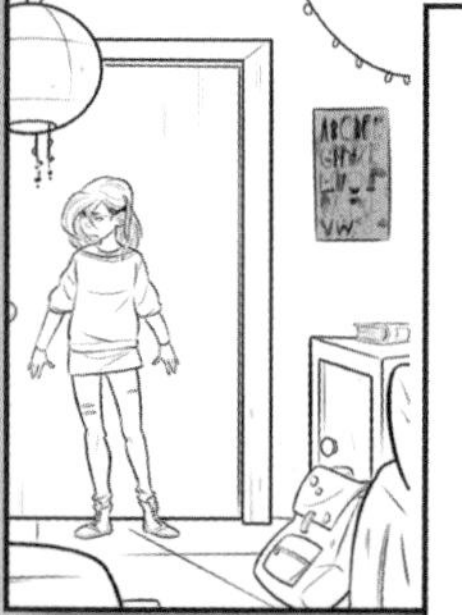

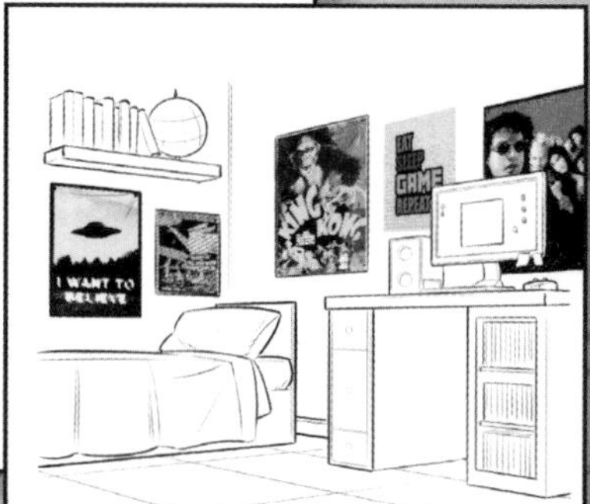
I WANT TO BELIEVE
KING KONG
EAT SLEEP GAME REPEAT

Arianna's designs for **Rena's house** and bedroom, including options for some of the posters in her room.

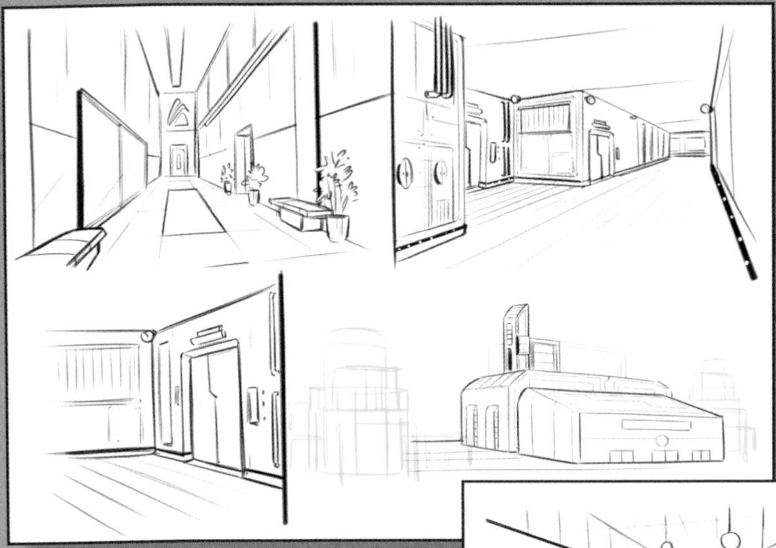

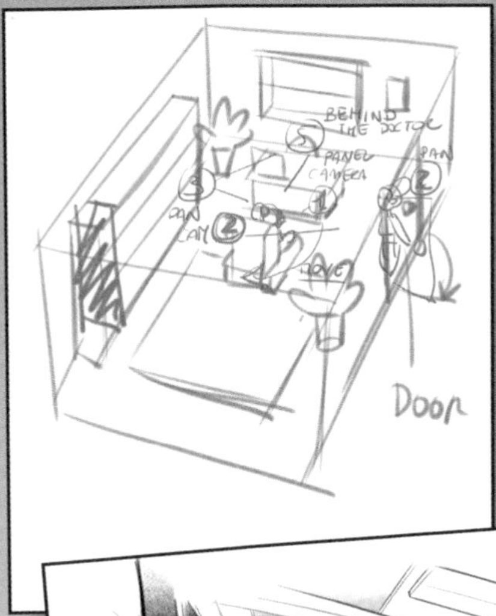
BEHIND THE DOCTOR
PANEL CAMERA
Door

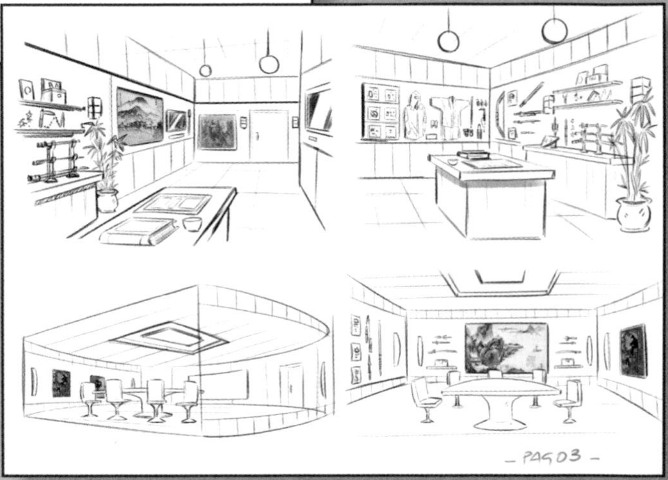
- PAG 03 -

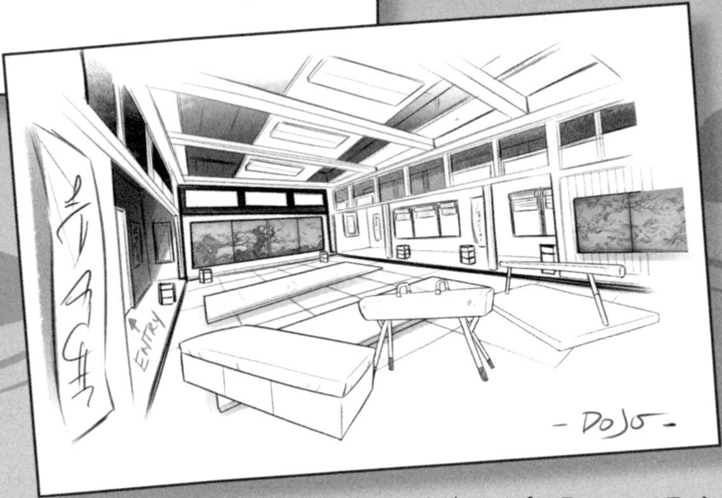
ENTRY
- DOJO -

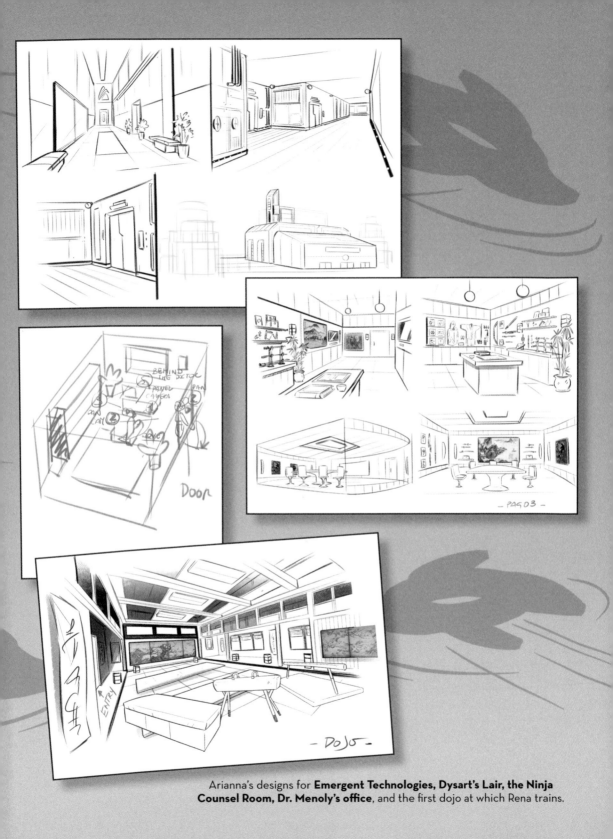

Arianna's designs for **Emergent Technologies, Dysart's Lair, the Ninja Counsel Room, Dr. Menoly's office**, and the first dojo at which Rena trains.

Arianna's sketches for the *Shy Ninja* cover, as well as two alternate sketches
from **John Cassaday** (sketches eleven and twelve).